FROM THE DEAD

FROM THE DEAD

By John Hilferty

Copyright © 2009 by John Hilferty
Cover photo © Ellie Hilferty

First published 2009

All rights reserved. No part of this book may be used or reproduced by any means, graphic, electronic, or mechanical, including photocopying, recording, taping or by any information storage retrieval system without the written permission of the author except in the case of brief quotations embodied in critical articles and reviews.

Chapter 1: PUTREFACTION

July 12, 1979.

The teenaged girl with the little Morgan horse was the only one Berardi could recognize. She belonged but the others didn't. She and the horse stood at the far edge of the circle outside the yellow tape looking in at Stanley Schweitzer and another special agent who stood talking to a Medford Township cop.

Schweitzer glanced at the battered black Toyota Corolla standing derelict in the center of the thirty-foot wide off-limits circle. Beyond was the mass of stubby pines, tiny trees no taller than ten or fifteen feet. Except for now and then clearings, they grew so huddled together they produced a thick, dwarfed forest of a million acres that had been giving a lie to this part of New Jersey for a millennium. The Pinelands.

When Schweitzer saw Berardi he beckoned with a curled index finger. Berardi's eyes were wide and confused. He stood stiffly, shoulders locked, hands in the pockets of his jeans. Just a few feet to his right, a state police corporal was checking the ground for blood stains, casings and footprints. There were still a few small puddles of rain water in the beige-colored sand from the thunder storm of the night before. Soon the July sun and the hungry sand would suck them dry.

Schweitzer broke off his conversation and with a pissed off look walked toward Berardi, who immediately ducked under the yellow tape to meet him. Schweitzer took Berardi by the elbow and walked him to the Toyota. Its front bumper was tangled with vines. All four doors were open. An officer leaned into the driver's seat with a powder jar in her left hand and a fine brush in the other, but Schweitzer knew there would be no prints.

Berardi copied Schweitzer when the agent grabbed his hankie and held it to his nose and mouth. When Schweitzer quickly opened the trunk lid, Berardi shook his arm away from Schweitzer and vomited. The FBI agent jumped backwards.

"Yo Stan," yelled a state police sergeant. "Nice move." Several other cops laughed. A Medford EMT who had been busy fussing with stretcher straps saw what happened and met Berardi at the yellow tape, helped him under and hastened him to the rear of the mobile medical lab, where she sat him down on the wide bumper, made him put his head between his knees and wafted a stick of ammonia beneath his nose.

Schweitzer, with his hanky still in place, took another look inside the trunk, looking at the little corpse who caused Berardi's breakfast to be deposited on his shoes and pants. The corpse was on its knees, bent in a Muslim-like prayer position. What remained of its face rested on a jack handle and a blood-dotted pile of rags.

This was a small person, thin in life, but bloated in death. The red-checked Bermuda shorts were down around the man's ankles. He wore sandals. Feasting around the crack of his rectum were flies and maggots, which combined with the sour, rotten stench had overturned Berardi's stomach. Berardi had not seen the handful of twenty-dollar bills that someone had lodged into the crack of the victim's ass, which Schweitzer knew was a calling card identifying the deceased as a rat who disclosed secrets for money.

When Berardi recovered sufficiently enough to breathe without gasping, a cop walked him back a hundred yards to a Medford police car parked next to the house that Berardi had been building for the past several weeks. It was peaceful there. Berardi looked haplessly at the bundles of shingles and then up to the unfinished roof that he wanted to work on today.

Stan Schweitzer arrived about ten minutes later, leaned into the rear window of the police car and said, "You really don't know what's going on, do you?

"What the hell does it look like to you?" Berardi answered, taking away the smelling salts from his nose. "I'm sorry I barfed on you."

Schweitzer opened the door and sat heavily in the seat besides Berardi. He was sweating and had taken off his jacket, undid the tie knot and wiped his face with a freckled forearm. Drops of sweat hung on the roots of his thinning slicked back red hair.

"You know who it is," said Schweitzer.

"I think so."

"Is that section of woods part of your property here?" Schweitzer asked.

Berardi nodded, then looked at Schweitzer: "I own sixty acres, all the way back to the cranberry bog. That's mine too." He paused to wipe his mouth again with the handkerchief. "Who found him?"

"The girl with the horse. Who is she?"

"Just a kid from around here. I let her ride here."

Schweitzer was about to say something else when a tall man in white coveralls came to the car and with a head motion asked Schweitzer to step outside.

"His chest is crushed and he has a Godzilla-sized bullet hole between the eyes that was caused by something powerful. I've seen this before. A four-eighty Ruger or a forty-four Magnum," said the State Police forensics examiner, Marty Rowland. "Something like that, something big. Dirty Harry must have shot this guy. But I would say this is a rather emphatic gangland execution." He opened a pack of cinnamon mints and one by one began putting several in his mouth.

"How long do you think he's been here?" asked Schweitzer.

Rowland shrugged: "Four, five days, maybe. And there's something else," said Rowland. "The body's covered with something salty. I'll call it sea water."

"Now you're telling me he was drowned too?" said Schweitzer.

"I'll never know until I get him to the lab."

Schweitzer opened the car door and motioned for Berardi to get out. "This is Vincent Berardi," he said to the medical examiner. "He owns this property." He nodded over his shoulder. "He's building this house here."

Rowland started to shake hands but Schweitzer put out a hand to stop him.

"Hold it Marty," Schweitzer said. He pointed towards Vince's hands.

Rowland looked curiously at Vince and said, "Let's see your

hands, if you don't mind."

Vince stuck them out and Rowland stooped to look for powder burns. He stood up and said to Schweitzer, "He's okay."

Rowland turned to go back to the crime scene just as the ambulance carrying the little cadaver was passing through the trees on its way to the lab in Hamilton. Rowland stopped with an afterthought and yelled for Schweitzer again.

"I assume you have some background on the victim. I'd like to know a little more than just his name. The state police sergeant back there identified...Let's see." He opened a notebook and read, "Anthony Trapetto. Do you know him?"

"Yes I do," said Schweitzer with something like a regretful sigh. "But I'll be in to talk to you later. When will you be doing the autopsy?"

"Right away, right away," said Rowland gleefully. "Haven't had one like this in months."

Berardi in the meantime had turned his back on the two and lifted a bundle of shingles, anxious like the forensics investigator to get back to routine measures of his life. He nearly dropped the bundle and felt his knees buckle when Schweitzer asked, "Do you own a gun, Vince?"

He looked at Schweitzer with a stare of resignation and fear, a cold wave of more nausea that he had to force back with every muscle tensed. His pulse rate spiked as he went to his pickup truck and from beneath the front seat pulled out the semi-automatic .32.

"The registration's at home," he said, his voice flat, handing the pistol to the FBI agent.

Schweitzer hefted the weapon, sniffed the barrel and bounced it upon his open palm as if weighing it and mentally comparing its abilities with the hole in Anthony Trapetto's face.

"When was the last time you fired this?"

"Weeks ago, at the range. I bought the thing after..."

"I know why you bought it," said Schweitzer, examining the weapon as though willing it to talk. "I'm taking this, Vince. You'll hear from me. And like before, don't plan on going anywhere."

Schweitzer leaned into Berardi's face and looked hard at him. Vince was about the same height, no more than five feet six, but stocky, with a thick neck, beefy calloused hands, a hard jaw and black curled hair turning lightly gray. His silver-rimmed glasses were fogged partially by sweat. But what Schweitzer saw in Berardi's eyes was the kind of fear that teetered toward loss of control. Seizing the opportunity, he whispered, letting his breath fall on Vince's face: "Now's the time, buddy. I'm still looking real hard for your friend Bannon." He watched as the warning floated through Vince's brain.

"What do you have to tell me?" Schweitzer asked, his chin hoisted like a stern schoolmaster cornering a frightened pupil.

Berardi studied Schweitzer's determined face — the thin line of his lips, his wide-opened eyes. Then he looked down, turned and walked away.

Chapter 2: TOUGH TIMES

July 13, 1979.

The next day's newspapers revealed to Vince and Julie Berardi facts and background that they already knew.

The *Philadelphia Inquirer* wrote: "The decaying body of a North Jersey Teamsters official who is a suspect in the disappearance of former Teamsters boss Jimmy Hoffa was found in the trunk of a car deep in the woods of the South Jersey Pinelands yesterday.

"The FBI identified the deceased as Anthony Trapetto, forty-six, a vice president of Teamsters Local 319 of North Jersey, whose partly decaying corpse was discovered in the trunk of a 1972 black Toyota Corolla, which was identified as being stolen July 6 in Piscataway.

"Trapetto is one of several North Jersey Teamsters aligned with the organized crime family of Rocco Scalesi, who is president of Local 319 with headquarters in Rahway. Shortly after Hoffa's disappearance on July 30, 1975, Trapetto was one of several Teamsters leaders called before a federal grand jury in Detroit. He took the Fifth Amendment fifty-two times.

"'It was a gangland style execution'," said New Jersey State Police spokesman Meryl Gagne, who said the crime scene was reported by a motorist alerted by a young girl riding her horse on a Pinelands trail.

"Other investigators were mum on details but *The Inquirer* learned from reliable sources that several twenty-dollar bills had been stuffed into the victim's rectum area, a gangland message that the deceased had been a paid informant.

"The heavily wooded Medford Township area where Trapetto's body was found is north of Tabernacle Road and west of Route 206 on land owned by South Jersey building contractor

Vincent Berardi..."

Vince put down the paper and and looked out through the screened-in back porch at the tidy rear lawn, where the plot of grass crept right up to the edge of a distant row of flowers. There the green stopped, in one absolutely straight line like a miniature cliff. No ragged edges to the lawn. No interfering with the daffodils and hyacinths, blooming magnificently against their woody little field of bark mulch.

No messes. As his life was once. As it was fifteen months ago before he got greedy. That's what he saw now. Dreams, ambition, the quest, and greed.

The money chase took only time back then, but the means would justify the end. He assured himself that the Vincent Berardi Construction Co. would get the $750,000 to begin building seven high-end post and beam houses in the Jersey Pinelands for one unarguable reason.

The Atlantic City casinos were now actual, their glass and chrome facades situated on the boardwalk facing each morning's rising sun. Like the waves pounding the sandy beach, a sea of money was pouring onto the revived Jersey coastline. Two casinos were built and already sucking busloads of customers from Philly, New York, Washington and Baltimore. A third casino would be up and running by summer's end. The shiny-suit executives transplanted from Vegas, London and the Bahamas will surely welcome the half-hour commute from their new, private and palatial homes in the woods, smack between Philly and AC. All that Vince Berardi had to do was secure the bank loan and build them.

But the money search had become as tedious and tiresome as this one, particular late-morning day of drizzle outside the First National Bank in Hammonton in the Spring of 1978.

Nearing lunch time, Mr. Dwyer, the loan officer, watched the clock over Vince's shoulders: "Times are tough for everyone. Eighteen percent consumer lending rates. Many, many defaults."

Minutes later, rejected and dejected, Vince sat in his new Bronco outside the bank. He picked up a glazed donut from its box on the passenger seat, bit hungrily through half of it and watched sugary flakes drop on his necktie and suit jacket. He looked down at the crumbs and decided to let them sit, to match the dishevelment of his loser's mood.

He touched the dashboard, fingered the radio knob, turned it on, turned it back to off, turned it on again. Off again. The voice of Elvis got as far as "You ain't nothin' but..." Tires hissed in the rain as traffic went by on Bellevue Avenue. He watched a young woman with wavy black hair cross the street, clutching her handbag above her head, using it as an umbrella. She began to jog and her breasts were jiggling beneath a silvery white blouse. Vince stared at her muscular legs as she ran, until she finally ducked into the protected alcove of the five and ten.

He sometimes chided himself for looking and lusting, but when he reached the Black Horse Pike and turned east toward home, the girl's sexy looks flashed again as he passed a farm stand on the south side of the highway. The shed was painted green, similar to the roadside vegetable stand that the Wolyniak family operated for the past two decades on Route 40 east of the small town of Buena.

The long shed and parking lot were backed up by several acres of flat, fertile fields — why Jersey earned the now out-of-date sobriquet, "the Garden State," supplying the ingredients canned by the Campbell Soup Company in Camden on the Delaware River. The Wolyniak shed was where the Berardi family, on nearly every trip back from Wildwood on summer Sunday evenings, would stop and load up on juicy Jersey tomatoes, freshly picked Silver Queen corn, cucumbers, carrots, lettuce and fruit. Young Vincent would sit often for the remainder of the car trip home to South Philly with a watermelon on his skinny lap.

The brief stops at the garden stand were the best fifteen minutes of the week. But while his parents moved between the wooden bins and bushel baskets of freshly picked vegetables, Vince stole stares at the perfectly luscious and ripened dark-haired beauty who stood behind the counter in a white apron. On hot days, he wished that he could stand beside her with a giant ostrich fan, waving the breeze upon her stunning face. He pledged a full life of slavery at her feet. It took him about a dozen shy visits before he was able to catch a glance from her, just a tad of a quizzical look.

Then that precious day, her customary smile broke to laughter; she invited him to talk. He hated leaving those teen-aged conversations and getting back in the car, and he went to bed on those Sunday nights with imaginary kisses on his hungry lips. They dated, and between his junior and senior year at Villanova, they were married in Queen of Angels Church, with a reception in a concrete block Farmers' Coop building between Vineland and Buena.

Chapter 3: THE WATERFALL

April 24, 1978.

The phone rang, Julie answered and handed it over. A soft drawl at the other end said, "Mister Berardi. This here is Oliver. Of Goddard's Southern Lumber. Just wanted to let you know your order is on the way."
"Oh, that's great news."
"And a reminder?" Oliver's voice slid up in range as though phrasing a question, which it wasn't. It was a South Carolinian's way of politely dropping a hammer on your toes. "Payment is due prior to delivery?"
"Well, thirty days you mean?"
"I'm so sorry, Mister Berardi. Since you are a first-time customer we just have to establish a good account from the get-go? I think you know how it is these days, the economy being so tight?" Vince agreed to the terms while his mind raced over a list of people who might tide him over.

Just a week before, Julie chastised him for going out of state for his building supplies. They argued. Vince won. Eastern white pine grown in Low Country soil has the quality of gold, not just because of its sheen; it is the best ever wood for framing post and beam. When planed, the wood develops only tiny checks, not the big gaps and cracks of hardwoods. And Eastern White Pine tends not to split or twist like the others.

"I guess our driver will be up your way about Thursday or so," said Oliver.

What a nice coincidence, thought Vince. The same day the mortgage is due, and the tuition to Nativity school for little Patty and Gloria. The lack of major capital that began as a large circle, was day by day closing in, soon to become a noose. On the coffee table was a stack of blueprints. Vince had gone over them just last night, seeking ways to cut costs.

The trick in construction was to increase the return by boosting the cost without too much impact on labor or materials. Enlarge some rooms, change the roof lines, add some dormers. With post and beam, you can do that with more options. Vince had studied the designs of old Pennsylvania barns, and read books and perused drawings of the medieval half-timbered homes of Old Europe. The best was when he spent a month in Vermont, taking Julie and the kids on a long, lolling vacation in the greenest and prettiest state he had ever seen, while he studied post and beam construction at a small school set up for guys like him.

He had told Andy Burke that he would have his house ready in the Pine Barrens in eighteen weeks, that construction could begin as soon as the weather cleared. The job site passed its perc test and was already permitted. Vince could get past the initial foundation work without the bank loan. But then he had to throw in the labor equation. He would hire some high school and college kids to work as soon as school was out. Cheaper labor? Sure. The tradeoff? A kid learns to build something solid, a construction skill that one never loses, always there, one of life's fallbacks, insurance against tough times. He had prepared for all of this, but the immediate deadline for the lumber payment was a jolt.

"I'm going out," Vince yelled.
"What about the Jungle Gym?" Julie yelled back. "You promised Patty and Gloria you'd get started on it."
"Can't," he yelled as the door was closing. He put on his suede jacket on the run.

Traffic on the Walt Whitman Bridge was light going west. A flood of trucks, cars and buses made their daily rush hour escape from the city going in the other direction.

He took local streets to the Philadelphia Navy Yard, passing red brick row homes lined in square blocks, smiling suddenly at the reminiscence of the famous Waterfall that he had built in one of them, the crowning construction achievement of a very young, one-man handy man. Instant fame descended upon him. Walking into Pork's Tavern on Catherine Street, guys yelling and laughing, patting him on the back. "Here's the guy who built Freddy

Bananas' waterfall!"

The accolades rang true because this was no ordinary outdoor waterfall, meant to dice up somebody's peewee lawn. This was an in-house waterfall, made of marble and granite, with some bits of pyrite for sparkle, piped-in Philadelphia water cascading from the third floor of a row house down two more floors to the living room below.

The customer was Alfredo "Freddy Bananas" Catalano, a trusted and productive earner of the Bruno crime family, a master hijacker whose field of operations extended from Harrisburg to Dover, Delaware, from the Jersey Shore and on up to Newark, where it invaded other families' territories who never-minded so long as they received a generous cut of the illegal proceeds. Freddy also smuggled cigarettes from North Carolina and was one of the most feared of loan sharks. His suits were hand-tailored. They made him regal; he used a fake grin to intimidate. Suckers behind in the vigorish found ways to pay up. Freddy lived high and he lived to pursue long-legged ladies who were not necessarily his wives, either present or ex.

Maddy Raynor, tall and willowy and the recipient of the waterfall, lived alone in the 300 block of Snyder Avenue. Freddy Bananas lived with his wife, Geraldine, only six blocks to the north, too far away to hear a shout. But in South Philly, the distance covered, that is, once the waterfall was up and cascading, it took only a couple of days of grapevine gossip to reach Geraldine.

For Vince, the rewards were not only monetary—"I'm sparing no expense," said Freddy Bananas. Vince's fame as a builder multiplied; the waterfall was legend. Soon he was building houses, initially small cottages at the Jersey shore, then larger homes, mostly in Delaware County and in South Jersey.

Vince's skills advanced with each project. Sometimes he reflected about the difficulty he had in placing the "moon" of Maddy's waterfall on the roof of the three-story row house. It gave Vince the most trouble, that is, angling the beam of the 500-watt spotlight from the third-floor ceiling above, getting it to shine on the cascading water into the small grotto on the first floor. That romantic moon became much too bright, figuratively at least, shining upon the baldish pate of Freddy Bananas. As he left

Maddy's house and canopied bed in the wee hours of an exotic evening, walking down the front steps from the porch, a bucketful of barn-red paint came his way, spraying its red and wet cape all over the camel's hair coat and a pair of Italian-made Oxfords handcrafted in Bologna.

The assailant was never publicly identified, and Freddie, who was not above shooting people for a living, did not retaliate. Mob guys deal with problems of the heart by bearing gifts. Thus did Geraldine earn an ankle-length sable coat and a dark silver BMW. Matching!

Chapter 4: FINDING FEENO

Vince stopped at the Navy Yard's massive iron gate and told the guard that he was a contractor with an appointment to see Vito Berardi at the No. 2 dry dock machine shop. A half-truth. Well, maybe one-fourth.

He turned left onto League Island Boulevard and took it halfway to the river. The Navy Yard was a little city in itself, with criss crossing flat streets, brick buildings, groceries, apartments, schools and day-care centers and playgrounds, long piers, tool sheds and mammoth dry docks. He parked in the lot next to the Navy Officer's Club. The aircraft carriers and battleships, mothballed since World War II, were faint silhouettes on the western horizon. It was about 4:30; the first shift of workers was letting out.

Membership in the Officer's Club was so lax in these peace-time years that the one-time blue and gold braid clientele had been compromised by men in Dickies and dirty work shoes. What hadn't been displaced were the portraits of Admirals Halsey and Nimitz on the wall behind the bar.

Vince ordered a shot of Corby's and a Schmidts on draft.

"Vito Berardi's little brother. Son of a bitch," said the bartender, whose name Vince could not remember for the moment. Then he recalled that it was "Sticks Gallagher," a member of a large family who had four other sons that he grew up with.

They caught up on who was where and doing what: "Shrimp, he's married, three kids, teaching school in Devon."

"Devon?" said Vince. "He went from South Philly to the Main Line?"

"Yeah, but he don't live in Devon."

"Where is Tweet?"

"Tweet ran afoul of the law. He'll be out this November,"

said Sticks, who moved away and rubbed the bar with a damp cloth. Vince decided not to ask about the fortunes of Ears and Honey Boy, the latter being his mother's favorite, who dealt with childhood teasing about his nickname with a swift poke in the nose.

After quaffing his fourth beer, Vince ambled to the Men's Room and when he returned, Sticks said, elbows on the bar, cigarette between two yellowed fingers, "Guess who I saw the other day."

Vince was not particularly interested.

"Remember Joe Bannon?"

"Feeno?"

"Yeah, Feeno. Ran into him a coupla' weeks ago up at the Teamsters Hall. Still fulla' bullshit."

"Yeah?"

"Like...he said he's workin' in finance now."

"If I know Feeno, that would be Advanced Bookmaking. I guess you could call that finance."

"'Nah', he said 'a bank.' He works in a bank. Hard to believe that guy in a suit and tie."

When Vince walked in the door about seven, Julie was already cleaning up the dishes. Her stiff demeanor forecast an impending storm. Vince turned to walk to the garage where his wood shop was.

"You're not going to eat?" Julie asked.

He looked hard at her face. When mad, her chin would tilt, her eyes would open wide. Her prominent cheekbones — her Magyar Warrior Princess look — seemed sharper and more threatening. But he witnessed now the softer eyes than five minutes before, and changed his mind. "Yeah, I'm sorry."

He helped put the girls to bed. Gloria, the youngest, urged him to "use your Pooh voice," when he read another exciting tale from the "Hundred Acre Wood."

When Vince and Julie settled for the night in the king-sized canopied brass bed, he finally told her what he had been up to.

"Vito never did show up. I don't know what the hell I'm going to do."

"Are you sure it's a good idea to borrow money from

Vito?" she asked.

"Well, him, or somebody else over there. I'm desperate."

She sat up in bed. "No, no, no! Don't tell me that. You're not going to borrow money over there."

"They know me. And it's short term. I know I'll get a legitimate loan."

Julie was known to both close and even distant friends as dependable, smart, generous, happy, good to be around. Women, in particular, sought her counsel on everything from gardening to raising children and handling husbands. Julie was the knowing one, with smiles, grins and loud laughter in abundance, the one not to get rattled, but the first one there when trouble strikes. There was one hot button, however, touched occasionally by smart people whom she loved but let their guard down. That was a weakness she could not tolerate.

Vince realized he had ticked that spot in her the seconds the words escaped — and they did escape thoughtlessly — from his thinned out, tired brain.

From her prone position in bed, she bent furiously toward him and said, with an emphatic whisper, "If you think you're going to go to a loan shark, say goodbye to me. I'm not kidding Vince. I'll take the kids and I'll leave. I will...fucking...leave."

The last two words were thuds on his ears. He could not see her eyes, only the black silhouette above him. He rolled over and pretended that he didn't need to hear anymore.

She whispered, angrily. "You're an ignorant ass. Your father. Your poor old dad. That's all I hear from you sometimes. You recite it to me, you recite it to the kids, you recite it to your brother! The great lesson. Remember?"

Her teeth were set, her jaw was tight. He felt her breath.

"Did you learn? Did you? Did you, Vince?

She talked to the back of his head, but he heard each word, and he heard from her voice, now trembling, the tears, the anger and the letdown. "I mean it, Vince. We will leave."

She threw back the sheet, got out of bed, and as she went to the bathroom, her bare feet padding heavily on the shag rug, he saw, maybe for the hundredth time in his life, even though that dark day happened before he was born, his father holding his hands in front of him, a jacket draped over the handcuffs so the neighbors could not see.

Julie ran the water in the bathroom, but Vince didn't hear.

What he heard was when he was sixteen, and his father told the story as they sat in the small living room on 11th Street after returning from Mass on a Sunday morning:

"I want you to know," he told his two sons. "All of it."

At the beginning of the Depression, when Piero Berardi was barely out of his teen-aged years and starting a family, he was drafted into the involuntary army of the unemployed.

Deciding to seize the opportunity to become independent, he borrowed money to buy an old flatbed stake truck, a six-cylinder Chevy, and went into the ice business. His tiny ice house, hardly bigger than an outhouse, stood in decaying shambles in a corner of the Berardi back yard in South Philly for most of Vince's childhood, a testament to failure. Vince did not learn until many years after his father's first telling of the story who were the major customers of the business — the speakeasies that dotted Prohibition's landscape from 1920 to 1933. In the mornings, Vince's father drove his truck to the Regal Coal & Ice Company on Oregon Avenue, picked up a truckload of huge and heavy cakes of ice, then made many back-alley stops to places that discreetly sold Canadian and moonshine whiskey, and beer brewed illegally in upstate Pennsylvania.

The business took in enough money to feed Piero's growing family but not enough to make the payments on the truck. So he did what was customary in those days, borrowed money from a bookmaker who did business around the corner, and when he fell behind in his payments, the bookie very generously gave him credit, month after month until Piero was forced to accept the deal — "do this one little thing to relieve your debt" — that reached the inevitable.

The Packard Convertible Sedan was an easy hot-wire, parked all day five days a week at the Paoli Railroad Station on suburban Philly's Main Line. All that Piero had to do was make delivery of the car to a man he knew only as "Spuds", dropping the bright yellow Packard off at the rear of a filling station on 69th Street in Upper Darby just west of the Philly city line. He got a friend to drive the ice truck out to the Main Line and drop him off at the station. By the time he got the Packard to Upper Darby, the cops were waiting. Piero took the fall, and because of his crime-free record at the time, did only six months in Moyamensing Prison. When released, he went to work for the coal and ice plant, doing forty more years of hard, but remorsefully honest labor.

    The story, as he laid in bed staring at the dim light through the window, played out in Vince's mind like the pages of a well-turned book. He turned to Julie, put his hand on her shoulder, but hearing her soft, deep breath upon the pillow, rolled back and stared at the dark, blank ceiling.

Chapter 5: NORTH JERSEY

April 26, 1978.

Vince, who was driving his pickup with the scroll lettering, "Vincent Berardi, Building & Remodeling" on the driver's door, found Unity Savings & Trust just off the Clifton exit of the Garden State Parkway. He drove east on Route 3, passing a country club and a couple of large cemeteries which made up the bulk of the greensward amidst a continuing facade of concrete and vinyl-sided malls and small stucco houses. In the distance were the still brand new, donut-shaped Giants' Stadium and next to it, the Meadowlands Race Track. Feeno's bank came up, a small whitewashed stucco building located in a strip mall, sharing a parking lot with Lotza Pizza on one side and Al's Home Furnishings on the other. Cars, buses and trucks sailed by with incessant noise, throwing up Jersey grit.

Vince vowed to himself that this was to be a social visit, to reacquaint with an old friend. He reminded himself that the loan application at the First Commerce Bank in Atlantic City was pending, and he might hear something any day now.

Inside, when the thick glass door closed behind him, the highway sounds were quieted to a muffled rush. Looking around he saw three tellers' cages encased and separated by a dark-stained plywood paneling. Sitting on the floor at each end of the lobby were two large baskets containing plastic rhododendrons of leathery leaves and bell-shaped blooms. Opposite the cages was a rack with deposit and withdrawal slips, and a stack of brochures with the headline, "Ask About Our Fabulous Rates." Yes, it was a bank, of sorts, humbled by location, but nevertheless a bank.

"Mr. Bannon?" Vince asked as a middle-aged woman with gray hair peered from behind the middle teller's window.

"I'm afraid he's not in at the moment. Can anyone else

help you?"

"Do you know when he'll be in?"

"Yes, he just went out for a moment. Said he would be right back."

Feeno had fixed their meeting "at ten sharp." Vince's watch read 10:02. He sat in a plush but inexpensive chair, perhaps purchased next door at Al's, and thumbed a *Skiing* magazine. Not just last winter's, but dated Fall 1977. The second hand of a large circular clock hanging high on the wall swept round and round.

Ten thirty came; ten thirty went. Ten forty-five; ten fifty.

Idle memories: childhood scenes of running to school, Feeno and Vince, always late. Standing on steamy summer nights on Two Street in South Philly outside of Murtaugh's corner grocery, swatting the mosquitoes that festered from the Delaware River marshland behind the dump. Feeno Bannon tall and thin. Large ears. Sloppy grin. Always talking, a funny kid whose easy pace and lack of concern disguised a buried intelligence, built and reinforced on cunning.

Feeno Bannon was one of those kids your mother warned you about. How did she know he was risky to be around? He talked fast and out of the side of his mouth at times, but she said, "It's in his eyes. I can always tell."

Vince hated that his mom knew more about street-corner culture than he did. Where did she acquire such insights?

But there was the time at the Bayer Playground pool. Hot day, Feeno and Vince about ten years old. Clever Feeno takes his pocket knife and carves a peep hole from a tiny nail hole into the girls' changing room.

"You oughta' see the tits on this one," he said. Vince's turn to peep. Vince gets caught, gets punished. Feeno doesn't. Moms, as always, know something.

"Did he say when he would return?" Vince asked the teller, rising impatiently from his chair. Since he had come in, a couple dozen customers had come and gone; their traffic seemed to match in human form the busy flow of vehicles out on Route 3. Customers ranged from young wives towing uninterested children to geezers cashing their pension checks. All, he guessed, were a K-

Mart crowd, except for two burly young men who swept in hurriedly. One with a crew cut wore only a black tee shirt above his jeans. The other had on a gray hooded sweat shirt above dirty overalls. His work boots were caked in mud.

"Where's Bannon?" one asked, and when one of the tellers said that "he should be back any minute," the two men turned and left in an obvious hurry to get somewhere else. "Goddamned nut!" one of them muttered as he went through the door. Vince watched the pair move toward a large, dark car parked outside. One leaned into the back window, gesturing as if in some kind of explanation to someone in the rear seat. All that Vince could see was a fat hand in the sleeve of a business suit. The hand, which held a cigar, waved up and down rapidly. The man who leaned into the rear looked down at his watch, and said something undecipherable to those inside. Then both men got in. The car raced away, spinning rubber on the asphalt, barely squeezing ahead of an eighteen-wheeler whose driver blasted angrily with his air horn.

When he returned to his seat and began his second hour of waiting, Vince felt again the slight breeze as the big glass door opened, and from outside, above the dull roar on the highway, he heard the familiar voice yelling to someone in the parking lot. "You ain't seen nothin' yet, pal. We got plans! Big plans!"

"I'm a son of a gun!" Feeno yelled loudly when he saw him. "Look who's here! Rita! Rita! See this guy, this goomba! Best friend I ever had. Girls, say hello to Vince Berardi!"

He slapped Vince's back and tousled his hair, grabbed him by the shoulder with one arm and gently swept him beyond the counter and into a tiny office.

"You're still skinny!" Vince observed.

"You're still a pissy-assed Dago." Feeno grinned and his freckled face seemed unchanged from youth. He sat down quickly in an office recliner and within the same nimble movement hiked his feet to the top of the desk, one ankle resting on the other, hands behind his head. He wore white loafers and apple green socks which matched the color of his polyester slacks and suit jacket, which he unbuttoned, revealing a white belt, and white cotton sport shirt. The top three shirt buttons were unattached, revealing two narrow gold chains draped across his thin chest. One chain carried a large Celtic cross. Its silver image stood out against Feeno's tanning parlor skin.

"I'm not looking at J. Pierpont Morgan here," Vince said. "You're a banker? Are you running the show here?"

"New aged! I'm a new-age banker. Times are changing. Gotta roll with the times. Look, I got a computer." He nodded to a wide desk in the corner. "Everything I need is in there. Records that filled twenty filing cabinets. In there. Except beer and sandwiches. I'm getting hungry." He looked at his watch. A Rolex, Vince noted.

"C'mon, let's go eat; it's stuffy in here. Then I got a golf date. You got your sticks with you?"

They were hustling out the door. Feeno chattering, Vince hustling to keep up with his long strides. In front of Al's Home Furnishings, a teen-aged boy was struggling, helped by a young woman, to lift a cumbersome upholstered chair into the rear of her station wagon. The chair was wrapped in heavy brown paper which tore and slipped as they tried to lift.

Without a word, Feeno jumped to the spot, grabbed one corner of the chair, and with the teenager managed to hoist it into the car. Feeno, again without a word, turned and returned to the driver's seat of his Lincoln Continental, nodding affirmatively at the "thank you" from the woman.

Seated beside him, Vince yelled above the roar of an eighteen-wheel semi going eastbound toward New York. "Where the hell are we going?"

"Upper Montclair CC. I'm a member."

"But I don't...!" Vince didn't finish the sentence. Suddenly, he felt winded, then resigned to let this be Feeno's day.

Feeno backtracked along Route 3 toward the parkway, then made a left into the country club.

They hardly settled in at the lunch table, ordered some drinks (Coke for Vince, tonic and lime for Feeno), when Feeno propped his elbows on the table, made a tent with his fingers and asked: "How much are we talkin' about?"

"What?" Vince stifled a choke, then laughed. "What are you talkin' about?"

"You sonofabitch, you," Feeno said, grinning, leaning back

in his chair. "I could read you when we were kids, I read you now." He leaned forward. "You're a lovable son of a gun! I bet your wife can predict everything you do, too. Am I right?"

Vince laughed and nodded sheepishly. Vince leaned back in his chair, looked him straight in the eyes: "Seven fifty."

"Seven hundred and fifty dollars. I got that in my back pocket." He grinned again.

"No, seven-fifty-thousand."

Feeno blinked, but kept his smile: "What are you building down there in South Jersey, your own casino?"

Vince gave him a few details on his project, and when he mentioned that his prospective homebuyers would foremost be casino executives, Feeno leaned forward. "How far from Atlantic City is your land?"

"About a half hour's drive, more or less, equidistant between Philly and AC."

"In the Pinelands," Feeno averred.

"Yes, in the Pinelands. Potentially beautiful home sites. Private, woodsy, isolated, but not far from civilization."

The waitress brought lunch: a big club sandwich for Feeno, a salad for Vince, whose stomach was beginning to get jumpy. He tried to subdue his feelings of anticipation and anxiety.

"I'll have to move this past my loan committee," Feeno said, deciding to change the subject from business to personal. "But a nice loan like that looks good on our books." He muttered, "Legit, legit, legit as he picked up a napkin and ignored Vince's puzzled look.

The main dining room of the country club looked out through a bank of wide and tall windows made up of small panes. White enameled tables and chairs added to the aura of lightness to the room. Ivy hung low from the outside roof top, shielding some of the sunlight.

"I know you're dying to find out how yours truly ended up with such a cushy white-collar job," asked Feeno, looking across at Vince with a devilish glare.

"Exactly my thoughts. I lost track of you after high school. I heard you joined the Army."

"I was drafted. What do you think I am? Nuts? Me join

anything? He took a sip of the tonic and lime. "Yeah, I went to Viet Nam and matured ten years in one day. An RPG — that's a rocket propelled grenade. It can do that to you.

"And after I got out of Nam, one day I was visiting my Aunt Annie up in Jersey City. Saw this ad in the paper, for returning vets, enroll at Seton Hall. So, I took my GEDs, got the high school diploma and learned Finance at Seton Hall."

"Finance?" Vince asked. "That figures. You probably devised more systems to play the horses, didn't you?"

"Actually, no; well actually, yes!" he said. "I fart around with systems, once in a while, but I don't play the nags anymore. Gave it up! Instead of going to the track, I'm a regular at Gambler's Anonymous. And on other nights, I go to AA meetings. And I quit smoking."

The waitress brought their jumbo shrimp cocktails and fresh rolls in a wicker basket covered with a little red cloth.

"So, how did you get to be a bank president?"

"Simple," said Feeno, lifting a shrimp and dunking it into the cocktail sauce. "I worked my way up from the bottom."

Feeno suddenly looked deep in thought and stared out the window.

"Well, who are your depositors in this bank?"

"Teamsters," he answered without hesitation, turning back to look at Vince. "Over a thousand individual accounts and the entire health and welfare and pension accounts of three different Teamsters locals. Solid security."

"Your bank," Vince said cautiously, "doesn't look like a big bank."

"Welcome to the New Age of finance," Feeno said. "Our bank. You noticed that we're right on one of the busiest highways in New Jersey. On purpose. Old banks? Look at them. Solid granite, marble interiors, all those big Greek columns. A goddamned safe as big as your house. That's capital. The real estate itself represents a big chunk of the wealth of the bank. They loan money against those assets. Hundreds of thousands of dollars.

"Today's bank? Mobile. Bring it to the people. Bring it right out on the highway where those truck drivers and their families can have access. You were sitting there. Did you notice our clientele? Hard-working families with a few dimes to square away. But they're able to get access to Teamster funds, for savings, loans, college tuition, mortgages, home building like you, renovations. That's why we're able to function with such little overhead.

"In your case? If you put in for a loan? You'd be borrowing against the largest Teamster network in the whole country. Do you have any idea how many trucks are rolling daily in and out of New York and North Jersey? Thousands upon thousands. A lotta' wealth, Vinnie boy, a lotta' wealth."

He ate the last of his salad and after both hastily gobbled their sandwiches, Feeno said he would drive Vince back to his car. "Besides, you have to pick up your loan application."

"What about your golf game?"

"Screw golf; I can play any day of the week."

As they left the restaurant, waitresses were setting up tables on the veranda, which was mottled with bright sunshine splashing through the maple trees. Feeno hailed a group on the first tee.

He walked toward them, with Vince trailing.

"Where the hell you been? We been waitin' for ya!" said a beefy man with a full head of hair made up of black ringlets and a neck that measured perhaps twenty inches in circumference, but only a half-inch between his shoulders and his chins. It appeared as if his head were resting on a barrel. His nose was large enough to have fallen from Mount Rushmore.

"Business, boys, business," Feeno yelled back, smiling at the group.

He made the introductions: "Vince Berardi, South Jersey super contractor, owns several acres of prime Jersey property. And my best old buddy from Philly."

One of the foursome stood out from the others. He wore baggy white knickers, "plus fours" they are called, with green argyle socks, a starched white dress shirt, long sleeves included, and a white cap, a la Ben Hogan. On his feet were spotless brown and white saddle shoes. He smiled and shook Vince's hand firmly.

A third golfer was muscular and middle-aged, with blond hair flattened to his scalp and black knitted tee-shirt deliberately tight to show off his gym pecs. A body builder supremo. He barely touched fingers with Vince. And the fourth was a small man. Everything about him was small. Eyes like raisins, a tiny mouth, hands and feet. Even his teeth were small and squirrel-like, slightly protruded. He nodded suspiciously in Vince's direction.

Small talk followed the introductions, and it was clear that the golfers were impatient to get on with their game, all except "Plus Fours", who eyed Vince with apparent interest. He wore a generous smile, tanned skin and his eyes sparkled. His name, according to Feeno, was Fred Russo.

As they drove back to the bank, Feeno explained that "Plus Fours" was an attorney, "obviously a flashy guy. You oughta' see his suits."

"Double-breasted, with a carnation," Vince imagined out loud. "Does he wear spats?"

"Hah, hah!" Feeno paused for a second, making a left past the stone pillared entrance to the club grounds. "You know his sister."

"I know his sister! I know his sister? Who is that?"

"You heard of Lena Russell, the singer? Velvet voiced. They almost ruined her, tried to make a rock star out of her."

"Lena Russell?"

"Yep, the same."

Lena Russell achieved popularity in the 1950s, recorded several platinum and gold records, appeared in some heart throb teen-age oriented movies, then faded from the stage, more or less, as time wore on. She had a low-pitched vibrato-free voice, which Vince remembered strummed your heartstrings, particularly when she sang Italian ballads.

"Fred is her younger brother," said Feeno. "Brilliant guy, out of Newark. Yale Law School. He's been representing the North Jersey Teamsters for a few years now. You should get to know him, Vince. The guy's got connections up the ass. Good buddy of Governor Gross; he's in with state lawmakers, represented some of the casinos at the Casino Control Commission hearings. He's one helluva fund-raiser too. There's this youth center up in East Caldwell..."

Feeno talked incessantly, but Vince had stopped hearing

half of what he said. He watched a refinery slip past the window, then another low-flying 747 piercing white clouds above Newark International Airport. Vince's thoughts, like the plane, were shooting to the sky.

Chapter 6: BUSTED

When he drove into the driveway, Julie was on her hands and knees, pulling at weeds and errant grass between the house and brick walk that went around the front and sides. She planned to plant periwinkle there. Patty and Gloria were pretending to help. A robin paced the lawn, his sonar tuned to the warm earth below.

"Daddy, daddy. Will you build our swing set now?" yelled Gloria. "Today, please, today?"

"Maybe baby." He picked her up and swung her in a circle, her little feet swirling and her still fat arms and hands posed as if in prayer.

Julie rose from the dirt, wiped her hands on her jeans and searched his face. "Where have you been?"

"Oh, just driving around. I was at the Burke site checking to see what the drainage looked like after the storm."

He went to the garage, which he built five years before as the envy of every auto-loving man in the neighborhood. There were bays for four automobiles, but only two were reserved for the Chevy pickup truck and the Bronco. The other two provided Vince's workshop, with a long rack of seasoned lumber against an outside wall, a table saw, a cutoff saw, band saw, jig saw, drill press, lathe, planer, router, and a long sturdy work bench with storage beneath for the smaller hand-held power tools. Attached to the outside wall of the garage facing the sun's path was a glassed-in hot house that contained Julie's Vince-built potting table and garden tools.

Vince began unraveling a clothesline rope from a cleat screwed to the side of a joist. The family canoe hung by the rope and pulleys in the garage rafters, stored for the winter. Letting it down to the concrete floor, he dragged it through the back yard to the lake and turned it upside down in the bushes. He returned to the workshop and hoisted the mechanical post-hole digger out to the back lawn.

"Daddy," asked Patty. "Is that for the swing set? Are you gonna build it?"

"You bet, sweetie pie."

The few days that followed worked in parallel with the warm days, with trees and bushes that had been full of colors that were pastel pink and brilliant white now giving themselves bright brushes of a pale green that would darken as the summer days advanced.

He called Rick Hayes, who owned the big back hoe, and advised him to start digging on the Andy Burke corner site.

Vince's properties were on the edge of New Jersey's proposed Pinelands area, a state and federal conservation plan to limit development by preserving and legally protecting much of the southeastern part of the state, except the communities fronting the ocean in the east and the Delaware River in the west. The move toward conservation only made peripheral properties like Vince's more valuable.

The Pine Barrens, as they were also called, contradict Jersey's image as a paved-over flatland of refineries and turnpikes, ruled by Mafiosi and shady public officials. But from Trenton south are a million acres of sand, supporting and growing a strange but hardy plant life of holly, laurel and huckleberry. There are miles of cranberry bogs, sand quarries and stubby pitch pines, barely ten feet high. The area boasts a mammoth underground aquifer, a body of virtually untapped fresh water; there are cedar-colored creeks of pure water, a few rattlesnakes and more copperheads, and some of the world's heartiest mosquitoes.

It took a full week for Vince to get all of his plans and financial data together to send to Unity Savings. In the meantime, he received a "sorry" letter from the First Commerce Bank in Atlantic City. He went to his local bank in Medford and secured a cashier's check for collateral of $36,000, almost tapping out his business account except for $10,252 that he needed for incidentals. Although he didn't have to, he expressed by overnight delivery the entire collateral, including the deed to his house, the construction plans and financial records up to Clifton. Feeno said it would take no more than two weeks for his loan committee to give the okay.

"It's in the bag, Vinny," he said by phone one day. "We're delighted to extend some business down to South Jersey. In fact, we're getting out a new sales brochure. I wanta' flood Atlantic City with 'em. I want your mug and your grateful quote on it. The satisfied borrower. Okay with you?"

Vince became so busy lining up carpenters that ten days went by without him thinking or worrying about the loan. Feeno had called a couple to times to check on some minor incidentals. Vince was impressed with his thoroughness. His maturity since his teenage days was astounding. No longer was he the kid searching for all the angles, the shortcut connections.

So it was that the two-week waiting period for approval of the loan came and went without a word. Vince trusted the transaction, trusted Feeno. Fifteen days went by, then eighteen, and with each episode of checking the mailbox, his concern became an itch. Nothing to worry about, just an itch. Feeno was so very unlike the half-dozen bankers who so far had said "No." Feeno felt no need to "size him up," like the bankers' eyes that shifted from Vince's tie and business suit to his fissured, worker's hands, scarred and overused.

Vince waited twenty full days without the word of approval; he decided to call. After a few rings, the operator came on and announced casually, "I am sorry, that phone has been disconnected."

"What do you mean, disconnected? It's a bank!" Vince was staring out the back window, looking absently at the half-built swing set. Some ducks were quacking loudly in the lake at the edge of the sloping lawn.

"I'm sorry, sir, that's all the information that I have."

"There's no other number? Connect me with Directory Assistance."

"What city, please?"

"Clifton, New Jersey. The number for Unity Savings and Loan."

But there was no forwarding address. No other number. "Check this name, 'Joseph Bannon, of Clifton.'"

"We have a Joseph Bannon, of 216 Carpenter Street. That number too has been disconnected."

Vince stared out the window. After a week of drought, soft rain was nestling into the thirsty earth of well-kept suburban lawns. Where they lived, Vince's property was an advertisement for serenity.

He called his local bank to check on his account.

"The $36,000 check that you refer to was cleared five days ago," said the bank manager.

May 24, 1978

As he drove north on the turnpike, in former fields of green were curving rows of homes, blurred into developments in lines that were as monotonous as they were confusing. South Jersey's few remaining farms were being ground up into a plane of single family dwellings and apartments. Strip malls proliferated. Developers were cashing in. He hit the gas pedal, propelling the pickup past a couple of tractor trailers hastening north. Counting the new developments just between Medford and Freehold recalled a Planning Commission meeting of several months ago when a green-clad woman berated the commission members for "allowing our beautiful farms to be eaten alive by greed." The woman looked at Vince as though he were a child rapist.

He welcomed taking leave of the turnpike onto the Route 3 traffic and finally into the paved lot of Unity Savings. A block or two before he arrived at the modest little bank, he had visualized a smiling Feeno Bannon at the door, arms outspread, grinning and saying, "Some joke, huh. Had you there for a minute. C'mon in, buddy, I got your money for you."

The otherwise truth was determined by the sight of a venetian blind in the main office window. It hung at a lopsided angle. No vehicles were in the parking lot. He got out and walked and was able to see that someone had begun to razor away the gold lettering on the front door. As he approached he could read only the letters "U-N-I..."

A paper sign was scotch-taped to the front door: "Closed by authority of the Federal Deposit Insurance Corporation." Vince looked in a window and saw an overturned chair, a stack of papers lying on the floor. So was a telephone. The phone that didn't work. Through the sun glare on the window it was difficult to see, but the door to Feeno's office appeared to be open to nothing. No furniture. No photos on the wall except, he observed by squinting and shielding his eyes, a citation honoring Unity Savings for its sponsorship of a local Little League team. Angrily, Vince smacked the door with the flat of his fist.

Next door at Lotza Pizza, the kid behind the counter was shoveling a pizza into the oven.

"Three days ago, I think. They were here one day and gone the next. Nobody knows where. Honest to God!" An older man came out of the back room, wearing a dirty apron and a Mets cap. "These guys were like the Baltimore Colts. Closed up and beat it in the dark of night. But nobody knows where. Nobody. We've all been talkin' about it. Hell, they were my best customers."

"Who were they, what were their names?" Vince asked fretfully. 'The girls who worked there. Feeno! Uh, Mr. Bannon? Did you know him? Do you know where he lives?"

On the other side at Al's Furniture the answers were the same. Nonexistent. Total perplexity about the sudden closing and vanishing of the bank was the consistent observation of the neighborhood of small businesses. All the while that he stood there confused and angry, the incessant traffic on the highway sped past, going elsewhere, making deliveries, carrying people to their jobs, kids to school, people on errands. Everyone and every thing was moving, except him.

Giving up, he asked the location of the local police station. An officer in a dark blue uniform ushered him into the office of Chief Reginald Quigley.

"Sit down," the chief said kindly, looking him over. He seemed less interested in helping Vince find out what happened than he was in finding out who he was, and finally he asked, "Were you a depositor, did you do business with the bank?"

When he told him that he was awaiting a large loan, $750,000 for his business, and that he had put up his house and $36,000 in savings, the chief's demeanor softened. He sat heavily in a swivel chair, placed his arms and elbows on the desk before him and said, "Bad news, friend. The bank was busted."

"Busted?"

"The feds. Strike Force from Newark. Closed them down and carted off everything."

"But the people! The manager? What happened to him? Bannon? Joseph Bannon."

"He's been arrested," the chief said, and before Vince could jump in with another query, he volunteered: "They, the feds, came to me right before the raid and told me what was going down. They wouldn't elaborate. They are not all that cooperative with local law enforcement. They didn't ask for my help at all. They didn't say it outright, but the message I get from the feds all the time is 'stay the hell out of the way'."

"For Christ's sake," Vince whispered, sitting down in a nearby chair and putting his head in his hands.

"Look, look," the chief said, holding up his hand like a traffic cop. "All I know is that this bank was funded by the Teamsters. Local 560 was one of them. That should answer some questions right there. Tony Pro! Ever hear of him? Tony Provenzano?"

"Maybe, I dunno." Vince's mind was spinning, only half listening.

"Sal Briguglio? Sally Bugs? Ever hear of him?" the chief asked.

"Uh, uh! No."

"Jimmy Hoffa. You hearda' him?"

"Of course," he said, looking up with a new concern.

The chief began twirling a pencil between his thumb and forefinger, then rapped it on his desk. He looked at Vince with his head tilted to one side.

Vince looked straight into the chief now. It seemed as if I was looking at a movie, watching a victim fall, and waiting for the next scene.

"I don't get it," Vince said. "What the hell does this have to do with Bannon, the bank manager?"

"You don't read the papers do you?" said the chief. "Where are you from?"

"I live in South Jersey."

"Well, this is what happened. Just a few weeks ago, two guys walk up to Sally Bugs over in Little Italy, in Manhattan, and put five or six slugs in his head. Nobody knows who did it. Briguglio was a Teamsters official, at 560. He was Tony Pro's right-hand man."

He continued: "And then the feds close this Teamster bank and pick up the bank manager. What the hell do you think's going on?"

"You're talking like it's the Mafia. This is a bank. It's not the Mafia."

The chief unfolded his hands and closed them again, letting them rest upon the desk. There was a faint appearance of sympathy in his eyes.

"There's no way Bannon, not the Bannon that I know, could be involved in anything like this," Vince said. "Just no way. I just can't believe this. I can't believe it. What the hell am I going to do?"

Chapter 7: "THEY KNOW"

May 20, 1978.

The banging on the front door grew louder. Feeno shuffled his feet into his slippers, glanced at "two o'clock" on the night table, scratched his head, wiped the sleep from his eyes and stared from the front window onto the otherwise silent, leafy street. The street lamp's diluted orange glow from a half-block away cast long shadows of two men on the lawn, and a dark van parked with its headlights gleaming. Feeno's eyes opened wide as two other shadows hustled toward the rear of his house.

He hurried downstairs as the pounding at the front door grew louder. His heart hammering, Feeno put one foot against the door and let it open a thin crack.

"Times up, Feeno! You gotta' come with us." The voice of the big-shouldered man in a business suit was familiar. Then Stan Schweitzer, the FBI agent, grasped Feeno's shoulders and easily pushed him back into the living room away from the light cast from the outside.

"What the hell's going on, Stan?" Feeno asked.

"They know," said Schweitzer, looking hurriedly around the hallway and up the stairs which separated the living and dining rooms of the colonial-type house.

"No they don't," said Feeno. "They shook me down tonight. I wasn't wearing..."

Angela Bannon hesitated at the top of the stairs: "Feeno?" She started down the steps, pulling tightly at the cord of the terry-cloth bath robe. She squeezed its collar protectively around her neck.

Schweitzer had left the front door open, paying no mind to the chilly night air. Two other agents, wearing dark blue wind breakers, walked in. Angela saw "FBI" pasted on their backs in yellow letters as one turned to his left into the dining room and one to the right into the living room. She heard the older man hastily clumping toward the kitchen. She heard him open the back door and looked to see two others entering through it. One was a tall woman with a clipboard.

Within a few minutes it seemed as if a small army of intruding strangers had taken over the Bannon house, where Feeno and Angela had lived in the relative comfort of a typical suburban couple for the past five years. The only difference from the other families on the block was that the Bannons were childless and the man of the house was up to his ears in a problem.

"Get packed!" said Schweitzer. Another man came into the house. He was close to six-feet, six and nearly three-hundred pounds. "This is United States Marshal Oscar Goldsborough," Schweitzer said, casually pointing to the huge man who smiled first at Angela, then at Feeno, extending a cordial and sincere hand to each:

"Sorry for the intrusion. I know this is a shock," said Goldsborough. "We'll try to make it as comfortable for you as possible. But we have to hurry. Pack one overnight bag, quickly. The marshals here will remove the rest over the next few days, everything you need, everything you want."

"Where are we going?" said Feeno, who had slumped into a stuffed winged chair in the living room. Nervous, he quickly sat up on the edge of the chair, looked down at the floor, and grasped his head. Then he stood up and hugged Angela as an afterthought. They held each other tightly. Angela looked about the room, taking in the stately old Grandfather's Clock, an expensive Rochester that Feeno had purchased as her Christmas present just last year, at the glass cabinet of curios she had collected, the tasteful stuffed furniture with large floral images. On the coffee table were Ski Magazine, Golf magazine, House and Garden.

"You better get packed!" Schweitzer said impatiently through his teeth.

Angela sat down heavily; she stared at the floor with a ghostly expression. "I'm not going," she said softly, as if to no one.

"Angie, this is no..." said Feeno.

"You heard me." Angry now, she stared at her husband.

"Why? This is all your doing." Her face began to screw up as if to cry.

Schweitzer said nothing. He stood and watched the two, his feet planted wide apart, his suit jacket open, revealing a leather-cased snub-nosed .38 on his hip.

"Angie, we have to."

"I don't have to do anything. This is your show. Your game. You invented it. You got yourself into this. Leave me out of it."

Schweitzer and Goldsborough looked on, saying nothing, letting the little drama run a short course before they would step in. The big marshal had come out of the kitchen, followed by the thin woman with the clipboard. "Get upstairs," Schweitzer ordered. The two turned and went up as if by a prearranged routine, knowing what they would be doing.

"Who's going to protect you?" Feeno pleaded, his shoulders tight, palms upraised toward Angie...

"My family, that's who."

"Hold it," Goldsborough interrupted. "That's the worse thing. Leaving Feeno safe and you exposed. I'm sorry, but your family..."

"What the hell do you know about my family?"

"Enough to know that they're related by blood to the Scalesis."

"They're cousins, that's all. And they wouldn't harm me."

"That's where you're wrong," Goldsborough said, taking a step toward Feeno, standing by his side. He started to speak again but Schweitzer interrupted:

"Mrs. Bannon, we have a list of about twenty suspects who pose a threat to your husband. Their lives, their future, depend on keeping your husband from testifying at upcoming trials, and half of them are named Scalesi. We don't have time for this. We've gone over this before. We all knew this day might be coming."

"I don't give a shit," said Angie, turning away and walking toward the sofa.

Schweitzer turned and spoke into the tiny mic in his lapel: "Judy, get down here. Now!"

As Judy was coming quickly down the steps, Angie turned

to her and knew what was coming. "Oh, is she gonna' be my escort?"

"If we have to do it that way, we'll do it."

Judy stepped directly up to Angie and with a ten-inch height advantage looked hard into her eyes. There was an obvious non-compromise. Angie would be carried out, gagged, bound and boxed if necessary, at least for the interim.

"If you are unhappy with the protection program, we can't force you to stay," said Goldsborough. "But it's our responsibility for tonight to see that you are safe." He grew serious: "And that we intend to do."

"So, I don't have a choice," said Angie bitterly. "So much for constitutional rights."

Goldsborough reiterated that she would have a later opportunity to officially withdraw from the program, but only after hearing the risks. He looked hard into Angie's eyes.

"All right," she said. "I see that I don't have a choice."

She started for the stairs and Goldsborough nodded to Judy to follow.

The stars were shining brightly above the budding maple trees as the black Cherokee van moved quietly away from Carpenter Street. Both Feeno and Angie looked for one last time at the home and the lives that they assumed by now they would never see again. Angie remained angry. Feeno felt safe for the moment, and also felt in free fall, spinning in a vortex, one that had begun when they were married three years before in a rush.

As the van moved rapidly through the darkened streets, he recalled how they met. It was through Fred Russo at a wedding for the daughter of Rocco Scalesi, the Teamsters boss. Angela Scalesi, who was the daughter of Rocco's first cousin, seemed smaller and was certainly quieter than the other bridesmaids, with a propensity for introspection.

"What's on your mind?" Feeno had asked as he guided the girl through a slow dance at the Passaic Country Club. The five-piece band was doing a fairly good job of imitating Lena Russell's "My Happiness."

Angela looked up at the tall young man holding her lightly and smiled, "Everyone asks me that."

"You're quiet," said Feeno.

"I'm a loner," she said. "I don't like loud parties. I'd rather be home reading a book right now than be here." She looked up suddenly, and laughed. "Don't tell anyone here that. I'll get dropped in the river."

Feeno knew what she meant but didn't comment. He initially had conflicted thoughts whether to attend a mob wedding. But he felt an energizing tingling up and down his spine as the big man at the door shook his hand and quickly and deftly patted him down. Feeno was at the precipice again, enjoying the fear of unsafe places. He was, in fact, beginning to feel comfortable in the presence of dangerous people, and they too were beginning to accept the smart young guy who worked in banking in North Jersey. He fit in perfectly. Just the perfect guy to replace the former bank president, who had quit in one day and headed off to the west some place.

As the black van headed toward the turnpike, Feeno put his head back on the seat as if napping, but through his sleepless brain emerged dates and printouts, ledgers and pay outs. Loans and more loans. Lots of loans. He would be doing his homework in the days and weeks ahead.

Chapter 8: LAWYERS

May 25, 1978.

Vince looked around Fred Russo's tidy, leathery law office, half expecting to see the white knickers and the 1930s golf hat hanging from a clothes stand. This was not quite the "Plus Fours" guy he had seen at the country club the day that Feeno had introduced them. It was not surprising that Russo was so elegantly garbed. But with a soft gray Armani suit with blue tie over a white cotton shirt, handcrafted black Oxfords and trousers with sharp edges, Russo exacted the appearance of Wall Street more than downtown Newark.

After extending a cordial greeting, the Teamsters lawyer removed his suit jacket, and using just the thumb and index fingers of each hand, carefully placed it on the back of his chair, a movement that revealed the white gold TAG Heuer watch on his wrist. The cuff links could have been solid gold too. Behind his large mahogany desk on a shelf containing heavily bound legal case books were several framed photographs, including one of his sister, the singer Lena Russell, and several more of Russo, plus a young and pretty Italian woman whom Vince guessed was Fred's wife, and three small dark haired boys, all of them mini-Freds. Vince had difficulty averting his gaze from Lena Russell's luminous face, which was simultaneously sexy and saintly, especially the long-lashed dark eyes, shining with liquid luster.

"You and your sister, you look alike," Vince observed.

"So I'm told," said Russo.

"Do you sing too?"

"No, not I. No real voice. My parents tried to get me to sing when I was little. You should know that all you have to do if you want to avoid singing in an Italian home is screech as loud as you can."

Vince smiled.

"They let me alone after a few of those sessions," said Russo, who offered Vince an expensive Cuban cigar from a desk humidor. As he gestured toward a seat facing his desk, Vince noticed that Russo's smile seemed to have been pasted on the lower part of his face, while his eyes could be hiding more serious thoughts.

"I know why you're here," the lawyer said.

"I'm glad of that," Vince said. He unloaded his rehearsed recitation: "To get right to the point. I want to know what happened to Bannon, what happened to the bank, what happened to my $750,000 loan, where is my $36,000 that I put up as collateral, and how long do I have before I lose my house? This thing has all but destroyed me, and once my wife finds out that I lost the bulk of our savings, my marriage will be gone."

Russo suddenly turned away to look out the window. Then turned back with a different expression. His face seemed drained and blank.

"You may be asking the wrong guy," Fred said, sitting down in his high-backed chair, "but look, Vince, you have genuine concerns and I'll try to be helpful. I represent the Teamsters though, not the bank, not Bannon. Just remember that. But I know you're a friend of Feeno's, so I'll try to help."

He spoke softly but directly about how he and Feeno had met, how he had not known Feeno before running into him at an Elks Club social gathering in Elizabeth. Through their conversation he learned that Feeno had been a loan officer at the Bank of Bloomfield where Teamsters Local 319 had an account. They began socializing, and took a liking to one another. Fred tested the young and eager banker, and sensed an intense ambition. It wasn't long after that that he and the Scalesis set up Feeno as the president and chief loan officer of Unity Savings.

Fred stood up and walked to the window. His office overlooked a section of Newark that was in the process of another gentrification, repeated and defeated before it even started. Some old brick and stone buildings about two blocks from the Federal Building were being gussified, but only a half block away were more tumbling structures, coated with generations of neglect and poverty. Between them were whole blocks of flat earth strewn with trash. They were lots proposed for more urban renewal. Newark remained one of the most rundown cities in America.

"Bannon," he said suddenly, turning around toward Vince. "He's in the Witness Protection Program."

When Vince's mouth flew open, Russo said, "Hear me out."

He began a tale that Vince knew immediately was law talk for the defense, except he wasn't too sure whether Russo was defending Feeno. Russo stayed focussed on Unity Savings Bank. "This was a small bank with a lot of assets, mostly Teamsters Health and Welfare funds. Pension funds and the like."

"Feeno told me that. I know about that."

"Well as you know, the federal government, the Justice Department, and the Teamsters Union aren't exactly sweethearts. It's been going on, the contention, ever since Jimmy Hoffa was president. The feud he had with Bobby Kennedy was famous. You know that Hoffa disappeared, three years ago, in Detroit. Hasn't been found. Well, naturally, there is a rather large investigation. And you might say that closing the bank is part of that."

"What in the hell would this bank have to do with Hoffa?"

"Hoffa was a Teamster. You might say he was THE Teamster, but he was the boss only right up to the time he went to prison. He was stripped of his presidency, and when he came out of prison he wanted to get back into action."

Russo moved away from the window and sat carefully on the high-backed leather chair. He opened a side drawer and lifted out a nail file. "Only trouble is there are people who moved up in the union. While he was in jail, and they have been running it in a respectable manner ever since."

"And they didn't want him back," Vince added.

"Sort of," Russo answered, smiling sardonically now. "This whole thing is under a cloud, Vince. The Justice Department, the FBI so to speak, have no idea what happened to Hoffa. They are fishing around, looking at everything, everybody. Local 560 here in Jersey is one of the largest locals in the country. So is 319, that's the local run by Rocco Scalesi. So they froze everything up, the feds did, closed this bank for instance, and have sent in the bank examiners looking for stuff."

"What stuff?"

"That's a good question." Russo said. "I think it's a fishing expedition, Vince. There's really nothing there."

Cocking his head to one side, Vince asked the next logical question: "And why is Joseph Bannon in the Witness Protection Program?"

"I think it's a ruse," Russo said. "The Justice Department is making it look as if Feeno was on the inside of some illegal action. I think they're just trying to flush out information, or make it look as though they know something and that some of the local Teamsters will volunteer to help them out to..."

He hesitated. "Look, it's no secret that Anthony Provenzano has had some problems with the law. It goes way back."

Vince knew nothing about the man they called "Tony Pro," but in the next few hours he would learn plenty.

Leaving Russo's office, he had intentions to drop in on the U.S. Attorney's office. But prior to visiting the Federal Building just down the street, Vince went to the local library. Once inside, standing and staring, not sure where to go, an elderly, gray-haired woman whispered and gestured from her post behind the heavy wooden counter.

"Newspapers?" he asked, but when the librarian smiled and nodded to a rack of today's paper folded over sticks, he corrected, "No, old newspapers. Archives, I guess."

During the next hour, once he mastered the microfiche machine, he began gathering a basket-sized file about the man they called "Tony Pro" — a caporegime in the Genovese Crime Family, and how Sally Bugs, who worked for Provenzano, was ambushed and shot to death on Mulberry Street in New York. And he learned about the Andretta brothers, Thomas and Stephen. All were connected to Teamsters Local 560 and had taken the fifth amendment during Grand Jury proceedings into Hoffa's disappearance in federal court in Michigan, as did a Local 319 official, Anthony Tropetta.

Hoffa had disappeared July 30, 1975, the same day that he was to meet Tony Pro at the Machus Red Fox Restaurant in

Bloomfield Township in Michigan. Hoffa and Tony Pro had been close Teamster friends at one time but had a falling out while both were in the Lewisburg, Pennsylvania, federal prison. The meeting at the restaurant was to heal those bad feelings. Anthony "Tony Jack" Giacalone, a Detroit mobster, was to have been the intermediary to patch things up between Pro and Hoffa. The background information reported in the *Newark Star-Ledger* and *Bergen Record* was that Provenzano and his Teamster playmates were skimming Teamster funds, milking them for personal use.

One of the other larger locals was run by Rocco Scalesi, described as the boss of the Mafia family that bore his name. It too had been charged with skimming union funds for its officers' personal use, and for friends in Las Vegas casinos. Vince read nothing in the news accounts about anyone named Bannon, but the picture was losing its shadows, coming in clearer to him than before.

As he walked into the Federal Building on Broad Street, he was certain his questions would surely be answered.

An Assistant U.S. Attorney named Shannon Cook came to an outer office to fetch him into her small office in the rear of the Justice complex. She seemed not too far removed from law school, pretty and young, except for the dark circles beneath her eyes. They went into a bare room that could have been for storage. Cardboard file boxes stood on the floor along one wall, along with a metal pail and a mop. There was a small conference table with six wooden folding chairs flanking both sides. She invited Vince to sit. She stood with her arms folded and let Vince know immediately that "we cannot disclose or discuss anything about the case involving the Unity Savings & Trust or its employees."

"I understand that. I just want to know a few things. When do I get my loan, if ever, and what happened to my $36,000 deposit as collateral?"

"I can tell you this," she said. "The bank funds have been frozen, but as the bank examiners go through the records and clear accounts to their satisfaction, those moneys are to be transferred to accounts in trust so that depositors can access those funds as they would normally."

"So you have a list of those deposits?" he asked. "What about loan applications?"

"Those we can't discuss"

"Listen, I am just a small business man from Medford, New Jersey..."

With the words just coming out of his mouth, they were interrupted by a tall man with a shock of high curly hair that stood out on his head like a fright wig. "This is U.S. Attorney Bianca."

"Ah, the boss?" Vince said smiling. "I am certainly glad to see you." He rose to shake the attorney's hand.

Mario Bianca looked at him and nodded to Cook to follow him to the hallway, leaving Vince alone to study things: President Carter on the wall above the national seal of "E pluribus unum." On the table across from him, a take-out menu from the Good Fortune restaurant, a couple of dirty, empty Styrofoam cups.

Five minutes later Cook and Bianca returned and the mood in the room changed from lukewarm to frosty.

"How well do you know Joseph Bannon?" asked Bianca.

"Practically all my life. We grew up together."

Bianca then started asking about Vince's business and his loan application. Cook left the room, but was joined a couple of minutes later by a third person, a man who Vince assumed was an attorney but who was not introduced. All three were staring at him but he confidently laid out all the information that he thought they needed in order to help him sort out this mess and at least get his money back.

But as he continued informing them of his plans to construct seven high-end post and beam homes on his woodland property just outside the Pinelands area, Bianca suddenly stood up, raised his hand for him to stop and said:

"I think we had better end this right here and now." He moved two steps toward the table and put one skinny hand upon the edge. "We want to have future discussions with you, Mr. Berardi, but I strongly advise that you have an attorney present."

"What?"

"In the meantime, I advise you to return home and go about your business."

"Wait a minute. I'm here to..."

"But do not leave the jurisdiction of New Jersey without advising us."

"What the hell are you talking about? Don't leave the jurisdiction. Are you crazy? What is this?"

Bianca had started for the door. Cook scooped up the Chinese menu and the styrofoam cups.

"That's all I can say," Bianca said coldly. At the door he stopped, turned and looked at Vince. "We will keep in touch. You'll hear from us."

Chapter 9: DOGS

May 27, 1978, Memorial Day weekend.

"**G**irls, girls! Come here I need you." When Patty poked her head into the kitchen, Julie yelled, "Go find your father!" She went back to chopping salad vegetables. The phone rang. To her sister-in-law, Julie said, "Oh, there's no hurry. Take your time. We're nowhere near ready yet. Vince wants to cut the lawn and then run to the store for charcoal. Which reminds me, if it's on the way, would you stop at the 7-Eleven and pick up some paper napkins?

"I know, I know he could get them, but knowing him lately, he'll forget," said Julie, lightly laughing. "Listen, listen. On second thought, you get the charcoal too. Vince has enough to do this morning. Lately, he's been forgetting half the things that he sets out to do."

She laughed. "When he gets those damn houses built he says he's going to get a secretary." A guffaw: "Vince Berardi with a secretary," I told him, "Yeah, make sure it's a *he* secretary, about six foot, blond and blue-eyed, with muscles."

While her sister-in-law laughed, Julie reminded, "And the napkins. Yeah, any kind, but you know, festive or colorful." She was wearing shorts, and already felt, looking up and noticing the speed of the kitchen ceiling fan, that the afternoon would be scorching.

Vince appeared. "Vincent," said Julie, holding a chopping knife loosely in her right hand. "The lawn?"

"Anything at all for a woman with a knife in her hand," he said and started out to the garage to wind up the mower.

As Vince yanked on the mower starter rope, Julie yelled from the window, "And Vince, Mrs. Hibberd's dog paid us a visit last night, so watch where you're mowing."

Not five minutes later, the warning came to bear as the

mower blades made contact with one of little Ginger's leavings. Except the cut was of a metallic "ting" and pitched something a couple feet in the air.

Vince bent to where it dropped to the ground. What appeared to be half of a dog turd, had a shiny interior. He stared at the strange piece of crap. Gloria, sitting on the picnic bench swinging her chubby little legs, was about to toss a popsicle stick she had just finished sucking on. "Hand me that, please honey."

He poked the turd. Not soft at all, unless Ginger had been having serious constipation problems. It was definitely hard, but still shiny, fresh and wet looking. By now he was comparing it to one of those novelty shop pieces of poop that could always fetch a laugh or two at a party. He found the nerve to actually pick it up with his fingers and hold it in the sunlight. It was made of soft metal painted light brown. Inside were tiny wires, one of them coiled, and a round metal object which could have been a battery or something. At one end of the turd was a hole that had been definitely drilled, about one-thirty-second of an inch in diameter. A what? A microphone?

He put the thing in a pocket of his shorts and carefully searched the rest of the lawn. He found two more turds. One laying next to a window well to the cellar. Another amid the leaves of last summer's petunia bed. All three turds had been placed obviously several feet apart.

He telephoned his brother-in-law, John Wolyniak, who was a cop with the Cherry Hill Police Department, and whispered him "to get over here as quick as you can." When Vince told him someone had bugged his lawn with dog turds, John asked, "Are you losing it?"

"No, no. I can see it. I chopped one in half with the lawn mower. A transmitter, mike, everything. No shit! I mean. Listen, just get over here."

When he arrived, they went inside the house, and as characters do in a movie, looked at all the lamp receptacles, took apart the phones, poked behind the radiators, the stove, refrigerator, and discovered nothing more unusual than a couple of marbles, pieces of Lego and cardboard puzzles, grocery coupons, a new golf ball that Vince had been searching for since 1973, and dust and lint.

The rest of Vince's afternoon played out in a fog. He cooked the hamburgers with typical care for pink, medium and well done, placing the buns on the upper grill at just the right time for toasting. He opened beers for guests, poured wine for the wives, attempted conversation, smiled without sincerity, all the time searching, not on the ground for eavesdroppings, but in enigmatic images.

Thoughts drifted north to Mario Bianca, the U.S. Attorney with the untrusting pinched eyebrows. To Feeno Bannon, aka Joseph A. Bannon, glad to see you. Was he wishing not to? To the man in silly Plus Fours, Russo the handsome lawyer, face engaged but eyes not.

When Julie was finally relaxing in a lawn chair and putting forth an effort to converse with her sister-in-law, Vince bummed a cigarette from Bert Worth, a neighbor from down the block who managed a local auto parts store. Sidling to the rear of the garage, Vince drew deeply and exhaled, watching guiltily as the blue smoke from his first cigarette in a month traveled skyward. Then came the recollection.

Two days ago? Was it three? As Vince had pulled his truck into the driveway and left to go inside, over his shoulder, he saw a car gliding slowly past with two men inside. Before he could ask if they needed assistance finding a house, or whatever, the car accelerated and was gone.

He could have, should have, jotted down the license number. All he had now was the neurotic suspicion nurtured by the sight of the pair, the driver fat, in what normally would be comic contrast to the man beside him. The glare came from the one with the small, knotted pockmarked face, the one from the first tee of the Upper Montclair Country Club, staring at Vince with pea-sized eyes that pointed from beneath a cap of dyed black hair.

Vince took a last drag, grinding the cigarette heavily into the ground with the heel of a sandal. Tomorrow he would accede to Mario Bianca's advice and would find and hire a lawyer.

Chapter 10: SHADOWS

June 1, 1978.

"If my client were part of any scheme to defraud Unity Savings, why would he apply for a secured loan? Not unsecured! Secured, mind you, putting up $36,000 of his hard-earned money, the money he had been saving for his children's college education, his and his wife's retirement, his mother's long-term health care. He lost that money, all of it. Does that sound like part of a scheme?"

Vince glanced at his lawyer, Bernie Samuels, to see where he was getting all of these ideas about what he might have done with his now missing collateral. They sat in U.S. Attorney Bianca's private office, a dignified step up from Vince's last visit. Lawyers work wonders; at least open doors, and Vince felt comfortable.

Samuels was about fifty-five, with a facile, distinct and flawless speaking voice, one that Vince, as a carpenter, could equate with driving nails with repeated accuracy. In this case, Samuels' pleadings were persuasions usually reserved for the courtroom and a jury, prompting Bianca, who was wise enough to see where Samuels was going, to overstep his opponent:

"Tell us about your father, Mister Berardi."

"What about my father?"

"Did a little jail time? Associated with the mob?"

"Woah, woah, woah," yelled Bernie. He stood up. "That's it. Thank you, gentlemen." To Bianca's assistant, Shannon Cook, he nodded, "Ladies."

Vince remained seated, but grasped the arms of the chair tightly, and began yelling: "My father made one mistake in his whole life; he borrowed from the wrong guy."

Bernie grabbed Vince by the shoulder.

"Quiet, Vince." To Bianca, he said, "Let's set some rules about surprises. My client is certain that once you examine all the evidence you will decline to lump him in with the people you are trying to incriminate. In the meantime, should you wish to indict, you have our contact information."

At the word, "indict", Vince twisted to see his lawyer, who stood behind him with a hand held firmly against Vince's shoulder. "You know and we know you will not go down that road." He flipped his business card toward Bianca, who picked up the card and without looking at it, stuffed it in his shirt pocket.

As they motored south on the turnpike, Vince closed the window to exclude the sulfuric bouquets of the refineries and other chemical plants that overwhelmed the natural salty stench of the remaining marshes. He turned the AC up high.

"Okay," said Bernie. "What's all this stuff about your father?" They had just passed Goethals Bridge, connecting the industrial neighborhood of Elizabeth and Staten Island.

"I wasn't even born yet," Vince said, looking up through the windshield at a fearsome Delta 747 that had just lifted off at Newark Airport and sailed just a few hundred feet above the turnpike. "My dad, Pop, was a young man. It was in the early years of the Depression." He told Bernie the story about the little wooden ice house in the back yard, the deliveries to the speakeasies.

"I didn't learn until I was a grown man what the business was about," said Vince.

"I remember those times well, even though I was a kid," said Samuels, not blocking a slight smile. "They sold moonshine and good Canadian whisky."

Vince continued: "Pop got behind on the truck payments. He made the mistake of going around the corner to a local bookmaker. And then he got behind on those payments. The bookie kept giving him credit. And then he pushed Pop into a corner. Pop had no choice."

"Anything else I should know?," asked Bernie. Vince shook his head.

The one positive they left the meeting with was the actual bill of indictments laying out part of the government's case against Unity Savings and the Teamsters. Included was Bannon's name as well as several union officials and others that Vince did not know or recognize.

Vince was driving slowly, attentive to Bernie as he read aloud some of the charges. The Garden State Parkway came into view above them, crossing the turnpike. There were huge cemeteries on each side of the highway.

"In July 1977," Bernie read, "Rocco Scalesi received an unsecured loan from the Teamsters Health and Welfare fund for $10,000 held in account in Unity Savings.

"Then there was another loan to Mario Scalesi for $20,000; a $25,000 loan to Philip D'Angelo for the purchase of a restaurant, followed by two $25,000 loans to the restaurant, the first of which Rocco Scalesi and Fred Russo used to buy out a guy named Edward Conway.

"A $20,000 loan to Margaret Scalesi and Scalesi's Hotel and Tavern, a loan for $125,000 to the restaurant on behalf of Rocco Scalesi, D'Angelo and Russo.

"And it says, 'Rocco Scalesi used his influence and incentive of union deposits to obtain loans for several other persons. Throughout this time, two certificates of deposit, one drawn on the Welfare Fund and one from the local's general funds, were continuously renewed, and an additional $100,000 deposit from the Welfare Fund was made in June of 1977.

"Here's a loan, citing a communication from the Central States Pension fund, directing Unity to lend $175,000 to the Desert Dunes Casino in Las Vegas, April 12, 1976. Again, no security.

"These guys didn't even try to hide what they were doing," said Samuels. "Remarkable."

"Where does Feeno Bannon enter this?"

"Well, that's pretty simple, isn't it? He's the chief loan officer of Unity."

"But what?" Vince asked. "What about? You know that police chief up here told me all this stuff about Jimmy Hoffa, the Teamster boss. His disappearance. What does it say about that?"

"No mention."

"How do you know? That thing's a half-inch thick." He took his eye off the road for a second and was rewarded with a blast from an air horn.

"Everybody's name who's involved is in capital letters and listed. There is no Hoffa here. No Tony Provenzano either, or the Local 560 officers. What we're looking at is a Scalesi indictment. The Teamsters hierarchy is mobbed up all over North Jersey. I think we're looking at only part of the picture."

"Fred Russo," Vince said as he slowed the accelerator to let line of three semis, all with the markings "Broadway Freight" on the sides, fly past them. He moved to the left into the "Cars Only" lane. "He's in there too. He told me there was nothing to the investigation."

"You said he was a lawyer, right?" asked Samuels.

Vince stole a sideways glance toward Samuels, then looked the other way, and finally tried concentrating fully on driving.

"Bernie, I'm sick. How the hell am I going to get out of this? My business. My home, all of it, it's gone."

"Whoah. Hey!" he said. "You're not going to lose your home."

"They have the deed. I put it up."

"Yeah, but you never got your loan, never got your money. There's no contract. It's void. Listen, listen Vince. You hired me to do your worrying. Of course, you can't put these things out of your mind, but quit sweating the details. We have objectives here. That's what you stay focussed on."

"Yeah, and what are the objectives?"

"First, to clear your name with the feds. Get them to believe you are an innocent in all this. You are a victim, period."

"Yeah, but you got up and walked the hell out just as I was trying to explain about Pop. You shut me up, remember. That's not exactly clearing my name."

He looked at Vince and laughed out loud. "You really are innocent, aren't you? Son of a bitch, clients are all alike," he said, suddenly shifting his weight to cross his legs. He scratched at the skin on his calf. "Listen to me, once Bianca gets on your ass, under your skin with an accusation, any accusation, true or false, relevant or irrelevant, that's when you keep your mouth shut. Kabeesh?" He made a zippering motion across his mouth.

"I'm sorry. What's the next objective?"

"Getting your collateral back. That's going to be the hard

part."

"Yeah, but once the feds see it as a deposit, won't they know, and return it to me? They're not allowed to keep that money. It should be insured by the FDIC."

"The check cleared, didn't it?" Bernie stated. "Where's the money? In escrow, where it's supposed to be? Or in your friend's pocket, or some other thug's pocket?"

"Some other thug," Vince repeated. By now, the mention of his onetime friend's name and the thought of his renewal of their friendship made his insides queasy with a mix of fear, disgust and betrayal.

Out of the corner of his eye, he thought he saw some compassion in Bernie's statement: "That money may be gone," Samuels said. "You might have to live with it."

"Gone," Vince said with resignation.

"Stolen property, Vince. Stolen property," Samuels said. "We may have to get in line, sue, to get it back."

"Christ. That's all I need."

Once past the Rutgers University campus on the right, the landscape became more South Jersey, with golf courses and parklands in view.

They approached Exit 7. "Are you hungry, Bernie? It's way past lunch time."

"I could eat."

"Let's stop."

They left the turnpike and headed south on Route 130, a busy four-lane, stopping at the Forge Diner. Vince's motivation was not altogether a need to eat but to schmooze some more with his lawyer. His thoughts were to get all his money's worth. *"How much are lawyers charging these days? A hundred an hour? Maybe Bernie would spring for lunch. Maybe he'd stop the clock while we ate."*

They walked to a booth with a window view of the moving traffic. The diner was authentic Jersey, decorated with faux plaster of paris objet d'art that reflected several thousands of years of various civilizations, from the Age of the Pharaohs to the Battle of Trenton:

Running along the middle of the ceiling were wagon wheels holding carriage light lanterns with yellow globes, and on a ledge running above the counter were trophies and plaster statuettes. One was of Moses holding the Ten Commandments; another was an elephant fixed with a howdah. A drum stood over a bas relief on one wall of two soldiers of the Continental Army. Next to it was a yellow-stained Sphinx and above a fake stone fireplace was a montage of plastic medieval knights holding swords and pikes. On flat spaces and other previously unoccupied nooks and crannies along the walls were vases of plastic flowers and dangling plastic ivy.

Even though it was a good two hours past the usual lunch time, the diner was crowded with patrons, sitting at booths and tables that were stained dark brown and illuminated with plastic Tiffany lamps shining on each booth.

"I'll have the Clams Casino," said Samuels to the waitress, a thin middle-aged woman with dyed red hair. "That come with bacon?" When she nodded "yes", he added, "and a little Tobasco sauce?"

"I'll have a cheeseburger," said Vince. "Make it a bacon cheeseburger." To Samuels he said, "My wife'll kill me if my cholesterol doesn't kill me first."

"Your wife's looking out for your well-being," said Samuels.

"I can't help it," Vince said. "My heart needs grease."

"You're not a fat person."

"I don't really eat much. I'm a light eater. Have you ever been on a cruise, on a big cruise ship?"

"Quite a few."

"All that gourmet food is wasted on a guy like me. Soup with pancakes floating in it? Egg noodles spritzed with broccoli and beet roots? Do you like beet roots?"

"I thought you were Italian," said Bernie. "Italians like their groceries."

"I like my mom's cooking and my wife's, but for Christ's sake, don't scare me with screwy looking food. On that cruise, I didn't even know half of what I was eating. We went to Italy a couple of years back and I almost threw up when I learned that I was eating a chicken's testicles."

When nearly finished their lunch and Samuels had summoned with a wave for the waitress to come with the check,

Vince stretched and felt the need for a nap, a feeling that vanished quickly as he saw sitting in a booth about fifteen feet away two men that he had recognized before.

One was the little guy with the face of a squirrel. He was staring at Vince, half-smirking while picking at his teeth. His was a presence that was unforgettably distinctive. Not just smallness and not just dot-like eyes that drilled, but a head of black straight hair with heavy sideburns that were the opposite of wings. They were combed straight forward instead of back, remindful of a page boy hairstyle on a woman. The cap of hair could have been a toupee; it fit his head like a helmet. Across from him was a heavy, older man who had sweat on the wrinkles of his close-to-nothing neck. He was the No Neck golfer that Vince had seen with the others that day at the country club.

The fat one seemed not to notice Vince, but the little one kept staring. Then they both got up, paid their bill and left. Vince decided against the urge to follow them, feeling a chill in his stomach.

"What's the matter? What are you looking at?" asked Bernie, turning his head. "You look a little funny."

"No, nothing. Just a little indigestion. I'm fine."

Chapter 11: VISITORS

June 14, 1978

With days getting warmer and bill collectors hotter, Vince took on some quick renovating jobs to generate cash. At day's end and on weekends he put his remaining energy into Andy Burke's four-bedroom house. He hired two college kids and a third boy still in high school, and after a few weeks found that he could keep up with the payroll. Some of his suppliers were understanding friends who agreed to pace payments over longer stretches.

On one of his solitary evenings, installing water supply lines into Andy's downstairs bathroom, Vince heard a crunch of tires on the pine cones out toward the sandy road. There was no sound of a motor. He listened. Nothing. Picking up an eight-foot length of half-inch copper pipe, he measured four feet, eight inches, and made the mark. His back was to the front yard. The slanting sun, which had cast a golden horizontal light through the woods, was dropping. The dark began to flow through the pines and the unfinished house; what light remained touched the thick barn-like timbers and cast skinny shadows upon the dirty floor. He turned on his work light. No doubt it was Julie arriving in her jeep with some dinner — a hoagie, a ham sandwich or tuna, a pack of TastyKakes, a couple of cans of Schmidts. On those occasions they would sit and talk, or simply listen together to the breeze through the pines, the birds settling for the evening and rabbits scuttling and snuffling through the leaves.

But his concentration now was on measurements, adding copper pipe lengths from one to the other to work their way through the floor and up vertically and horizontally toward where the fixtures would be placed. Vince measured, then heard the noise outside. So he remeasured, marked and measured again.

He fixed the pipe cutter over the copper, tightened and

began twisting, careful not to let the round, sharp blade begin to travel. Probably, no one was there; then came the sound of breathing. Heavy breathing.

He turned, but the work light was blinding his eyes to anything beyond its globe.

"Julie?

"Who's there?" he asked, feeling a quickening of the pulse. There was a mass chattering of red-winged blackbirds settling for the night in the solitary maple tree nearby.

"We're friends, Vince."

The sound was of a high, raspy tenor, of someone who could have had a stick stuck in his voice box.

Vince reached out to grab the light to turn it toward his visitor. A strong, bony hand grabbed his wrist and held it tightly:

"Don't move, Vincent, don't move. Nobody's gonna get hurt."

Another hand, unseen, a fatter one with small drops of sweat around the wrinkles of the wrist, grabbed the work light handle and detached it from the nail holding it to a joist. The fat hand pulled the light back several feet. Vince blinked; he stood, throwing up his arms and hands against the blinding halos.

"I said, 'Don't move.'" A hand poked out of a blue serge suit sleeve. It held a gun. It's all Vince could see, just the snub of a revolver aimed at him with a steady, determined hand. The rest of the arm and body was in dark shadows.

"We just want you to answer one question."

Vince stood silently, blinking into the stabbing light.

"Where is he?," the voice asked.

"Where is who?"

"Your friend, Feeno."

"He's not my friend anymore...and I don't know where he is," Vince said in stutters. "And if I did...if I did, I'd make surer than shit that I'd get there first."

"Join the crowd."

There was silence for several seconds. A faraway owl asked "Whoo?"

And Vince: "Who are you guys? Do you want to identify yourselves?"

The pistol cracked his skull in a blinding split second. He fell backward. A flash of lightning exploded before his eyes but there was no sound other than the meteoric swish of the gun and the arm and then the crack above his left ear.

He held his head with both hands.

"You don't ask no fucking questions. Is that clear?"

Vince heard only half of what was said. Blood oozed between his fingers and into his eyes. His glasses had fallen to the dirty floor.

"Once more, where is he?"

Blinding light, blinding pain. Vince put up his arms to ward off the blow, crouching, yelling, "I don't know. I don't know!"

But there was no blow. He put his arms over his head and kept low, working his feet backward. One foot struck the blow torch, knocking it over. He looked to the floor quickly. Was it leaking gas? He fell backward over his tool box.

On his back, he looked and saw the work light move. And then the hand that held it, that fat hand covered with sweat, hanging it on the nail. There was shuffling of shoes, hard heels against the plywood sub-floor, growing distant. Silence, except for the owl.

Thirty-seconds passed. There came the double sound of two car doors slamming. A crunch of pine cones and needles as the tires dug into the soft earth, and slowly backed away.

Vince waited, breathing deeply. Against the still-blinding light, he felt for his glasses with trembling, bloody fingers. From his knees, he grabbed at the work light, pushed the switch. The blackness was immediate, and for several seconds he saw halos of ingrained brightness, then shadows and hazy forms --- of joists and studs, the opening of the uncompleted window, the black trunk of the maple tree on the lawn, its leaves and branches not moving in the dark night.

He sat on the dusty plywood floor and listened, trying not to breathe, then stood and made half steps slowly to the door. With a leap, he bounded down the two by ten that served as a ramp and jumped on the sandy earth, running toward his truck, opened the door, jumped in, locked both doors from inside and looked toward the rearview mirror facing the road where the intruders had left. Vince's breath came in uncontrolled gulps and his head throbbed painfully.

Darkness. He started the engine and drove slowly down the sandy lane toward Stokes Road. His eyes searched frontwards and backwards, ahead to find the narrow path through the stubby pines, then into the rear view mirror to see what was behind. Nothing, except an awareness of movement back towards Andy's house. Then a shape. They were following.

He felt the Chevy pickup lunge as he hit the gas. Fifty yards behind him, two headlights came on. They began wobbling as the car struck potholes in the dirt road.

The truck clawed and jumped another quarter mile, weaving and dodging the upright stubby pines and fallen branches. The sand roads were next to invisible. He drove by instinct, by rote, having traced all of these shifting, crisscrossing intercourses through the woods many times before. He knew where he was going, his pursuers didn't.

He aimed toward an opening at the bottom of a small berm, gunning the accelerator, the four-wheel drive kicking at the dirt and rocks. The truck hit the creek with a thud and splash, tires spinning, then grabbing the rocks beneath the shallow water and propelling the truck forward across the creek and into the woods.

Behind him he heard the undercarriage of the car smack the ground. Then the headlights grew distant, and a minute later disappeared.

He took his foot from the gas, allowing the truck to come to a stop on its own. Simultaneously, he shut down the lights. And waited, sweat and blood pouring into his eyes. He wiped them with the sleeve of his work shirt and winced as the cloth rubbed across the open cut. He touched the side of his head and felt more liquid covering his fingers. Yanking the patterned blue handkerchief from the back pocket of his jeans, he pressed it tightly to the cut and drove with one hand the rest of the way.

He pulled into the driveway about 9:30. The kids would be in bed and Julie would be watching TV. He slipped through the back door and snuck quietly into the downstairs bathroom off the laundry room. In the mirror he saw a giant red welt and a deep yellow cut, now caked with dried blood, which he washed away as carefully as he could. Nearly passing out, he collapsed against the wall.

"Vince?" she said. "Oh, you're in...Ye gods, what happened to you?"

She grabbed his shoulders and forced him down on the toilet seat.

"I fell," he said, not looking up.

"You fell?"

He felt her breath quicken, and could see the breasts before his eyes heave beneath the blouse, the ministrations comforting and warm. He would not look at her eyes.

"Missed the ramp. Pushing the wheelbarrow down it. Awful dark out there." He tried to laugh and felt pain.

"Jeesus, what on earth did you land on?" Carefully, she pulled his bloody hand away and with warm water running from the tap, gently dabbed with a wash cloth.

He winced and tried to grab her wrist.

"Ohh, honey, I'm sorry. Oh my God. Look at this. My God. What in...?"

"Pile of lumber," Vince said.

"You have to get stitches," she said, and was reminded, "The kids...I'll have to call John."

John Wolyniak, Julie's brother, the cop, came over and drove Vince to West Jersey Hospital in the Cherry Hill PD Crown Victoria which he kept parked overnight in his driveway. They were made to wait their turn before Vince repeated the wheelbarrow story for the emergency room doctor and nurses. The admitting nurse repeated the act of putting clean gauze on the cut and let Vince do his own bleeding control as one by one the emergencies ahead of them were looked after — a little girl holding her tummy, an old man with rheumy eyes brought in by an attentive daughter, a Little Leaguer in a dirty Hap's Service Station uniform clutching his elbow.

As they rode back, Vince said, "John, I'm going to tell you something. I don't want Julie to know. Okay?"

"Let's hear it." John kept his eyes on the road. He was five years older than Julie, with the same curly black hair, but beginning to gray at the temples. His profile showed similar sharp cheek bones but also a ski nose, broken by a Youth League baseball bat as the young catcher was learning the position, squatting too close to the batter.

John looked at his passenger as the tale of the night unwounded. He could imagine the fright deep in the woods, with no help around. "I'll call Medford PD today."

"No, Christ, she'll find out."

"Don't be a jackass. You need protection," he said, turning left onto Hopewell Road. It was late and many of the suburban houses on their little lawns in the woods had their lights out. As John drove into the driveway and braked, he grabbed Vince by the arm when he opened the door to get out. "I got a friend I want you to meet. I want to tell him. I think he can help. He's an old ATF guy, retired. Lives near you and he worked all the pizza arsons. Are you familiar?"

"You mean those places that burned down? They bought the wrong kind of cheese or something?"

"Yeah, those pizza joints. The Gambinos were involved. Lots of Sicilians. Anyway, listen, Vince, I want you to talk to this guy. Name's Clyde Woolen. Good guy, I mean it."

Vince had been surprised the next morning that he had slept so well the night before. He had awakened two or three times and it felt good to simply touch the fat clean bandage on his temple, which still throbbed. But he fell back to sleep each time, finally awakening to the welcoming smell of brewing coffee, then bacon, as it wafted up the stairs.

At the kitchen table, Vince said, "I didn't even hear the kids go out to school."

"You slept," Julie said. "I could tell."

He felt the hot coffee jump start his stomach. The usually loud ticks of the big Regulator Clock above the door to the dining room were silent against the crackling, frying sounds on the stove. Everything seemed normal and warm. Julie took big plates out of the dark-stained cabinet on the wall that Vince had built from wainscoting gleaned from an old Victorian he had renovated on Spring Valley Road.

Decorative plates of funny-shaped cows done by the artist Warren Kimble hung in a double row along one wall next to the cork board of announcements and household reminders. Vince rested his hairy arms on the heavy, light-stained maple table, picked up *The Inquirer* and put it down again when the headlines began twirling all on their own. Funny, because he had no headache. He picked up the ice pack and held it gingerly to the wound.

"Julie, I...I...ah...have to tell you something. I didn't fall last night. I didn't land on a pile of lumber."

He told her what happened. She sat down across from him and as he talked she slid her hand up to her chin, and then the front of her throat. Her soft voice was hoarse: "Who were they? What did those men want?"

"I couldn't see them. I can only guess who they are. They think I know where Feeno is hiding.

"That's not the worst of it, Julie." Tears filled his eyes and he caught his breath. "The money. Our money. From the savings account. I put it up as collateral."

Julie got up from the chair and over to the window, putting her two hands on the sink, looking outside at the sunlit, cheery lawns and yellow forsythias blooming down the street.

Without turning, she whispered, "All of it?"

He couldn't look at her, and had to clear his throat. "Most of it. Thirty-six thousand."

"They have to give it back," she shouted. "They have to give it back. You said it was a bank. They can't keep it. It has to be insured."

She looked at him, her eyes wide with surprise and fear. "Doesn't it...doesn't it? Vince, answer me!"

He looked up into her eyes and shook his head. "I don't know. I don't know, Julie. I'm sorry. I am so sorry I did this to us."

Chapter 12: CLYDE WOOLEN

Bernie Samuels, called a few days later to relate the results of the news that he had passed onto the U.S. Attorney's office.

"I talked first to Bianca and he handed me off to an FBI agent named Schweitzer. I told him that the attack on you was evidence that you have no connections to the evildoers at Unity Savings," Samuels related. "He said they would look into it."

"What about the feds? What did the FBI, what did this Schweitzer say when you told him?"

"It doesn't matter; he really said zilch, said he would look into it. Your real worry now is not the feds, it's the mob. Look, Vince, you had better take precautions."

"I'm getting a gun," Vince said.

"I can't advise you on that," Bernie said. "I don't like guns, especially around kids." He quickly added, "Keep your doors locked and don't go anywhere alone."

When Vince was a boy, his father once told him that fear involves things that we cannot see, that what lies in the darkness is magnified beyond proportions. Never was that so pronounced for Vince than the night that the visitors shined the work light in his eyes, staying hidden in the black void behind. Temporarily, his father's advice about fear made him feel somewhat secure in his own neighborhood, where things — houses, trees, cars, neighbors, everything — were familiar and understandable. Nothing to be threatened with. If someone tried to sneak up on him or his family, he told himself, he would see them. But it was a false assumption that came with the pendulum swings of his mood, one that eventually vanished, replaced by a sickly tumbling of the gut. Vince was approaching a zone where he did not know what to do nor where to go. The fear and wonder deepened.

It was why he flinched when he saw the stranger approach

his home on that Saturday morning. The man wore red suspenders over a plain white tee shirt and had on baggy plaid shorts which angled down in the front, unable to fully grasp his protruding stomach. His large feet, which walked in a way that Vince and his friends used to call "east and west", were clad in sockless leather sandals. The man was bald except for a half-halo of gray hair above a pinched, wizened face that held small but smiling eyes. Friendly dots. He held a leash which had attached at the sidewalk end a small dog, about as big as a banana, covered with curly fur.

"Vince Berardi?"

Vince stopped himself from snarling, like George Raft, "Who wants to know?" He simply nodded.

"Clyde Woolen," the man said, extending a large hand.

"Oh for God's sake, Clyde. I beg your pardon," said Vince, extending his hand. "John told me about you. I'm sorry I was a little hesitant."

"It's okay," said the man. "I think you have a reason to be jumpy."

What Vince had not expected was an older man who looked more like an elderly Pillsbury Dough Boy than an investigator, particularly a retired ATF agent who had made an adult lifetime of pursuing the murky underworld of guns and explosives.

"Wow, you took a wallop!," Clyde said, looking at the reddened and yellowish swollen left side of his face and head.

"It hurts," said Vince, "but not as much as the other pain."

They walked to the backyard where Vince invited Clyde to sit at the wooden picnic table. "Wow, this is a nice house. You build it yourself?"

"About six years ago now. It's already too small."

Clyde looked around the surroundings with approval. Modest man in a modest neighborhood. Kids, wife, troubles. "You were talking about some other pain. What's that?"

"That other pain," Vince repeated. "That's the one where the feds think that I'm on the same side as the bastards who beat the crap out of me."

Clyde didn't respond for a while. He collected his thoughts. "I know it's hard to swallow, but the feds will probably come around. It takes a long time sometimes for those guys to sort things out. That's often what happens with a Strike Force." He opened red beefy hands wide, then folded them on the table.

"They can sometimes act quickly because there are a lot of investigators. They got the FBI, the state police, the ATF, the bank examiners, postal inspectors, even immigration guys. When they share and coordinate information they are a pretty powerful bunch. The problem is when they have to sort out evidence, especially when there is a lot of it like the case against the bank, multiple defendants, the Teamsters and the Scalesis."

"That's no solace to me," Vince said. "Just because the bank manager is my — was my — personal friend, they think I'm part of it."

"Give them time," said Clyde. "I know how you feel. It's creepy, but they'll come around. Its taking so long because each branch of that Strike Force is assigned something and takes exclusive possession of it. Like your problem that your brother-in-law told me about. Right now, it's the bank examiners that are going through tons of stuff. I made some phone calls and was told they even rented a house in Nutley to put all the records in. They got four full-timers sorting out the bank accounts."

Julie came out and was introduced. She went into the kitchen and returned with a pitcher of iced tea. As they talked, Clyde's little terrier named Yipper paced off circles on the lawn, sniffing flowers, old footprints, the one-time presence of electronic dog turds.

"That's such a cute little dog," said Julie, bending to pat the little creature, which shivered under her loving hand. "What kind is he?"

"Yorkshire terrier. He's a Yorkie."

"He's a darling."

Vince smiled, happy to see a change in Julie. After she learned of their losses, her beatific smile — the smile that rarely shut down and was bestowed on everyone, stranger and friend alike — had disappeared. For a week Vince heard no more her laugh, her loud guffaws at something funny. TV wasn't funny. She sat, smiled sometimes at "Fawlty Towers" or "The Jeffersons." All was glum, until that very morning when she awoke, looked into the bathroom mirror at the deep circles, washed her tired face, dried her hands and said, "Shit!" Aloud. Then silently, weary of her self-appraisal, to herself she counseled, "Get over it."

Clyde had retrieved and secured Yipper to one of the nearby lawn chairs.

This was a high-sky day, yellow sun beaming, and breezes from the lake below gently bending branches of willows and pin oaks. About a block away in a small playground, some young girls in a group were singing Beatles songs while they sat on the swings. Patty and Gloria Berardi were among them. Vince looked at his watch. He had a lot of yard work that he wanted to get done today and had planned to meet a couple of neighbors by 5:30; they were going to the Phillies game at Vet Stadium.

"Listen, I'm grateful that you're here," Vince said. "You seem to know a lot already."

"That's the benefit of old age," Clyde said, his face crinkling. "I know just about every mob guy in Jersey and Philly and a lot in New York.

"I've only had my private license for six months." Clyde laughed, showing a gap in his mouth in the right side of his mouth where a molar was absent. He yanked on the leash and pulled Yipper away from one of Julie's rose bushes just in time to prevent it from being pissed on. "But I didn't retire my brain and I still like to schmooze on the phone with some of my old buddies." He paused and stared hard at Vince. "I checked you out."

Vince stared hard at Clyde and felt a mutual communication. A two-way path. Maybe he had struck a mother lode of ways to find things out. When Woolen asked about where Vince found the dog turds that turned out to be listening devices, Vince eagerly showed him.

"Wow, they weren't taking any chances, were they?" Clyde said as he toed the grass as if looking for more. "Do you still have them?"

"Yeah, there were three of them. One is pretty chewed up where I hit it with the mower."

"Let me see one. One that's still intact."

As Vince left to go into the house, Clyde added, "And do

you have an Exacto knife? If you don't mind."

Vince returned with all three dog turds and laid them on the table. They made sounds like dropped marbles. "Aha!" said Clyde. "These are familiar-looking babies."

He picked up one device, pulled reading glasses from the pocket of his tee shirt. The dark-colored device he held in his hand was about as big as his thumb. Leaning, he carefully made a slit with the knife along the horizontal side of the phony feces. Then at opposite ends of that line he, again carefully, cut two short lines of the soft metal, and with the knife point, peeled back the colored cover.

"Yeah, just what I thought," said Clyde. "See these?"

Vince stood up and came around the other side of the table for a closer look.

"Three little batteries. You got some transistors here and there are diodes. This little hole here? That's the mic."

Clyde pulled back from his close examination and sipped his ice tea. "I've seen these before. In fact, we used 'em one time, just like this, up in Schuylkill County in Pennsylvania. A bunch of Ku Klux Klansmen and American Nazi Party guys had a camp up there, way deep in the woods. They were practicing their military shit gettin' ready for the big race war."

"This thing here," he said, palming the fake turd. "It'll pick up a conversation from within twenty feet and it's got a radio range of about six miles."

"Who do you think planted these in my yard?" Vince asked.

"Not us, that I know. I mean not the feds. I checked. There's no warrant."

"But you can't tell me who planted them here?"

"Just a guess. Who wants to find your friend Bannon?" He raised an eyebrow, sipped his ice tea, placed it down on the picnic table and spread his opened hands apart, a gesture that said, "Who else?"

"What can you tell me about the bastard who did this to me?" Vince asked, pointing to his sore head.

"My guess is the same Scalesi guys. They're in the most trouble. They have the most to lose in upcoming trials. It's not just the Teamster phony loan business. You must know they're under indictment in the drug thing."

Vince flung back his head. "What drug thing?"

"Smuggling heroin in from Salerno, on Alitalia freight. Through JFK. There are about twenty-five defendants. Probably ten of those guys have taken it on the lam. Or were flipped and are informing on the operation. A couple guys disappeared completely. My guess is they were whacked. And I know that a couple have gone back to Sicily. Some of these were Sicilians.

"These are desperate assholes, Vince," Clyde warned. "I don't want to scare you anymore than you are, but be careful. They suspect everyone is out to get them now. The Scalesi bosses are facing big time in prison if this shit goes down against them."

"Is it all connected with the Teamsters? The bank, what does the bank have to do with it."

"What's in a bank? Money. It's always money, and the best money to the mob is laundered money. A bank does that better than anybody. All those loans, going out this way and that. I know you know about the Hoffa stuff. If Jimmy Hoffa was killed, and he mostly likely was, and his body was disposed of, which it appears to be because they can't find him, somebody gets paid for doing those little jobs. Where is the money coming from?"

"Well, I heard that Hoffa is buried under Giants Stadium in the Meadowlands. Is that the Jersey connection?"

"Hoffa's buried in Jersey?" Clyde said, laughing out loud. "I don't think so. That's bullshit. Hoffa was most likely bumped off in Detroit. Nowhere near Jersey. Who in their right mind would take the chance of smuggling the most easily recognized labor leader in the whole world and take his body across — what is it, five hundred, six hundred miles? — just to bury him in the middle of the country's largest metropolis, right in the middle of ten million people? I think Hoffa's body is in Detroit.

"Tony Provenzano, the Teamster boss in Jersey. He was supposed to meet Hoffa in Detroit that day he disappeared. Tony Pro controls the biggest pile of Teamster funds in the whole country. He and the Scalesis. And it's all deposited in Unity Savings."

"So the payout came from Unity?" Vince suggested, beginning to grasp the enormity of what was going on.

"The payout came from Unity," Clyde repeated, shaking his head in the affirmative. "I don't know that for sure, but that's where this thing seems to be going."

Chapter 13: MO HENRY

Neptune County Detective Maurice "Mo" Henry had had a busy week, performing the part of investigative work that he enjoyed the least — dealing with potential witnesses. Sometimes it is easy. Getting a store clerk to identify a shoplifter is trouble-free. It is another task altogether to convince a frightened, ordinary citizen that it is his or her civic duty to stand in front of a crowded court and finger a man who could just as easily blow your brains out as tell you what time it is.

Mo Henry's first contact in the case against Joseph A. Bannon was a furniture dealer from Bergen County who lost $20,000 collateral to Unity Savings in February of 1978. Another was a builder, Steve Smith, from Pennsylvania who dropped $25,000. Both were easy to convince and it was Smith who told the Neptune County Prosecutor's office about Vincent Berardi down in South Jersey. Berardi was the one who would be the most trouble. Mo Henry was convinced of that.

"And why do you think that?" asked Prosecutor Arnold Rosenstein, seated at his large desk sipping coffee while studying the Markets Data Center of the Wall Street Journal. Mo leaned against the office door. He peeled the wrappers off two Doublemint gum sticks and chewed as he talked.

"This guy is a big buddy of Bannon's," said Mo, referring to information obtained during the phone call he had made to a state police buddy on the Strike Force in Newark. "His may be one of the phony loans. But nobody's sure. Apparently this guy, on the other hand, has been screaming bloody-ass murder against Bannon. So he could be easy, he could be difficult. He could be off our list completely if he figures in with the Teamsters and Bannon."

"Well, go after him anyway," said Rosenstein, without looking up from the newspaper. His eyes went rapidly up and down the market columns.

This was the part of the job that bothered Mo Henry the most. He had been a thirty-year cop, first with the Brick Township police and for the past twelve years with Neptune County. He had served under three different prosecutors now and was the wariest about Rosenstein, who had political motives which often seemed far detached from the work of the office. Rosenstein had been a major supporter and fundraiser during the gubernatorial campaign of Gov. James Gross. So much of a buddy had he been of Gross's that the state Attorney General's job seemed his for the asking.

And Rosenstein asked, and he asked some more, each time getting more confused and hotter under the collar at Gross's snubs. When the governor-elect would no longer answer phone calls and when the papers announced that Gross had appointed Madeline Pelligrino as A.G., Rosenstein began wheedling for the U.S. Attorney's job, an appointment that was in the hands of the President of the U.S. through the head of the Justice Department. Politically, the governor's recommendation would be considered among the front runners, but once again, Rosenstein was bypassed.

The scuttlebutt over the politics was brought to light in a column written by a State House correspondent in Trenton for the *New York Times*. Rosenstein had subscriptions to every daily newspaper serving New Jersey: The *Times, Star-Ledger, The Record, New York Daily News, Philadelphia Inquirer, Trenton Times, The Trentonian, Camden Courier, Atlantic City Press, Home News & Tribune, Asbury Park Press*. Three TVs at his home were tuned to each of the networks. No news escaped the prosecutor.

The column that dug into the background of the governor's appointments explained that Gov. Gross was acutely sensitive about the threat of Mafia activity taking hold in the new Atlantic City casinos. So he wanted out front some prominent cops with Italian names in both the U. S. Attorney's office and in his own A.G.'s office. The appointments were also meant to appease the large population of Italian Americans living in New Jersey who felt tainted with a social stigma because of an over emphasis of Italians as a synonym for mobsters. Now, Gov. Gross could explain, and probably correctly so, that for every Italian-made member of La Cosa Nostra, there was an Italian cop on the other side dedicated to putting his ass in jail.

Mo Henry cared not either way. He didn't particularly like Italians any more than he liked blacks and 'ricans. He considered himself a practical man. So he did more investigating, calling local cops in New Jersey to test the character of Vincent Berardi. No arrests, no convictions. A Medford Township detective said, "He's a pretty solid guy, well liked in the community. As far as we know, he's clean. We would know if he had any associations."

It was enough to half-convince Mo that the man he would be dealing with is probably not connected with Unity Savings and in particular, Joseph Bannon, other than that of a legitimate borrower and long time friend. Mo's instincts would tell him within five minutes if Berardi were dirty.

When Mo drove up the dirt lane from the main road to the construction site in Medford Township, he didn't realize immediately how fortunate he was that his car had a "Neptune County" identification brightly written on the front doors.

Vince stood in the uncompleted dining room. He leaned the piece of sheet rock he had been struggling with against two joists. Immediately his hand dropped to the nail pouch of his leather tool belt where the semi automatic .32 rested. By now, he had become accustomed to packing the gun whenever he worked on Andy's house, which since the nighttime visitation of a couple of weeks before was never after dark alone. During the day, he had the company and apparent security in numbers of the boys who were helping him build the place. Today they were putting in wiring and next week they planned to be fitting the doors and windows.

"Are you Berardi?" asked Mo Henry, waddling up the plank walkway to the inside of the house.

With his right hand in his tool belt and his eyes fixed on the stranger's hands, Vince said, "Yeah."

"Maurice Henry," said the big man, extending a hand. "You can call me 'Mo.' I'm with the Neptune County Prosecutor's office."

"Now what did I do?" Berardi asked.

But Mo talked, and Berardi stood speechless for the ten or fifteen minutes, hearing the details of a case that Neptune County was building against Joseph A. Bannon and Unity Savings. The charges were fraud and the victims were Berardi and a few others who had sought loans from Unity Savings only to lose their collateral and all hopes of a legitimate loan.

"But Bannon is in the Witness Protection Program," Vince pointed out.

"We know all about that," said Mo. "It doesn't matter."

"But how can the Justice Department, the FBI and all those guys stand by and watch you prosecute one of their informants?"

"It's easier than you think. We are a different governmental entity. There are New Jersey citizens and others just like yourself who were fleeced in our county. It's the duty of law enforcement in that county to protect its citizens and bring guys like Bannon to justice. We don't care who he works for."

"So, you want me to testify against him?" Berardi asked.

"Yes."

"But what if I say no?"

Henry looked about him at the stacks of sheet rock, piles of lumber and bags of concrete mix. Then his eyes took in the heavy barn-like framework. "Nice house. This yours?"

"I'm building it for a guy in town," he said. "It is supposed to be one of seven post and beamers I have under contract, but the other six are on hold unless I get some money."

"And you're not gonna' get money from Unity Savings," Mo said. "That's the story isn't it?"

Mo walked over to the kitchen area and scraped some mud he had tracked onto a piece of two-by-four laying on the floor. A teen-ager was screwing hardware onto some cabinets and said, "How ya' doin'?" Mo said nothing, just looked around as if admiring the layout. He turned to Vince: "How are the feds treating you?"

"Not good," Vince said. "They suspect, they think...well I don't know what the hell they think, but it's like they're trying to link me up with Bannon."

Mo turned and placed his hand idly on a cutoff saw, thumbing the sharpness of the blade. "How would you like to get your money back?"

Vince stared at him.

"I'm talkin' about the $36,000 that Bannon took from you."

"How would that happen?"

"A trial," Mo said quickly. "A judge, a jury. Full-blown courtroom proceedings. Coupla' days trial, that's all. This guy's guilty; he owes you big time. He stole from you. I think you'll get your money back."

"What if he can't pay? What if the bank can't pay?" Vince asked. "The Justice Department has everything tied up."

"He's employed by..." said Henry, stopping in mid-sentence because he changed a thought. "Right now we don't know who he works for, or even where he is. But I can tell you this. If we indict, and right now a grand jury is looking into it, who do you think is going to put up this guy's bail money? To keep him out of jail? The feds, that's who. The good old American taxpayer.

"That's the first step. You know, or should know, that if Bannon has to spend one night in a county lockup, he may come out on a stretcher. There are a lot of guys who want to kill him. The Strike Force will do just about anything to protect their boy."

Vince noted Mo's baggy trousers and shirt. Though looking out of place in the woods and heat of August, he saw no sharpie, maybe no bullshitter. *The guy is offering a way to get my money back, maybe my respect and my reputation back.*"

"I have to think about this." His voice rose a pitch as he foresaw the possibilities. "In other words, I would have to incriminate Feeno in public."

"Is that hard?" Mo asked. "What has he done for you lately?"

"I'd want to talk to Feeno first."

Mo picked up a piece of hardened concrete and tossed it unconsciously in the air. He smiled. "This guy was a buddy of yours at one time, right?"

"One of my best friends."

"Let me give you a little advice, Mister Berardi. If you don't mind, that is. It's not my...and I apologize."

Vince's nod told Mo it was okay to talk.

"Your wife and kids. They matter now. Friendships. Old friendships. Sure they mean something. But you got a family now, buddy." He looked toward the dusty plywood floor. "That's what

I'd be thinkin' about."

"Well, I'll promise you this," said Vince. "I'll discuss it with my lawyer, and maybe you can keep him informed about the case. About the particulars. Where it's headed. All that."

They shook hands and Mo ambled to his car and as he had his hand on the door handle, yelled to Vince, "Hey, you got a nice lookin' house here. You do nice work." He hesitated as he ducked into the driver's seat, and yelled once more before shutting the door. "I mean it! Nice job!"

Despite the new and unwanted overtones to his life, Vince noticed that the summer moved quickly. At times even rhythmic, especially at the job site, with the envisionment of creating, planning and tinkering, the actual building of it, watching Andy Burke's new home going up before the weather changed, ready for occupants, with a coat of white paint and green trim on the wraparound porch. A lofty moment of this over-all sad summer was when Andy's lawyer handed over the check at settlement.

Vince now could start on a second home on a plot just down the road, but deeper into the pines, for an ob/gyn M.D. from Haddonfield. The doctor had some big bucks and didn't have to convince Vince that a 6,500 square foot home was not overly large for a family of four.

As for old business, Bernie Samuels was working with the remaining customers to nullify the contracts that were already signed. And the director of security of the Bally Casino in Atlantic City had stopped by to look at a lot. One plot had a stream going through the back yard, to connect with a larger stream feeding into Squaw Lake. It was choice property, surrounded by Pinelands.

The Berardi family turned to summer routines, taking off a couple of weekends to stay at Julie's Aunt Margaret's cottage in Stone Harbor. Lying on the beach, tempting the torrid August sun to burn a body to cinders was like a game. Lie there as long as you can, feel the searing heat upon your back, thoughts tuned to kids playful shouts being muffled by the charging surf.

With a leap, a run and a headlong dive into the cold Atlantic, the breaker iced the burn from your body and with a furious tug at your thighs forced you deeper into its refreshing embrace.

    Then, with the sand castles built — the Berardi structures being the envy of the beach — he'd watch the tide approach and with little swirls create moats around the castles. Your feet on the hard sand would tickle as the water fled back to whence it came, undercutting the gray Jersey sand. And the sun would beat once again upon your shoulders.

Chapter 14: THE IRISH TENOR

On a rainy Friday morning in late August Vince stayed home from the job. The ground was a mud swell. He was tired. He sat on the back porch with the day's mail in his lap, putting the bills to one side, flipping the junk mail to the seat of a chair. The rain was pounding down heavily on the porch's metal roof. He slit open the envelopes with his jack knife. All the Acme Market ads and applications for credit cards, solicitations for contributions to Father Flanagan's Boys Home and the donations for the Nativity School bazaar went into the junk pile. Charity was guiltily listed last in these parlous times.

There were a couple of post cards advertising local businesses like insurance protection, specials at the hardware store, nurseries advocating that "autumn is the time to winterize your lawn." And one from Fortino's Restaurant in South Philly promoting the upcoming appearance of a new singing waiter.

"You're going to love this fantastic tenor," was the endorsement of Albert Fortino, the owner. "Giuseppe Banone has come all the way from Busseto, Italy, the boyhood home of Verdi, to sing for you. Sunday, Sept. tenth."

The guy must be good to be singled out among the tenors and baritones who struggled with their careers while serving up linguini and tortellini at Fortino's. Yet it seemed odd and out of place that a decent tenor would migrate from Italy to the U.S. just to sing at a small Italian restaurant in South Philadelphia.

He left the porch and went to the kitchen, found a thumb tack in the beer-nuts catch all jar and tacked the Fortino's postcard onto the cork reminder board.

He checked his watch, noting that Julie's aerobics class would end in a half-hour, and was he or she supposed to pick up Patty and Gloria at the summer soccer camp?

"Jumping Jesus Christ," he said aloud. He rushed to the

cork board, grabbed the postcard and stared. "Giuseppe Banone — Joseph Bannon." To sing at Fortino's.

The two-and-a-half weeks that followed the arrival of the postcard and the intrusion of Feeno back into his life advanced slowly and unbalanced. An expectant euphoria that at last he could verbally expunge his old friend from his life was replaced by fear.

An unavoidable problem occurred when he failed to remove the postcard from the Berardi household public view. Julie saw it.

"Hey, let's go," she said. "We can take your mother." She did not make the connection re "Giuseppe Banone" being the present family nemesis.

"I don't think I want to go," answered Vince quickly, searching for the proper lie to allow himself to go alone.

"It's been so long," she said. "We need a night out. You've been tense as hell lately. So have I, both of us. Let's go, Vince. Call mom."

The risk was evident. How would Feeno appear? Not as a waiter, never as a waiter who sang for his supper. How? What other hunted and hated man with a contract on his head would show up in a neighborhood where the Mafia had a presence on every other block?

By Sunday afternoon Vince had convinced himself that there was nothing he could do but to go ahead with it. Uninviting his mother and his wife to a Sunday evening outing of canolis and arias was not an option. He tried to convince himself that Feeno would not show. But he and Julie ended up picking up Momma at her condo in Voorhees. They arrived at South 11th street about 7:30.

Momma, with a new, boiled blue "permanent" hairdo, grinned as she walked up the brief stone steps to the corner entrance. She waved to two women sitting on the steps to another row house a half block away. They were watching warily three young boys play step ball, as if they would have the athletic prowess to intercept any tennis ball heading for a living room window from across the street. It was a game usually accepted by most adults as being a necessary risk. There were few playgrounds in South Philadelphia.

Rules in the closely packed neighborhoods were necessarily bent to accommodate the social needs, as on hot summer days when someone would wrench open the valve of a fire hydrant. Laws against the widespread theft of city water during heat waves were not quite enforceable, so the city came up with sprinkler heads to be turned on and supervised by the local Democratic Party committee man or woman.

Fortino's took up three former row houses whose walls had been punctured with wide doorways or torn down completely to accommodate several rooms of dining tables. The inner walls facing the streets at the corner were stripped of plaster, leaving a brick facade upon which Al Fortino had painted pastel scenes of the Amalfi Coast, including a montage of Naples and Capri. The most popular of the three dining rooms was the Blue Grotto.

When the Berardi party entered, Fortino was standing behind the small bar, pouring Chianti from a wicker-encased bottle into glasses. He waved and motioned Vince to come over. "I saved a table for you next to the stage."

Vince fingered the postcard invitation in his pocket but wisely chose not to inform Fortino of its presence or lack of authenticity.

Working their way to the rear of the room was a slow parade. "Look who's here?" said a gray-haired gentleman to Rosa Berardi. "Oh, Rosie," said another who had remained a resident of South Philly, not joining the exodus like Momma and other seniors to the quieter climes of South Jersey and Pennsylvania suburbs.

Julie too received the recognition deserving of a doe-eyed young woman with an attractive figure and smile. Vince received hearty pats on the back and cries of "Where 'ya been?" and "How 'ya doin'?"

A short, young waiter who was definitely not Feeno Bannon pulled out the chairs for Rosa and Julie.

Vince forced a smile, and interrupted, "Oh, leave that one for me. Against the wall. "

He sat, assured of a good view of the room. Behind his head were landscape prints of St. Mark's Square in Venice and the Roman Forum.

"What's wrong with you?" Julie asked. "You're as jumpy as a cat."

Vince ordered a bottle of Zinfandel, but Momma grabbed his arm: "Vincent. Nebbiolo? Please."

"Mom, Zinfandel is just as good as..."

"Vincent!", corrected Julie.

"Nebbiolo," the wine steward smiled as Vince nodded acquiescence to the Italian model.

He sat back, searched the room for any man standing over six feet three. The wine was brought, tasted and approved, and the Zuppa del Giorno arrived and was sampled, Vince felt the warmth of his stomach reach up to soothe the brain. He felt more relaxed. The movies are right. You can't comfortably rest in the chair on Death Row without quaffing down one last favorite meal. But he hadn't gone halfway through his Pasta alla Caruso when Al Fortino approached. "Vince, telephone for you."

He jumped out of his seat and followed Al to the bar. "No, not here," said Al. "Go out in the hallway. I'll hand the phone through the waiter's station."

Vince whispered to Al, "Hold my dinner in the kitchen will you? This may take a while."

In the hallway there was a modicum of privacy. A staircase led to the second floor. Vince nervously looked up and down and back and forth before picking up the receiver. He cleared his throat and said, "Hello" in as strong a voice as he could muster.

"Vince the Prince," came the voice, neither forcefully nor happily as usual, but subdued and expectant.

"What do you want, Feeno?"

There was a long pause at the other end: "I don't blame you for being pissed."

"Pissed isn't the word, Feeno! How about fucking destroyed." He whispered as loudly as he could without being overheard. "That's what you've done. My money's gone, bad-ass buddies of yours are beating me to shit and lurking at every corner." Between the teeth, his voice rose, "Do you know what you have done to me, my family?"

"You should be in my shoes for a day, buddy."

Vince kept quiet, waiting for the explanation.

Feeno was standing in a gas station phone booth adjacent to a vast, head-high field of corn. The evening sky was white with heat, causing the straight, asphalt road to shimmer.

"Your loan was approved, all set to go. It fell apart in one night. One night, that's all. The bank trustees, the Scalesis. I could tell they were on to me. We had our weekly meeting. I put your application on the table. I had already stamped it "approved." That's when the shit hit the fan."

Chapter 15: THE COMMITTEE

Feeno, leaning half-in, half-out the phone booth, began telling of the night only four months ago back in Jersey that changed everything, his life and Vince's life, and the lives of everyone immediately around them.

Feeno had told Angela he would be late. Truthful, so far. The evening as outlined was to meet the loan committee members for dinner at a restaurant always of Rocco Scalesi's choosing. Then on this particular night the committee would adjourn to Unity Savings, and with stomachs gorged with fine food and drinks, enjoy the remainder of the evening routinely studying and approving a short list of low-risk, legit applications like the one for good old Vince Berardi, the kid who built shacks and waterfalls and who now created mansions.

The Hof Brau was located on a cliff overlooking the Hudson River near Sneden Landing just off the Palisades Parkway, over the state line into New York. A party of seniors, men and women dressed in formal wear, was stepping from a limo to go into the side restaurant entrance. A yonder-aged class reunion, most probably.

Feeno, arms folded, scratched the ground with the sole of a shoe as he leaned against the fender of his Lincoln. He checked his watch. Next to him was a brief case containing the transactions of the evening.

He checked his watch again. They could already be inside at the bar. But in a minute, a red Buick drove up beside him.

"Get in," said Trapetto.

"What's up?" asked Feeno, bending to hear the little man sitting in the passenger seat next to the driver, Arnold D'Alfonsi.

Trapetto pointed with his thumb toward the back seat. The door opened. Fred Russo moved over. Feeno climbed in and no sooner had his long leg left the ground and he reached for the door handle, Fonzie hit the gas and the Buick left the lot with screaming tires.

They drove south, back into Jersey, reaching Passaic about 7:20. "It's on Monroe Street, a block and a half up," said Trapetto, picking his teeth with a match book.

"Ah, Passaic, the birthplace of television," Russo said, sitting in the middle, his Armani suit scrunched between the wide-bodied Rocco and long-legged Feeno.

"What do you mean, birth place of television?" Feeno asked.

"Remember DuMont?" answered Russo. "The DuMont Television Network? Right here. Right here in good old Passaic, New Jersey."

"Park here," yelled Trapetto, noting a single spot in the crowded block of small storefronts, a mixed neighborhood of a yeshiva on the corner, a Polish deli and Cantonese restaurant. A broad wooden sign above a small shop read, "Guatemalan Imports."

The five men got out of the car as a woman hauling a plastic basket full of wash stopped to let them pass. She then proceeded to the Quality Laundromat. A dingy bar with a facade of fake stone was next door. Beside it, from a typical Church of the Open Storefront, came a piano's jazzy, rhythmic sound of "How Great Thou Are." And on the other side of the church was a small store with Asian writing on the window panes flanking a wide center door. The door opened before Trapetto had even reached it.

A man, even smaller than Trapetto, greeted the men with a cautious smile and a stiff bow. He wore a green smock with lettering, "Asian Noodles Wholesale Imports" scrolled over the heart. He ushered them in and motioned for them to go between an opening in a long, wooden counter. No lights were on and the evening sunset cast long shadows from both wooden and cardboard boxes. A ceiling fan turned slowly above tables of large round jars filled with what appeared to Feeno to be curled pasta. And on shelves behind them were both twiggy and ground spices, also in jars.

Inside the back room were floor to ceiling shelves, mostly

filled with bright yellow and red, dragon-decorated boxes of noodles. In the center of the room beneath a dangling bright light with a green, metal shade was an octagon-shaped table with a flat surface of green felt in the middle.

"Are we gonna' play cards or get down to business?" asked Feeno, imitating a smile. He looked at his Rolex, then from Rocco, to Russo, to Trapetto. "I wanta' get home in time to see the Mets game."

"Sit down, sit down, Feeno," laughed Rocco, both amused and pleased at the banker's impatience.

"We're gonna' get down to business, then go out to eat," said the Boss. "Business before pleasure tonight."

He sat, pulled a leather pouch from a suit pocket and with a cigar-clip containing a single diamond, nipped the end of a Bolivar Corona, and twirled the other end above the flame of a jeweled Zippo.

"All right, whataya got?" asked Rocco, his voice, typically for him, hoarse and falsetto.

"First off, a big one," Feeno said, pulling the file for Vince Berardi. "Seven-hundred and fifty-thousand. We probably will have to lay off part of it, maybe a major part, with Central States, the pension fund. But this is good. Really, really secure. I've known this applicant, Vincent Berardi, all my life. He's a..."

"Stand up," Rocco suddenly yelled at Feeno, pointing with the corona. Rocco stood, as did Feeno, startled. "Over here," he motioned. Fonzi stood also and pushed with his boxer's arms and muscle-bound fists against Feeno's chest.

Feeno yelled as both his back and his head smacked into the hard edges of shelves. Boxes of noodles fell to the floor.

"Check the front," yelled Rocco to Trapetto. The little one hastened to the door to the front room and looked as the oriental man pulled down a shade. The oriental turned and nodded, "Okay."

"Stand him up," yelled Rocco, who stepped forward and with two hairy hands grabbed Feeno's shirt fronts and ripped them open to the sides. Fonzi grabbed Feeno's sports jacket and with one hand twisted him and yanked it off. He grasped the rear collar of Feeno's shirt and yanked it down to his waist.

Fred Russo, the lawyer, stood to the far side of the room and watched, his eyes wide.

Rocco grabbed a handful of Feeno's cotton tee-shirt at the collar and yanked. It split. With both hands, Rocco split it more.

Then they stared. At Feeno's thin but violently pumping chest. Angrily, Rocco snatched the gold chain with the Celtic cross and broke it away from Feeno's neck. It flew across the room, hitting an upright vacuum cleaner and dropping to the floor.

Feeno, sweating and with his chest heaving, gasped for air and when he found it, yelled with as much bravado as he could muster, "What the fuck are you looking for?" He pushed hard with the heel of his right hand against Fonzi's shoulder. Fonzi barely flinched and raised his fist.

"Hold it, hold it, hold it," said Rocco, dropping his cigar. "Easy, guys. Easy, easy, easy."

Feeno, who stood six inches taller than the tallest thug in the room, stood panting, his face formed in now legitimate anger. "You sons of bitches. You bastards. I work my fucking head off for you creepy pricks. And this is what I get."

"Hold on," said Rocco, backing up. He looked toward Fonzi. "Make sure. Remove the pants."

He looked at Feeno. "Remove the pants, Feeno. You heard me."

Feeno began to comply, but Fonzi grabbed the belt buckle, yanked and pulled Feeno's trousers to his ankles. He turned Feeno around, one way, then the other. He bent to the floor and examined the pockets and even put his fingers into the cuffs of Feeno's green and white checked socks and Italian loafers. Fonzi looked up at Rocco and shook his head from side to side. "Nothing."

"All right, up," said Rocco, his treble voice lowered an octave from before. He walked back to the table. "Everybody sit down. You too, Feeno."

Feeno, tucking in the clothing he had left that was not in tatters, took a seat at the poker table opposite Rocco. His angular face was flushed crimson, panting and sweating. He looked at the men on all sides, then at Rocco sitting across from him. When he could breath, he sensed a slight restoration of Mafia honor; he smiled, thrusting his chin, eyes brightened. He laughed, lightly just once: "You cocksuckers had me going."

Rocco stared, his eyes and brow hard and wrinkled.

Fonzi snickered once, still pleased with the roughing up of a man he never liked; he involuntarily snickered again, chuckled and began roaring, mouth wide open. Soon, tears were falling from his squinting eyes. Even Trapetto's squirrel-sized face broke, his little pointy teeth laid bare with amusement. Russo sat down heavily, wiped his brow with his handkerchief, loosened the ninety-dollar tie at his neck and said, "Whoosh!" He grinned, looked at Feeno, and laughed loudly, slapping his knee.

As the laughter died, Feeno stole glances at Rocco's face, dominated by the hooded eyes of a serpent, a slightly smiling serpent. The others stopped laughing and waited.

"Okay," yelled Feeno, relieved to be in control. He shot his sleeves confidently but grasped the Vincent Berardi folder tightly to keep his fingers from shaking.

"Vincent Berardi."

"We ain't approving this loan," said Rocco, his face pointed downward for a moment, examining the Corona.

Feeno blanched, his mouth flew open: "But it's okay. The guy's good; I've known him all my life. He has equity. The return on this? Seven-hundred and fifty-thousand. It'll be seven years. Seven. It's all calculated. At 8.7 percent. It's a winner."

Feeno's brain raced threw particulars of other loans he and his committee had put up and stamped "approved" with no consideration. Loans to Teamster friends, Mafia-run restaurants in Jersey, casinos in Las Vegas, a multimillion dollar loan to a high-end Teamsters resort with a golf course and spa in California, loans to mob-owned trucking companies. All still awaiting full payment.

"Half of the loans we put out this year won't see payments. Ever!" He dared not mention the money doled out to Rocco himself and the half-dozen other relatives in the family. Over Rocco's shoulder, through the inner door, he glimpsed the oriental man fingering the green shade of the front door, still peeking outside.

"The heat's on, Feeno" said Rocco. "That fuckin' Strike Force. Why do you think we shook you down?"

"But this is legitimate," Feeno asserted, standing up and slapping the folder on the poker table. "For once we got something real and you guys..." He stopped himself, then added, "So what should I do?" Feeno asked. "Return Vince's money? He put up – let me see what it is?" He shuffled through the papers in front of him. "Thirty-six grand in cash. The collateral, sixty acres of prime, halfway between Philly and Atlantic City. His houses. He put up his own house, a couple rentals, an apartment house."

Russo, a reasonable voice who often brought calm to angry sessions such as this, offered, "How many other investors are involved in this project?"

Rocco shot him a warning glance: "You keep out of this, Fred."

Feeno's head swiveled from boss to the lawyer, the lawyer to the boss. "None. No one, just himself."

"He ain't gettin' the cash back," said Rocco. "We need all the cash we can get before all this shit falls apart. We gotta' pay something toward that last shipment of 'H' that came into Kennedy before the feds cracked down. The cousins in Palermo are getting edgy." He stabbed the table with a heavy forefinger, letting his raspy voice shower the room. "I want that cash and the other cash wired to Cayman tonight. We're cleaning everything out."

As Vince leaned against the metal wainscoting of the restaurant hallway, listening to the summary of events that Feeno related, he held a finger in his opposite ear to mute the raucous, in time clapping of hands in the restaurant, initiated by an inspiring waiter's rendition of "Funiculi, Funicula."

Far away at the other end of the phone line, Feeno stepped from the overheated booth in the middle of nowhere and yearned for a nonexistent breeze. He wore a yellow "Guinea tee," the sweat sticking to his bony skin. He continued telling Vince in a hushed and hesitant voice that he left the meeting that night determined somehow to set everything right. "At least to see that you got your collateral back. But I never got the chance."

"Louder," Vince shouted. "I can't hear you."

"I'm going to get you your money back," Feeno hollered.

Outside the gas station lube pit, a man in dirty coveralls unloading tires from a pickup truck looked Feeno's way and smiled.

Feeno continued with a few details of how, that same night that the Scalesis shook him down, the FBI swooped up him and his wife into the Witness Protection Program.

"It was over, Vince. Ended, kaput!"

After a very long pause full of stormy and confused thoughts, Vince finally asked, "What the hell am I going to do?"

"What the hell are we going to do? We're in this together."

"Where the fuck...?" Vince shut up as a heavy man came puffing down the hallway stairs carrying a load of linen. "Where the hell do you get we, Feeno?"

"Ah, Christ, Vince, I'm sorry. I'm so fucked up. Everything, my life." Standing inside the overheated phone booth, he kept open the sliding door to keep from being boiled and baked in the excruciating, unforgivable summer heat. He looked about at this strange flat horizon, bleeding cornfield green to the west, a busted-up asphalt road running to the south, the clapboard gas station just over his shoulder with an ancient "Tydol-Veedol" sign leaning up against a tilted, broken garage filled with greasy detritus.

"What I mean is...To me it's spiritual," Feeno continued.

The operator interrupted with the message that he needed more coins. His stack in front of him was dwindling. He waited until the jingling quarters fell to the bottom.

"You saved my life that night, Vince."

"How?" asked Vince.

"Yours was the only loan we were considering that night. The only one on the table. Because of that I didn't wear the wire. Didn't need to. I told my control, the FBI guy. He agreed. But that night, when I got home is when they yanked me and Angela into the program."

He began describing his days as a federally protected citizen, but wouldn't disclose his whereabouts or what his new identity was or his occupation.

"All I can say is that it's far from urban where we live. My wife is going nuts. Vince, she is filing for a divorce as soon as she gets the chance. She hates me, even though she was partially responsible for me getting into this."

Puzzled, Vince asked what he meant. "She's a Scalesi, Vince. A beautiful person, really. Not mobbed up at all. But I fell for her and..." Here he hesitated. "You know me. I always was fascinated by mob guys growing up in South Philly. I liked to hang around, you know. So here, I saw an opportunity to get a rush. I had no idea how much of a rush it would be. I thought originally that the bank loans to close friends of these guys would certainly be repaid, that they were just a little thing under the table. It got deeper and deeper. They said that I was one of their best earners. It went to my head. The money was good.

"But Vince," he continued, pleading now. "I can't hurt you; I can't hurt the people I grew up with. I'd give anything to turn back the clock."

Vince couldn't help saying, "That's what everybody says when they get into hot water."

"Vince, I swear, I'm going to make it up to you, with interest, I promise." Vince heard him choke, then cough. He sensed that this was genuine remorse coming from Feeno. Vince told him though about the federal pressure being put on him.

"They think I'm part of it, Feeno. They think I'm dirty, like your fucking friends."

"I know, I know. Vince, I told them a thousand times that you're clean. You're innocent. I think they half believe me, but Mario Bianca, the U.S. Attorney in Newark. He's a first-class prick. He said they'll get to you when they get to you, meaning he has to have proof after the bank examiners go through all the evidence that you're not involved.

"Vince, I'm taking an awful chance talking to you, calling you like this. If I get caught I'm in deep shit trouble. You can't tell anyone about this phone call. No one. Please, you have to promise."

Vince reiterated that he wasn't feeling too safe about the conversation they were having either. "We're both in trouble," he said.

"We're both in trouble," Feeno echoed. "And we're going to get out of it. I promise."

Feeno said goodbye, hung up and left the booth. Before Vince returned the phone to Fortino and went back to his table, he asked for a double shot of Bushmills, which he downed in a second, then asked for another. He went to the men's room, and looked under the stalls before taking a much needed leak. He thought about the impending fraud case in Neptune County against Feeno and was half glad he didn't tell him about it. He will know soon enough, and he'll know that Vince could very well be the chief witness against him.

Chapter 16: WHITEHAVEN

Sept. 3, 1978, Labor Day weekend.

"Blow your nose, you crazy bastard!"

The goose sailing overhead answered Feeno's request with another nasal "Ah-Honk, Ah-Honk" before splashing into the marsh flats. Several more of the big birds pecked and crapped on the lawn sloping down to the river. Feeno picked up an oyster shell, threw it hard toward one of them, then watched the winged visitor from Canada waddle three feet and crap again.

"Why the hell don't you fly back where you came from?" Feeno yelled.

"Why don't you leave those ducks alone?" asked a woman's voice from inside the small white clapboard house, which had been built on wooden piers above the lawn and hard-sand driveway.

"They're not ducks, Angela. They're Canada Geese and they belong in Canada, not here. Look at the shit they leave." He pointed here, there. "Everywhere. I have sensitive feet, you fuckers. This is my yard. Am-scray."

Angela, inside now at the sink washing vegetables, smiled. And at the thought of nothing being allowed to touch her husband's tender feet except socks, slippers and shoes, she grinned, then chuckled, her shoulders shaking.

She watched as the former banker from New Jersey walked to the skiff twenty yards away, stepping delicately into the water, like a man on a tightrope. Plopping into the skiff. A few strokes of the oars put him in open water. He had learned to crab, tying chicken necks onto twine and letting them soak awhile before slowly pulling up the salty, green critters.

The only thing he hated about the crabbing routine was keeping his eyes alert for goose poop as he walked. Lately the crabbing, as he became acquainted to life in this flat and unpretentious landscape, replaced the internal gnawing that he felt since the beginning, when the Witness Protection Program resettled him and Angela on this rural haven far from the murderous eyes of the Scalesis.

Each day Feeno was going through copies of accounts removed from Unity Savings, linking the transactions to persons involved, identifying them as best he knew, according to their relationship, either through blood or Teamsters connections.

The Justice Department and other law enforcement agencies determined the investigation to be paramount because it was so far-ranging — from the payoff from Teamsters funds to the men who made Jimmy Hoffa disappear, to the importation of heroin into the U.S. from secret labs in Italy.

The loans, payouts and the money laundering all centered on Teamsters health and welfare and pension deposits intended for the benefit of thousands of dues-paying truck drivers and other freight handlers and their families. They were workers who had such obeisance and loyalty to union officials that most didn't suspect they were being defrauded of their savings.

At least once a week Justice lawyers made the trip from Washington across the bay to Whitehaven, located on a stubby little river, one of two in Maryland that are named "Wicomico" that feed the Chesapeake Bay, the other being near the Potomac.

The preparation for the upcoming trials was erratic, seemingly going forward, then being put on hold for reasons that Feeno was not informed about. Both Feeno and Angela had the time to work jobs under their new names in nearby Salisbury. Feeno worked as a bookkeeper for a small accounting firm, handling accounts of clients, doing payrolls and other chores, while Angela worked in actuaries with an insurance company. Their names were now "Joseph and Ann Yarnell."

Typically after work, when the quietness settled on the lawn and small house, Feeno would walk down toward the river working his pooper scooper, ridding the lawn of goose leavings, hurling them into the cattails.

The ritual came to offer a loosening of tension. As a new born rural caretaker, he began to feel comfortable, especially in the small white home on the river, which probably belonged to and was used for vacations, he surmised, by someone in the Justice Department, no doubt a lawyer.

White was the color of choice in all the rooms, except the kitchen, whose wood work bore a dark but handsome stain. The white rooms reflected a homey lightness, an ease, a quietness.

Feeno sometimes stood in the middle of a room, perfectly still, as if to detect any noise at all. Most times, he heard buzzings of insects, chattering songbirds, a putter of a small-engined boat upon the river, an a-honk from a goose.

A small brick fireplace in the parlor was flanked by floor-to-ceiling bookcases, also painted white. There were books on the U.S. Constitution, three copies, all of them worn, of *Black's Law Dictionary*. Many dull books: *Loan Loss Coverage, Charitable Gift Planning, Dispute Resolution*.

At once bare locations on the walls were old portraits. One of an old man in mutton chops with a woman whose severely combed back hair was flattened to her head. In one wooden frame hanging over an old sofa (with doilies) was a piece of white embroidery with red, Old English script lettering:

> "The Secret of My Success
> Is That At An Early Age
> I Discovered That
> I Was not God."
>
> ~ Oliver Wendell Holmes, Jr.

On a Sunday, an early morning gray sky was being painted by streaks of gold against blue as the summer sun travelled over the rivers and bay. On the river, a work boat with two men puttered slowly downstream toward Fishing Bay. Feeno had come to recognize the locals by now and he waved to them. The men waved back.

"How about coming with me for a spin on the river?" Feeno asked Angela, who had slumped into the hammock on the porch and was examining the Lifestyle section of the *Baltimore Sun*.

She didn't answer. On her lap was a book titled *Midnight Express*, about an American guy, a hashish smuggler who spent time in a brutal Turkish prison. It's a book that Feeno had started reading, but stopped because details of the cruelty of Turkish prison life made him uneasy. Angela dropped the newspaper and picked up the book and began reading.

"Whataya say, Ange? Before lunch." He watched her small behind pushing down on the hammock cords. She touched the little wooden table next to her and pushed, setting the hammock slightly swinging. Still she did not answer.

Feeno swung away and walked toward the skiff. Angela's silences were customized by now. Her non-replies were a stronger communication than the shouts and crying of their earlier arguments. Stone silence sometimes dealt blows that bruised deeper than words. Angela's boredom and discontent seemed to grow stronger day by day.

Not all days passed thusly, with her sulks and aches, her distances from him. There were occasions when she made sincere attempts to be at ease with the man she married. Once, Feeno hooked up the outboard and the two of them went downstream seven miles toward the bay. They anchored about one hundred feet from a sandy beach and swam and splashed in the warm water.

Before lying down on a blanket, Angela's eyes searched the high grass and wide expanse of water. She looked up and down the narrow beach before taking off her bikini top. Lying down on her back, the sun blinding in her eyes, she removed the bottoms and welcomed him in.

Sitting on the beach after putting on their bathing suits, Feeno popped a cold beer from the cooler and handed it to Angela. He pulled out a bottle of Coke for himself. They ate hard-boiled egg sandwiches.

"Why did you want to join the Mafia?" she asked, brushing her hair back in the breeze. Three turkey buzzards circled overhead, steadying their flight upon a dead target in the brush. He watched the silhouette of a tanker heading up the Chesapeake Bay toward Baltimore.

He looked at her, trying to puzzle it out. "That's a funny question."

"That's a funny answer," she said.

"I never said I..." He began again. "First-of-all, I'm not in the Mafia. You know that. I'm not Italian."

"That's not what I mean. I mean – you came from Philly. Poor family. I know all about that. Then you go to college and get a degree. That's pulling yourself up. I would think you were at the top, maybe of the pinnacle of something in your life. Then you decide that's not enough."

He sifted sand through his toes and took a big swig from the Coke bottle.

"I mean," she said, "what's in you that makes you want to stand on the edge and dare yourself to jump? That's what you do. You do it all the time."

"Ah, I'm restless."

"Restless isn't the half of it," she said, her voice darkening. "Here I am, I'm trying to break away from a family connection that has caused me embarrassment all my life. And at the same time you're busting your ass to get into it."

"I didn't bust my ass or anybody else's ass, Angela. All right, I took to it. I liked what I saw. The lifestyle, the money, the glamour. What else do you want to know?"

"You liked the thrill too, didn't you."

"What the hell are you saying, Angela?" He looked hard at her, at her eyes squinting against the sunlight. She looked away out toward the bay, and turned to look at him.

"I'm getting tired of Schweitzer and his cronies trying to get information out of me."

"How do you think I feel?"

"You don't get it, do you? They're after me to flesh out the family tree. They want to know all about Rocco Scalesi, his wife, his daughter. Who else is involved? My parents. And me! I feel like crap after one of those sessions."

"I'm sorry," said Feeno, "but I didn't get you into your family's problems."

"You may not have," she said. Her face reddened and tears began to fall. "But you've done all you could to destroy my connections, my..."

"My parents," she said. "I can't even see them again. This

is where your fucking thrill got us. On a deserted beach in the middle of a fucking nowhere."

She got up hastily and waded to the skiff.

The next day, Monday, he dropped her off at the American General building in the center of Salisbury. He leaned toward her with an intentional goodbye kiss, but she slammed the car door. Rush hour traffic was heavy. A big fertilizer truck changed gears as it moved past. "Pick you up at five?" he yelled as she hurriedly walked away.

She turned. In the noisy background, he caught the words, no more than scratches. "No. Getting a lift. See you at..."

At his own desk, minutes ticked with no remorse. He shuffled through the day nursing routines. At five, he stuck the payroll records of Ferguson Hardware into a folder and dropped it on a clerk's desk for filing. To the walls, he said "see you tomorrow."

At home, he let the screen door slam to announce his arrival. Silence again, so he droned around the kitchen, biting an apple, putting it down and transferring the breakfast dishes into the dishwasher. He began wiping the table and shelves with a damp dish rag, picked up the *Salisbury Times* from the table and read, "Mayor Seeks Tax Cut", and "Poultry Prices Down," He dropped the paper on the table.

Outside the evening air was still, warm and quiet, with flies silently buzzing A few warblers un-warbled as the sun, no more than a tiny, brightly red crescent, lipped over the water. He carried an aluminum lawn chair to the far end of the driveway off to the left where it was partly concealed by lilacs. A squadron of barn swallows dive-bombed the lawn, raking insects for supper.

The car, foreign to the neighborhood, drove up fifteen minutes later, just as the sun had had it for the day, passing off the sky to the twilight. It stopped near the mailbox at the end of the lane where it joins Water Street.

He watched them. Angela leaned toward the driver, a man of about thirty, wrapped her arms around his shoulders and kissed him on the lips. She opened the car door, but turned again, rose up, and with her knees on the car seat, held the man's head in her hands and kissed him hard, smearing his face over and over with her lips. Feeno could see him reach behind her, grabbing at her ass and back, trying to pull her hard into his body. She shook her head, "No," then jumped from the car, shut the door quietly, and leaned through the open window for the goodbye kiss. Looking around, she smoothed her dress in front, smoothed her dark hair with one hand and with the other reached into her handbag for a tissue. She wiped the smeared lipstick from her mouth and walked toward the house, chin held high. Feeno sat motionless. His head dropped slowly. He stared at the ground as she got to the house, climbed the porch steps and went inside.

Chapter 17: CHRISTMAS

Dec. 24, 1978.

Vince had put the airplane tickets in an envelope with a Christmas card depicting a pastel scene of the Nativity, with the Holy Mother, Baby Jesus and — standing off in his usual corner — Joseph, Vince's stand-in, a small family struggling to make ends meet.

The next day, in the living room next to the Christmas tree, Julie hugged him, smiled and let out a yelp. Patty and Gloria, who had been tearing into their packages, looked up surprised. "Oh, great man," Julie said. "I'd rather go to the Caribbean. London and Paris can wait." She stood, shaking the sleeves of her heavy robe, and gave Vince a sincere smooch.

"I'm sorry we can't do it the way I planned," he said, bending to pick up torn wrapping paper. "It's a little less elaborate."

"Baloney," she said. "Girls, we're going to Virgin Gorda."

"What's Virgin Gorda?" asked Gloria, holding her new Barbie by the feet, as if it were a club.

"An island in the Caribbean," said Julie. "British Virgin...British? Right?" She looked at Vince, who had reached behind the couch to turn on the Christmas tree lights.

"Yeah, British," he groaned from the difficult angle. He was relieved over how well Julie accepted the scaled down, one-week only Christmas present. His fantasies, his blooming dreams, padded and accented over the previous months, of having under contract a half-dozen timber-framed beauties in the woods, with happy customers shelling out major dollars for them. Gone — dreams reduced to one house at a time.

They had tried to forget, except at times it was pushing against water. He reminded himself that Feeno Bannon had been friend at one time. Still a friend, still a distant friend in trouble,

Vince often told himself. Julie had different feelings, but they tried not to discuss them, tried not to argue or differ about them. She avoided the "I told you so."

Just after Thanksgiving, Mo Henry had phoned. Vince recognized the jowly man with the high-pitched voice as the Neptune County detective who had visited him in August.

"I want you to talk to somebody, Mister Berardi. She's Hope Eversham, an assistant prosecutor here. She's going to be in charge of the case against Joseph Bannon."

Associating warm bedroom voices with soft, pretty faces is not an exact science, so Vince, who had been feeling seduced for months, tried to think of the woman as neutral. Beyond the introductions, Ms. Eversham buttered it on.

She stood, pacing her small office on the fifth floor of the courthouse, looking out on a park of now dead leaves blowing across the barely green lawn. "Vince. May I call you Vince?" She sat on the edge of the desk.

He said that she could, and immediately she began outlining a case against Joseph Bannon, her words coming easily and as matters of fact, leaning towards assumptions that Vince was compliant, ready and willing to testify.

Suspecting the hesitancy of this potential witness, she used the psychological trick of easing him into place by assuming that he had already signed onto it, that this would be no more complicated nor consequential than a trip to the dentist: Testifying against your lifelong friend, calling him a liar and a thief was a routine matter. Done every day. No sweat.

"We'd like to set up a time when you can come up and talk to Prosecutor Rosenstein. What day suits you best? We have Monday and Friday open?"

She heard silence.

"Mister Berardi? Vince?"

"I have some misgivings," he said finally, and began telling her in hesitant steps about his phone conversation with Feeno at Fortino's in Philly.

"You did what? You talked to Bannon?" She rose and placed a finger on an intercom, hesitating though about pushing it.

"You talked to Bannon? He what? He called you? Hold on a minute."

Seconds, then minutes passed. Vince studied his watch. He had told her that he had only a half hour to get to Haddonfield for an appointment with the doctor and his wife to go over plans for their new oversized home.

"Vince, I want to give you my phone number. Will you call me, please?" She emphasized "please," then repeated it.

Vince caught on, recognizing a sudden need for secrecy. He was wondering for weeks if his phone were tapped.

He had no hesitation about talking to the prosecution seeking to nail Feeno and the bank. The reason was simply that he would explore anything that led to getting to the bottom of the mystery, plus getting his money back.

He hopped into his pickup, drove to Willingboro and from the shopping plaza there phoned the doctor and said he would be a little late; then he called the number that Eversham had given him.

The strange but oiled voice of a man came on the phone. "Vince, how are you? Arnie Rosenstein here. I understand you talked to Bannon. How is he doing?"

Vince related everything about the conversation with Feeno, how it wasn't his fault that he didn't get the loan, that the Scalesis were behind the fraud and that Feeno was almost tearfully repentant.

"I can understand all of that," said Rosenstein. "One of the hardest things that a prosecutor runs into is a witness who is reluctant to finger a best friend. That's understandable. But I have to ask..." The prosecutor was at ease. He leaned back in his swivel chair, and with his feet put the chair in rhythmic, half-swings back and forth.

"Only trouble is, Vince. How do you know you can trust...Even best friends can be deceitful."

Vince's chest was now heaving. "They beat the shit out of him. He told me that. He told me that Rocco Scalesi, he's on the loan committee of the bank. He's the one who refused my loan. He's the one who stole my money."

Rosenstein replied with some questions that took Vince back to reality. "Do you really, really know that?"

"What do you mean?"

"Did Feeno ever lie to you? Look," he said before Vince could answer. "We don't know what happened. Neither you, nor I, nor the FBI. We have second hand information. We have assumptions. We don't know the truth, but I can tell you this. Word is out that the Scalesis are putting it all on Bannon. He's the bad guy. He's the one."

"But," Vince said, now quickly. "That's all the more reason why I go back and forth. There are days when I don't want to nail him. If it's not the truth that Feeno is telling me, how the hell do you expect me to participate?"

"Listen. Vince. Who's the president of the bank? Who's the head of the loan committee?"

"Feeno."

"Yes, our friend Feeno. Joseph Bannon." Rosenstein ran his hand flat, front to back across his head, flattening the dark, smooth hair that no longer covered the middle. "You have two things to clear up, Vince. Number one, there's the money. I'm talking about the collateral you posted. Not the loan. Forget about the loan. You'll never get it, not from Unity anyway. But the collateral, what was it, thirty-five thousand?"

"Thirty-six."

"Thirty-six thousand dollars. A lot of money. Do you want to get it back?"

"Yes."

"Okay," the prosecutor said, "I'm going to make sure that you do. No judge in this state, no jury either, is going to let a swindler, especially a bank, get away with fleecing a law-abiding citizen like yourself out of that kind of money. No way, Vince. No matter who was the culprit. Right now it appears to be your friend."

"What's Number two?" he asked.

"Number two, clearing your name. It's that simple. The Justice Department, the Strike Force. They have a blanket over everybody connected with Unity, everybody who ever received or applied for a loan. You're under that blanket. They cast doubt about your innocence. They have suspected you of being in on the illegal activities. If you don't go through with this, it'll hang over you for the rest of your life. Think about your family, think about your business."

Rosenstein was warming up now.

"Before anything like a verdict is decided, there's also a blanket of innocence," the lawyer said. "You're innocent of everything. There are going to be reporters at this proceeding. Here's a guy, Vincent Berardi, a family man who makes a living building homes for other families, caught in a tide of accusations that have nothing to do with him, except as a victim. A huge victim. Listen, I know how these mob cases work. You're one of the fringe guys who gets tangled up with the mob through no fault of your own. Your reputation is soiled by these suspicions. These FBI guys, the prosecutors, they're human, Vince. They suspect everyone, especially, and I'm sorry to say this, guys with Italian surnames whose South Philly father did some prison time. This is the one big chance that you will get to clear yourself.

As an afterthought, "And your dad."

Chapter 18: THE GRAND JURY

Jan. 21, 1979.

"C'mon Franco, you son of a bitch, run. Up the middle. He runs. He's in. Touchdown!"

From the kitchen, Angela yelled, "Who's ahead?"

"Pittsburgh. My babies," answered Feeno, raising the volume on the new 24-inch Sony color TV purchased especially for Feeno and Angela by the American taxpayers.

"Why are you cheering for the Steelers? Aren't they in the other conference?"

"They are."

"But you said that in the Super Bowl you always root for the team in the same conference as the Eagles. And the Eagles aren't in the Super Bowl."

"I know. They lost to Atlanta in the Wild Card game."

"So you should be rooting for Dallas to beat the Steelers. That's what you told me. You root for the team in the Eagles'..."

"That's the general rule, Angela. But this is the exception. Eagles fans root against Dallas. Always. All the time. Forever and ever. Until hell freezes over." He turned to see her bringing in another plate of cheese. "Always. It never changes. No exceptions. We hate the Cowboys."

"But they're in the same conference as the Eagles."

He didn't answer because Angela didn't understand. The misconception made him sorrowful and lonely on this Super Bowl Sunday. A year ago, they had half the neighborhood at the Super Bowl party in their family room. This year they were a disjointed twosome, and Angela as a halfhearted fan, and a spiritless wife and companion.

Both had suffered on Christmas Day, except for a bright period when he presented his gift to her, a brown ball of puppy fur, a Chesapeake Bay Retriever, who now lay at Feeno's feet and began barking happily when Franco Harris put the Steelers ahead 28-17 halfway through the fourth quarter. Feeno walked away from the TV after the Steelers scored again within seconds after a fumble recovery.

"Game's over," said Feeno, but he watched anxiously as Dallas scored two more times. He finally pumped a fist to the ceiling when the Steelers' Rocky Bleier fell on Dallas's onside kick with seventeen seconds to play, sealing the score and the game in the Steelers' favor at 35 to 31.

When the game ended, Feeno stretched his long body upon the heavily padded leather couch in the lawyer's den, staring absently at the rows of legal volumes in the bookcase. He tried focussing on the future, then on reality past and reality present. Tomorrow, the Justice lawyers and FBI would visit to set up school again. Once more, he would be asked to decipher numbers, dates and transactions, to decode mob talk, the whys and wherefores, to listen to another mile of tape and fill in the language gaps, if at all possible.

He closed his eyes, hopefully to lure a nap. But his evening's sleep was pushed away by recollections of the last visit:

Why should the Desert Cactus Casino in Las Vegas receive $125,000 to be used for landscaping from an insignificant little bank in New Jersey? Who is Margaret Franelli, who owns a restaurant in Poughkeepsie, N.Y.?

"Did you know she was cousin to a Bonanno when you approved that transaction?" asked Stan Schweitzer on his last visit.

"Let's go over it again, Feeno, about what happened the night of March 10, 1976 at the Alitalia warehouse at JFK?"

"How did you guys know I was there?" he answered.

"That's not an answer," said Shannon Cook, the Justice Department lawyer with the puffy eyes.

"We know you were there because Alex Greene laid it out for us."

Alex Greene was, like Feeno, another informant, the Alitalia employee who was flipped after law enforcement discovered he defrauded an insurance company by torching his Cadillac in 1975. He wore a wire the afternoon that a Scalesi capo handed him another $20,000 to leave a side door unlocked the day of the theft. The amount was the same as one the week before when he forklifted crates of olive oil to the highest parts of the tall warehouse. The false bottomed cans contained heroin of the richest sort, of an unsurpassed street value in metro New York.

Schweitzer and Cook arrived on Monday before noon. They were joined by two Justice Department Organized Crime attorneys and a stenographer who made the drive from Washington via Annapolis and the Bay Bridge before picking up Route 50 and eventually the isolated roads leading to the obscure village of Whitehaven.

Assembling in the den, Cook noticed the stuffy air and crowded conditions. "Let's take a ride," she said.

"I'm staying here," said one of the visitors from Washington. "We'll be picking up where we left off."

Cook nodded and motioned Feeno and Schweitzer out the back door to the car, which Feeno noticed had Maryland plates.

"Where'd you get the car?"

"Rented it in Salisbury," said Schweitzer. "We don't want recognizable Jersey plates hanging around here."

Cook appeared serious as she shut the driver's door behind her. Feeno sat in front beside her, Schweitzer in back. They drove back up the sandy road toward the main highway, but turned onto a smaller road going west toward Bivalve, one of the fishing hamlets along the Nanticoke River. It was a chilly, damp day, fields flat and full of stubs of cut corn stalks, dead as the winter itself. Pools of ice collected in pot holes in the road. They passed an old cannery with weather-beaten tin siding and a rusted roof. The road dead-ended at a boat launch on the river, flat, gray and hardly rippled, some crows cawing in the distance, ducks landing in the marsh.

"There's a problem," Cook said, facing Feeno.

"There's always a problem," said Feeno. "What now?"

"Neptune County Court in Jersey," said Cook. "Do you know the prosecutor there, Arnold Rosenstein?"

"I know of him. What's this about?"

"Rosenstein ordered a grand jury investigation. Into the bank. You're involved."

"Yeah, and what's that mean?"

She turned sideways to him and stared. "It means you'll be a defendant in a fraud case in the Neptune County court." She began explaining to him about a few loan transactions that never materialized. Two of them involved builders.

"There's the one in South Jersey involving your friend. Vincent Berardi."

"I know, he never got his money," said Feeno, and we — Rocco and the others — sent his deposit offshore. His collateral. We went over that. I had nothing to do with that."

"That's not what Rosenstein thinks," said Cook. "He's coming after your ass. You're the bank president, you're the loan officer."

Feeno rolled down the window and looked out. He suddenly needed air. "Well, if I have to testify, I will. I'll just tell them the goddamned truth."

"These are the problems," said Cook, lifting her voice. "It means exposing you to all kinds of danger. And it's not just the danger from the Scalesis. You may as well face it. It won't be easy."

She paused and waited until Feeno turned toward her. "The chief witness against you," she said, "will be your old buddy, Vincent Berardi."

Chapter 19: SEATING ARRANGEMENTS

June 3, 1979.

The cabin cruisers and fishing boats sailed slowly past Gull Island through the Manasquan Inlet, heading out to the presently tranquil ocean. "Carmelita II," a thirty-seven-foot cabin cruiser, sailed with water lapping close to the gunwales. Collectively, nearly a ton of mobsters was crowded on board; the seven men sat mostly on the rails in a horseshoe facing the cabin, where Rocco Scalesi stood on the cabin's top step facing the stern. The waist of his Bermuda shorts tugged at an ample stomach, pregnant with the good life. His massive chest, as wide as it was deep, was covered with curly gray fur, making a bearish appearance that was accentuated further by his leathery face and half-closed eyes. They were eyes with reptilian lids, appearing soft and sleepy to friends and loved ones, but cold and threatening to others. Beneath the hooded eyes was a half-smile so constant that it probably appeared in his sleep. It was a smile coming from a man who knows something that you don't.

"Tomorrow's the court date. I want all of youse there."

"Jesus Christ, Thumbs, you can't be serious?" asked Mealy Piglitano, whose real front name was Emileo. "I got warrants."

"What, for punchin' out your wife in the nightclub? Parking tickets? If they was after you for them, they woulda' got you by now." He waved an arm toward the bright sun as the Carmelita II, with the little man known as the Squirrel at the helm, passed a port-side buoy. "Besides, this ain't federal. It's Neptune County. Rosenstein, that prosecutor, whether he knows it or not, is doin' us a favor. We're gonna' be eyeballin' Feeno Bannon. I want him stared down."

"How the hell we gonna get in the courtroom? They'll be stickin' a metal detector so far up your ass it'll come out your fuckin' nose." piped up Georgie Fortunato, a young, well-chiseled wanna be who was close to becoming buttoned. Not out of his twenties, he already had two notches on his belt for murders that he secured against defectors of the blood oath.

"This is America," said Rocco. "You're a citizen. You're allowed to sit in a courtroom. Just don't pack no heat. One more thing, this guy Berardi, the witness. We know he's scared shitless."

"You want him stared down too, huh?" asked Georgie.

"No," Rocco said quickly, popping ashes into the sea and smiling. "Tomorrow he's our buddy. Tomorrow he's one of us."

"Yeah, but what if Feeno takes the stand and discloses what we did with that guy Vince's money? He could kill us." asked Mealy.

"Our lawyers say that Bannon most likely won't take the stand. He'll be exposed to too many questions that the feds aren't prepared to answer yet. This is good luck for us. This is a county court. The feds, the Strike Force, they're as good as defendants here. They gotta' protect Feeno." Rocco tossed the stump of his La Corona cigar into the sea. A gull sailed down to look, but backpedaling his gray wings two feet above it, he sailed on, joining the other gulls, diving, climbing, hovering and swooping, making laughing sounds.

June 4, 1979

Riding the back elevator down from near Rosenstein's office were Rosenstein, Eversham, Mo Henry, Vince Berardi, and two sheriff's deputies, all crowded against a metal shopping basket containing blue binders of evidence and yellow legal pads. The other handful of witnesses, all of whom had been fleeced by Unity, were already in the courtroom.

Eversham nodded to Vince to sit in the front row behind the prosecutor's table where the stuff from the shopping cart was being unloaded. The courtroom was already half-filled with curious spectators. Looking around, Vince recognized none of the faces until about five minutes had gone by and some of the attorneys and federal marshals had entered the room. Just outside the swinging double door in the hallway, a sheriff's deputy played a metal wand over everybody, head to toe.

Once seated, Vince searched for Feeno, while at the same

time he rehearsed in his mind the details of his friendship with the defendant, how he had been promised the loan and subsequently lost his collateral. He had no idea whether things would go well. He had, in fact, fantasized sometimes at night, lying in bed, that thugs began standing in the courtroom, firing bullets into Feeno Bannon's unprotected skull.

"How ya doin', Vince?" said a portly man in his forties wearing a strong, cheap cologne. He placed a hand on Vince's shoulder and smiled broadly. His mouth was small and oddly pert for such a large man. "Fun day, ain't it? Ain't seen ya' for a while. So how's the wife and kids? Doin' okay?" The beefy man talked loudly, letting other spectators hear his voice. Vince saw a neatly dressed man, a lawyer in a striped suit at the defendant's table, look his way.

Vince was sitting still, stunned by the beefy guy's theater, when on the other side of him another man approached. He was the weasely little thug he had seen before. He wore an expensive suit with a blazingly loud green and yellow tie. His hair was combed in flat strands forward. Helmet hair over his small head. His ears and eyes were mere buttons. He too patted Vince's shoulder; he smiled with tiny, straight, pointed teeth. "Whadda ya' say, Vince kid!" Vince had a recollection of heavy metal cracking his head above the ear.

Vince looked toward the prosecutors, but all were busy, looking down at papers and talking in low voices, unaware of the scenario going on directly behind them. But within a minute a feint shadow coursed overhead, and Vince heard a forceful voice whisper to the small man: "I think you gentlemen might be more comfortable sitting somewhere else."

It was Mo Henry. His stare fixed firmly on the beefy one, then at the little one; Mo's eyes were unsmiling. When the Squirrel tossed his head and cocked it as though challenging Mo, the detective whispered again, this time more loudly: "Right now, you little prick! Get lost!"

Both rose slowly, stared threateningly at Mo and moved to the last row in the courtroom. At about the same time there was a flurry of movement at the defense table. One lawyer shrugged his shoulders and gave another an "I-don't-know" look. The other lawyer looked at his watch. It was 10:20. The session had been scheduled to start at ten sharp before a judge who demanded promptness. The lawyer suddenly raced toward the entrance door, pushing aside a woman, jostling her handbag. She appeared shocked and annoyed and stared at the lawyer as he hurried toward the door.

The jurors by now were being led in from a corner rear door. Six women, six men. Two blacks, one obviously hispanic and others white. Half of the jurors were middle-aged. One young woman had brightly dyed red hair and wore a light blue and red tie-dyed blouse. A husky young man with a shaved head looked like a Marine. It was an all-American jury which stood to attention at the sound of "All Rise" when the judge entered from what appeared to be nothing more than a varnished brown panel behind the bench. He sat down heavily and waited for the shuffling and occasional cough to quiet.

Looking directly at the jury, Judge Napolitani said in an even but firm voice, "Members of the court, distinguished members of counsel and members of the jury: I am sorry to announce that this proceeding is being postponed indefinitely." He shook the large sleeves of his black robe and folded his hands before him. He leaned forward, his face mostly blank except for a slight trace of annoyment. "There has been an unexpected development which is being looked into and hopefully, things will get back on track within a short period of time." He smiled reassuringly, then frowned: "I cannot say when, however." He pronounced the last sentence in a strong voice, barely able to control an obviously rising anger.

Rosenstein and Eversham glanced at each other and then at the defense table, where an attorney for the government answered their unspoken questions with a shrug. Everyone else in the courtroom except the defense counsel and U.S. marshals, looked at each other in wonder and surprise.

"Before dismissing the jury for the interim, I wish to announce that I want to see all members of counsel in my chambers immediately," the judge said, staring down hard at the defendant's table where the lawyers behaved as though naked. He rapped once with the gavel: "The jury is dismissed."

Minutes later the lawyers gathered in camera in the judge's secluded office: "Let's cut the crap right now, Mizz Cook," said Judge Napolitani, leaning back against his high leather chair and staring hard at the Assistant U.S. Attorney, who was standing against a paneled wall, arms folded. Behind the judge was the usually impressive collection of beige law books with red titles on the bindings. Napolitani slapped the mahogany desk, rattling a small American flag, an engraved pen and pencil holder and a framed picture of the judge, with an attractive middle-aged dark-haired woman and two smiling children, a boy and girl.

"What happened and where is he?"

Chapter 20: FORT DIX

June 3.

The day before the trial was to start, a delicate breeze floated above the Wicomico, scarcely wrinkling the water surface and barely stirring the leaves of the shoreline trees. Feeno stood watching the river flow out toward the Chesapeake. He tossed the remainder of the hot coffee in his cup toward the lawn.

He needed no caffeine on this day of jingling anticipation. Angela came up silently behind him and stood by his side. He looked at her. She wore green shorts, sandals and a tank top, which was starkly white against her tan.

She looked up as he folded one arm over her shoulders, then returned his embrace, but kept one side of her face pressed against his chest as he kissed her hair, which he smoothed softly with his fingers. He gently pushed her shoulders back and sensing that she wished to kiss her lips, she pulled him to her again and rubbed his back.

Feeno looked beyond her to a pair of grosbeaks, husband and wife. They flew and fed together, and now were dining on the red berries of the crab apple tree in a corner of the yard.

Angela gave him one last pat and went inside. Feeno walked down the lane of crushed oyster shells, turned right on another sandy road and stepped aboard a broken down pier, splintered and dark with its half-destroyed shed hanging dangerously above.

From there he could see the small, flat ferry that crossed "on demand" going over to the barren road that went to Princess Anne. The ferry had no schedule. A beep of the horn on either side of the river fetched it. Feeno waved and Charles, the ferry man, waved back.

Peters and Kelly came around two o'clock, parking the

black van with tainted windows at the edge of the drive. Both looked around them in all directions as they left the car. Peters wiped his neck and face with a handkerchief, it was so very hot and humid. The landscape was flat and contained few features like buildings or even trees. But the tall marsh grass worried the two marshals.

"I bet you hate to leave this place, even for a day," remarked Kelly, a narrow-faced man with thinning sandy hair as he walked up to the porch. Feeno said nothing and neither did Peters, an all-business federal officer who scoped constantly, his eyes hidden by dark sunglasses. He was bulkier than Kelly, and older.

A second van containing four marshals with sidearms had pulled to the end of the lane. Angela said her goodbye from the door. Peters and Kelly both noted that her farewell was casual, not impressive for a wife seeing her husband off to several days in a strange court.

The drive north on this lazy Sunday afternoon took them past long flat, sandy fields of tomatoes, then cucumbers, past low-profiled chicken coops. Feeno recalled Frank Perdue's squeaky-voiced commercials announcing with high-pitched pride: "It takes a tough man to make a tender chicken."

Half way through Delaware, Feeno fell asleep, his head resting on the tinted glass of a rear window. He did not waken until a strong breeze entered the open window. Feeno saw that they were high up, crossing the bridge from Wilmington over the Delaware River towards Jersey. He remained awake and sat up straight just before the van pulled under the big overhead sign that identified "Fort Dix Military Reservation. U.S. Army Training Grounds."

"I knew it," Feeno said. "Good old Fort Dix!"

"Whadda' you know about Fort Dix?" asked Peters, turning to face Feeno sitting beside him in the back of the dark van.

"What do I know? I did my basic training here. Sixty-nine."

Peters, looking out the window, said, "I can't imagine you doing basic anywhere."

"Oh yeah!" answered Feeno. "What do you mean?"

Peters turned his head the other way and talked as though

to no one outside the window: "I thought you'd be one of those guys who took off for Canada."

After a long delay at the security gate, where MPs bent and peered into the open windows, the van followed a jeep escort and pulled into a cul-de-sac, stopping at a small white clapboard building near a sign that read, "Doughboy Circle." Feeno got out and handed his suit bag and duffle bag to Kelly.

"What's with Peters?" Feeno asked.

Kelly grinned, quelling the rising spark. "Old school," said Kelly. "Don't mind him. He's a good guy. He just has this thing about white collar..." He bit off the word "crime."

Inside, Feeno was assigned a small room with a single cot, bureau, desk and reading lamp. The remainder of the one-story building contained three unfurnished rooms, including a kitchen with a refrigerator. Kelly opened it and was pleased to see that the light inside was on and the thing was humming. When he heard a loud banging in Feeno's room, he hurried in and said, "What the hell are you doing?"

"Trying to get some air in here," said Feeno. "I don't think this window has been opened since World War II. You don't suppose the taxpayers can cough up for an air conditioner while we're here." He strained and managed to lift the sash about four inches.

"We're going to have to live with it," Kelly said. "It'll cool off at night."

"Yeah, I know. I loved this place at night. Crickets. Lotsa' crickets, my favorite summertime sound. That and frogs. I was here in the spring during basic. Did you ever hear peepers? Baby frogs? What a great sound that is! We're in the middle of the cul-de-sac." He sat on the cot and rubbed his fingers over the taut khaki blanket, then stripped it from the bed with a sudden yank

Kelly listened with interest to Feeno's description of the vast forest of scrubby trees that he had seen on their approach to Ft. Dix. Kelly, who was from Indiana, was surprised that such a wilderness of sandy soil and shrubs could exist in a state like New Jersey.

"I thought we'd be up against an oil refinery," he said.

"Naw," said Feeno. "Not this place. This is heaven. These

woods stretch nearly all the way from the Delaware River to the Garden State Parkway and the shore. Miles and miles of sandy roads and rivers. Isolated. I did a lot of canoeing and fishing in this place on my days off, when I was in the Army and at the bank."

That afternoon he was visited by an adjutant general at the military camp who was more curious about the strange visitor than helpful. He asked him if he needed anything.

Later that day, Feeno drove with Peters to a PX where they both purchased small cans of shaving cream. Feeno bought a small vial of insect repellent, *Time, People and Golf* magazines and a half-dozen Milky Ways. Peters lifted two six packs of Rolling Rock from a cooler. On the way out, Feeno's eye caught sight of a table top window fan. He grabbed it and placed it on the checkout counter.

"You got any more of them?" Peters asked the girl at the cash register.

Toward evening, rather than eat in a cafeteria, Peters brought in trays of hot food and a large thermos of ice water. Night began to settle on the camp like a soft blanket. The day's haze lifted, moving away to allow the darkness to take its place. Where Doughboy Circle was, there was very little sound, except for insects buzzing and chirping and birds snuggling for the night. The sky overhead was a diorama of planets. They numbered zillions. But on the northern horizon was a reddish glow from the lights of Manhattan and North Jersey.

All three men said "good night." The marshals each had rooms on opposite sides of Feeno's. There were only two outside doors to the clapboard building, one in front and another opposite in the rear facing the expansive lawn and forest. The rear door had a deadbolt lock with a key inside. Feeno saw Kelly lock the door and remove the key and stick it in his pocket.

Peters, before taking up his watch for the night, went outside and walked around the barracks, flashlight in hand. He searched beneath the cellarless building, then shined the light on the trees beyond. Pretty secure place, he reckoned. In addition to the MPs at the gates, cyclone fences with razor wire encircled the drill fields and gunnery range nearby.

He completed his circuit and stopped at the front of the building closest to the street. He sat on the wooden steps, lit a Marlboro, inhaling deeply, figuring this would be the first of many he would light before Kelly replaced him as sentinel four hours later.

Kelly, sitting on his cot in the room at the rear, removed his shoes and massaged his feet. He stretched and laid down on the cot, turning the pages of his *Popular Mechanics* toward the one feeble light at the head of the bed. Minutes later he nodded, deeply involved by now with the tranquility of the summer night.

Toward midnight, Peters, still sitting on the steps, was surprised to hear a movement behind him. His hand automatically moved to the holstered luger on his right hip. But it was Feeno:

"Having trouble sleeping, it's so goddamned hot."

He handed Peters a beer and sat beside him. Peters probed: "Where's yours?"

"I don't drink," said Feeno. "Gave it up. Part of my trifecta."

"Trifecta?" echoed Peters, looking at Feeno, who sat down heavily beside him on the steps.

"Yeah, I quit the horses, quit drinking and quit smoking, all in one week."

"How the hell did you manage that?"

"It was easier than I thought it would be. My wife, Angie, threatened to leave me if I didn't stop the booze and the gambling. I didn't want that, so I quit."

"Not just like that," said Peters, snapping his fingers.

"Not really. I was going to a shrink at the time, a little Korean guy. Doctor Chang, my shrunken shrink, I called him. I was going to him because my nerves were bad, I couldn't sleep. The shrink was part of a testing program at Beth Israel Hospital. They advertised for people with insomnia, bad nerves. It was some drug company doing it. Half the patients in the program were given placebos. You know what a placebo is?"

Peters said, "Yeah," although Feeno wasn't sure about the strength of Peters' vocabulary.

"Well, the other half was given a real drug — to calm the

nerves."

"What was it?" asked Peters, now fascinated.

"I don't know. You weren't supposed to know. But that's beside the point. I was between banking jobs. All of this happened right before I was hired at Unity Savings. I saw that job as a big opportunity, and when Angie got pissed off at my boozing and stuff, I was afraid I'd lose it all. She's related to the Scalesis you know."

"Yeah, I heard that."

"Yeah, and she could derail everything. Everything. So I had to quit boozing and I asked Chang to help me. You know what he did?"

"No," said Peters.

"He hypnotized me. It took a few sessions, and he put me on Librium. You hearda' that."

"Yeah."

"Patrick Henry, remember? 'Give me Librium or give me Meth.'"

Fred Peters laughed for the first time that day.

"The librium helped, and so I took a pledge. Quit the booze, stopped smoking and haven't been to the track or a bookie since then. Except, I do go to Gamblers Anonymous and for a while I was going to AA."

Peters was beginning to feel a sliver of respect for his ward. In his sixth year as a custodian of witnesses, who were mostly criminals, he had studied strange behavior-patterns. Particularly, he saw how difficult it was for many of the Mafia who had turned on their brethren to give up or surrender certain patterns of behavior, particularly ones like theft and deception.

He had one witness under his care who was arrested three times by local police for No. 1, stealing a car; No. 2, assault on a woman, and No. 3, writing bad checks. At the same time, the turncoat was responsible for putting away more than a dozen mob guys in trials where he was the star witness.

"Nice night, except for the heat," said Peters after a while of gazing into the dark sky sprinkled with white dots. He and Feeno listened while the cicadas beat a steady harmonium in the trees.

"I gotta take a leak," said Peters, who rose and moved toward a high bush next to the house. His back was turned.

"I'm goin' back to bed," said Feeno.

As Peters grunted, "See you tomorrow," and watched the stars, Feeno, keeping his sight on the marshal, carefully slid from the steps and ducked toward the corner of the building, keeping low. Within a second, he had disappeared. Still bending, he moved to beneath the window of his room. He heard the fan whirring inside. He stooped to where he had dropped his clothes out the window, put on his sneakers, sweat pants and hooded gray, sweat jacket. He stuffed his wallet, money, insecticide and small flashlight in its pockets and scrambled to the far end of the building, keeping low as he passed beneath Kelly's bedroom window.

At the far corner, he stopped, slightly panting, listening, watching. Once free in the yard, he ran as hard and as fast as he had ever run in his life.

Chapter 21: WHAT HAPPENED?

June 4, 1979.

Shannon Cook was trying to appear unworried. She still stood with her back to the wall throughout the judge's questioning.

"The marshal said that he and the witness..." She paused, and substituted "defendant...had been seated on the front steps of the building where they were staying for the night. Bannon said 'good night' and went to bed. That was the last time he saw him."

The room grew quiet as the lawyers and the judge thought about it. Finally, Napolitani said, "Do you think it's possible that Bannon might be dead? That someone got to him."

"Well, there is no evidence of any kind of shooting or violence in his room, where he was being kept. Could he have been kidnapped? Possibly. But the window was open only about three inches. And there was a fan on the table blocking it."

"So the alternative is that your defendant took off on his own," said the judge.

"It's possible."

"And the marshal. Asleep on the job?"

Cook didn't answer.

"And why wasn't I told about this sooner?" asked Judge Napolitani. "From what you have said when this incident occurred, it was about eight or ten hours ago."

"Quite honestly, we didn't know where he was and we didn't know if he had been nabbed by someone, or if he just ran on his own. We thought...he could have gone for a walk."

"Without telling the marshals?" the judge erupted. "You had U.S. marshals taking care of him."

"We thought we would get him back, and believe me, if we had, he would be here. The marshals didn't want to panic until there was a thorough search."

Rosenstein, sitting in a corner of the judge's leather-bound office, leaned back with his legs crossed. His right elbow was on the arm of the Windsor chair and his fingers stroked his chin in his impression of The Thinker. Rosenstein, for once, was eager to remain silent. On one hand he was disturbed that the trial he had prepared for so long over the past weeks may never take place. But he was also enjoying the drama of federal attorneys squirming in the judge's chambers.

"We have an APB and search parties out in all directions," said Cook.

"If he disappeared when you think he did," interjected Napolitani, "that was hours ago. He could be anywhere."

"Fort Dix is a big place," said Cook. "It would take time for someone to hustle him out of there, and if he left on his own, the same thing. He can't be far from there, but we have alerts out all over Jersey, Pennsylvania and New York. If Bannon left on his own we think he may be headed to Philadelphia; that's where he's from originally."

"And you're not the only ones looking for him, I suppose," said the judge. "There is a contract out on this man's life?"

"There is," said Cook. "He should be protected. He can't outrun the Scalesis forever."

Vince had heard the summary of the fiasco in the succeeding hours from both Rosenstein and Hope Eversham, the assistant prosecutor. Everyone was on hold for the time being, suspended in time and place. The judge ordered everyone to stay where they were in the courthouse and wait until further notice.

By now, the courthouse was in chaos. As soon as the Scalesi men had heard that Feeno was missing, they began edging toward the door of the courtroom, some rather quickly.

"Stop right where you are, sir," said a deputy, tall, thin and commanding. He reached and grabbed the arm of Anthony Trapetto, holding him firmly. Trapetto and three other Scalesi gang members slumped in the last row of the courtroom.

Vince was ushered out a side door, down a hall to a small room where a sheriff guarded the door. Hope Eversham joined him. Rosenstein had gone back to his office.

"Where do you think Bannon is?" she said, lighting a cigarette and offering it to Vince, who hesitated, shook his head, then grabbed it from her, drawing deeply and watching the blue smoke waft toward the ceiling. "Do you think Philly maybe?"

"Maybe, I dunno," said Vince, trying to put two and two together, picturing Feeno Bannon in his old neighborhood, lounging, laughing, talking. Always talking.

"I don't know," Vince continued, pushing back from the small table and crossing his right ankle over his left knee. He grabbed his shoe, yanked it off and rubbed his foot. Very hard he rubbed his foot. "I don't know, I just don't know." He chuckled slightly.

"What's funny?"

"What's funny? This whole thing is funny. I've been preparing for this day in a cold sweat. Every goddamned day as it got closer, I'd sweat. Look at my kids, couldn't smile. Couldn't smile at my wife..."

"You've been scared?"

"Goddamned right I've been scared." He laughed again. "Now I'm relieved." His grin broadened as he looked at Eversham. She turned away.

"Feeno's gone, Feeno's gone."

He dragged deeply on the cigarette. "You think Philly. Right? You think Feeno fled to the old neighborhood?"

Eversham looked again at him.

Vince smirked, shook his head. "He's nowhere near Philly. I'll bet."

"Where do you think he is, then?"

"Feeno Bannon? He's somewhere where you'd least expect him."

"Where?" yelled Cook, taking a step toward Vince and leaning both hands on the table. "Where?"

"I have no idea," said Vince softly, smiling. "No idea at all."

It wasn't until late in the afternoon that they were permitted to leave. Vince called Julie to tell her what happened. "In some ways I'm glad," he said. "I wasn't looking forward to sitting in that witness stand and identifying Feeno as the man who stole my money."

"That's probably one reason, maybe the only reason for him to take off, if he did take off," she said. "He couldn't handle it, watching one of his best friends accuse him of fraud or whatever."

When Vince walked out of the Neptune County courthouse with Eversham and Mo Henry he felt as limp as a puppet.

"Let's go get a drink," said Eversham.

For the next three hours, Hope, Mo and Vince drank and then had dinner in the Cockatoo Restaurant on Broad Street around the corner from the courthouse. Vince called Julie to tell her he would be late, that they had to go over strategy, what next to do.

It was nine o'clock by the time Hope and he got up to leave. Mo had said goodbye an hour before.

Outside, the night air offered a different world from the stuffy insides of the courthouse and restaurant that had Vince trapped all day. Breathing it made him dizzy. He said goodbye to Hope and turned to walk away, but stumbled into a potted evergreen which stood beside the door. He was hammered. Six, seven, eight. How many vodka martinis had he introduced into his blood stream?

"Keys!" said Hope.

"Wush?"

"Keys, you're not driving."

She stuffed him into the front passenger seat of her Honda Civic, where he fell asleep. Some time later, he felt someone tugging at his shoulders, shaking him awake.

"C'mon!" she said.

"Where are we?"

"My place."

All that he could determine was a brick facade which seemed to stretch for infinity, and that they went through a door at the end unit of the condos.

Vince recalled being led to a couch and dropped on it. Someone took off his suit jacket, loosened his tie, removed his shoes and unbuckled his belt. He looked up and saw two cute blondes bending over him, one superimposed on the other. He felt cool, soft lips on his forehead, then the words, "Good Night," before he dropped into darkness.

Chapter 22: THE PINE BARRENS

June 4, 1979.

Running hard never figured in any part of Feeno Bannon's life except when urging the four-legged kind at Garden State Park and the other tracks in Jersey and Pennsylvania. Witnessing was the closest he got to exercise. Running as swiftly as he did, the blood pumped through Feeno's brain in cadence with a horse-racing mantra, Damon Runyan's immortal poem about the jockey, Earl Sande: "Gimme a handy guy like Sande bootin' them babies home."

"Bootin' them babies, bootin' them babies, bootin' them babies" Feeno whispered with deep breaths, arms pumping, knees high, even as he stumbled through the shadows. He would run and run and run until someone stopped him.

From the woods came an unceasing treble of cicadas. He pumped harder, running in as straight a line as the landscape afforded. There had been only one building in his path, a small maintenance shed which appeared empty. Outside it, parked in neat rows, were several Patton tanks and Armored Personnel Carriers. A flagpole appeared, pencil thin in silhouette, standing dumb sentinel on a flat parade ground. Then at the perimeter of the Army installation was one bivouac after another, and some bushes, trees and in the feint distance, a cyclone fence. He would scale it, tunnel it or run right through it.

At the fence, he stopped and looked from side to side until he found what he needed, a small branch that had fallen from a pine and lay half-embedded in needles. But it was fat enough and strong enough to dig through the soft sandy soil. Soon, he wiggled under the fence through the hole he had dug, and was off again, breathing hard. He ran quickly across two deserted asphalt roads about a quarter-mile apart until he stopped, exhausted, leaning forward, hands upon his knees, gulping the hot, wet air, which included in a gasp a bug of some sort. He coughed, stood straight, and with a great deal of effort, removed the sweat-soaked shirt. He reached into a pants pocket, grasped the little plastic jar of OFF and applied some liberally to his face, neck and arms. The mosquitoes had found him and welcomed him to the safety of the Pine Barrens.

He took out the small compass and pen light from his pants pocket and waited for his breathing to subside to a level he could handle. It was important for him to keep heading to the east or southeast in as straight a line as possible. A whippoorwill called and as Feeno listened, there was — louder now — the drilling sound of tree-dwelling cicadas. The males played tiny drums with their wings, luring girl bugs to bed.

Feeno's plan was to keep to the east until coming to the nearest paved highway leading toward Atlantic City. As he walked on through the dwarfed pines, he encountered dozens of sandy, one-lane roads, crisscrossing hither-thither, some circling and some dead-ending. His compass offered the only route to be trusted.

Within a half-hour, some moonlight splashed down, affording light enough to illuminate a sliver of silver up ahead. It was a stream flowing to the east, and served as a watery border to a small cedar bog of drowned stumps.

Though the Pine Barrens can be as flat as a dining room table, it had its own miniature continental divide, pushing water flow either to the west and the Delaware River, or to the east toward the bays which joined the Atlantic.

"Eastward Ho," he whispered, following the rapidly flowing water, taking care not to meander away as it coursed snakily through the woods, which by now were taller cedars and pin oaks. The stream had widened to a fifty feet width and sparkled clear in the half-light.

Feeno stopped when up ahead loomed the outline of a shack. He moved to the right and then left, looking for any sign of lantern light from inside the small cabin, which he knew could easily have been inhabited, either by a fisherman or poacher out to shoot a deer not in season, or it could have been lived in the year long by a man or even a woman.

The year-rounders were known as "Pineys." Many of them

were descended from original settlers going back to the Revolutionary War. Outsiders heard tales of Pineys wedding and bedding close cousins, breeding down to featherbrained, blind albinos.

Feeno feared not; his magnanimous personality could win over a cyclops. He reasoned too that a Piney would be the least likeliest person to question why he was alone in the woods at night.

The mapless pigmy forests drew all sorts of humankind, from hunters and campers to lovers, fugitives and gangsters. Skeletons lay buried in the sand, never found nor identified, their interments witnessed only by owls and raccoons or deer. Mobsters from Philly, Jersey and New York put most of the corpses there.

Keeping his distance, Feeno, as quietly as he could, circled the shack, which he could see had no outlying amenities like an outhouse or wash tub. There was no car nor pickup truck, but at the edge of the river, half-hidden beneath a huckleberry, Feeno could see the prow of an old canoe.

He approached carefully and quietly pulled it from the underbrush enough to flip it over. There was no paddle. He walked back to the cabin, stopping every five feet to listen.

The crowds of cicadas were beginning to sound like a chorus of tiny engines as Feeno listened for any human sound above the din. His mind's eye witnessed the abrupt appearance of a 12-gauge aimed at his groin by a bearded Appalachian type in long underwear. But there was nothing. No human sound nor visage, and luckily, no lock on the cabin door.

Feeno carefully pushed it, lifting it up at the latch to unstick the bottom edge from the dirt floor. He shouldered it aside and let his flashlight search the interior. A broken down lime green icebox stood in one corner, smeared with the dirt of decades.

A camp bed was a few feet away. Its ripped, fragile canvas had not held a body in many years. An upturned Windsor chair had three legs. A tiny shelf attached to the wall near the ceiling held a rusted can opener, a large lead spoon and an empty jar whose torn label identified it as Miracle Whip. The floor was dirt, pounded flat. As he entered cautiously, crouching low, Feeno found what he wanted behind the door: A canoe paddle.

As he set the canoe in the water, holding on to its gunnel to keep it from drifting away, Feeno felt the cold stream pull at his socks and shoes, his ankles and calves, massaging away the heat and sweat. He searched for leaks in the canoe, pushing it down hard into the water and rocking it from side to side. Satisfied, he stepped in and knelt with the small of his back against the rear seat.

The canoe took to the water, its prow seeking the downstream current, and for the first time in several hours, sailing under a protective canopy of trees, Feeno breathed normally and deeply, switching the paddle from starboard to port, steering with the swift flow.

After a while, satisfied that his craft seemed to know where it was going, he lay on his back, getting as comfortable as he could, his thin knees poking towards the dark sky, hopefully pointing to the North Star, which would be at the end of the handle of the Big Dipper. He knew no other constellation. He couldn't find it, so he closed his eyes and listened to the night songs of the woods.

Music. Faintly, then louder, with a distant light. A murmur of voices grew louder. Laughter. Around a river bend the campground came into view, with silhouettes moving around a fire on the dirt.

A boom box let loose "Born to Run." Never more appropriate. A small wooden dock lay ahead about fifty feet from mid-channel. Two figures, a teenaged boy and a girl, sat talking, their bare feet hanging and dipping into the water. The boy waved; Feeno waved back.

"Catching anything?" the boy yelled. The girl laughed.

"Bugs," Feeno answered. "Lotsa' bugs." The girl and boy laughed. "Good luck," yelled the boy.

Out of sight, Feeno lapsed to a reverie, lying down again in the bottom of the canoe: He saw Angela asleep in peace, free from his entanglement; then he saw her awake, next to a man in the bed. Feeno blinked, stared at a star and closed his eyes again.

He had no sense about how many miles he and the canoe had drifted. It was still dark when the canoe thudded gently against something in the river. He awoke and saw that the canoe had lodged beneath a bridge.

He decided to sit awhile before advancing. A minute or

two later a car came and went from overhead, its tires banging a crack in the bridge surface. He figured from the sound that the road was paved with asphalt. He would wait until dawn.

The pickup truck went fast past him, apparently ignoring his thumb, but then stopped with a shudder of brakes, skidding on the stony, sandy berm. The driver put it in reverse as Feeno scrambled toward it.

"Hop in," said the woman. She saw the hooded sweatshirt and sweat pants, sneakers caked with mud, Feeno's hair plastered with sweat to his forehead.

"Where ya' headed?"

"Atlantic City," he said. "I was taking my morning run. I like coming out here in the morning. Then lost my car keys, couldn't find 'em."

He felt safe with the woman driving the pickup, who said she would take him as far as Brigantine Boulevard. She drove fast, slowing only to put another cigarette in her lips and light it with a Zippo which she kept in the console between the driver's and passenger's seat.

Her hands were red and raw where they weren't stained with nicotine. There was a band-aid on one thumb.

"I hate bein' late for work," she explained. She had a sagging, fleshy chin, red face, dark stringy hair, streaked gray.

"Where do you work that you have to be there this early?" he asked. The upper lip of the sun was beginning its crawl up the wall of grayness that hung over the road and endless pines.

"Marina Casino," she answered. "I'm the cleaning super. Usually, most of the gamblers sleep late, so that's no problem, but I hafta' do laundry work as well. I had a helluva time with my kids this morning," she said, drawing deeply on the cigarette and shifting down to absorb the punch of another pothole. "It's always that way at the end of the school year. They start fightin' every morning when I'm tryin' to get them up."

Feeno commiserated silently, occasionally staring out at the friendly forest as the truck sped and bumped along the old county road. He unwound the window and gulped the morning air. Like most reformed smokers, the burnt stench of her cigarettes repulsed him.

But he was thankful that the cleaning super had a lot on her mind. She only shrugged at his story of parking his car in the Pines to go running and losing his keys somewhere on a back road, necessitating a trip "back to AC" where he allegedly resided.

As minutes passed, the traffic increased. One vehicle got to within about 1,000 yards and blinked its headlights. Feeno noticed a dome on the top of the car. His eyes tallied back and forth. He fingered the door handle, ready to spring it open.

The police car with the lettering "Galloway Township" on the driver's door slowed and stopped beside the cleaning super's. The two drivers rolled down their windows and looked across.

"I can't pick up the kids Friday night," said the officer sheepishly.

"Shit, Ray! You know I go out Fridays!" she yelled.

"I'll get 'em Saturday morning. Sorry!" He sped away before rolling up the window and hearing the obscenities.

As the police car gathered distance behind them now, she calmed down and murmured to Feeno: "My ex! He does this to me every goddamned time. I go to Chatsworth to the dance every Friday night and he knows it. Now I gotta' get me a baby sitter."

She slowed the truck as it entered Absecon, turning left off of Route 9 and onto Absecon Boulevard, the final stretch before skimming the marshes and entering Atlantic City. At Brigantine Boulevard she stopped and apologized: "Sorry, I gotta leave you off here. If I wasn't late I'd take you on into the city."

"That's okay," Feeno said with a well-meant smile. "You have no idea what a favor this is." He had only about a mile to walk to get to downtown on what was a sunny looking day. Clouds were gone and the pale, white sky in the East was changing into blue.

As he walked, Feeno kept deliberately to the Inlet Area. Acres of dusty, urban renewal lots lay on each side of the street, littered with old tires, cans, empty wine bottles and the rest of poverty's detritus, except for one corner garden plot off in a distance, where bean poles and tomato cages were visible. This part of Atlantic City was abandoned, as yet, to the destitution which was supposed to be eliminated by the casinos only a few blocks away. Housing was still decrepit. He crossed Mediterranean Avenue and then Baltic Avenue, two stops on the Monopoly Board that few were anxious to land on. They represented the cheapest real estate now as then.

This would be a warm day. He removed the sweat shirt, pulled a small twig of pine out of a crease at the elbow. Nearby, two homeless residents of the neighborhood were curled atop cardboard sheets in an alley separating two abandoned cement block houses. One of the sleepers was protected by a dirty, thin blanket, the other by a torn blue vinyl tarp. The top of a head with black and twisted frizzy hair suggested that this was a woman.

Feeno stepped past the sleeping pair and sat down in the alley, which had dew-speckled grass growing in its middle, flanked by bald dirt tracks where vehicles had once driven. It looked like months since the last vehicle had entered this place. He put his back to the wall, peered at his watch, and waited.

By ten o'clock the stores would start to open on Atlantic and Pacific avenues. Already, the commuters were heading to work. Feeno saw a small pack of four middle aged women, wearing shorts and tee shirts and running shoes, walking rapidly with their fists pumping, heading for the boardwalk. A couple of bicyclists went in the same direction. At this time of day the boardwalk and hard-packed sand beach flanking the roiling surf were the greatest outdoor gyms to be found anywhere.

From where he sat, Feeno could sniff the fresh salt air. Realizing he was terribly thirsty he sprang to his feet and found a deli just a half-block away. He bought a cold, pint bottle of water and drank it down hurriedly, then bought another and drank it down before buying a bag of cashews.

"You don't know, do you," he asked the clerk, a perky, big-busted woman of about fifty at the cash register. "Is there any thrift shop near here anywhere. You know, for clothes?"

She grinned widely. Large circular earrings bounced at the sides of her face. "What'd they do, clean you out at Caesar's last night?"

"How'd you guess?"

"I'm just kidding, honey," she said. "Yeah, there's one just a couple blocks on up the street, on the left. But I don't know if they're open."

Feeno smiled as he shopped. First he bought a pair of plaid lightweight bell-bottomed wool slacks, then a cloth woven belt and a brilliant red and yellow striped dress shirt. Only the shirt was the correct size. He couldn't wear an uncomfortable shirt. He came to a necktie rack, choosing a black string tie with a longhorn cattle clasp.

Now, the sports jacket. One with brown large checks and gray stripes fit perfectly, so he hung it back on the rack, then found one similar in color and design that was two sizes smaller. In the "dressing room", which was packed with cardboard boxes, and grocery and shopping bags full of donated clothing, was a narrow and cracked but full-length mirror. Now fully clothed and reflected was a tall gangling man who could have fallen from a pickle truck.

"Whoops! A hat! And the bathing suit. And the thongs!" he remembered as he deposited the pile on the long counter near a cash register. "And where's your underwear and socks?" A teenaged boy with zits was folding clothes and writing sizes on small sheets of paper which he stuffed in the pockets or pinned to dresses and other garments. Feeno walked to a hat rack and chose an almost new black baseball cap with the grinning Indian Atlanta Braves logo on its front. The pale blue bathing trunks that he bought, and which he put on right away in the dressing room, fit as they should have and were almost new.

He also purchased two large beach towels, one of which had inked within its nap a great, colorful cockatoo. The other advertised "Duff's Restaurant" in Myrtle Beach, South Carolina.

Two more stops and he would be outfitted for his day at the beach: At a Rexall drug store, he asked a clerk for "the strongest sun screen known to man, in particular a freckly Irishman like me. And zinc oxide, for the old nose, you know." He peered into the small, wavy mirror attached to the top of a revolving sunglasses display. One after the other he tried to imagine how he looked without the annoying little price label that dangled over his nose. He chose a wraparound pair.

At last. With all of his new purchases deposited in a cloth athletic bag, he headed for the twenty-four hour diner across

Atlantic Avenue.

"Coffee, bacon, eggs, toast, home fries," he ordered.

"You want the Number Two: The Waker-Upper."

"You got it, the Waker Upper."

A half-hour later, Feeno Bannon, late of the captive world, stood on the beach in his new bathing trunks and looked into the surf pounding noisily and rhythmically onto the flat, beige-colored sand, ebbing to tiny rivulets at his feet. The water felt ticklish, cold and good as it wrapped around his ankles. He gulped salt air, held it in his chest, and running and splashing toward Spain, dived into a tall breaker of rushing ocean.

Chapter 23: THE DIAPER

Borne upon the backs of breakers, wave after thumping wave, he felt the anxieties of the night and day before being scrubbed away. He stood now in shallow water, knuckled salt sea from his eyes, and scanned the beach.

A thin and fit young man ran past on the hard sand. An older couple, he with white hair, she gray, both potbellied, walked north, their feet in the ebbing water. Dark brown and green seaweed marked the high-tide line where soon the tide would ebb. A good two blocks south, a figure leaned back in a small canvas chair, wiping sunscreen on his or her arm. Feeno could not make out the sex.

The sun appeared pasted over with humid air, the start of another searingly hot day where the sky loomed white. Beach and bathers, and Steel Pier to the south, shimmered in the distance. Out in the iron green sea, two tiny dashes were silhouettes of ships, a freighter going north, a tanker south.

People were arriving, mostly women, and a few children, tugging beach umbrellas, coolers and folding chairs. A Boston Whaler lifeboat, its clapboards painted white with "ATLANTIC CITY" printed in big red letters, was parked on wooden rollers, facing the surf. Behind it on the life guard stand a bronzed, blonde girl with a pony tail, sat with her eyes sweeping the near sea.

Feeno moved away from the water, back to the small pile of new worldly possessions – the bag of clothes and towels. He sat, took one last glimpse to the boardwalk and beach, finally stretching his long body on one towel while he awkwardly covered himself with the other, shielding his delicate Irish skin from the sun's wrath, except for his head and from the knees down.

He imagined himself in the moonlit ride of the night before, the canoe gently bumping on the river that bore them to freedom. He slept long and deep, awakening in mid-afternoon.

Before him stood a vision, a child in a diaper, staring down at him, licking a chocolate ice cream cone. From his thin hair to the tops of his little sunburned reddened feet, the toddler's body was coated with gray sand. Chocolate smeared his inquisitive face, dripped from his chin, dribbled in brown trails down his raised sandy forearm to the elbow. Drops of chocolate ice cream fell upon the sand.

Feeno propped himself on an elbow, looked about the beach and back to the dripping boy, whose diaper, stained with poop and pee, hung at half mast on his knees.

"There you are," yelled a woman hurrying through the sand. "Thank God! Oh, God, look at you." She stooped to hug, but hesitated. She knelt and grasped the boy's shoulders. He stared at her, nonchalant, licking the remains of his ice cream. "Oh, God, you're a mess."

Absorbed by the domestic scene and wondering why people had children in the first place, Feeno watched the hesitant fussing over the mess of a child. She wore a bikini, starkly white against the brown of her legs, shoulders and the small of her back. Her legs were relatively short and just a little heavy, but her waist was thin. Short, wavy hair of a shade betwixt blonde and brown. Plastic glasses were sliding down her pert nose. The little boy's hair was thin and straw-colored. The toddler pulled away from the woman's grasp, yelling "No, no!"

Grasping the boy's left arm and attempting to remove the ice cream cone from the other, she groaned because simultaneously the diaper, sagging heavily from pee and poop, sunk ever lower toward the sand. She let go one hand and tried to pull the diaper up. The boy swung his arm. Now the woman had stripes of chocolate on her firm belly.

"Oh no. Now what do I do?"

Feeno rose hesitantly, wincing at the burning soles of his feet upon the hot sand. "Can I help?"

"Yes you can!," over her shoulder. "Would you take the ice cream and I'll take his diaper?"

The toddler yelled, No!"

"I don't have enough hands," she said. By now, the tow-headed boy was screaming and pulling with more strength to get away.

Feeno grasped his tiny wrist, then wrestled from his fingers the dripping cone. The woman stood straight, panting heavily. With just the thumb and forefinger, she held the diaper; with her other hand she held the arm of the offensive child. Confused and defeated, the woman yelled to Feeno, "Can you take the diaper too, and throw it into that trash can?"

Feeno obliged. He also held the diaper with two unwilling fingers.

"Throw the whole thing away," the woman said.

Confused, Feeno was about to ask her to repeat, but she shouted: "Throw the whole diaper away." He deposited the mess into the trash can and wiped his hands on his new bathing suit.

Now the woman had the naked child in the water and attempted to rinse away the filth — sticky sand, poop, pee and ice cream. She held the boy with one hand, and scooped too little water with the other. She lost her balance and fell on one knee. The child ran toward the beach, but into the path of Feeno, who said, "Here you go, kid!"

He grabbed the screaming, kicking boy under the armpits, staggered a few steps into deeper water and dunked him up to his neck, once, twice, three times. The child's screams turned to giggles. Feeno dunked the child totally in the water, lifted him out and tossed him in the air. The lad was ecstatic, opening wide his little mouth.

"Oh, God! I don't know how to thank you! That was horrible."

The woman stood tall, but at full height came up to Feeno's mid-chest at best. She tugged strands of hair from her eyes and squinted up though her glasses at the stranger. "Never again!" she said. "This is my sister's boy. She asked me to take him to the beach. She's at work. I never thought. Never!"

She laughed now and the cadence of her voice gave away that she was from somewhere in the South. Small freckles stood on a small slightly turned up nose and tanned face. She could not have been more than twenty-five.

"You had a handful there," said Feeno. "What's his name?"

"Gerald."

"Gerald," Feeno repeated. "Hi, Gerald. You're a pretty nice little guy. Whataya think?"

"I'm really grateful to you," said Gerald's flustered aunt to Feeno. "He disappeared. I was paying the ice cream man and turned my back. A few seconds." She grinned. "The little devil took off and I went the wrong way. Oh, my God, I was scared to death."

"Well, he really didn't go far."

Feeno and the girl exchanged more small talk. Looking up, she shielded her eyes with one hand, holding the, by now, gently behaved Gerald with the other. "Thank you again," she said.

Feeno watched with a little longing as the pair headed north, the girl stooping from time to time to rub Gerald's head and shoulders with affection. She picked the boy up, squeezed him tightly in her arms and kissed his hair as she walked through the sand.

After four o'clock, bathers began to leave. Feeno felt hunger, looked at his watch, then to the boardwalk. Beyond, Resorts International, Atlantic City's first casino, which opened the year before, got itself ready to welcome its guests.

Funny, he thought. Years ago, where hotel patrons walked on wooden walkways on the sand to get to the beach, now the boardwalk stood as a barrier. The hypocrisy of the hype: the casino brochures bragged in full color the roiling Atlantic and welcoming sands. But gambling rooms are tombs and have no windows to the east. Don't look at the sea, the surf, the sky beyond. From the inside, concentration is demanded upon pulling the handles of jingling, flashing slot machines, tossing dice at the craps, sneaking looks at "the hand" and staring hopefully at spinning, clicking roulette wheels. The gamblers could as easily convinced themselves that they were on Mars rather than two hundred yards from the Atlantic Ocean.

Feeno picked up his things and walked along the beach to the north and the Inlet area, away from the casinos. He stooped beneath the boardwalk. Should he get dressed here? Remembering Gerald, Feeno's body, sticky with salt, said not. A block away he saw what he really needed. There, in a tidy row of small cottages was a small, white rooming house with a green roof. He saw an outdoor shower against one wall.

Hastening across the avenue, he faked nonchalance; he walked across the yard whistling, put down his clothes, quickly jumped beneath the shower head and pulled the chain. He gasped as the cold water splashed upon his overheated head, hair and shoulders. With one hand pulling the chain, he held open his bathing suit with the other, letting the cold water do its job. In the back yard about sixty feet away, a gray-haired woman was hanging bathing suits on a clothes line. She looked suspiciously at Feeno. He smiled and waved. She smiled and turned away.

Five minutes later, in the dirty office of the Chevron station that stood on a corner of Oriental Avenue, Feeno asked if he could use the men's room.

"Can't allow it if you wanna' use it as a bath house," said the skinny teen-ager on duty, looking at the tall, skinny man at the door. He was wiping grease from his hands on a dirty shop cloth.

"I understand," said Feeno, who watched as the boy walked out the door to the gas pumps. When the kid returned he looked at Feeno's outstretched hand, stopped and looked both ways, stealthily grabbed the five-dollar bill that Feeno had offered, and put it in his pocket. Then from a nail on a counter behind the battered desk, the boy grabbed a child's small baseball bat which at the end held the bathroom key, attached with a leather thong.

When Feeno showed up fifteen minutes later with the key, the kid stared at the transformed gangly man in an Atlanta Braves baseball cap, wearing a loud checked sports jacket which failed to match his striped bell bottoms. The trousers were, the kid noticed, "high waters", where the pants bottoms stood a good two inches above the man's white socks. On the stranger's feet were brown Keds sneakers, circa 1950s. The one adornment to the latest style were the large dark sunglasses which wrapped the man's upper face and hid his eyes. The glasses sat on an irregular nose to begin with, but it was slathered with white paste, zinc oxide to heal the sunburn.

"Thanks, buddy," said the reinvented man formerly known as Joseph A. Bannon. He walked away, waving to a man selling paintings of Elvis on velvet at the corner. "Beautiful stuff," yelled Feeno, "Just beautiful."

Chapter 24: FARM BOY

Feeno had a nice soft hand before him, an Ace and a five. Flicking an index finger, he signaled a hit. Another five! Boffo, twenty-one the first hand. Resisting deep breaths of anticipation, he kept his lips shut, his eyes and concentration fixed on the table and on the dealer's cards directly opposite. Between Feeno's protective wrists stood a major stack of chips, most of them of the $500 variety. A small crowd gathered behind him.

A blonde holding a drink and wearing a thin-strapped gown that set off the gold of her skin whispered to her companion, a middle-aged, well-dressed type with steel-gray sideburns: "He looks like a bum, but I guess he knows how to play blackjack."

"It's a disguise," said the man. "Some of these card sharks pretend they're hicks, rubes. They like to look like pigeons."

"What's a pigeon?" she asked.

"Ah, somebody who's unsophisticated."

Just an hour before, Feeno had entered the casino through the boardwalk side. His senses absorbed the glare and jingle, bells and dizzy lights ringing and blinking, and people whooping as they crowded the slot machines, paper cups in hand, oblivious to all but the machines they were partnered with.

The security guard at the door gave the new visitor a single glance. All manner of species visited these premises. Ah, the humanity — mahogany-skinned men wearing turbans, women in veils and burkas, occasionally an Old World pince-nez, older women with blue, puffed hair, oriental men wearing dark blue business suits, cowboys in ten-gallon hats and string ties, native Americans who didn't look like native Americans, and guys who just fell off a pickle truck.

On this desperate day, lying on the beach that afternoon, thinking scenes of past and future, Feeno forced his brain to the evening ahead. Walking into the lion's den of Harrah's was a major risk, quickly over with if he ran into a bad guy, someone from the Bruno gang who recognized him through the corn-fed falsity, or worse, a Scalesi or Genovese.

But the odds might be with him because of the New Jersey Casino Control Commission's vigilance in keeping a black list upon which was written the identities of most known made members of organized crime. From the outset, the commission was determined not to repeat the mistakes of Nevada by letting the OC people get a toe hold in control of the casinos.

The system wasn't perfect. The mob was making inroads into the bartenders' union and laundry services, and a heavy push into bricks and mortars, the construction trades remaking the city by the sea. But indoors, in the plush-carpeted betting rooms where the real money was to be made, much of the Mafia was outside and because of the black list, just looking in.

Feeno searched for a "safe" blackjack table, one with gamblers who were quiet. At the first table only a few steps past the raised corridor connecting to the slots, an older man with a beet red nose was obviously steaming over his bad luck, doubling down almost on every hand, even when his face cards glared with pathetic numbers. Next to the man was a heavyset woman wearing a pound of lipstick and rouge. She kept asking the man who was standing behind her, "Now what do I do?"

"Stay, stay, don't do nothing," whispered the man, or "hit me, hit me."

Finally, Feeno found a table with an impassive dealer, a face of stone who displayed all the emotions of a sea turtle. Feeno noticed with dismay that four decks were being used. Not good. The last time he played blackjack was in Vegas where he scored well at a two-deck table. That was just before the incipient fall, where his hot streaks led him to baccarat, a game played in deep and dangerous waters best left to genuine high rollers.

Feeno recalled those days aloud at many Gamblers Anonymous meetings in the basement of St. John the Baptist church in Piscataway. "All I want to do before I die," he once said, standing before the crowded room of penitents, "is go to a casino, play one game of blackjack, drink one glass of beer and smoke one cigarette." Most of the people in the room told him he was an idiot. He had changed much since those days.

He looked up momentarily as two men in suits flanked an obviously drunk gambler, half carrying and half-dragging the happy-faced man to the outside and fresh air. As his game progressed and the chips kept mounting, Feeno resisted the amateurish urge to count his winnings. He was hot and knew it, doubling down his bet on every count of ten or eleven, and splitting, taking a gamble, when the dealer was showing any card less than seven.

People in the crowd behind him were murmuring now, sometimes shouting as Feeno took in one hand after another. He decided to bet low on a few hands, which he deliberately lost with determined, sloppy play.

Some of the crowd dissipated. Feeno finally slouched back, resting. Behind the dealer, a waitress, dressed in black hot pants and platform shoes, was wearing the kind of bunny suit top that squeezed her breasts to near exploding; she winked at Feeno and hoisted her tray in his direction. She smiled and her lips said, "Want one?" He shook his head, "No."

Time was passing quickly as midnight approached. But most gamblers were oblivious. Time always stands still on a casino playing floor. There is no outside world. Nothing exists except a confusing mix of hopes, fulfillment, anxiety and despair, one big room where patrons took turns experiencing heaven, hell or limbo. Feeno was just beginning to enter the latter when he felt a hand on his shoulder. Without looking up, he heard the whisper, "Would you come with me, sir?"

He sat perfectly still. He watched the dealer's eyes look up at the man behind him. The dealer's eyes revealed nothing as he automatically washed the cards across the felt table, mixing them as casually as a cook stirring a broth.

Feeno felt the hand on his shoulder squeeze ever so slightly. He stood up, determined not to look at the man behind him, who whispered again, "Bring your chips please." Before Feeno was given a tray to carry them in he tossed the dealer a $100 toke.

"Thank you, sir," said the dealer. "And a pleasant night to you, sir."

Feeno knew exactly where he was going. By now he was able to glance behind him at the two security men dressed impassively in light green suits. They followed about four steps behind to the cashier's cage. Feeno expected that he would find more security at the cage awaiting him. Or most certainly the FBI or AC police. He looked left at a wizened old man with a limp. To the right was a young couple, smiling happily as a slot pumped out coins. Looking up, Feeno saw a balcony with broad marble stairs, carpeted in red velvet. Two quick steps and he could be up them, going fast and out.

He measured his chances as he walked, risked a glance behind him. One of the guards was tall, lithe, obviously swift. The other, probably slower but built like a linebacker. Feeno pictured his chips scattering on the velvet stairs, his face pushed into the marble railing. People screaming, staring, perhaps some laughing. He decided to walk, to stay pat.

"Would you like a check or cash, sir?" asked the woman behind the cage window. She had on a crisply starched white blouse and a red bow tie. She pushed a cashier's receipt across the counter. Feeno read the figure, "$12,650."

"Cash," said Feeno, who repeated, "cash" louder because of a nervous catch in his throat. The heaven he had been in ten minutes before was swiftly collapsing into the fiery pit. He knew the FBI would be waiting nearby. Feeno watched as the woman counted out the bills and placed them in a manila business envelope.

"Thank you," he said, placing it in the inside pocket of the ridiculously checked sports coat.

They walked past the ornate lobby and a noisy disco bar, where flashing strobes showed blinking nanoseconds of people dancing. One of the guards stepped in front of Feeno and held the glass door tightly in one hand. "Stop a minute," he said to Feeno. Standing up close, he grasped Feeno's elbow and said commandingly through his teeth, careful not to be overheard:

"Take it someplace else, farm boy! We don't like counters in here."

"I don't count cards!" Feeno yelled. By now, he was totally unnerved and desperate, his eyes tracing the outside, where the boardwalk was bathed in a soft, orange light from the street lamps above. Up in the sky, a couple of searchlights bounced an advertisement, "Copper Glow" suntan lotion off of the clouds.

Should he make a run for it? How many were waiting for him? How far would he get?

"Just get the hell out of here and don't come back," said the guard, who pushed Feeno out the door. Feeno took a look around, then looked back into the casino. The guards had vanished. On the boardwalk, a young man pushed a wicker rolling chair with a young couple huddled inside. Other boardwalk strollers ambled slowly in both directions. The humid, salt air pasted itself to Feeno's sunburned face, but it felt exhilarating. He felt like screaming with unrestrained joy. There was no FBI, no cops. He had been kicked out of a casino because of being a suspected card counter.

That's all, that was it! It's a perfect world, and he had a cool twelve thousand bucks in his pocket to prove it.

Chapter 25: "I'M ONLY DA BOOKKEEPER"

On North Carolina Avenue he hailed a cab, directing the driver toward Route 40 east, one of the direct routes to Philadelphia. The city of Feeno's semi-wasted youth was about an hour away but he had no intention of going there. Several blocks later, a string of lights came into view. "Ah, the low-rent district. Stop right here."

Twenty minutes later Feeno came upon a Ford pickup with a slide-on camper parked at the far end of the open-all-night "All Aces" Used Car lot. The truck was painted black, with 120,000 miles on it. An elderly man in coveralls approached. He had a pistol strapped into a holster around his waist.

"Security," the old man laughed, slapping the gun. "Gotta have it back here in the backwash." The lot was closed in by the highway on one side and the broad marsh and back bay, laying black at night, on the other. Ten thousand moths and fellow insects dive-bombed the strings of bare yellow bulbs above the cars for sale. Down the highway as far as the eye could see was a string of billboards, brightly lit, advertising the diversions of the city: Don Rickles at Resorts, Sinatra at the 500 Club. In the far distance, an outline of a trumpet and Miles Davis.

The truck's camper cab contained a small refrigerator, a little sink and faucet, a propane gas supply and a 100-125 volt electrical system. Most appealing was a bed which seemed large enough to accept Feeno's long frame. "I think this one will do."

Inside the office, which was a small converted mobile home, the man accepted Feeno's three thousand and gave him change of fifty-six. He asked to see Feeno's driver's license and said, when the paperwork was done and he handed over the keys, "Thank you, Mister Peters. I know you're going to enjoy this vehicle."

Driving his new truck west on the Black Horse Pike, Feeno came upon another island of lights, this one from a shopping mall with an all-night sporting goods super store, whose business was elevated these days by an influx of camping tourists, including many Canadians and out-of-state job seekers looking for cheap summer-long housing. The twenty-four hour Gold Rush economy was a phenomenon new to Atlantic City, thanks to the casinos. Not only were players adrift in a timeless world, employes who worked the casinos in three shifts contributed to a round-the-clock stream of consumers. Doors did not open and close in this seaside town; they revolved.

Feeno picked out a sleeping bag and mat, a two-burner Coleman stove and lantern, a tank of propane, a collapsable plastic water jug plus bottles of water, more bug repellant and a topographical map of the Pine Barrens. He unfolded the map and began applying his brain to it as he wheeled his shopping basket up to the cashier. A voice broke his deep study: "Going somewhere?"

She was behind the counter, quickly bending and reaching into his cart to help unload the goods. Her face was lit with a sunrise smile that countered the cold fluorescence of the superstore. He noticed the bare skin of her back as her cotton shirt lifted with her movements. For a split instance, his fatigued mind did not recognize her, mostly because of the glasses. He stared at the soft, light brown hair and inviting smile.

"Well, I'll be darned," he said. "The lady on the beach."

She laughed.

"Little Gerald's aunt. How's auntie tonight?"

"Auntie's fine," she said. Auntie's name tag beneath the collar of the shirt read, "Edna Fowler."

"Edna, I guess," he said. "You're Edna."

The conversation that followed seemed to Feeno, as he reflected later, to have lasted long into the night, although it could have been only ten minutes. There were few customers in the store so they had the little cashier's checkout to themselves. Edna's easy speech confirmed that she was from the South. North Carolina in particular. She had come to Jersey to join the casino slow-track employment line.

"If you're from out-of-state you have to establish a six-months residency before you can get hired," she said. "Jersey residents have first dibs." She was living at the Bayshore Motel just down the road and spent her days taking courses at the Garden State Casino Academy. In her idle time she hung out at her sister's apartment in nearby Pleasantville.

"We're kinda in the same boat," said Feeno. "I came here for the big bucks too, except mine's in construction. At least I want to work in construction. Home is Pittsburgh. Economy's shot out there. Employment prospects seem better here," he said, aware that his self-conscience behavior was muted by the fact that Edna seemed not to notice, nor care, that his duds — particularly the undersized, check sports coat over a ridiculously loud, striped shirt — represented a style not worldly wise nor urbane anywhere except perhaps the the deepest reaches of Appalachia. She was a Southern girl.

They said their goodbyes and Feeno drove up Route 9, turning left onto a county road with pockmarked evidence that it was little used. Within a mile, he turned left again onto a sandy road. About twenty minutes later he guessed that he had driven at least two miles from the nearest paved road. He was about four miles above the old town of Atsion. By his map he reckoned he was somewhere near Hampton Furnace, east of Indian Mills.

The truck wheels met softer sand, causing some bumping and swaying. The forest thickened. Feeno knifed the truck into a space within the trees barely big enough to fit, so surrounded by such dense brush that he had difficulty opening the door.

Reflecting on the events of his most unusual day, forefront was the pleasant recollection of the Ace and the two fives, delivered by Providence on the very first hand of blackjack dealt at Harrah's. And next best was the serendipitous meeting with Edna, both on the beach, wrestling with little Gerald, and in the store several hours later.

Now his tired mind, as he lay in the limited confinement of his new home, began its process of mapping a solitary future. What was he to do now ? How would he redeem the harm done to Angela, to Vince? Foremost of his goals would be to return Vince's money. He played in his mind the dread he certainly would have felt, having to sit in a courtroom and listen to his one-time good friend paint him as a thief. Being there was not an option. Running was.

Thoughts were of Angela, of their last embrace on the deck of the small house in rural Maryland, with the Wicomico River flowing near the back door. The picture of his wife faded as he envisioned her with the new man.

Underlying all of the distress was the more serious matter of how deeply he was trapped in the banking scheme, one created by men who were skilled at deflecting things like guilt onto other people. How could he be responsible in any way for the disappearance of Jimmy Hoffa? That was a puzzle he could not solve while trapped in the falsity of the Witness Protection Program.

"My role was small," he said as if to a jury. He recalled a line in a movie. Was it Al Capone's accountant? He couldn't remember, but the guy said, "Don't look at me, I'm only da bookkeeper."

"Don't look at me," he whispered as he drifted into sleep. He was barely fifteen miles from Fort Dix.

Chapter 26: NEWARK

June 11, Newark.

The little room in the North Ward's Second Precinct police station had a metal desk and three folding chairs, one on one side and two on the other. Sholanda Griffin sat on the lone chair, head down, studying her nails. Would she be able to file her nails in prison?

She looked at her watch. Mickey Mouse, given to her by her grandmother, one single, sweet legacy of a childhood that was mostly bad. She sat up straight, sighed heavily, folded her arms on the table and rested her head on them.

Detectives Brice and Williams entered, took the seats across from her. Brice pushed a box of tissues Sholanda's way.

"How is she?' Sholanda asked, wiping her eyes.

"She'll live," said Williams, sitting back heavily, crossing his arms and staring at Sholanda, who had been picked up for stabbing a "sister" in the gut outside a tavern on Lower Broadway in Newark.

"We know this is tough," said Brice, a veteran cop who broke the male-dominated detective bureau gender barrier five years earlier. Brice tilted her head and with an understanding nod, told Sholanda that she had a daughter "much like you. A little wild. Prone to trouble. I know what it's like. Bad friends, bad circumstances."

Now, she asked, "You want to tell us what happened, Sholanda?"

The woman stiffened, squeezed her stiff upper arms toward the middle of her chest, pushing out her breasts, accentuating the cleavage. She wore an emerald green dress which stopped at the top of her thighs. The front was splotched with dark stains.

"We know what the witnesses say," continued Brice.

"There were three of them, standing no more than ten feet away. Eyewitnesses. They're in this building. They're here."

The cops waited. Thirty seconds, forty-five. Two minutes.

"How much time am I...?"

"Five years, maybe ten," said Williams quickly. "It's a long time to be off the street." He leaned across the table. "Listen, good looks like yours don't last forever."

"Oh, cut that shit," laughed Brice, punching Williams arm. "Don't listen to him, honey."

"I don't know what I should do," said Sholanda, looking up at the ceiling, which held a cold, florescent light.

"He's right, though," said Brice. "We have aggravated assault, assault with a deadly weapon, carrying a concealed weapon. Add it all up with the probation violation, and..." she said, pointing to Detective Williams, "he's right. Some long time, some long time. It's up to you; you want to get this over with? Tell us exactly what happened. Tell us the truth, sign it, and we'll help you. It could go a lot easier on you."

The detectives waited. The quiet in the room was worse than the befuddled thoughts in Sholanda's head. Quiet is the worst kind of pressure. A full two minutes elapsed. Brice looked at Williams and nodded. They both got up and left the cramped room without another word spoken.

Brice went to her desk to pick up the phone, while Williams walked to the coffee maker and grabbed a styrofoam cup. Both were interrupted by a uniformed officer who had been standing outside the interrogation room door: "She says she wants you back."

Back in the room, facing Sholanda, again the detectives remained silent, sitting, waiting, staring at the prostitute, who curled tissues in knotted fingers.

"I know something," whispered Sholanda finally.

In a voice full of hesitancy and fear, she told about Eddy French, a bartender pimp who had been shot to death on Seventh Avenue one night about a year ago.

"Eddy French, your old procurer?" said Williams, not too eagerly.

"Yeah, I know who shot him." Sholanda stole a glance at

Brice, studying her impression. Brice's face was impassive.

"Little late with that, aren't you, Sholanda? That was what? A year ago? Two years?"

"I don't remember when, but I was there."

Detective Williams sat back in his chair and folded his arms again. Brice leaned towards Sholanda.

Eddy French held a daytime job as a bartender at the Lotus, a grubby bar on Seventh Avenue. By night, he ran a string of a half-dozen girls. A sweet-talking manipulator with a "don't-fuck-with-me" attitude, he ran a steady, lucrative business. The hit took place on the sidewalk outside the Lotus, after Eddy had repeatedly reneged on protection payments. Eddy was determined not to take shit from the little mob guy he knew as "Squirrel" any longer, and the day that Eddy gave Squirrel the finger was the day that guaranteed Eddy's future, which a week later was zero days.

"I saw it," said Sholanda.

"Did we question you on this when it happened?" Williams asked.

"Shit no, I ran and I ran for a week. I don't need no trouble from them."

When Sholanda finished her story, Brice rose, leaving Williams behind. She returned five minutes later and spread several photographs upon the table.

"That one," said Sholanda, jabbing an index finger, touching with emphasis a portrait in the middle of the pack.

As Sholanda was led away, wrists cuffed behind her, Williams returned to his desk and dialed the phone:

"FBI," said the voice at the other end.

"Agent Schweitzer, please," said Williams, who waited and when Schweitzer got on the line, said, "I think I got something for you guys."

Chapter 27: BASS RIVER

June 20.

Schweitzer started the engine, reached over and closed the passenger-side window, did the same on his side, then turned on the AC, feeling the rush of cool air upon his face and arms. Out on Lake Absegami, two girls were shouting from their respective canoes. Way far out a Sunfish sailboat turned toward the breeze. Lazy day, oh so lazy, hot and tranquil.

Schweitzer settled in, knowing that Trapetto would be late. He picked Bass River State Park because the Garden State Parkway passed right through it, an easy drive from South Amboy, where Anthony Trapetto lived.

The best moments of an investigator's life were the lucky breaks, like this case. Dominoes. Get them lined up and give one a small push. Somebody pushes the whore, and see her push the Mafia guy.

Three p.m. Slowly, the big black Eldorado came up in his rear view mirror. Schweitzer saw Trapetto's wee head above the dashboard and smiled.

Trapetto walked nervously, darting eyes to the lake and ring of pines. Schweitzer grinned at the boy-sized figure in red Bermudas with green socks pulled up to the knees. The mobster wore a plain white tee shirt and a Yankees cap, the brim pulled far down over his eyes.

"So what time is the viewing?" Schweitzer asked when the Squirrel had finally nestled into the seat beside him.

"I don't know," said Trapetto, shielding the flame from the cigarette lighter blowing in the air conditioner's wind. "We're supposed to meet in the back of the bakery about eight. Thumbs wants to go as a group."

Schweitzer chuckled, then laughed aloud. "You guys always

go in groups, don't you? It's great togetherness. You gotta' admire that."

Trapetto paused, pushing smoke from between thin lips. "I don't know if I can do this."

"That's what they all say in the beginning," said Schweitzer. "You'll get used to it. All we want are for you to use your eyes and ears. You'll become comfortable with it."

"I ain't ever gonna be comfortable with it, and you know it."

Schweitzer continued unheeded: "Don't write anything down at first, not until you get to a safe place away from your buddies."

Trapetto looked over at the redheaded, heavy man and asked, "What'd you say I'd get if I just pled guilty to that hit? Eddy French was an asshole. He couldn't be worth much. I did society a favor."

Schweitzer ignored the question: "You can work your way out of this, Anthony, just by being a good guy for a change. Let's cut the bullshit. For instance." He turned towards him. "Where do you think Bannon is now?"

"At the bottom of this fuckin' lake, maybe," said Trapetto, finally smiling. "Why don't you get your bathin' suit on and go get him?"

Trapetto lit another cigarette, inhaled and opened the window, letting a huge breath of smoke disappear in the humid air. "Feeno Bannon is long gone. He ain't nowhere around here, you can bet on that."

"Do you think he went to Philly?"

"No way. That guy's scared shitless. He took off; way off, probably to Mexico or Canada."

"If that's the case," asked Schweitzer, turning his glare on Trapetto, "why are you guys still pressuring Feeno's friend, the builder guy from South Jersey, Berardi?"

"We ain't pressuring him," said Trapetto, peering straight ahead out the windshield.

"Oh yeah, who put the shiner on him? You or your fat friend? Somebody pistol-whipped the guy."

"I had nothin' to do with that."

"If you had nothin' to do with it," yelled Schweitzer, "how the hell do you know what I'm talkin' about?"

Trapetto didn't answer.

Schweitzer unwrapped a tube of Certs and put one in his mouth. His offer to Trapetto to take one was waved off. "How involved is Berardi in this? We know he got money from Unity Savings, from the Teamsters funds."

"I don't know nothin' about that," said Trapetto. "Don't even ask me."

Schweitzer's grin was sardonic.

"And I don't know nothin' about that Hoffa shit," said the Squirrel. "We weren't involved in that."

"Oh, yeah, who was?"

"That's Tony Pro's people. Different union."

"You're all Teamsters, Anthony."

"Yeah, but different locals. All we share is the pension money. Health and welfare. Stuff like that."

"I know, it's all deposited in the bank in a lump."

"Don't look at me," Trapetto answered. "Feeno Bannon's the guy who controlled all that money. He set everything up. He's responsible, he's the mastermind."

"You're all part of it," said Schweitzer. "Same funds."

"Yeah, but you heard me. Different union locals," answered Trapetto quickly.

After a long pause, Schweitzer looked at his watch. It was 3:32. "What time is that viewing?"

"I already told you; I don't know. All I know is when we're meetin'" said Trapetto. "And don't get any ideas. I ain't wearin' no wire for youse guys."

Carrying a live microphone taped to his body, Trapetto knew, was akin to pocketing a rattlesnake. Even if you don't get found out directly by your thug friends that you are a rat, a deserter, one who breaks the blood oath, sooner or later the word gets out. There was even a New Jersey law providing that subjects or suspects are to be notified ninety days after the completion of an investigation where a wiretap or body mike is used against them. Trapetto was aware of that law and felt that his days on earth were in countdown.

Evening in Bayonne, the sun beginning to squirt behind the low buildings. By the time the Scalesi men arrived at the Gramowski Funeral Home on West 29th Street, the line of mourners was beginning to reach backwards toward the front door and out the street. A breeze coming from the bay and Staten Island kicked up street dust, scattering it through the neighborhood of small shops and homes. The funeral home stood on a treeless corner.

Visitors shuffled slowly beneath a green canvas canopy that covered the front steps. There were genuine mourners, family and real friends of the deceased and his family. And there were associate "mourners," men of respect who were commanded to be there. Rocco Scalesi, wearing a dark, tailored suit, white shirt and black tie, advanced patiently in line, hands clasped lightly in front of him. Suddenly, one of the funeral home employes came to him:

"Mister Scalesi," he said deferentially. "How good of you to come, sir. Mister and Mrs. Gambini are expecting you. Please come."

Rocco stepped out of line while the mortician made a path for him through the other mourners, most of whom nodded to the Don with the most heartfelt respect. Rocco reached the bronze casket, genuflected and crossed himself while staring at the young dead body, laid out in deathly purity — a white tailcoat and trousers, a white shirt with a starched wing collar and white bow tie, a white pique waistcoat and white patent leather shoes. The hands, wearing white gloves, were clasped, holding a blackthorn rosary. All that was lacking was a halo.

The deceased was barely a boy out of his teens, handsome, the image of an angel; his skin had been buffed with makeup to conceal the acne. He had shoulder-length black hair. The burnished brass casket was banked by an entire wall of flowers, the odor of their sweetness enveloped the deceased and the room.

Standing next to the casket was a beautiful woman, mother of the corpse, dressed in black. She stood tall, proud and defiant even in grief. Her dyed black hair was the only feature that indicated her age as being beyond forty. Her olive textured skin was creamy and her eyes, even in sorrow, were lustrous. Her hands were knotted in front of her, except when she greeted some of the mourners she did not know. Those she shook hands with. The ones she knew, like Rocco, she let kiss her on the cheek. Rather than weep, her face was fixed in confusion and anger.

"Find the one, Rocco" she whispered to Scalesi, her lips close to his ear. He felt a mix of sympathy and pride, a quiet thrill, the latter because he, like the other men in this room, had admired the untouchable Concetta Gambini from afar, keeping the respectable distance of Old World Mafia, whose code was not to covet another boss's wife. He looked deeply into Concetta's eyes and squeezed her hands. The search of his eyes dropped to the front of her black silk dress and the fluff of taffeta that embraced her heavenly breasts, then moved to the left to a weeping man who was sitting in a wheelchair. Concetta's husband, Joseph, had been put in the chair after a shooting in the groin five years ago. He clasped Rocco's hands in both of his and said nothing. His face, twisted in genuine heartache, echoed his wife's plea to Rocco, who nodded gravely and moved away to the next room.

Anthony Trapetto took an aisle seat and nervously looked right and left. His new government sponsored assignment would be simple, according to Schweitzer. He was to note who was and who wasn't there. Were the families out in force? Many people, many men in dark suits, smelling of sharp cologne. From Jersey were the DeCavalcantes, Genoveses, and Scalesis. The Bruno family from Philly and Atlantic City was represented, as were most of the New York families.

The majority of the men stood outside on the funeral parlor steps, oblivious to the grief, both genuine and put on, that was going on inside. Squirrel put together so many faces and names that he soon quit the impossible task, trying to discover instead which bosses were absent.

Standing outside at last away from the perfumed air of the parlor, he heard, "Yo, Ant'ny! Over here!" One of the Brunos. Wiseguys from Philly prefaced greetings with "Yo!" He walked to the man named Davidio, standing broad-shouldered with a beefy pocked face and dark mustache, his gray hair cut short and bristled.

The over-all conversation on the funeral parlor steps dealt with how Richard Gambini, the kid in the casket, "got it."

"Christ almighty! Right outta' college!" said Davidio, talking to a small group.

"No, he flunked outta' college," piped up Julio Girard.

"That's what I mean, right outta' college. He was going to a high school prom with Joe Grease's daughter. That's when the bastards whacked 'im. He was steppin' out of a limo at the country club."

"No witnesses?"

No, not even the girl or the driver. She was steppin' out of the other side."

"What was the reason for whackin' this kid?" asked Nicky Nuts, a Mafioso from Atlantic City and a longtime soldier in the Scalesi family.

"You don't know?" asked Freddy Dots. He guided Nicky to the edge of the steps away from the others. He looked up and down the street, knowing full well that the feds were around, watching, taking notes. "The kid, Richard," said Freddy. Nicky, smelling garlic, took a step away.

Freddy grabbed his lapel and pulled him close enough to hear his whispers. "The kid was pushin' 'H'. He got Joe Grease's daughter addicted. She was a nice kid before she met him. Beautiful young girl. But she was hooked. Then the bastard makes a skin flick with her, fuckin' her blind, front and rear, gettin' her to suck 'im off. It's all on film. So whataya' think happened when that little movie got circulated?"

When the Squirrel met Schweitzer the next day at the lake he was carrying a light fishing pole and small green tackle box.

"Going fishing?" asked Schweitzer.

"Yeah, fishin' for you," said the Squirrel. "I wish youse guys would do your own fuckin' fishin'."

"So, whatta' you got?" asked Schweitzer.

The Squirrel took a deep breath on a Camel and flicked it onto the grass. They sat side by side on a tarred horizontal log separating the parking lot from a small beach. "They were all there, everybody." He started naming families. "Genoveses, DeCavalcantes, and individuals, Budsy Russo, Al Carini, Bart

Malosinni, on down the line."

"How about New York?"

"Everybody!" He looked at the FBI man sitting beside him. "Except maybe one, as far as I could see."

Schweitzer shuffled uncomfortably on the log, turning to get a closer look at the small man beside him.

"I didn't see no Colombos," said Trapetto. "Why, what do your guys say? They were there. I saw 'em; everybody saw 'em. They stand out like sore thumbs. Takin' pictures."

"They were there doing their job, just like you," said Schweitzer. "Only difference is they don't know all the made guys from the street crews."

"What makes you think I know 'em all?" asked Squirrel, turning to look at the lake, which on this midweek work day was nearly empty of boats.

"Aw, you don't give yourself enough credit Anthony. Okay, continue. The Colombos weren't there..."

Chapter 28: ENCORE

June 20.

Vince grunted, struggling alone to hoist the four-by-eight sheet of wallboard in place in the doctor's unfinished dining room. The two college boys who had been working with him were at the lumber yard picking up new bathroom and kitchen fixtures that had just come in that morning.

Vince fingered the Browning pistol in his nail pouch. Never fired outside the range. Never fired with purpose. Occasionally he hefted it, even pointed it at a cat once, and said, "Gotcha!" He wondered if he would ever have the cold nerve to pull the trigger. Replaying the slap upside his head in Andy Burke's house now made him angry. He fantasized lying on his back on the the dusty floor, pulling out the gun and firing at the two cowardly mobsters hiding behind the blinding work light. He could hear their grunts as the bullets tore into their guts, spilling their bad blood, curses from their throats.

To reality again, Vince looked forward to a full day of work without the pestering of another reporter looking for a fresh angle on the bizarre case of, as the *New York Daily News* had put it, "Mob Banker on the Lam." The connection of Joseph A. Bannon to the multi-million dollar Teamsters funds and loans going out to mob compadres in Las Vegas and other ventures was in full-fledged disclosure.

So was the political mayhem launched by Neptune County Prosecutor Arnold Rosenstein and his audacity to compel an FBI informant who was in the Witness Protection Program to stand trial for fraud.

Vincent Berardi, the star witness who never got a chance to testify, was described as a victim of Bannon's stealth. His lifelong friendship with the banker added a layer of drama to the story.

Then the bombshell that "informed sources" revealed that Berardi was himself under investigation. For what? None of the media could say. But the *Camden Courier* had dug up the one-time association of Vince's father with the kind of notoriety which hung around a person's life and revisited after death. Identities through buzz words? "South Philly Italian" being prominent. "Stolen car." "Moyamensing Prison." All true, all in the past, and, after the facts, all counter to a man's being .

Vince's father had been out of jail twelve years before Vince was born, and by the time of Vince's earliest memory, that terrible chapter was all but erased from the family history. The man that Vince knew was of quiet speech but stern behavior. A man who foreswore liquor, beer and wine, gambling, socializing, womanizing and chiefly important, hanging around with or even saying hello to mobbed up men.

Vince did not learn until manhood why this street corner or that tavern or club was off limits, not to be visited, not even to be looked at. The father never borrowed a dime nor accepted a loan from any other person for the rest of his life. He worked forty-eight hours a week at the coal and ice plant, never tardy, never absent. Nine o'clock mass every Sunday he passed the wicker collection basket from pew to pew, and slowly, so very slowly, habits led to a lifestyle that allowed a man to die redeemed. Until now.

"Hey there," a voice interrupted. Vince with his back turned, dropped the wallboard against the unfinished stairs to the second floor.

Clyde Woolen stood with a smile clamped on the stub of a cigar, hands in the pockets of his overstuffed bright green shorts.

"I thought I'd stop by to see how you're doing," he said, and though Clyde looked around the unfinished building in admiring glances, Vince caught the edge to his meaning and let him know with a thin smile: "You mean the house or my miserable life in general?"

"Seriously, how you doing?" They shook hands. Clyde dug into his shirt pocket and produced a Havana.

"Thanks, I'm not smoking."

"Go on, go on," said Clyde. "I can tell you want a smoke. Try one of these babies. You'll never go back to cigarettes again."

Vince took one and accepted Clyde's wooden match, which he lit with a quick swipe on the brick fireplace. Remembering how his dad did it, he bit the small end off, twirled the cigar's business end over the flame. He drew in and breathed out, letting a veil of blue smoke drift to the ceiling. "C'mon, let's go in the kitchen." There was a cooler. He reached in, clutched two silver cans of Schmidt's. Wet and cold with melting ice, they felt good to grab.

Clyde leaned against the counter for the as yet uninstalled sink; Vince sat on a much-furrowed wooden saw horse and stared at Clyde as if wanting to say something and not making up his mind. Clyde stared back.

Sometimes slight looks reveal something another man can trust. Clyde had soft eyes. He didn't need to speak.

"I'm going to tell you something," said Vince after a while. "Something that stays with you." He walked to the open wall to the outside and spit on the ground, but looked about at the wild expanse of trees, noting only a kicked up breeze which made the skinny twigs of shrubs dance in the air.

"This stays here," Vince said, turning. "Here, you got it?"

The big man nodded, letting his smile disappear.

"I talked to Feeno." He paused, looking for Clyde's reaction. There was none.

"I won't tell you how or when."

"Was this before or after..."

"Well, it was before. Before he disappeared. And then he got ahold of me just yesterday."

Clyde's eyebrows lifted, eyes opening wide: "Yesterday?"

"Yeah," said Vince, shifting his feet, poking with his index finger to drop some ash from the cigar to the floor. He rubbed it with sole of his heavy work boot. "I can't tell you how."

He drew again on the cigar. "Ah shit," he said, digging into his sweat-stained shirt pocket, pulling out a much-handled postcard and thrusting it toward Clyde.

Clyde took it and turned from the photo on the front of a skinny Italian with a straw hat holding his big oar in the water at the stern of a gondola. The other side showed writing in a flourished cursive. He read, flipped the card from front to back. "I don't get it."

"Look on the back," Vince said, smiling slightly. "Giuseppe Banone, the tenor."

"Jee-sus Christ!" He looked at Vince, trying not to laugh aloud. "Is this guy a clown?"

"No, he's a tenor. Irish tenor."

They both laughed.

Clyde listened silently to Vince's story, then very calmly asked Vince to tell him the next time that Feeno got in touch. It came within only a week:

When Al Fortino handed Vince the phone through the waiter's station out to the hallway, there was no "Vince the Prince" greeting.

"It's me," Feeno said.

"I hear you."

"Listen. This is hard."

"Tell me about it."

"I had to get away," said the fugitive.

"That's pretty obvious." Looking up the stairs and in both directions in the hallway, Vince felt his nerves becoming undone. "Listen, stop a minute," he said through the phone to Feeno. "Listen, I have to say something right out. Don't tell me where you are. I don't want to..."

"What the hell do you think I am, Vince, crazy or something?"

"Yes, in fact, I think you are crazy."

"No, no, no. Listen. What I've gotten you into...How do you think I feel? No way are you going to find out where I am. Nobody knows. Nobody who knows me knows. Sometimes, even I don't know where I am."

Feeno waited for a reply, but heard none. Vince stood next to Clyde and shook his head negatively.

"Vince? You still there?"

"Yes." He felt, or detected not just the urgency in Feeno's voice, but fear.

"I don't know what I'm doing, Vince."

"Why the hell did you call me?"

"I had to. Look, I'm at the end of my rope." Feeno stood in a lonely phone booth at a general store deep in the pines, surrounded by stubby green-needled trees. A black pickup was at the gas pump. A man in a green tee shirt walked from the store, lugging a six-pack toward the cab of a large semi, its engine quietly throbbing. Feeno looked at the man hard, then at the door which bore "Ocean Spray" in blue letters, but was relieved to see him climb into his cab. He heard a deep-throated bark of the engine as the truck moved slowly down the dirt road.

"I need help, Vince."

"No shit. Don't we all."

"I was scared. I ran because I couldn't stand to sit there in that courtroom and listen to you condemn...to testify against me. Vince, why did you...?"

"Listen, Feeno. What do you think?" His voice got softer, but his anger mounted. He looked directly at Clyde. "My life. My wife's life. My kids. People look at me. Now, all of a sudden, I'm a mob associate. Under investigation. I can't even get my money back, thanks to you."

"I know," Feeno interrupted. "It's one reason I wanted to talk to you. I know about it. I know what the feds have dropped on you.

Vince frowned, puzzled that Feeno was aware of what the papers had printed. How the hell could he know unless he was nearby. Pennsylvania, New York, Delaware, Jersey?

"I will," Feeno said. "I swear to Christ, I will get your money back. I'll clear your name."

Vince yelled, "Do you know what?"

Clyde put his hand out, finger to his lips.

Vince breathed deeply: "Do you know what it's like?" Softer voiced, he told Feeno how his business had suffered, the hell he was going through.

Feeno answered: "I'm going to help you, but I need your help first. Somebody's help. Anybody's help. I can't do anything. I have to get moving again. There are places I have to get to. There are records I can't get to anymore. I can't defend myself this way. I can't help you either unless you help me, Vince. We are in this together."

"Don't give me that together bullshit, Feeno. I've had enough fucking togetherness."

"All right. Forget it. Just fucking forget it!" He squeezed the handle of the phone booth door, strangling it. He was sweating heavily. He looked down at his dirty khaki pants, noticed his dirty hands. His last bath was in the Mullica River, at night, about a week ago.

Clyde suddenly pointed to the phone in Vince's hand, then pointed to himself, tapping his chest.

"Feeno, hold on," Vince said. "Hold on." He stopped as a woman with dark glasses came down the steps and walked toward the restaurant kitchen, rife with the engaging odor of frying onions. She ignored the two men, who stood in shadows. "Feeno. I think there may be somebody."

"Who?"

"He's a guy I know. A detective." Feeno looked directly at Clyde who again gestured that he wanted to talk to Feeno, but Vince shook his head, "No."

"A detective? What kind of detective?"

"Private," said Vince. "He's a former ATF agent. Knows about organized crime. He has investigated organized crime. Right now he's the only guy I can think of who can help you, help both of us."

"How do you know he's not a setup?" asked Feeno. "He's a fed isn't he?"

"How do you know anything, Feeno? Maybe you're going to have to trust me for a change. You can take it or leave it."

Silence at Feeno's end. What he could see out of the phone booth now was his new, entire world. A woods, with rednecks for acquaintances and advice. He watched a squirrel sit up at the trunk of a maple tree, looking up at a bird feeder, nervously chattering, little head moving, swiveling, watching out for trouble. The squirrel climbed the trunk, stuck out a paw toward the feeder, couldn't reach it, reconnoitered, suddenly jumped toward the bird seed, and fell to the ground. And ran away.

"Vince," said Feeno softly. "Eight o'clock tomorrow."

"Where?"

"Right where you're at, you dummy."

On the way back to Jersey, going over the Walt Whitman bridge, high above a tug pushing a barge full of gravel. A 747 roared overhead in its takeoff from Philadelphia International Airport.

Clyde opened the window, threw out the match he used to light another Havana, breathed deeply and looked over at Vince: "Why didn't you let me talk to him back there while we had the chance?"

"He was scared, Clyde. He would have spooked. I know it. It wouldn't have been a good idea."

They drove without talking, picked up Crescent Boulevard and headed north on 130. Vince pulled into a Pathmark and asked Clyde to wait while he got some hamburger patties and rolls.

"I'll make your supper in the backyard and tell you all about it," said Vince.

Heading back on the highway, he asked, "I have to know, Clyde. You seem anxious to help out. I'm curious."

"Curious about what? Oh, you think I'm hungry for work or something?"

"Well, I dunno. I guess I'm puzzled."

"Okay," said Clyde. "I can see where this is going. I'll be honest with you. This is an interesting case. To me it's like an open window. But it's just open a tiny crack. You don't know, you and Feeno, where it's all headed."

"What do you mean?"

"Here's what I mean," Clyde continued, relighting the cigar. He scratched his neck in thought. "You have a Strike Force investigation. Not just into mob activity. You have the Teamsters Union. You have a mysterious runoff of bank funds. You have money being shifted all over the goddamn place. You got cops, accountants, bank examiners, informants. And not just Feeno Bannon. You got informants that need protecting. You got investigators whose hands are tied.

He turned to look directly at Vince, who by now was listening with full attention. "And one other thing."

"What?" Vince asked.

"You got Hoffa. Jimmy Hoffa," he said loudly and smiled. "Who killed Jimmy Hoffa? Where is Jimmy Hoffa? You think he's in Jersey?" Vince asked. "You yourself, you told me, he's not buried in Jersey, even if he is dead."

"Oh, he's dead all right," said Clyde with emphasis. "And he's not in Jersey. But the guys who did it – the ones responsible. They're here, they're right under our noses. A good, old Jersey connection if there ever was one."

He stopped for a second, took another deep drag. "And maybe I'll be the guy who finds out just who and where."

Chapter 29: A FAMILY PICNIC

July 8.

A parade of small boats funneled from the Atlantic into the Manasquan. The men who were gathered beneath the tent-like canopy could see, if they wished, the upper lip of the setting sun, red and dime-sized against a graying sky. They were concentrated on other matters. Rocco Scalesi's getaway summer home afforded a wide view of the river and tidal bay. His was the sole house on the sandy point, built high enough on the dunes to let one see the stone jetty leading to the ocean beyond. On the land side, a dirt lane flanked by waving dune grass led for a curving half-mile from the stone and shingled home to the road beyond.

A large window of the house faced the ocean. It allowed the morning sunlight to flood the deck and wide kitchen. On the south side was a short lawn kept fertile almost daily by the swish-swish of a water sprinkler. The lawn led to a wooden dock where "Carmelita II" was tied up in a short and very private canal, nearly hidden in the tall green rushes. The canal's land end held a clapboard shed with gray shingled roof. The shed was wrapped around on three sides by a stout wooden pier

Rocco's home was new and exclusive, with not another building in sight for a half-mile. It was built in spite of regulations limiting construction on barrier islands and peninsulas, thanks to an unsecured loan from Unity Savings & Trust to the local official who had the last word.

Between the dock and the house, a half-dozen men sat on lawn chairs under the tent, protected on all four sides by mosquito netting. A folding table within easy reach held several bottles of wine, whiskey, salsa, chips and peanuts. On the ground was a cooler of ice and bottled beer. Fred Russo sat at the table, holding a loose-leaf notebook in his lap. A hand-drawn spread sheet had listed on it various corporations, charities, foundations and trusts. He pointed to one, shifting in his seat to allow Rocco to look. The women and kids, chilled by the evening air, began moving inside.

Rocco read, "Marian Medical Clinic" with the initials written in pencil "CP, Cal." in the border.

"What's that?" Rocco asked.

"Cactus Pines," said Russo, not having to explain about the exclusive Teamsters retreat, complete with casino and golf course very close to the Cal-Neva line.

"This one should be hard to trace, at least in the short run," said Russo. "So should some of these others."

"What the hell do you mean? Short run! What's that mean?"

"It means the feds aren't that dumb. Sooner or later..."

"Jee-Suz Christ!" said Rocco. "Sooner or later? That's not what I been payin' you for, Fred."

"Easy, easy, Rocco," said the lawyer, sitting back and taking a sip from a crystal wine glass next to a bottle of Bordeaux, which was exclusively his. Two other wine bottles on the table being sampled by other guests were of the Sneaky Pete variety. Nunzy Batdorf, of Paramus, an acting capo since last November when Louie Costa was sent up, lounged nearly flat in a folding canvas beach chair; with the June issue of Playboy magazine spread over his sleeping face. Angelo Crupi, aka "Doggie", was similarly inclined, but awake and studying the Racing Form. Petey Boy Sergio stood, examining the ocean and combing back his slick black hair.

Sitting at the far corner of the tent, looking out to sea, taking frequent sips from a glass half full of straight rye was Anthony "The Squirrel" Trapetto.

"It's going to take them months to get through the stuff they have stored in that place in Nutley," said Russo, who brushed a few flakes of ash from Scalesi's cigar off his neatly pressed white shorts. Russo was wearing Egyptian-made leather sandals and a white yachtsman's cap. "The dummies we set up are intricate, hard to trace, but nothing's foolproof. Even so, it'll give us time to shuffle things around and hide them even more."

"Yeah, but Feeno Bannon is going to fuck us royally. If he

ever comes in again and if we can't pin most of it on him." Rocco took another gulp from the glass in front of him and yelled, "Hey Anthony, get over here. I wanta' hear what you got on that Berardi guy."

Trapetto for a moment almost lost his grip on his glass of whiskey. He got up slowly, swung his chair around and faced the table. He half-stumbled as he walked the three steps to Rocco. He started talking nervously before he got there. "I ain't on it all the time. I ain't had the time that I used to. I been busy cleanin' up that mess in Elizabeth. I asked Nicky Nuts to follow Berardi."

Rocco stared at the Squirrel. His face grew darker: "Askin' Nicky Nuts to do somethin' intelligent is like tryin' to put pants on a flea."

"Yeah, but he's down there in South Jersey, Thumbs," said Trapetto. "Atlantic City ain't too far from where Berardi lives and has that house he's building," said the Squirrel. "This much we know. I don't think Berardi and Bannon are in close touch. What I mean is we ain't any closer to finding Feeno than we were the day he took off."

"You stay on it," yelled Rocco. "I want both of youse, you and Nicky, to keep the pressure on. Berardi may be our only chance to get at Bannon."

The Squirrel returned to his chair to face the inlet. Rocco lifted his wine glass and yelled again at him: "And I want a report every day. From both of youse. Got it?"

Trapetto nodded.

Just a few hundred yards off the point of land a small fishing boat with an enclosed cabin sat at anchor. While a man with a fishing pole and line in the water lounged at the stern, the two men inside were wearing ear phones. Both leaned forward as Russo and Scalesi began talking about the financial tie-in with the Cactus Pines. Both frowned when the conversation shifted to the whereabouts of Feeno Bannon.

Russo laughed and interjected, "Feeno Bannon is probably somewhere on the Amalfi Coast right now drinking Schweppes."

"Good," said Rocco, "we got guys in Italy that'll snuff that prick in one day."

Nunzie Batdorf, who had awakened, suddenly waved to his

boss, put a finger to his lips and pointed toward the house. Rocco turned, and his face brightened.

"Here's my babe," he said as Nancy Scalesi pushed open the netting, ducked her head and entered the tent. "Sit down, dear." The girl, about twenty-five, wearing white tennis shorts and sleeveless blouse, had a white headband over curly black hair. Like her father, she was short in stature, more broad than thin, muscular. But where Rocco's eyes penetrated beneath half-mast brows, Nancy's brown eyes shined with welcoming brightness.

Nunzie, feeling guilty as he looked at her tan legs and arms, which glistened with a slight sweat, grunted to get up from the low-lying beach chair.

Fred Russo arose and bowed, "Hello, gorgeous." She offered her cheek, which he bussed lightly.

"Hi, handsome," she said. "I love that hat." She turned toward her father, who grasped her face with both hands and kissed her forehead.

"Sit," he said, pointing to Fred Russo's chair.

She slumped back, reached to the small table for a salsa chip and dip. "What are you lazy guys up to?"

Russo quickly picked up the papers and binder from the table and walked toward the house, wishing he could stay to chat socially with the affable young woman. A sometimes exception to the exclusion rule, Nancy was welcomed into the inner circle of these Teamsters officials, though kept out of the sordid side of the business dealings. Russo watched her grow from a teenager when she had accompanied her father to work and to various labor meetings. She was permitted free rein to run around his big office in Rahway, where Rocco also kept a box of toys for her to play with. Her high school summers were punctuated with brief employment periods at the Teamsters office, ostensibly clerking but often doing nothing but her nails.

Nancy, blinking away a stab of setting sunlight, shaded her eyes and said. "Oh, Daddy. I need a car tonight. The Springsteen concert."

"Where? "

"It's at the Garden," she said, flopping in Russo's vacated chair.

Rocco thought a second or two, sipped his seltzer: "I don't like you driving over there. I'll send one of the boys..."

"Oh, daddy, c'mon," she erupted in genuine horror.

"Who's going with you?" he asked.

"Connie and Joanie."

"I don't like you in the city. It ain't proper for a proper young woman. Women."

"Daddy, daddy, daddy! What AIN'T," she said loudly, emphasizing the bothersome grammar, "is to be escorted by one of your..." She hesitated: "Associates."

"Okay, okay," said Rocco, throwing up his hands. "You can go."

He looked toward Petey Boy: "Call Jimmy at the office and tell him to get a car over here."

To Nancy, he pointed a stubby index finger: "But promise me you'll park at the Port Authority, and take a cab. I don't want you driving there."

She beamed, rose from the chair. "Thank you, Daddy. You are such a special man." She leaned and kissed her dad's baldish head, patting it, and left.

Petey Boy jumped up also and held the tent fly. Nunzie grinned, bemused, shaking his head.

"What are you laughin' at?" asked Rocco.

"You know what I'm laughin' at...? said the loyal capo. "This is you," he said to Rocco, holding up his right hand. "And this is your daughter.", showing the little finger of the other. He wrapped his hand around the pinkie, and smiled, very pleased with himself.

Rocco grunted, resigned to the obvious. Nancy's congeniality and responsive warmth to other Teamsters besides her father endeared her to the tough men surrounding him, whose affection toward Nancy was demonstrably changed when he became a widow in 1965.

Nancy was the switch who could turn her father's ruthlessness to a state of calm. In turn, she saw only endearment from the man who loved and protected her.

When Rocco was indicted on a manslaughter charge seven years ago for the death of a rival mob associate, and it appeared that Rocco may go to jail, the Teamsters showed no hesitancy in appointing Nancy to his post as secretary-treasurer of the local, even though "as acting." Called to explain at the trial how and why that happened, she straightforwardly explained the reasons. In doing so, her soft tones and frankness charmed some members of the jury, and may have helped to convince them that her father was not guilty. He walked.

"I don't think those union members would have cared if what was written or said about my father was true or not true," she said in court, "because they know what he did for them.

"I often heard them say, 'Look what Rocco did for me. He gave me a pension, he gave me and my family eyeglasses, he gave us a dental plan. If he saw a Teamster on the street, he'd take them to a bar, buy them a drink. He remembered a guy's wife's name, he would ask about their kids. There was a young girl who had a concussion after an accident. My father visited her, sent flowers. He always asked, 'What can I do for you?'

Nancy had looked up at the judge and told him, "There is something about my father, sir — not that you can't get mad at him. You can get mad at him. But there is something about the man. I mean you can't understand until you're like one of the guys from the local. They just — I would have never believed it, if I wasn't in those meetings and I didn't hear those people go wild about him. That's how I got to be a trustee in the union. I have no illusions about it. I am simply Rocco's daughter."

A behavioral psychologist might say that people of Rocco's personality had pendulum mood swings, bipolarity matched in magnitude on either side. Rocco Scalesi's kindnesses, his acts of generosity, when swung the other way, would be manifested in uncaring brutality. He was careful that Nancy and her friends saw only the one side. Her closest friends thought that no way could this man, Nancy's father, be a big shot in La Cosa Nostra. One newspaper photo a few years back of Rocco in handcuffs prompted one of Nancy's friends to call her and cry, "How can the newspapers say those awful lies about your father?"

The party was breaking up as darkness filled the sky over the Atlantic. All of the wives and kids left earlier in two cars, the women knowing when they were not wanted. Only the hard core, inner legion of men remained, camped under the canopy, by now making small talk, joking and drinking. Russo lit a cigarette and sipped his Bordeaux; Crupi reached for two cans of Coors Light in the cooler, handed one to Petey Boy, then they settled down to a game of gin on the card table. The humidity had lifted, stars were starting to wake up, and on the ocean and bay, pin prick lights of fishing and pleasure boats were fixed to the dark sea. Trapetto stared at each, sitting uneasily, coaxing the liquor to dull the drumbeats inside him. When Rocco got up and went inside without excusing himself, and his capos and the others paid no heed, the Squirrel relaxed some.

Rocco stepped through the kitchen, reached down and picked up Benny, an orange tabby, whom he held to his ear to hear the purring. He departed toward the far end of the house into a dark study, shut the door and walked to a large mahogany desk, with just enough light from the window to see the dial on the telephone.

He guessed correctly that Joe Gambini, being confined to his wheelchair, would not answer, and let the slight echo of Concetta's soft, low voice create a pause before answering in return. His back was to the interior of the room. He faced the seemingly unending ocean of dune grass, now dark but waving in the foreground. Miles away were dots of light from the populated part of the island.

"Concetta?"

"Oh, Rocco," she said. "I got your flowers. You shouldn't have sent them. How did you know it was my birthday?" Her voice was a smile that caught Rocco in mid-breath. He sat back, stroking Benny. "You are too kind a man. You are too, too generous."

"I wanted to keep in touch, Concetta, to see how you are doing," he said.

"We are all well. As well as can be," she said. "It's been tough at times. Sometimes so hard. I think of Richard every day. I know you know that," she said. "It never leaves. I try to think of the good times." Instinctively, she glanced at the small table of photographs: Richard on a merry-go-round, Richard in Little

League, and Richard, the smallest in a group photo of siblings. And the most recent, Richard in high school cap and gown, long dark hair touching his shoulders.

"And you, Rocco. How have you been? It has been so long."

She asked about his daughter, Nancy, running up and down a line of niceties. Both were skilled at playing the charade of touching and not ever touching, each aware of the other's feelings of something that is almost, something not quite, something not able, yet always there with promise.

Rocco slathered it on thickly: "I know," he said. "I know the loss, and I want you to know that I am at your side, every day, Concetta. I think of you every day in your sorrow. You know that I am here for you. I will never leave your side."

Outside, Nunzie opened the flap of the tent with his heavy forearm, belched and walked to the edge of the lawn, where he relieved himself in the rushes. A floodlight came on, sweeping the yard with a light so brilliant, it caused Petey Boy to blink and shade his eyes.

"Hey, you fat asshole, you triggered the light. They can see you all the way to Red Hook. Nunzie ignored the jibe by turning toward Petey and pretended to pee on him.

The men left the tent, walking to their cars laughing. They had to skirt the sand dunes to get to Rocco's garages where their cars were parked.

"Get the fuck off my fender," said the Squirrel to the teenaged cousin of Petey Boy, a gofer, a wannabe who stood watch at events like this. The Squirrel was wobbly, tripping over a lawn chair but righting himself by catching the branches of a holly bush and hanging on.

"Woah!" laughed Petey Boy. "Hey sailor, you're drifting to port."

Trapetto didn't hear. He stumbled forward. When he began groping his pants for car keys, Russo said, "Hey give me them, Anthony. You're not driving tonight. I'll take you home."

"Get the fuck outta' the way!" he whispered, pushing Russo aside and stumbling into his driver's seat.

Before the others could persuade him otherwise or even to

grab the keys, he was roaring out the driveway, the tires spitting out sand and small pebbles.

"What are you gonna do?" shrugged Angelo, who laughed..

"He's fuckin' blind though," reasoned Petey Boy. "I watched 'im; he was hittin' that stuff pretty hard all day."

"Well, somebody should catch up to him," said Russo. "Follow him, or pull him over. Make sure he gets home."

Angelo and Petey Boy got into the latter's Caddy and hurried from Rocco's house. They were not a mile from the lane, heading north on the paved road, when they heard the car horn in the distance. It started and wouldn't stop, just one incessant blast, growing louder as they sped toward it.

The Squirrel's car had hit the wooden guard rail at the curve in the road head on. The heavy Eldorado had passed through it and out the other side; the front end was embracing a thick oak, which was pushed back into the engine. No houses or buildings were nearby, only woods. The Squirrel's head rested on the top of the twisted steering wheel. He was so small that his nose was doing the horn blowing. Petey Boy quickly pulled open the car door and gently grabbed Squirrel's shoulders and pulled him back in his seat. Blood was dripping from his nose and mouth; he was unconscious and his legs seemed trapped beneath the steering wheel and dash board.

"Christ, I think he's dead."

"Take his pulse, is he breathing?'

Unable to find the little man's carotid artery in his neck, Petey Boy reached under Trapetto's ribs, ripped open his shirt and felt for the heart. "I think it's beating," he said. "He's alive."

He also felt something hard, probably a holy medal. But larger and round in his fingers, not oval. He pulled, looked down at his bloody hand. Then he yanked. In it was a small medallion and a loop, and a piece of white surgical tape, messed with blood and black hairs. Petey Boy held it all up to the fading light for Angelo to see. Russo came up. The car horn had stopped blowing. The men looked at the wire, and said nothing, but Russo felt his heart drop to his stomach, his pulse quickening.

Extricating the little gangster, whose legs were trapped, was difficult, accomplished only when the men were able to secure a rope around the back rest of the front driver's seat, between the back rest and Squirrel's body. The loose end of the rope was passed through the rear door and attached to the suspension of Petey Boy's car. Petey put his Lincoln in reverse. There was a strain on the rope and a loud crunch as the back rest was pulled out of its mechanism. They laid Squirrel on a tarp from Russo's car, wrapped him up with only his head showing.

Nunzie opened the trunk to Russo's red Maserati.

"Yo," said Russo. "Not in my car!"

Nunzie and Angelo, carrying the Squirrel between them, bowed to the executive privileges of the consigliere; they stopped.

"Put him in my fucking car," said Nunzie, slamming the trunk door of the Maserati and flashing a dark look at Russo.

Rocco stepped from his hot tub on the deck when the men returned and laid Trapetto on the lawn, staring at the body, then at Rocco and back at the body.

"He was wearin' a wire," said Petey Boy, holding it up for Rocco to see.

"Put him in the boathouse," said Rocco, referring to the one-story shed built between two piers and sticking out over the water. A short boardwalk wrapped the three closed sides of the shingled building. Water lapped at two boat fenders attached to the pier.

The Squirrel groaned but was obviously in shock as he was carried into the boathouse. Blood dribbled from his mouth and nose, which was bent and yellowed.

"Put him in that chair," said Rocco.

"He's dyin', Thumbs!" said Angelo.

"Put him in the fuckin' chair, I said."

Russo stood at Rocco's side, glancing at his boss, then at the dying informant.

Rocco had a .44 Magnum at his side, waiting.

"What are you gonna do?" asked Russo.

"Here, do you wanta' do it? You wanta' earn your bones? It's about time." Rocco reached the gun out to the lawyer, who backed away.

"No way, no way. Look, I think the guy's dead."

Squirrel started to tumble forward. Petey Boy grabbed him

by his bloody hair and tilted his body back against the aluminum chair. With Squirrel's head resting on the chair back, Rocco, three feet away, aimed and put a bullet almost perfectly between the eyes. The impact drove the small body back, tilting the chair and Squirrel into the water. The little dead man remained fixed in his chair, which bobbed and floated, then sunk to the bottom.

"Pick 'im up," said Rocco to Russo, who was shaking, but did as told, reaching into the gray-green water to grab Squirrel's shoulder. The water was no more than five feet deep. Petey helped pull the Squirrel up to the dock again, laying him down. Blood and water mingled, dripping through the cracks of the wooden dock, back into the sea.

Rocco pulled a switchblade knife from his front pocket, snapped it into a weapon, forced open the dead man's mouth, grabbed his tongue, pulled it, and cut. Russo turned away and faced the ocean, fighting nausea.

"What the hell are you doin, Boss?" asked Nunzie, his broad heavy face distorted.

Rocco held up the tongue. Blood trickled down his hairy forearm: "Saint Anthony, Saint Anthony. That's who this little prick was named after. In Padua. That big cathedral there. Saint Anthony. He was a great orator. Did you know that? They got his fuckin' tongue on display there, behind the altar."

He swung back his arm, and with a heave, threw Trapetto's tongue into the reeds. He turned and walked back to the house, cursing.

Chapter 30: ONG'S HAT

To describe the Pine Barrens and what was there — towns and geographical features named Apple Pie Hill, Penny Pot, Martha and Hog Wallow — a person could hardly be convinced that this could be somewhere in the megalopolis of the Northeastern United States. This forest existed in spite of itself, with spans of dwarfed pine trees resting among cranberry bogs and abandoned iron forges, and all of those sitting delicately upon an underground reservoir, a lake of seventeen billion gallons of pure water. New Jersey? Never in a million years. And reporting that these so-called "barrens" measure more than one million acres, or one-fifth of a state dominated by turnpikes, refineries and jammed housing in the suburbs of New York City and Philadelphia sounds as logical as a Benedictine nun running a nightclub.

Only a few highways travel through the pines, with not many travelers paying heed to its ghostly history of crossroads towns that often were named for a particularly odd occasion or resident, identifying a happenstance that may have occurred in a single night or single day.

Over the years, the curious names remained unique to the history of the place.

In the Pine Barrens, the apocryphal origins of the place called "Ong's Hat" involved several versions, all revolving around the single night of a man named Ong, who some time in the 1800s threw his hat into the top of a tree, where it remained for several years. The major version of the story is that Ong got drunk and that his hat got tangled in a tree top only after he angrily threw it there because of a tiff that he had with a Piney prostitute. The stories differed according to the possible ethnicity of "Ong." Sometimes Ong is Chinese, sometimes Dutch and sometimes the hat is most illogically a "top hat" worn by a gentleman.

Today Ong's Hat, like many of the ghost towns of the

Pinelands, exists in a flavorful lore only, commemorated by a lonely road between Buddtown and Early's Crossing. It's a Pine Barrens neighborhood that, despite inevitable incursions, maintains its character still close to the description of an *Atlantic Magazine* article published about the Pine Barrens in 1859:

"It is a region aboriginal in savagery, grand in the aspects of untrammeled Nature; where forests extend in uninterrupted lines over scores of miles; where we may wander a good day's journey without meeting half-a-dozen human faces; where stately deer will bound across our path, and bears dispute our passage through the cedar-brakes; where, in a word, we may enjoy the undiluted essence, the perfect wildness, of woodland life."

The undiluted essence of Feeno Bannon's life in the Pines was a house built upon the back of a pickup truck, which moved from one remote sanctuary to another, depending upon the human faces encountered during the day. Those who made him wary were almost always hikers, fishermen, a Boy Scout troop, or solitary inhabitant, like himself, just one more lonely Piney man who asked no questions and harbored no grudges.

Clyde Woolen stretched from inside his front door to the mailbox attached to the post. Bills, a subscription reminder from *Sports Afield*, a birthday card from his ninety-two-year-old Aunt Hannah in Delaware, and another business-sized envelope, also with a General Delivery postmark from Delaware. He plopped heavily in a faded green wicker rocker on the porch, and opened the strange piece of mail first. He read the cursive scrawl: "Ong's Hat, 7/12, 10 p, 2.5 m. fr. Ridge Rd." Through Vince, Clyde and Feeno had struck a deal that would take them as far as — who knew where? Would the relationship end in as much mystery as the beginning?

The first conversation between Feeno and Clyde occurred when Feeno phoned two days before. Feeno was alarmed and breathless about the news of Anthony Trapetto's mangled, rotting body being found on Vince Berardi's property in Medford.

"What's it mean?" Feeno had asked.

"It means that Scalesi's trying to pressure your buddy. Putting the squeeze on." Clyde took a few minutes to calm Feeno down, who was anxious, worried and confused.

"All because of me."

"You want me to hear your confession, or do you want to do something about it?"

"Vince doesn't know where I am, does he? I mean if he does..."

"Even I don't know where you are, pal, and let's keep it that way."

Feeno, leaning up against the dirty plastic enclosure of the phone booth outside of the Chatham General Store, plugged one ear with his finger as a large cement mixer rumbled down the country road.

"I guess I have an idea," he said finally, turning away as a couple of men in work clothes passed and entered the store's creaking screen door. Feeno glanced quickly to see if they were looking at him. They weren't; they were laughing, unconcerned with the gangly dude in the dirty Farmer John's and wild beard, wearing a painter's hat.

"I guess its time we had a look at those records," he said to Clyde. "I'll send you something this week."

Clyde, with a map beside him on the front seat, drove north on Route 206 until he came to the barely existing village of Beavertown. He looked in both directions into the black night before turning right onto Ridge Road and driving three miles to Ong's Hat Road, where he "zeroed" his odometer, turned southeast on the narrow but paved road and drove exactly 2.5 miles to Feeno's prescribed meeting place in a forested sea of nowhere. He waited in the darkness, ticking off the lonely minutes. No cars or trucks passed. With his flashlight, Clyde saw that it was 10:17 o'clock. Vince had warned him that Feeno was never on time for anything.

Clyde yawned and hunched down to nap but was brought to attention by the tapping on the passenger door window. Though Clyde had not known exactly what to expect about a man he had never laid eyes on before, he was stunned by the visage: A shadow, a beard in the light, eyes that gleamed.

"I hope you're who I think you are," he said, rolling down

the window. "And you're supposed to be the president of a bank?"

"Pretty good disguise, huh!" said the bumpkin who jumped in beside him, the knees of his lanky legs banging the dashboard. They shook hands. "Wow, I like your taste in automobiles, buddy. What is this, a Mustang?"

"Yeah, my baby," said Clyde, "GT-350."

Clyde was more interested in examining his new passenger than he was talking about his Mustang. He shined the light on Feeno, who wore his Atlanta Braves cap, a heavy flannel shirt buttoned to the neck and wrists. His shoes were scuffed work boots, but most outstanding were the Farmer Brown overalls draped on his tall frame. A Piney indeed. Clyde's flashlight momentarily lit the face of a brown beard striped with wiry strands of gray.

"So, you found out that this place is in Nutley, huh." Feeno asked, as Clyde headed the Mustang back to the turnpike. "What is it, a house where you said the bank examiners are?"

"Yeah, the FDIC rented the whole vacant house where they can examine your bank's records paper by paper. Are you sure you can find what you're looking for?"

"Who knows," said Feeno. "But I need to look and I need to think. Re-think is what I need to do. There's something I've been missing." He pulled a Slim Jim from an upper pocket and unwrapped it. "Supper," he said. "Want one?"

"Thank you, no," said Clyde. "I already ate."

After a pause, Clyde asked, "How long were you connected with Unity Savings?

"Two years. I replaced the first president. Guy named Battista."

"What happened to him?"

"I dunno, really. He just up and left is the way I heard it. Went west or some place."

"Do you think he was involved in the bank shenanigans?"

"No, I don't think so."

"That's not a very good answer," said Clyde.

"But," said Feeno. "It's something you would pick up. I know that when Russo hired me and introduced me to Rocco, they told me that the bank was going to expand. Go places. Right off the bat, the Teamsters locals offered me big-time certificates of deposit. All they wanted, they said, was a couple of sureties. For loans. So, big deal. That's standard bank procedure."

He put his head back on the seat, closed his eyes. "It all happened so fast. The good times. All gone. What puzzles me about all those months is what in the hell did the bank have to do with Jimmy Hoffa? And what in the hell connects me with Hoffa? What in the hell is it?"

"Do you think there's something there that happened when the other guy, Battista, was president?"

"You got me."

"You knew Hoffa?" asked Clyde.

"Met him a couple of times. At banquets, dinners, testimonials and stuff. Whenever he came to Jersey. He was a buddy with Provenzano back then. Way before they fell out."

"That happened in jail, I understand," said Clyde.

"Yeah, power struggle. Imagine that, those guys never stop."

The scenery changed from pitch dark night to distant lights of housing projects, refineries, TV towers. North Jersey unofficially begins with a line stretched from Trenton, the state capitol on the Delaware River, along I-195 east to Seaside Heights, a jaded little ocean town.

They left the turnpike and drove to Nutley, a New York City suburb of nice homes and shops, and welcome shade trees. Cruising down Franklin Avenue, Clyde turned left on Centre Street, looked for Union avenue. A sloppy rain had begun falling, giving street lights through the windshield a wobbly, drunken look. "We're looking for Floral Park," he said, squinting through the wiper sweeps. "Wipers. That's the only thing that doesn't work right with this car."

"There it is. Two blocks past." He drove slowly past a white-painted bungalow with green trim, shining black in the rain. The property had a small yard and old iron fence, similar to those that embraced school yards in years past. Clyde circled the block, mostly tree-lined with other small houses and a Citgo station on the corner. He went twice around the block and parked.

"Let's go," Clyde said, slamming the driver's side door and

holding a newspaper over his head.

"Where the hell are we?" asked Feeno. "I thought you said it was back there."

"It is back there."

They walked in the rain, two blocks back to the bungalow. Feeno poked his shoulders up, trying hard to push his head down into his shirt collar.

"This way," said Clyde, when they had reached a lot full of weeds and a cellar hole of a torn-down building. The rain came down harder by the time they reached the back step of the house.

Clyde examined the lock on the back door, pulled a thin piece of brick strap from his jacket pocket and slid it between the door and the frame, jiggling it until he felt the metal and the click. They were inside.

"I'm surprised they didn't have more security on this place," said Feeno wonderingly.

"Don't sweat it," said Clyde. "I doubt if everything in this building is an original document. These would be working copies. The original records are probably stored in an Evidence Room somewhere."

They donned surgical gloves and walked through a kitchen that was a real kitchen, with a refrigerator, stove, table and chairs, plus dirty dishes in the sink. Their flashlights, which they kept aimed low toward the floor, picked up a dining room full of filing cabinets. Same as the living room, which also had two computers sitting on stands; there were four tables and chairs, all of them strewn with papers. Feeno looked around, his brain quickly picking up a system. One area for deposits, another for loans with subsets for "secured" and "unsecured." The latter is where they would begin. They ignored the computers after unsuccessfully trying to type in a variety of passwords.

Up against one wall of the dining room was a stack of industrial shelves, each containing cardboard file cartons. Feeno read: "Asset Backed Securities, Account Control Agreements, Balloon Loans, Capital Markets." All familiar stuff. But what?

He and Clyde bumped shoulders: "What the hell am I looking for, Feeno?"

"Fuckers got all kinds of systems going here." Feeno said.

187

He half-sat on the edge of a battered metal desk. "How many guys did your buddy say were working here?"

"Three or four. All bank examiners."

"All FDIC?"

"I dunno," said Clyde, who froze suddenly. He put a finger to Feeno's mouth and switched off his flashlight. Feeno did the same.

They stood still in the dark. From outside, a shadowy light rolled around the room through the window. A passing car, tires hissing in the rain. Then came a rasping sound of metal against wood. Scraping, pausing, scraping again. It came from the kitchen area.

Clyde signaled for Feeno to stay where he was. He rose and subconsciously patted his left breast, his reassurance that the .38 was there if needed, something he had done on a countless number of occasions in hundreds of crime scenarios as an ATF agent. Considering that this was an initiation into the nether side of the lawless line, his heart thumped loudly. To be busted by former associates in the FBI or by the local police would be an ignominy he didn't deserve.

Clyde's back hugged the wall as he inched toward the kitchen. He froze next to the kitchen window next to the back door. Semi-shadows wheeled again around the room, cast by distant headlights. When the traffic occasionally subsided, the kitchen was painted in near darkness.

He waited. Whoever wanted inside had finally forced the screws of the flimsy window lock to tear from the frame. The lock fell to the floor. The window slid up and a single leg in jeans stabbed into the kitchen. Clyde waited. A jacketed arm came through, then a shoulder followed by the back of a slender figure. Clyde saw the lettering, "Regal Aces" written blood red on the black leather.

When the head appeared is when Clyde thrust both hands into the neck of the jacket, hauling the intruder quickly through the window. He spun him around and pushed whoever it was up against the wall.

The boy, probably about sixteen, shuddered, his eyes were pie plates. His cap bounced to the floor.

"What's your name?" whispered Clyde, his face only two or three inches from the boy's.

"J-J-Jermane!" he answered.

"Where do you live?"

"Over there, the projects!"

"I see," said Clyde, relaxing his grip on the front of the boy's jacket, only to subsequently tighten it. The latex gloves created added leverage in lifting the frightened boy nearly off the floor.

"Jermane, listen carefully."

The boy nodded.

"I'm gonna let you go, but if you come through that window again I'm gonna cut your nuts off! You understand?"

"Yes, yessir!"

"Get out of here, and remember nothing. You were never here tonight. This place doesn't exist."

As he loosened his grasp and the boy began to relax, Clyde grabbed the boy's hand and pressed it against the lapel of his jacket, where the kid felt the outline of the gun. "You understand, Jermane?"

Within seconds, the kid was out the window and racing to the cyclone fence at the rear of the property. In a single leap, the flat of his right sneaker touched the top of the fence and he vaulted over. Clyde switched on the flashlight and checked his watch. "After midnight. Let's get the hell out of here."

By the time they crossed Route 1 leading east to Jersey City, the rain had stopped. "That son of a bitch! That kid. Did you see him jump that goddamned fence? One single bound, and he's over it. I'd like to lock these kids into a gym somewhere so they can do nothing but play basketball."

"I'd like to lock myself into that house and be invisible for a couple of days," said Feeno. "That's what I'd like to do."

The night, the foray had been a huge disappointment. They stayed silent until the Mustang turned onto Ong's Hat Road. It was after three a.m. and they were tired.

"Wait a minute," Feeno warned. "Stay here a minute. We have to talk. We have to go back."

"For sure we have to go back," said Clyde grinning. "You never get what you're looking for on the first try."

Feeno was jumpy. "Just before that kid came along, there was a box I was going after. It had 'California' written on it."

"What do you think?"

"I think they divided the country."

"Well, we're not going back up there tonight."

"No, not tomorrow either," Clyde said, looking at the time once more. "We need time to think. We also need someplace where we can talk without the phone. Is there a place we can use as a message drop?"

Feeno directed him to drive about 100 feet ahead. "Okay, turn right here."

"Turn right?" said Clyde. "There's nothing there but trees."

"Trust me, turn right now," ordered Feeno. Suddenly, as the headlights hit the pines, an opening barely wide enough for a car showed itself. There was a definite road of sorts. Clyde drove in and within five hundred feet his car was enveloped by dark forest. He stopped, doused the headlights and observed a night and scene that was dense with foliage and devilishly dark.

Feeno removed his baseball cap. "Here's the mailbox. He got out of the car and folded it into the junction of branches of a pitch pine. The significance of Feeno's Hat in the tree was lost on neither. They both laughed.

Over the next two days Clyde made phone calls; he spent time in Newark going over old indictments. He gleaned from old friends in the FBI and the Strike Force the necessary background information in the Hoffa case. He knew a couple of state cops who were part of an undercover team a year or two ago, setting themselves up in a phony trucking company in Parsippany, working the North Jersey roads and the transport system, diagnosing familiar hijacking locations and ways and means. The state cops even had their own softball team, which played in a league of other trucking companies. Clyde picked up names. Who was a good Teamster, who was a bad Teamster?

He examined OC charts, past and present, both in New York and Jersey, studying diagonal connection lines from one photo of a bad guy to another, then to another and so on. Some charts had so many crisscrosses they appeared to be designed by a drunken spider.

Three days later Clyde and Feeno met again at the mailbox in the woods.

Looking at Feeno, who was seated beside him, he said, "We need a third person; we can't go in there again without a lookout at the window."

Feeno looked at him blankly. "No, nothing doing. You're not getting Vince into this."

"I'm not sure we have a choice," said Clyde. "Besides I already asked him. And he's rarin' to go. He's a tough little bastard. Before, he was scared, now he's pissed. He wants to find out what's going on with this crap as much as you do."

"I don't think it's a good idea, him knowing that I'm around here. I got the guy in enough trouble already."

"What difference does it make? He still doesn't know where you are. Even I don't know where you are. Going into that goddamned pinelands is like jumping into the middle of the ocean."

Chapter 31: NUTLEY REVISITED

Feeno emerged from the thicket of needled trees like a dark specter, unrecognizable even after slipping into the back seat of the Mustang behind Clyde, who did a U-turn on Ong's Hat Road to head to the turnpike. Not a single, other vehicle passed in either direction.

Vince, from the passenger seat, turned and stared. Finally a half-smile overtook the face that had been full of curiosity and bewilderment. "You always were bizarre."

Feeno wore a gray cotton jacket above worn jeans, and from his shaggy head the logo of a toothy, happy Indian on his Braves baseball cap stared back. Vince noted that the whole vision was loopy.

"I take it there's no Gap outlet where you're living," Vince said.

Feeno answered, "None." His smile was weak.

There remained silence for a half-mile, with Clyde content to let the two once close friends analyze their present relationship. Feeno leaned toward the front seat, laid his hand firmly on Vince's shoulder: "Buddy, I don't know how to express this."

"Don't, just don't. I don't want an apology. Leave it. Leave it." Vince looked hard at Feeno and just as deliberately, faced the windshield and studied the passing scene, a 7-Eleven next to a laundromat in a little strip mall.

As Feeno slumped back into the seat, Vince asked Clyde, "Just what is it we're doing, anyway?"

The car jumped onto Exit 7 of the turnpike, which was another marker of the unofficial boundary of South Jersey from the chemical and concrete north. Places like Cranbury Station and Grover's Mill, where Martians landed in Orson Welles's old radio hoax, slipped by, which were just a few miles from Princeton, the Ivy League seat of learning just down the road.

"I got some background we should go over," Clyde said, steering the conversation as well as the car. He turned into the off ramp of the Joyce Kilmer Rest Center. Stopping in a remote, dark corner of the lot, away from the tall lights glaring down above the parked cars and trucks, he turned the key and felt the engine of the little Mustang tremble to quiet.

"Who wants coffee?" Vince asked. Both partners said yes. Feeno yelled, his voice catching up to Vince, who was already a hundred feet away: "Hey, get me a cheeseburger. Everything. Raw onions."

Clyde tapped the steering wheel with his heavy fingers. Headlights beamed in both directions on the highway, backed on either side by woods and small houses. "You wish you could go in there too, don't you?"

"How'd you guess? It's pretty lonely in the woods."

"What do you do all day?"

"I work on how to get out of this mess. And when I get tired, I do horses."

"Horses?"

"A system, system. I've been doing systems since I was a teen-ager."

"I had this one once. Using jockeys. Got seven years of records of performances, averaged them out, worked out probabilities."

"It worked, of course," said Clyde, sardonically as he turned to look at Feeno.

"It did, it did. I played the jockeys, not the horses. Only trouble was..."

Clyde grinned, his small mouth widening enough to show the molar gap on the right side. His eyes crinkled. He enjoyed Feeno, could see easily how people tried to take in the rush of Feeno's personality, his capricious funniness, the unpredictability of his thought track.

"The system necessitated being at the track every day. You had to put down your bets every day. I stopped it when I almost got hit by a train racing to get to the crossing before I did. I was late getting down to Delaware Park."

Clyde was chuckling aloud: "The horses can kill you, can't

they?"

Vince returned. Feeno took big mouthfuls of his cheeseburger and sipped the hot coffee.

"So, Feeno," said Clyde after a while. "You want your freedom restored. Vince, you want your reputation back."

"Yeah, the good one," answered Vince.

"The key to everything," said Clyde, starting the engine and backing away from the wooded boundary of the lot, "is, I believe, Hoffa. We find out what happened to him and we get both of you guys off the hook. Just figure it out. Why all the intensity on New Jersey for a labor leader who was most likely done away with in Michigan? What role did the Jersey Teamsters play in it and when you break that down, we find out what role your bank played in it."

"Well, what's the real Jersey connection?" asked Vince.

"It starts with when Hoffa was sent to prison by Bobby Kennedy. One of Hoffa's jail mates was Tony Provenzano. He was the boss of Local 560, up in Union City."

Clyde began summarizing the facts he had gleaned from other investigators, plus newspapers and records that were public knowledge.

"Hoffa spent four years in Lewisburg for jury tampering. And then Nixon pardoned him in 1971."

"Why would Nixon pardon him?" Vince said, sipping his coffee.

"Well," said Clyde, looking left before gunning the accelerator to join the swift flow of northward-bound cars and trucks. "The Teamsters were longtime supporters of Nixon, and besides, why wouldn't Nixon like to turn the tables on a Kennedy? Pardon Bobby's worst enemy. Either way, Hoffa now figures he's going to get back into business, get back the Teamsters presidency. What he didn't know is that the pardon included a provision that he never be allowed back into union politics, never hold office again. This doesn't stop Hoffa. He's one of those guys, you say 'no' to him, that just lights his fires. So he gets his lawyers busy, then he tries to enlist his old buddies into going to bat for him. That includes Tony Pro from Jersey. But Pro and Hoffa — when they were in Lewisburg prison together — they had a major falling out. Hoffa blamed Pro and all the other Mafia guys connected to the

Teamsters for causing him trouble, attracting attention. He called Pro 'a bum.' I heard they had a real fight, somebody had to separate them.

"Nevertheless, Hoffa gets out and he needs Provenzano, plus Russell Bufalino. He's the head of the mob in northeastern Pennsylvania and a big shot Teamster. Hoffa, I think, signed his own death warrant. He kept bad-mouthing all the guys whose help he needed. Behind their backs. Said he was going to clean up the union. Throw the mob out, probably starting with the Genoveses and Tony Pro's buddies.

"I thought Tony Pro was a Teamster," said Vince.

"He was, but he's also a capo in the Genovese family. And Sal Briguglio and the Andretta brothers. They're all in Local 560.

"Hoffa was a magnet," said Clyde. "He attracted trouble all around. Who the hell needed Jimmy Hoffa now? Nobody, absolutely nobody. All of his successors, starting with Frank Fitzsimmons, who took over after Hoffa, were just as capable of stealing money as Hoffa was. So who needed Hoffa? But he kept trying. The more he tried, the closer it got to him being whacked.

"So, finally Provenzano and Hoffa agreed to a sit-down. That was to happen July 30, in '75, at that restaurant outside of Detroit, the Red Fox restaurant. This was a meeting arranged by a go-between, Anthony Giacalone, the Detroit mobster and friend of both Hoffa and Provenzano. So, Hoffa's on time for the meeting, always on time, but he waits, and he waits. That's the last anybody sees him.

"When the FBI comes in, after Hoffa's disappearance, they bring tracking dogs, pick up a scent in the back seat of the car owned by Tony Jack's son. That car was there, at the scene of the disappearance. And that's when it ended. Hoffa vanishes. Poof. Into thin air. Jersey connection? Yeah, big time Jersey connection."

The Mustang picked up speed, switching from one lane to the other. The Jersey Turnpike was a northward flowing river, running from four lanes in the south to as many as a wide, twelve-lane mess through the New York metro area. The men in the car were nervously eager. Vince sat stiffly in the front seat, not listening to the rest of Clyde's retelling. His heart was going like a jungle drum. He thought of Julie, and little Gloria and little Patty.

"You know how it all points to Provenzano?" Clyde said. "He never left New Jersey on the day Hoffa disappeared, even though he had agreed to the meet. He alibied. A too tight alibi. Stupid and simple. He was playing cards in Union City, he said. But Sally Bugs, Tony Pro's right hand? He was there. He was in Detroit. He was witnessed in the parking lot of that restaurant. He may have been in the car when Hoffa took his last ride. He took the fifth before the Grand Jury. About a zillion times. And he gets killed in Little Italy in New York just this year."

"So what happened next?" Feeno asked. "Was Hoffa killed in the car or...?"

"The FBI thinks he may have gone along in that car only with people that he trusted. Was he killed in the car? I doubt it. There was no blood evidence, no bullet holes. So he may have been taken some place else and killed."

When they reached Nutley and parked two streets away from the little house, Vince's throbbing heart caused the sweat to stand out on his forehead and drip from his arm pits. He was to stand sentinel by the front window, on the alert for anyone approaching. It was an easy enough task, but his palms were damp and his stomach cold. Every car, every truck idling by on the quiet tree-lined street scared him.

In the living room behind him he could hear Feeno opening and shutting filing cabinet drawers as quietly as he could, and in the dining room Clyde was going through the same process, looking at the labels on filing boxes.

"There's gotta be a pattern here," muttered Feeno, half to himself, trying to put his banking expertise in the brain of an FDIC accountant. "How would they go about this?"

He decided not to go through any of the cardboard filing boxes piled on the metal shelves until he studied every label, looking for a system. Fifteen minutes passed when Feeno said softly, "Here's something." He had pulled down a heavy box labeled "SAR." "Clyde, that reference sheet there on the table, the one we think is a key."

Clyde fumbled the papers, finally finding the one they

needed: "Here it is." Scrawled in cursive on the outside of the folder were the words, 'Suspicious Activity Reports.' "Here it is."

He and Clyde huddled. Vince heard one of them say "Michigan drawer" and Feeno said, running his finger down the list, "here's a Giacalone. Wasn't that...?"

"Tony Jack Giacalone," said Clyde. "He's the guy who arranged the meeting. What's it say?"

"Nothing," said Feeno, who had turned to the large file box. "It's just a written memo with an address and phone number."

Feeno continued thumbing file folders toward the rear of the carton. "Here's another Michigan address," said Feeno. "Central Sanitation, Ham-tram-something. I can't pronounce it, but it's in Michigan. This is a loan approval. Wow! Eighty-five thousand dollars!

"I swear to God," Feeno added, his mouth jumping open. He felt a curl in his gut. He stared at Clyde, eyes popping. "I have no memory of this."

Clyde took the papers from Feeno's hands. "It doesn't say what Central Sanitation is. Sounds like some kind of laundry. Eighty-five thousand? What's the date?

"It's a scribble," said Feeno. "Can't really read it. It's not my handwriting. It's not Carmen's either. She's my secretary. Was my secretary. It looks like seventy-five. Can't read it."

"Who signed for the bank?," Clyde asked. He looked up, staring at Feeno, who looked at the papers. On the last page, where the signature was needed for approval by the bank, it read clearly, "Joseph A. Bannon," listed as "President and chief loan officer."

"I swear to Christ," Feeno said. "I have no knowledge of this. Let me look at that signature."

After a minute of study, he concluded in a tone of resignation: "It looks like my signature. I don't know."

"Well, we don't have the luxury of arguing about it." said Clyde. "Give it here."

He put the papers on a table, then pulled out a miniature Minox camera. While Feeno held the light, Clyde snapped pictures.

Hastily, they searched other areas in the file cabinets. Clyde asked Feeno to find other documents where his real signature was affixed. Clyde took six of those papers and photographed the signatures.

Busy bending over the desk in the dining room, neither paid much attention when Vince whispered hastily, with determination: "Somebody's out front."

Two men were shuffling past on the sidewalk about forty feet from the front door. They appeared to be talking to one another but with the traffic noise, Vince could hear or discern nothing. But they walked on, and by the shuffling and slowness of their pace, it seemed that both were drunk. FBI guys pretending to be inebriated?

"Okay," said Clyde. "I think we have enough for now. Let's get out of here."

Heading south, the three men remained silent for most of the trip, each thinking separate thoughts. Finally, Clyde said: "That signature. Your signature, Feeno. I'm thinking just how clever those bastards were."

"What do you mean?" Vince asked.

"These guys are smarter than we give them credit for," said Clyde. "They have insulated themselves, because it's the bank that is making the loans, not the Teamsters, not the Scalesis, not the Provenzanos. It's you, Feeno! I don't like to say it, pal, but you're the one everybody is going to be looking at."

Vince looked hard at Feeno and could tell by his blank visage that he already knew how deeply in trouble he was. But Feeno said, "Yeah, but I got the other Aces."

"What's that?" Vince asked.

"The tapes, miles and miles of secretly recorded tapes. I know about the heroin they smuggled from Italy, the extortion of trucking company executives. I got all of that. Scalesi. You know he pissed in the mouth of a dead guy? He put another guy's eyes out. Did you know that? That's why they call him 'Thumbs'. And not just all those loans. The loan sharking. They threatened one guy who didn't pay up by tracking his kids going to school. Then they let him know about it. And the hijacking. They stopped trucks and swiped dresses and shit the minute they drove through the tunnel from the garment district. And guys they whacked.

Jesus Christ, that list is as long as your arm.

"It was all right here," said Feeno, tapping his chest. "Right in the little wire. I wore a wire for so long it's a miracle I have any skin left."

Chapter 32: ENDANGERED SPECIES

Inside his truck camper, by the light of the Coleman lantern and using the folded up camp stove as a desk, Feeno studied his signatures from different directions, tilting his head as he observed them. Florid and distinguished, he thought. He had transcribed "Joseph A. Bannon" several times on different sheets of paper as Clyde had instructed, then put the papers flat in a plastic bag, which he rolled and secured with a rubber band.

Clyde picked up the signatures the next day at the "mailbox" in the Ong's Hat tree. Feeno had substituted the Atlanta Braves hat, which had been the first mailbox, with a waterproof canvas bag, colored dark green to match the foliage of the pine tree. The bag could not be seen from more than a few feet away. Each time he fetched the bag, Clyde grunted and squirmed to reach it, scratching his face on the pine needles and branches.

By now Feeno was growing accustomed to his over-all surroundings, but like a bird changing his neighborhood, rarely parking the camper in the same secretive place for more than three days. He moved the first time after voices awakened him from sleep. It was morning. Wispy layers of fog had lapped over the trees. He put one eye up to the small window. Perhaps sixty feet away the undergrowth of bushes trembled as two men picked their way through it. Feeno thought he saw a thin fishing rod being carried, and perhaps a tackle box.

The voices grew distant, then could not be heard. He waited an hour, then drove away, learning later as he became more familiar with the woods that a pond about one hundred yards wide and twice as long lay only a quarter-mile from where he had slept. The source of the pond was not a stream or brook, but came from deep within the soil, as part of the magnificent aquifer which in some areas was believed to be seventy feet deep. Joseph Wharton, the Nineteenth Century industrialist who founded the University of

Pennsylvania's Wharton School, purchased one hundred fifty square miles of the Pinelands in the 1870s and had a plan to export pure water to Philadelphia. The state of New Jersey said nothing doing.

Because of the acidic soil from a million pine trees, the water in most places was tea-colored but transparent and clean. Another of New Jersey's anachronisms. Some paths in the forest were so narrow the shrubs and brush grasped the fenders of the truck as it rocked along. These were paths to nowhere which Feeno liked because they hid his truck so cleverly that only an eagle or osprey could find it. The deer that flicked across these paths were gone in a flash. Likewise, raccoons and muskrats which surfaced on the river banks could count on thick vegetation for protection. Feeno never saw any of the Pine Barrens tree frogs, although he heard their crazy nighttime din. They were among the more than one hundred endangered species in the Pinelands. He counted himself among them.

His first explorations were by foot, oriented only by careful study of the geodetic maps that he laid out each night on his sleeping bag in the truck. As he walked the sandy roads, he carried his newly purchased engineer's compass in his right hand, consulting it frequently to make sure he could find his way back. Occasionally the road split to avoid dips and troughs carved into the sand by previous travel. Most times the paths would join again several yards later, or remain separate, never to join again and taking the unwary hiker in directions that tended to encircle several miles of consistent forest.

Feeno was led in this manner to a town on the map named Hampton Furnace. He knew it was one of the old and abandoned iron forges which made cannonballs and shot for the Continental Army during the American Revolution, but he was surprised to see an interchange of multiple sandy roads and paths, meeting and continuing as haphazard paths in all directions, a tumbled spaghetti thoroughfare that was as equally as confusing as the multiple connections of turnpikes and parkways just forty miles away in North Jersey.

In the midst of this interchange was nothing except a broad field dotted with birches, pin oaks and pitch pines, with no trace of the forge and buildings that kept busy during the days of the bog iron industry. Like the paper mills, grist mills, saw mills and glass works, they vanished over time. Occasionally Feeno came across an abandoned clapboard building, its wood siding now weathered almost black, leaning against or hanging on for life to a brick chimney whose days were also numbered.

In case of an emergency such as pursuit by someone, he mapped a major escape route paralleling the Mullica and Batsto rivers which flowed southeast toward the Atlantic shore. There were dirt roads through the pines leading between Route 206 at Atsion and Route 542 in Batsto. Atsion and Batsto were major Piney towns in the more civilized industrial decades of the area's history. Feeno avoided Batsto, which had been turned into a restored tourist attraction of several old buildings reminiscent of that period in the town's life when it had manufactured iron at its busy forge.

Atsion attracted tourists also to its large lake for swimming and several campgrounds nearby. Where the town center had been there remained only the shells of the huge old cotton mill that had stood there for years, along with a fallen down ice house and store. Nearby was the Atsion station of the Central Railway of New Jersey, which operated until the 1920s.

At night Feeno's mind wrestled with the truth about how much longer he could endure nothing but his own company. He often had to force himself away from the easy conversation that he enjoyed at the Chatsworth store where he bought his provisions. Every few days he purchased ice, fresh fruit, lunch meat and bread. The store was fairly well stocked with supplies and equipment indigenous with the outdoors. But it didn't have everything. It was time to make another visit to the all-night sporting goods super store.

A mirage of heat shimmered from the parking lot asphalt as Feeno drove to a corner flanked on one side by a marshy field of cattails. Beyond the wavering low gray sky was the outline of Atlantic City.

He gasped with welcome relief as the blanket of cool air fell upon him inside the store. His eyes scanned the bank of cashiers as he walked to the aisle containing green and butt metal camp stoves. He chose two gallons of Coleman fuel and six packs of wicks for his lanterns. His disappointment at not seeing the small, cute girl named Edna was surprisingly profound until he remembered that she worked nights. Still, he had a hard time concentrating. He finally chose a new lightweight sleeping bag to replace the heavy duty one he had originally purchased, which experience had now taught him would have been good enough for survival at the Arctic Circle.

He returned to the front of the store slightly dejected until, with surprising delight he saw her, stuffing a large plastic bag for a portly camper who had two kids in tow. Edna chatted and smiled at her customers.

"Are you always so cheery this early in the day?" asked Feeno as he dumped the camouflage clothing on the counter.

Her smile faded to a puzzled look, then "Hi!" Her greeting was high-pitched and sincere with surprise. It made him feel good when she added, "What a nice beard. I didn't recognize you," and added, "I wondered if you were still around."

He wanted to take some time and look at her tanned arms, neck and face, the line of slight freckles upon her fantastically pert little nose.

"I'm still out in the woods; I like it there."

"I'm not a woods person," she said. "I like to hike in the woods and jump in a lake on a hot day but that's it for me."

She keyed the items into the cash register and began thrusting the sleeping bag into a large yellow bag marked with black letters, "The Great Outdoors."

"I need a bath and a bed every night," Edna added. "I don't know how people can stand all those bugs and stuff."

"You get used to it," said Feeno, grinning broadly.

Two more customers pulled their shopping baskets behind Feeno, who hated breaking off his brief conversation.

He paid cash and as he was starting to walk away, he turned and asked, "What are you doing here in the daytime; don't you work nights anymore?"

"Not this week," she said. "One of the other cashiers went on leave to visit her mother. The woman's ill. So this week I'm working days."

"That's great," said Feeno. "Well, take care." He paused, and added, "Edna."

"You too," she said.

He got to his truck and placed the purchases on the front seat beside him. Before driving off he scanned the parking lot, searching to see if the kind of people who could end his freedom were approaching. As he drove away, he said to himself, "She doesn't even know my name." He hit the brakes, skidding to a stop in the sand pebble drive of a Sunoco station. Looking both ways in a hurry, he sped back to the store.

Edna was bending beneath the counter to pick out a clean register tape. As she rose Feeno stood there.

"Edna," he asked, and hesitated, scratching his chin and beard. "What time do you get off work? And by the way, my name is Bob."

Chapter 33: THE DRIVE-IN

Far away on the big outdoor movie screen, Sylvester Stallone was kicking high down Delaware Avenue, wearing a gray sweat suit, pumping his fists, running and shadow boxing to the heart-pounding theme of "Flying High Now," which Feeno noticed at a glance put tears in Edna's eyes. Feeno thanked Rocky as Edna squeezed into his shoulder, dabbing at her wet eyes. He smelled her hair and kissed it.

When the screen flashed a large bag of popcorn and frothing soda in a big paper cup and the "Intermission" message appeared, people began opening car doors. Some of the girls smoothed their skirts and dresses with their hands. One hurriedly buttoned her blouse.

A line of chattering, mostly young moviegoers stood and waited to get up to the order window of the low-pitched, whitewashed concrete-block snack bar. When Feeno spotted a cop in dark blue leaning against a car fender, he moved out of line and went to the Men's Room, hiding in a stall for a couple of minutes. Was the cop staring at Feeno or was he simply myopic?

Coming back to the truck, Feeno carried the floppy cardboard tray carefully, both hands beneath it, eyes on the cokes wobbling above the cheeseburgers and large fries. He settled into the truck's front seat with a grunt, balancing the tray on his sharp knees, then readjusted the heavy metal speaker on his side window. Edna took delicate, small bites of her cheeseburger. Feeno was starved and ate his in four gulps. Anxious. There were a thousand things he wanted to tell her, and so much he couldn't say, especially about his firsthand knowledge of the narrow streets of Philly in the *Rocky* movie. He wanted to tell her that he had seen a Van Gogh exhibit at the Philadelphia Art Museum just years before, and that he had worked on the docks on the street where Rocky ran.

Just recalling the recent lie that his name was "Bob Price"

brought a grimace. *"Bob Price, Jesus Christ! Is that the best I can do?"* But the story that he was camping in the Pine Barrens while working in construction was a fib he could live with.

Edna's recent life's tale was delivered unremorsefully, with a matter of dull factness that revealed she had told the story of her marriage and divorce a few times before:

"My marriage lasted, believe it or not, six months," she said, retrieving a crumb that had dropped to her chest, picking it carefully with the tips of her thumb and forefinger and dropping it onto her tongue. "He told me he worked in NASCAR and that he was a substitute pit crew member who went from team to team whenever there was an opening." Her mind's eye drifted to the night time races at Darlington. She showed up just to surprise him, that new husband, even paid extra to get into Gasoline Alley and watch him. She had pictured him in tight-fitting coveralls with sewn-in labels. Then she saw him, standing behind a plywood table set on saw horses, "selling those little doodads, matchbox cars and tiny trophies and checkered flags and all that stuff at some guy's trailer.

"He'd been lying to me all that time. And that wasn't the only thing he lied about. Flora Jean, Flora Jean! I found out about her through some bartender."

Edna said her decision to start life over in Atlantic City was an easy one to make. Her sister and brother-in-law had come to Jersey from Las Vegas where they had worked as dealers. They wanted to return to the East Coast.

Sitting in the drive-in's exit to Route 130, keeping his eye on the traffic cop waving his arm in a circle, Feeno resisted the urge to ask Edna if she wanted to stop for a drink. As dark as it was, the headlights from the heavy traffic made him uncomfortable. He had already had too much public exposure for one day. He told her that he had to get up early, but driving back to the east, before they reached the Bayshore Motel, she had begun chattering on about her "nice view from this little dock" attached to the rear of the motel.

"I want to see your dock," said Feeno as he parked the truck in front of Room 102, which was one of a half-dozen lined in a concrete row with wooden pots of plastic geraniums fancying up the front. A long metal green and white canopy covered a sidewalk in front of the rooms facing the highway. It was midnight and still cars and trucks, Atlantic City traffic, whizzed by in constant movement.

The tide in the darkened back bay had ebbed to low and from the dock they could smell the oddly sweet stench of the marsh, an odor that excited newly arrived visitors to the Jersey shore. The eastern sky was flooded with the lights of the city. Feeno slapped at a mosquito but vowed that no bug could destroy this moment, this single night of respite from running and hiding. They kissed. Edna turned with her back to Feeno and let him fold his arms around her stomach. He could feel her breathing increase. He pressed closer and pulled.

She put her head back onto his shoulder, looking up at the dark sky, then closed her eyes. And she took his hand and moved it to her breast where he felt it move in rhythm with her hurried breaths. The softness of the breath made him put his lips deeper into her neck, kissing it over and over. He put his other hand between her legs and rubbed, first lightly, lifting the skirt with his fingers.

Not even the quick fear that his truck might somehow be recognized as that of a fugitive could stir him too swiftly from the bed, even though the camper truck was parked out of view of the highway on the south bay side of the motel. Sunlight crept around the edge of the building and began its slow climb to the west. She was asleep on her stomach, with one arm beneath her head and face, which was turned away from him. Her small back and shoulders were tanned golden.

He lightly touched and noticed how different they were from Angela's. Edna had a little meat on her bones, which he liked. Small white dimples appeared when he pressed with his finger. On her back were two small bug bites, tiny red welts that would heal in a day or two. He laid his hand across her skin, feeling the heat of her shoulders flow into his fingers. He kissed the gold of her back and her hair, then carefully left the bed. She slept still. He dressed quietly and left.

Chapter 34: HAMTRAMCK

Daylight was fading over the cold, old buildings sitting in an abject row on Moran Street. From what little he knew about the town, Clyde had figured that Hamtramck, Michigan, had been named for some Eastern European luminary from decades past. Besides having a large Polish representation, Hamtramck melted a slew of ethnics. So he was surprised to learn that the honor for the city's origins belonged to a French Canadian, Colonel Jean Francois Hamtramck, who had been the commander of the Continental Army in Detroit when the British were defeated and kicked out of the area in the American effort towards independence.

Moran Street ran north just a few blocks from the big Cadillac assembly plant. Clyde parked his rental car across the street from the building at 8215. He had flown into Detroit only two hours before and though late in the day, he felt anxious to dig some truth. There was too much to learn and too little time.

He looked long and hard, pleading with the two-story nondescript building to give up its secrets. What he observed was a cement wall on the ground floor; with a second floor facade of some kind of white metal. An overhead door that was painted gray and appeared capable of welcoming large trucks was in the center of the building, with "Central" painted in black letters against an orange background above it. On each side of the door were two grimy concrete columns, whose white and orange paint had faded years ago. Above the pillar on the right was printed, "Community Service." The one above the left read, "Good Neighbor".

"What they hell do they do here?" he asked himself. *"And what would a bank in New Jersey be doing lending this joint eighty-five thousand bucks?"*

Checking his watch, he walked across the street and tried the front door, guessing correctly that business hours had concluded for the day. He began walking around the block, thankful for the exercise after two-hours in the knee-cramping space of the coach flight from Philadelphia. As he strolled, he took in a neighborhood that ranked between squalor and indifference. He rounded the block and stopped outside the Corner Bar & Grille located a half block from Central Sanitation. A closed-in delivery truck, "Murphy's Beverages," stood next to the curb. A man was unloading metal kegs of draft beer, tilting them on their sides, and carefully and deftly guiding each one to the street, letting them bounce on a heavy pad at his feet.

The Corner Bar & Grille was constructed of brick that had been painted an uninviting black. Two tiny windows advertised "Schlitz" in cursive yellow neon in one and in the other, a red tube of "Budweiser".

Clyde was a man of vast experience who knew the good sense of inhaling outside air one last time before pushing open the door to a dark barroom veiled by the thick cigarette smoke of shots and beer drinkers. The wooden bar itself was dented and dirty, stained with rings of beer glasses, scarred with burns from dropped butts, while from a corner juke box Rod Stewart pleaded, in his appealingly grating treble, "Do Ya Think I'm Sexy?"

The bartender was heavy set and baldish except for a dyed black comb over. A waist-high apron bore a week's worth of grunge. Clyde set himself up in mid-bar. Not trusting the presumed cleanliness of a glass, he ordered a bottle of Coors and drank directly from it. On the TV, Ronald Reagan, who was being touted as presidential, was seen smiling and waving over his shoulder as he limped down a hallway.

"I like Reagan," Clyde said to the bartender as he hefted a handful of peanuts to his mouth, "but he always walks like he just fell off a horse."

"He probably did," said a short, skinny little fellow whose ancient acne was half-concealed in a half-week beard of gray thistle. He grinned, bearing old teeth that were beige in color. He wore a guinea tee stretched tight over his thin frame.

Another graybeard, perhaps a retiree, said, "He rides a lot. I read it in a magazine. He's a real cowboy. For real." He looked around for confirmation.

"Bullshit. He's a fuckin' actor."

"Bullshit. He's got a ranch in California. Big goddamned ranch. Rides them palominos."

"No, you're thinkin' Roy Rogers," said a fat middle-ager in a Detroit Tigers cap. "He's the one that rode palominos."

"Trigger."

"Yeah, Trigger." The man thought carefully, looking away from the TV. "You know how many Triggers there were?"

The bartender smiled. "Probably a lot. Horses don't live too long."

"Seven," the other man said. "Seven Triggers. That's what Roy Rogers had."

"I bet chew can't name Gene Autry's horse," said the fat man.

"Champion," yelled a man sitting in a booth against the wall. He nearly choked with a mouthful of pickled egg. "Champion could do tricks."

"I seen Champion and Gene Autry when I was a kid," said another elderly type. "At a rodeo in Detroit."

Clyde smiled broadly at the man, thoroughly enjoying himself. He hoisted his Coors, toasting the bartender. "Have one on me."

"Thanks," said the bartender, and as he reached into the cooler, Clyde asked him casually, "Hey, that place down the street, Central Sanitation, what the hell do they do there? What is it, a laundry?"

"Laundry?" The bartender smiled and leaned back against the bar. "Nah, they're into waste disposal. Commercial waste, mostly. Big trucks, big loads of trash from all over."

"Well, how do they get rid of it there?" Clyde asked.

"They got one of those big shredding machines," said the bartender. "And incinerator. Ask Al. He works there." He nodded toward a muscular man about fifty wearing a black tee shirt. Dirt was engrained in the elbows he had propped on the bar. His nose was big and veiny, pink kind of veins. Eyes dark and recessed. No smile on this guy. Next to an empty shot glass was a half-filled beer which Al grasped lightly. The beer lacked a foamy head, telling Clyde how poorly was the dishwashing in this emporium.

"We got a compactor too. Takes trash and squeezes it into a small cube."

"Yeah, and an incinerator," piped up a third drinker sporting a malicious smile. "To take care of what the shredder can't do." In the mirror behind the bar, Clyde saw the man wink at the bartender, who smiled and looked down at the floor.

The next morning Clyde visited the city Bureau of Records. After ten minutes of shuffling through an indestructibly heavy book with a red leather binding, Clyde made a discovery which was, insofar as his clients were concerned, of biblical importance. Listed as the owners of Central Sanitation, Inc., were Raffael Quasarano and Peter Vitale, two Detroit mobsters whose reputations were potent enough to make every Mafiosi organizational chart in the country.

A half-hour later Clyde stood in the small office of Central Sanitation and was able to see in the back and beyond of the building a large lot with bales of paper, dumpsters full and half-full of scrap metal. Other piles were of compacted refrigerators, stoves, cars and indistinguishable waste material. A couple of front-end loaders and a fork lift were presently standing idle. At the far end of the lot was a massive steel structure with balanced weights, hooked up to a diesel engine, and next to it, a two-story brick building with large iron fire doors, and a tall brick chimney which Clyde observed could be an incinerator.

Surely, the man named Al whom he had overheard the evening before was yanking at the drawer of an old green metal filing cabinet. He appeared to be wearing the same black tee shirt from the day before, and another day's growth of wiry whiskers. Different about his appearance was a pair of rimless reading glasses.

When Clyde started talking about how he had just purchased a large office building near Wayne State Stadium Al, unsmiling, showed no recognition.

"You taking on new customers?" he asked.

"Depends on who your hauler is," said Al. "We contract by hauler. We don't care where the waste comes from. What kind of cubic feet are we talking about?"

Clyde noticed that Al's right hand shot up to his temple, which he rubbed hard with his fingers, as if massaging away a headache. His face was blotched and his fingers trembled slightly. Al could be seen as a man in need of a drink.

"Well, give me an idea of tipping fees," said Clyde, looking over Al's shoulders through a dirty window towards the mysterious interior of the junk yard. "I just want to know if it would be worthwhile to have my crap trucked out this far."

"If it's just office trash," Al said, "it should be no big deal."

Clyde said he would have to get those figures later. Al handed Clyde an oil-stained leaflet. He had to shout as an unseen piece of machinery started up with a roar. "Call that number on the bottom there when you're ready."

As he drove the crowded streets toward the interstate for the short trip back to center city Detroit, Clyde wondered silently how much of the old energy he could amass for this investigation. Was this the final push? The beginning of the end of the final push, or the beginning of the end of nothing?

As a younger investigator long ago he adopted a code, words to live by: *"I am the last person on earth who can answer these questions. I am the last person on earth who can solve this case. I am the last one who can put these assholes behind bars. Nobody else. Just me."*

As ridiculous as it was, Clyde let the words serve as a mantra for telling himself that *"it's on me. Me and me alone. It's my case."* Making the extra phone call, the one more interview, the one more long drive somewhere on a hunch paid off countless times for Woolen, earning him several citations. But the oath turned fable more than once, leading him many times to dead ends. But when that happened it was an automatic jump to the next procedure: *"Find someone who knows."*

In his hotel room he called room service for lunch, not wanting to waste even the few minutes it would have taken to consume a quarter-pounder at the MacDonald's down the street. After loosening his tie and sitting on the edge of the bed, he dialed the FBI office in Philadelphia and asked for Agent Hightower, who was, like himself, a trusted old-timer. His question was simple: Are any agents that he knew in Philly working now in the Detroit office?

Hightower mentioned Ernie Silvestri.

"Sure, I know Ernie from way back," said Clyde.

A half-hour later, after what seemed to be another trip down a blind alley, Clyde removed his shoes and lay back in bed. Silvestri was off today, which was a Friday and wouldn't be returning to work until Monday. The logical step would be to call the airline and get on the next plane back to Philly. Instead, Clyde scoped the phone book, discovering thirteen Silvestris but only one named 'Ernest,' in Dearborn.

"Ernie's not home," his wife answered. Clyde left his name and hotel phone number, sunk back into the pillow and slept.

At five the phone rang and jolted Clyde awake. It was Silvestri. The two men exchanged greetings and after catching up on reacquainting, Clyde told the FBI agent why he had come to Detroit; he disclosed that he was working for a banker who had been in the Witness Protection Program and needed help. He never thought about lying to Silvestri or leading him astray. You never burn a buddy in the business.

"What can you tell me about Central Sanitation? I know it's owned by Raffie Quasarano and Peter Vitale."

There was such a long silence that Clyde for a moment thought the phone had gone dead.

"Jesus, Clyde, you don't want much, do you?" Silvestri finally answered. He sighed.

"Listen, Clyde. I'm relieved that you called me about this at home. No way I could talk about this in the office. In fact, I can't even talk now." Then, balancing the value of friendships over protocol, he said, "I'm gonna have to meet you."

When Silvestri picked up Clyde at his hotel about an hour later, Silvestri looked grave and worried. He decided to drive to an underground garage on Russell Street and there he parked in a remote darkened corner. Office workers had vacated for the weekend and only a few other cars remained in the hollowed-out parking tomb.

"For your eyes only," he said, dumping onto Clyde's lap a stapled pack of mimeographed sheets.

The cover sheet read, "THE HOFFEX MEMO."

"Internal," he emphasized, then looked at the far wall of the garage before turning and staring hard into Clyde's eyes. "It's gonna come out some day, maybe. The higher ups are reluctant to make it public. You know the bureau. The presumptive evidence rule. No corpus delicti, no case. At least not yet."

Clyde looked at his old friend, whose face told the simple truth: An investigator who works his butt off only to run up against a legal system that can be a maze of frustrations: Knowing the truth is not enough, proving it is the burden. Silvestri also gave Clyde a copy of an FBI affidavit for a search warrant for Central Sanitation which was, concerning the tie-in with Feeno's bank, even more enlightening.

"You're going to see an informant's name in there," said Silvestri. "Be careful with it. I know that one of the other major reasons why the bureau doesn't want this stuff to get too far out there is that we have other informants working with us. Too much information gets out?" He showed his right hand as a gun. "Bang, bang, they're toast."

Chapter 35: THE HOFFEX MEMO

Clyde showered, rubbing his baldish, red-skinned head vigorously, brushing up the brain cells. Night was deep in downtown Detroit, black and relatively quiet, streets all but deserted. The St. Clair was a motel complex a half-block long, squeezed between two small restaurants. Clyde smelled fried food, thumbed through the yellow pages. He ordered "anything hot and a lot of it" from the China Moon, just two blocks away.

The air conditioner clanked and made a loud hum, but it cooled.

He lay on the bed and read.

The facts were chilling, but what impressed Clyde most about the Hoffex Memo and the search warrant affidavit was not just the details and time line, but the void left in their wake. The Hoffa investigation was a long, dark, uphill trail through the fog of judicial uncertainty. It was an impact made double by the fact that the information, though incriminating, had not reached the conclusion of arrests or confessions even though the information had been put on the table in January of 1976, six months after Jimmy Hoffa vanished. Three years since then had elapsed. Three years, thought Clyde, the memos lay in a bottom drawer, their information salient only to a small cadre of frustrated mob hunters.

He recalled Silvestri's exasperation: "No corpus delicti." The inability of investigators to push their evidence over the top and into the courtroom is equal to rolling a ten-ton stone uphill.

Clyde blinked away the thoughts. His immediate concern was toward his clients, particularly Feeno Bannon who faced considerable jail time if accused and convicted of overtly taking part in the disposal of Jimmy Hoffa, a man who at most was a remote figure in Bannon's life.

Clyde read the memo three times that night, marking with a hi-lighter the more striking information.

Hoffa's movements on July 30, 1975, appeared casual, from the time he left his home in Lake Orion, Michigan straight down Route 24 to attend what he thought was to be a meeting with Anthony Giacalone and Anthony Provenzano at the Machus Red Fox Restaurant in Bloomfield Township. Both Tony Jack and Tony Pro were active members of La Cosa Nostra. Clyde read on about some things he was familiar with. About the role of Giacalone to be the intermediary to patch up the long-standing dispute between Hoffa and Provenzano that began when both were serving time in Lewisburg Penitentiary in Pennsylvania.

While Hoffa was in prison for attempting to rig a jury, the leadership of the Teamsters Union was taken over by underlings, notably Frank Fitzsimmons, who adapted quickly to the perks and powers of being the boss of the most powerful labor organization in the world, one that was capable of shutting down major portions of America's economy simply by stopping the trucks from moving.

Hoffa's determination to regain control of the union was not only uphill, it had reached dead end. Though they hated each other, there was mutual need between Tony Pro and Hoffa. Pro was angry at Hoffa's refusal to assist him in gaining Teamsters pension funds. Conversely, Hoffa blamed his own troubles with the law on his association with bums like Provenzano.

The memo continued: About 2:30 in the afternoon he disappeared, Hoffa phoned his wife to tell her that Giacalone and Provenzano had not shown up at the restaurant. From that moment, the trail that Hoffa traveled was through the mixed mire of probability and supposition, with evidence furnished by distant informants, plus witnesses who were unfriendly to Hoffa, and casual eyewitnesses who made identities which could be easily challenged.

Clyde's attention was drawn to a page of "Suspects Outside of Michigan." They included Tony Pro, Steven Andretta and his brother Thomas Andretta, Salvatore "Sally Bugs" Briguglio and his brother Gabe, and Frank Sheeran, president of Teamsters Local 326 in Wilmington, Delaware. Sheeran was a longtime friend of Hoffa's, but he also was a friend and protege of Russell Bufalino, La Cosa Nostra chief of Eastern Pennsylvania who also didn't want to see Hoffa coming back to control the Teamsters.

Bufalino's power extended into New York's garment industry, which was nearly totally dependent on truck transportation.

Of that list, all but Sheeran and Bufalino were associates of Local 560 under Tony Pro's leadership. Both Briguglios and Thomas Andretta were thought by the FBI "to be involved in the actual disappearance of (Hoffa)."

Clyde thumbed through the Hoffex Memo for information that would tell the tale. The suppositions were that Hoffa was lured into the back seat of a car, perhaps shot. But by whom? Sally Bugs? Clyde recalled that Sally Bugs met death by gunshot in New York's Little Italy only a few months ago.

"Informant 1, on many occasions during the past ten years, has identified RAFFAEL QUASARANO and PETER VITALE as Detroit syndicated crime figures utilized by the Detroit syndicate for murders and disposal of bodies in matters of extreme importance to the Detroit syndicate. Informant 1 has advised FBI Agents, as recently as August 7, 1975, that he has personal knowledge, obtained directly from persons present, that at least (10) murder victims have been disposed of by QUASARANO and VITALE through and by the facilities described herein."

It went on to describe the shredder, the compactor and the incinerator at their business on Moran Street in Hamtramck, the small incorporated city which was actually surrounded by Detroit.

"Informant 1 has advised that he believes HOFFA to be the victim of such a murder and that he believes HOFFA's body to be totally destroyed by means of the aforesaid facilities." The informant reinforced his beliefs with the account of his personal observation of Teamsters President Frank Fitzsimmons at a "clandestine meeting with QUASARANO and VITALE...at Larco's Inn, a notorious syndicate hangout" in Detroit.

Clyde searched the affidavit and Hoffex Memo for any information connecting Feeno's bank with Central Sanitation. He couldn't get out of his mind that there was a sinister connection between the bank and the disposal company. Small banks in Jersey just don't routinely hand over $85,000 to small companies in Michigan. How much Feeno Bannon, the chief loan officer and bank president, knew about it and what was his culpability was still a puzzle to be solved back in Jersey.

Clyde turned on the TV, switched between re-runs of M*A*S*H and The Waltons, finally to the eleven o'clock news. He fell asleep as the sports announcer was enthralling over the Tigers' 4 to 3 victory at Toronto.

The next morning, Clyde had plans to get back home to Philly on the first available plane.

But first, one more try.

He recognized Al's voice on the phone and was surprised when Al said, "We ain't open past noon."

Clyde hung up, assured that Al neither recognized nor cared who he was talking to.

In the front seat of his rental car, Clyde read and reread snatches of "The Hoffex Memo" as he kept his eye on the refuse company a half-block away on Moran Street. Only six or seven trash trucks showed up the whole time. Then, about 11:45, Al emerged from the office, pushed closed the massive doors to the yard and snapped a heavy lock. Clyde was not surprised to see him walk directly to the Corner Bar & Grille.

Clyde drove and parked near the corner, waiting to see if Al would emerge from the bar. About 12:30 Clyde entered the bar, which was more crowded on this Saturday than the the day before. The bartender was pouring a double shot of Schenley in a small glass in front of Al, who sat and stared at the TV, then reached and grabbed a battered copy of The Citizen newspaper that had been left on the bar.

A waitress came out of the kitchen. "Al," she said. "Your beef stew."

Keeping his attention on Al through the dirty mirror behind the bar, Clyde waited.

"How ya doin?" he said, walking to the booth as Al was wiping his mouth with a paper napkin. "Remember me?"

"Oh, yeah, sure. You came in the other day. Yesterday was it?"

"Name's Clyde Woolen. Yeah, I think I'd like to do some business." He sat and nodded toward the waitress, a frazzled-looking mid-life woman with early osteoporosis and tired gray eyes. "Two more here."

"You know, all you gotta do is hook up with a hauler in

Detroit," said Al.

Clyde waited. "That's not all that I'm interested in," he said, voice a little more gravitas. He drummed his fingers on the beer-stained table. There are other disposals I'm interested in. And I'm sorry, I didn't get your name."

"Al Marvin, and what do ya' mean? What other disposals?"

"July thirtieth, nineteen seventy-five."

Al's face clouded; he put down his fork, but before he could rise, Clyde reached across and grabbed a forearm.

"Give me five minutes."

"Who the hell are you?" asked Al angrily, but not loud enough to be overheard.

"I'm a private investigator," Clyde answered, gambling that the truth in this instance would gather more trust than subterfuge. Al, he could tell, was tired and confused, and had been down this road before. "I'm not from Detroit. Not from the government. Not from..."

"I been before the grand jury on this."

"I know."

"Bullshit, you don't know nothin.' Grand juries are secret."

"I know that too," said Clyde, who had folded his arms and leaned closer.

"About thirty times you were in and out of that room, talking to your lawyer, taking the fifth."

"I said nothin' and I'm tellin' you nothin'."

"Here's my question," said Clyde. "The eighty-five thousand that Raffie and Vitale got for taking care of that little disposal that day. How much did you get?"

Al stiffened, staring hard at Clyde, who could see Al's anger rising. He knew he had hit the nerve.

"You're the guy," whispered Clyde. "You're the guy who did the dirty work, but you weren't in it alone. Look, Al, I'm not going to ask you any questions. You don't have to say beans." He opened his coat jacket, lifted his shirt. "No wire, nothing. I'm not going to bullshit you. You don't have to say a thing."

From the inside jacket pocket, Clyde pulled out an envelope. "Just point, Al. That's all I ask," he said, as he spread several photos on the table, looking quickly to the bar to see if they were being observed. Nobody paid attention.

Al pushed the half-finished bowl of stew to the corner of the table. "I ain't playin' that game." But he couldn't help looking.

"Just point."

Al looked at Clyde as if he did not understand, but his eyes were drawn to the head shots of several men laid out before him like a hand of cards.

Al at first looked at the photos with only sideways glances, mentally dismissing them one by one. A couple of the men could have been accountants, or dentists, wearing glasses, benign expressions. Two others also looked alike, but were younger, in their late 30s, with shocks of thick, black hair, prominent Roman noses, small-mouthed and weak-chinned. A fifth was downright sinister, with hooded eyes not very well masked by the aviator glasses he wore. This was Tony Provenzano, and the other four were his associates, Salvatore and Gabe Briguglio, and Thomas and Stephen Andretta. A sixth man also had dark hair, handsome features, soft blue eyes. This was Fred Russo, the Teamsters lawyer, brother of the singer Lena Russell. Another was a beefy man with light, gray hair and Irish features, Frank Sheerin, the Teamsters leader from Delaware. Two other photos were of Joseph Bannon and Vincent Berardi. A tenth was a thin-faced man with small features, his black hair strangely coifed from back to front, like the helmet of a Roman legionnaire, Anthony Trapetto, the one called "Squirrel."

Al stared, looked up at Clyde, who stared back hard. Al lifted his glass, which though small, had a double shot of Schenley's in it. He took it down quickly, sighing as the warm stuff hit his stomach.

Clyde watched as Al said nothing, but looking into the dirty man's brain, he could tell by the flicking of his eyes and the quick look to some of the other photos that the man in question was Trapetto.

"This guy, right?" said Clyde pointing to the Squirrel's photo.

Al smiled finally. It was a strange smile, but he said nothing, as Clyde kept tapping.

"Ma'am," yelled Clyde to the waitress. "Another for my

buddy, Coors for me."

Al had stopped eating, pushing the plate to the side. He gulped down the latest shot and as Clyde waited, now it was Al's turn to size up the man across the table. He looked at Clyde, feeling better inside, then began to talk.

"He called," said Al.

"Who called?" asked Clyde, surprised to hear Al's voice.

Al tapped Trapetto's photo, which by now had fingerprint stains upon his likeness.

"And...?"

"And he said, 'It's off. They weren't comin''"

Startled, Clyde almost yelled, "What do you mean by that?"

"That's all I got to say," said Al, who wiped his mouth with a paper napkin and sat back in the booth, staring at Clyde, who by now shifted uncomfortably from one heavy haunch to the other.

"You pointed to this guy; how do you know him?"

"He came in the day before. Said he was from back East. Said he had a delivery coming the next day. Disposal of some trash, he said. I thought nothin' of it when he called the next day and said he wasn't comin'. Then I read the papers and put two and two together."

"You think they took the body someplace else?" asked Clyde, trying not to reveal his frustration.

Al shrugged, kept his mouth shut for a few seconds. "That's all I got to say."

He started to rise, and as Clyde tried to grab his wrist, pulled away and without looking back, walked to the bar and deliberately placed himself in a small circle of men who were laughing and talking.

Clyde followed Al with his eyes, deciding whether to pursue. He sat for five more minutes, took a final swig of beer, took out a couple of dollar bills, left it for the waitress, got up and left.

Chapter 36: KNIGHTS OF THE ROUND TABLE

The clock hanging above the gold leaf laurel encircling the fresco of a bare-chested Roman girl carrying a jug of wine on her shoulder read "8:06." Feeno was startled to realize he had been sitting at a poker table in Harrah's for five hours, with the only break being the mandatory twenty minute shutdown for the vacuuming of the carpet. Five hours and he was still behind. Not much behind but surely this would not be a positive day at the poker table.

In his hand were a three and a nine of clubs, two and seven of hearts and a jack of spades. He threw them down and rose: "Gentlemen." He turned to the one woman, who could have been a Nigerian tribal queen, head dressed in a winding turban flecked with blue stars. "Ladies," he said, bowing.

As he walked towards the men's room, he stopped frozen. Coming down the padded marble steps were two men. One, who was about thirty-five, he had seen from the bank. A minor Teamsters official. The other, dressed in a Mexican-type flowing sports shirt, was also a bank customer. Feeno's eyes met the Teamster's and locked for a split second. No time for faking little fantasies.

The Teamster in particular was startled when he heard the tall fellow at the bottom of the stairs slide past and say, "How you all doin' today?" in a voice of southern syrup, face bearded, streaked with gray, loud but dirty sports jacket with alarmingly large checks, gray rumpled slacks too short above his sneakers, white socks, baseball cap.

The Teamster, mouth gaping, stopped and stared as the southern man slid along. "You know that guy?"

"What guy?" asked his partner.

"That guy, that skinny guy. Over there." But where he looked was an empty space. "He ain't there now. Nobody, I guess.

Nobody."

In the bathroom, hurriedly splashing cold water on his face, Feeno wanted fresh air. He left the casino by a side door, turned left on Kentucky Avenue and walked the one block to the boardwalk.

The laughing gulls welcomed him, the two joggers running slowly caught his envy. Running is what he should be doing instead of hiding. Running. For real running. *"I am running,"* he thought. *"Running from everything and everybody. Running from my entire life."* He stretched to one side as he pulled the small wad of bills from his pants pocket. Squinting into the morning sun he counted three hundred, twenty-seven dollars. He had not had a good day at blackjack, poker or craps for two weeks. He would need money fast. Money and information. Where is Clyde Woolen? Feeno hadn't heard from him in a week.

He leaned his head back against the wooden top slat of the bench, closed his eyes and quickly opened them again. He looked nervously in both directions. Unable to sleep the night before, he had picked up and headed here from the deep woods of the Pinelands, which had started to spawn apparitions.

He had awakened in sweat two nights ago, seeing in a warm haze of heavy rain — through a clap of thunder and lightning flash — a tall man, dressed in white, standing motionless, staring, smiling, mouthing a message: "I'm waiting...."

Feeno looked at his watch, then at the beach, with his mind's eye remembering Edna wrestling with little Gerald and his shitty pants. He looked again at his watch, got up and walked to his pickup truck parked on Atlantic Avenue, with the promise of a long, long nap after his long, long night of nothingness.

At about the same time, one hundred miles to the north, a dozen men and two women shoved themselves and their chairs up against a large oval table in the federal courthouse in Newark.

As a fly on the wall, Feeno would have been impressed with the Strike Force steering committee meeting about to get under way in his honor.

U.S. Attorney Mario Bianca sat in the middle of one side of the oval shaped table. At his side was Assistant U.S. Attorney Paul

Murdoch and next to him, another assistant, Shannon Cook. On the opposite side of the table were a half-dozen representatives of the various Strike Force components, including Oscar Goldsborough of the U.S. Marshals' Office, George Woerth, representing New Jersey Attorney General Madeline Pelligrino, FBI Agent Stanley Schweitzer, and New Jersey State Police Capt. Paul Cooper, among others.

"Let's go through this from the ass end today," said Bianca. "I want an update, Stan, on The Squirrel's unfortunate demise."

Everybody familiar with the discovery of the twisted little informant with the twenty dollar bills stuffed in his rectum cheeks laughed aloud.

The laughter turned to guffaws when Goldsborough asked, "Don't they ever write checks, these guys?"

Papers ruffled, chuckles subsided and the seriousness returned with Schweitzer's reading of the autopsy report on the late Anthony Trapetto.

Schweitzer shuffled through several sheets of paper in front of him, and put on his reading glasses. They hung in jeopardy of falling from the tip of his thin nose. He related that the Squirrel suffered blunt force injuries to the face and chest "like from an automobile accident. He was badly cut up in the face and upper rib cage." Schweitzer hurriedly ticked off injuries and causes: "damage to mid-sternum. Bilaterally over the anterior something — Iliac spinae. Myocardial contusions. Pulmonary contusions. In other words, severe damage to the heart and lungs.

He paused, looked at Bianca, who said, "And the wire..."

"We know that the transmission from the wire he was wearing went dead at nine-oh-three. We can also assume that Fred Russo or Angelo Crupi or Petey Boy Sergio — any one of them could have found the wire. We also know for a fact that Trapetto took a single four-fifty-seven Magnum right between the eyes, which may have been administered after the Scalesis found the wire."

"A coup de grace," said Capt. Cooper.

"Hah!" Schweitzer laughed. "No coup de grace was needed."

"You mean that this was a message from the mob. Right?"

asked Murdoch.

"You got it," said Schweitzer. "The guy's as good as dead. Scalesi still thought he needed a message sent. It was meant to make an impression on the other Scalesi guys. 'You don't get away with screwing with us.' It's like getting in the last word."

He continued, grasping the report tightly in both hands: "And besides the gunshot wound...

Here he paused, looked around the table. George Woerth appeared to be nodding, but jolted upright.

"...somebody cut his tongue out"

Murdoch: "His tongue? Out? Cut out?

Goldsborough: "What the hell is this? The inquisition."

Schweitzer: "No, it's Rocco Scalesi. Cruel to the max. Scalesi is a sociopath of the first order, with an unbelievably violent temper. I'm telling you...I'm sure you all heard the story of how he put a guy's eyes out with his thumbs."

"Yes, Thumbs Scalesi," said Cook with disgust, looking down at her blouse, trying not to imagine what the Mafia boss might do to a woman who crossed him.

"What else do we know?" asked Bianca, steering the conversation back on track.

Schweitzer tossed the report to the middle of the table. Goldsborough picked it up to examine.

Schweitzer added, "The autopsy said too, that Trapetto was soaked in sea water. I guess that was their way of cleaning him up before stuffing him into the trunk of that car."

"So," said Bianca, scratching the short black mustache above his lip. "They know now that we flipped Trapetto. And they don't know how many more are working for us. By this time, my guess is that Thumbs is on the verge of panic. He has his own crew to worry about and he also has Feeno Bannon, who is the only one for sure who can put him in jail."

Bianca also asked about the status of Berardi. "More specifically, Stan," he said, looking at Schweitzer, "what's your impression of the Berardi guy?"

"I'm more and more convinced that he's clean," said Schweitzer, quickly looking around the table, waiting for someone to disagree. "The guy threw up his breakfast when he saw

Trapetto's body. You can't fake that."

Goldsborough interjected: "Did you expense a new pair of shoes, Stan?" Once again there was laughter.

"Let's get serious, guys," said Bianca. "What about Berardi? South Philly! His old man was in the can, mobbed up."

"Berardi's father apparently was a loan shark victim," said Schweitzer. "He couldn't meet the vig and was forced to steal a car. He went up for it."

"It's typical," said Murdoch. "Poor desperate guys on the fringe who get sucked in."

"You mean like Feeno Bannon?" interjected Bianca. "Let's face it. Our boy Feeno was different; he was a wannabe right from the start, fascinated with mob guys. Even married to the mob. So they sucked him up as an earner."

"He ain't no wannabe now!" said Cooper, slapping the table and starting to rise from his chair. A serious stare from Bianca made him sit again.

As is typical of any large bureaucratic brainstorm meeting, the discussion slipped and slid from subject to subject and back again.

"If Berardi is clean and he's being pursued by the Scalesis, maybe he belongs in the witness program," said Murdoch.

"Not yet," said Bianca. He picked up an empty styrofoam coffee cup and squeezed it until it broke. "But let's put somebody on him. From what we know, he's been in contact with Bannon. Let's do a 'round-the-clock.

"And now let's get back to our friend, Feeno. Stan?"

"As usual, we have had several quote-unquote 'sightings'. Some of them in Philly. We checked them all out and we're convinced that he's not in Philly. Every airport security in the country has been alerted, as well as APBs to law enforcement. He honestly could be out of the country."

"What about Jersey, what about here?" asked Bianca. "Let's go back to the day, that day he disappeared."

"Christ, we've been through all that," said Cooper, irritated.

"Think about why Bannon fled," said Bianca. "Think about it. He knows his best friend, Berardi, is going to disclose in court about stealing all that money from him. Bannon knows he faces a state rap for fraud. He runs also because the Scalesis had him backed to a wall. If the Hoffa investigation comes to a whodunit conclusion, Feeno's the one who authorized Teamsters loans to pay off the perps. He's the fall guy. So he runs from the Scalesis, he runs from the charge in Neptune County and he runs from us. He hasn't got a friend in the world, or so it seems. My feeling is that he took it on the lam alone. He's by himself and he could be anywhere."

Schweitzer interrupted: "I agree he could be anywhere. We're checking every lead. I got one tip just yesterday. I'm going to check it out today, this afternoon."

"And what's that?" asked Bianca, only half-listening, as he began gathering up papers in front of him.

"We got a call from a patrol officer in Galloway Township. That's outside of Atlantic City. Seems his wife picked up a hitchhiker. I think it was a day or two after Feeno jumped. The cop said his wife dropped the guy in Atlantic City. That's all he knows."

"Sounds like a wild one," said Bianca, standing up to signal that the meeting is over. "Atlantic City doesn't sound like a logical place for a fugitive to hide out. But check it out and let me know what it looks like."

As the meeting broke up and the attendees wandered off in different directions in the federal building, Bianca motioned to Schweitzer to "join me for a minute." They walked into Bianca's office. Bianca shut the door firmly and asked Schweitzer to sit down.

"I think it's about time we sprung a little leak," he said in a whisper.

Chapter 37: ROCCO AND CONCETTA

Concetta Gambini attached a plain gold necklace over her white silk blouse, a small touch that with the shiny white of her bulging blouse helped to accentuate the deep olive of her skin. The black slacks she wore made her look even taller than her five feet eight. In a world of many, short Italian men, Concetta was a towering physical presence. It was one that she used to an advantage, a prop to a personality that was proud, wise and elegant.

She deferred to no one, not even to her husband, Joseph, who, before a bullet put him in a wheelchair, was and still is one of the most powerful men among Northeast Mafiosi. Also included in the coterie of tough and violent men who looked up to Concetta was Rocco Scalesi, who picked her up at a cafe in Morristown about an hour after his phone call to her French style Manor House, hidden in the woods above the Somerset Hills Country Club in Bernardsville. Concetta left a note on the bed table next to where Joseph was napping, saying she was going to town to do some shopping and wouldn't be back until before supper.

They drove west on Interstate 80, the blue Alpha purring smoothly, in no hurry. They crossed over the Delaware River at the Water Gap and into the Pocono Mountains of Pennsylvania about mid-afternoon.

"I want to show you some forest land that I just purchased," Rocco said as he buttoned off the radio driving through East Stroudsburg and out to the north on Route 447. At Analomink, he drove the Alpha onto a dual road that led northwest into the forest. Upon reaching a small lake, he diverted to the south onto a dirt road that curved around the eastern edge of the water. The road had for years serviced a few clapboard cabins that still stood at water's edge. Most had docks with gentle water lapping at small boats with outboards.

On a bluff to the north of the lake he stopped. The

summer air was still. Out on the lake were a few rowboats with fishermen.

Pointing, Rocco said, "After these trees are taken out, you'll be able to see the sunsets from here. A nice high point here, Connie." He watched to take in her raptured approval. "This is where the main lodge will go in, just high enough above the lake to catch the breezes. There will be cottages here," he said, pointing to his right, "and over there on the far side. In between goes the golf course, a championship course."

All about them stood tall spruce and hemlock. In the distance, the haze created a shimmer in the lower sky. Concetta shielded her eyes with her right hand.

"It's beautiful," she said, smiling and tossing her long dark hair. "You are a wise son of a gun, Rocco." He extended his hand to help her step upon a sturdy rock affording a better look. Her hands were soft and welcoming. Their fingertips lingered.

The compliment from Concetta warmed him to his toes. He looked at her and wished. Oh how he wished! But he forced the lust in his mind to transfer to those of business. He, after all, perhaps alone among men, would not compromise the honor of this beautiful woman, married to a man of respect, *a compatriota* who was his just and deserving equal. Sometimes Rocco enjoyed bathing in his pain.

He had purchased six hundred acres, he told Concetta, in anticipation of building a major gambling casino that some day he was convinced he would build on this gorgeous property, less than a two-hour drive from both New York City and Philly. "It's only a matter of time, Connie," he said. "I have a few friends in the Pennsylvania Legislature and they say, "Not now, but wait. It will come.

"Pennsylvania is different than New Jersey. Quakers run this state. It was not long ago that they allowed Sunday drinking, and they just got horse racing within the last ten years. And even that ain't thoroughbreds, just harness."

They drove to the main road. Rocco checked the time on his watch and decided to stop for a drink and a bite at a small roadside log cabin inn. He requested a table on a verandah near which ran a small but powerful mountain stream, rushing and gurgling over the rocks. The air temperature seemed to drop ten degrees. It was refreshingly cool, a perfect balance to this beautiful summer day.

Before they ordered, Rocco drank a double martini, then beckoned the young waitress for another. Concetta drank burgundy. They both smiled when the bartender himself came with their drinks, and explained, "The waitress is only twenty; she's not allowed to deliver your drinks."

Concetta smiled again later, half laughing at Rocco. "I never saw you quaff a drink so fast like that."

Rocco forced a smile, leaned back in his chair and then leaned forward, his elbows upon the checkered table cloth. He placed a hand over Concetta's. "I have something to tell you."

She was still smiling, teasingly now, and amused. She watched him cough. He seemed embarrassed.

"I found the one who murdered your son," he said.

The breath left Concetta so swiftly, she withdrew her hand and put it to her throat, then brought up both hands to her cheeks. Her face had fallen and was suddenly thin, drained of blood.

She tried to speak, but Rocco, grasped her forearm and squeezed. "Don't," he said. "Let me tell you all that I know.

"This is the most desperate part of it, Connie, the one I am ashamed of. I have difficulty telling you this."

She looked, pleading with her eyes for him to continue. They now brimmed with tears, but she could not take her eyes off of Rocco, listening to what he was going to say, her mind willing the details from his lips.

"Richard was killed, I am so very deeply sorry to say, by one of ours," he said. "But as soon as I learned of it, I took care of it. The man who killed Richard will kill no more."

Concetta's spine stiffened. She released his grasp and sat back in her chair, her expression changing from remorse and sadness to anger.

"It was Anthony Trapetto, Connie, a man I have trusted all my life. He took the contract from the Colombos unbeknownst to me. I knew nothing about it. He defied the rules of our family, and of the commission. So did they. It has never happened before."

"How?" she asked. "How?"

"This man who requested Richard's killing, I know him only as Joe Grease," said Rocco. "It was something to do with his daughter. I know nothing."

"You mean Joe Grease ordered the murder of his daughter's...Rocco, they were going to her high school prom! They were going to the prom!" Her arms stiffened as though to hoist her from the chair. She sat again and wept now. Rocco was glad that they had taken a table far from other prying eyes. Concetta's back was to the dining room and from the terrace no one could hear her sobs.

For the moment, he couldn't comfort her, but let her cry. When she felt composed, she asked, wiping tears with the hankie he withdrew from his pocket. "How did you resolve this?"

"I'll explain to you in the car, on the way home. Come, Connie, we best go."

"There wasn't much to tell," he said to her in a low voice as the car jumped into eastbound traffic on Route 80. In the westbound lane, traffic sped cross country, with eighteen-wheelers bound for as far away as San Francisco, Omaha, Salt Lake City and Chicago. "He was dispatched in the usual way. With a bullet to the head. I took care of it myself."

That evening, Rocco sat in the dark alone in the office den of his shore house. There were three calls on the phone answering machine, one from Aaron Vinokur, his lawyer, a second from his daughter Nancy, and a third from Fred Russo, the Teamsters lawyer. Nancy's message was brief — an invitation to dinner on Sunday at her new apartment in Manhattan. He felt not in the mood for returning the other calls. Business could wait.

Rocco's seaside home was close enough to see the ocean but not hear it when the wind was blowing out to sea. Late in the summer when nights were cooler the fog would creep across the inlet, smothering visibility to the south and penetrated only by the melancholy horn warning ships and boats of the danger of nearby shoals.

Rocco replayed over and over the quiet sobs of Concetta. Despite the sadness of the day, her emotional needs thrilled him perhaps even more than the fantasies of lying in her bed. He wished her dependence more deeply now. The newly found control that he had gained this day made his spine tingle.

The reverie, as he sat in the darkness sipping chardonnay and smoking his La Corona, was halted by the urgent ringing of the phone. He let it ring twelve times before picking it up.

"Rocco," said the familiar voice of Aaron Vinokur, his personal lawyer. "Where the hell have you been? I've been trying to reach you all day."

"I was busy," said Rocco. "What is it?"

"We may have some bad news."

"That's all I get is bad news. What the hell is it now?"

"Bannon," said Vinokur. "Feeno Bannon."

"What about Bannon?" asked Rocco, bracing himself and putting down the glass he was holding.

"He's back in custody. But we don't know whether he's in jail or back in the witness program. Either way the feds have him." He paused. "Listen, Rocco, I haven't nailed this down yet, but the information I have is pretty solid. Once again, we just don't know where he is. But we can't take chances. We have to start getting organized on this one. There's no telling when more indictments will be coming down or when we go to trial. We're going to have to meet tomorrow. I want you to call Shirley and set up a time. In my Manhattan office."

When Vinokur hung up, Rocco sat staring toward the sea under the darkened sky. Was Vinokur trying to cough up another fancy fee for himself or was this really urgent? Was Feeno really in custody? Rocco tried to imagine where. He concentrated on a prick of light way out, way far in the ocean. He thought, poured himself another drink, sat back in the cordovan chair and dialed the number of his dependable old soldier in Atlantic City. Nicholas Campanio, the ruthless one, the fearless one they called "Nicky Nuts".

"Nicky," I have a job for you."

"Yeah, what is it?"

"We'll meet. I'll explain it to you. Come up here tomorrow. No, day after tomorrow."

Nicky returned the usual assurances of an underling

impressed with being needed. In return, what Rocco wanted now was old-world loyalty, Nicky's toughness and ruthlessness, his ability to finish a job that others were afraid to start.

"Listen, there aren't many that I would give this assignment to," Rocco said. "It's important. You are the only one I can trust who can pull it off."

Chapter 38: CONFRONTATION

Alone at night in bed, Vince and Julie Berardi nestled and whispered, getting out in the open the faults, the setbacks, and sometimes the bright moments of the day. When they were married fifteen years ago, Julie's father lifted his champagne glass toward the bride and groom: "Never go to bed mad, never go to bed sad."

Everyone laughed when he added, "If you can keep that one, let me know. I'll try it myself."

Julie said, holding onto Vince's shoulder under the covers, "I may have found out what's been bothering Patty. Why she doesn't want to go to soccer camp."

Vince turned to Julie and frowned in the dark, anxious to hear whatever mother-daughter confidence might shed light on the sudden turnaround in their eleven-year-old daughter's behavior. The previous fall she beamed, telling her parents how she couldn't wait for warm weather and soccer again. She had shined that past season, scoring more goals and making assists that brought smiles to her face and pride to her parents.

"What happened?" Vince asked.

"I've been after her and after her," Julie said. "We know she's shy. I told her it's harmful to keep things bottled up. I asked her again what happened to make her suddenly not like soccer. She got pissed and yelled for me to leave her alone. About twenty minutes later she came out on the porch and sat next to me in the glider. She put her head on my shoulder. I didn't say a word. I wanted her to open up, you know."

"Yeah," said Vince, rolling over toward his wife impatiently. "What happened?"

"All she said to me," Julie continued, "was 'Mom, what's the Mafia?'"

"What?"

"I know. I didn't know what to say, but I was afraid. She must have heard something. Read about it in the paper. When they found that Trapetto guy's body on our land. I bit my tongue for a second. I asked her, 'Who's been talking to you about the Mafia?'

"She wouldn't say, and I said, 'Tell me.' I said it nice; I tried to stay calm.

"And finally, she said, 'The girls.' Then she said somebody asked her if her dad was in the Mafia."

"Jesus Christ," Vince yelled, jumping out of bed.

"Shh, Vince."

"What the hell?" he said in a loud whisper, turning on the light. He turned it off, went to the window and looked out at the street light, the dead quiet neighborhood, the light yellow glow of the Philly night sky across the river to the west. He walked downstairs, made a cup of tea and sat on the back porch, waiting for dawn.

Julie joined him, sat down beside him. She grasped his hand and squeezed. Her hand felt warm but clammy. "What should we do?"

"We have to turn it around."

"But how."

"It's been on my mind. First, Mister Fairchild, now Patty."

"Mister Fairchild? You mean the guy from Bally's?"

"Yes."

"Oh, no, Vince." She turned in alarm to look at his face, but in the darkness discerned only a silhouette. "Don't tell me. He signed the contract, didn't he?"

"He tore it up. On Tuesday."

"Tore it up?"

Vince summarized what happened. He had gone to Atlantic City to finalize the plans for Fairchild's new home on land that the casino executive had just purchased on the eastern boundary of the Pinelands at Wading River.

Fairchild, recently over from England where he had directed Entertainment for The Ritz Club outside London, had not been returning Vince's phone calls. Vince had prepared the blue prints for a six bedroom manor house in the woods a half-mile west of the Garden State Parkway.

When he caught up with Fairchild, who was having lunch with a half-dozen other Bally executives in a private dining room of the casino, Fairchild, a corpulent, usually ebullient man, turned white when he saw Vince standing in the doorway, hands at his side in a "what's up?" gesture.

Fairchild laid down his napkin, excused himself from the table, walked to Vince and grasped him by the elbow, half dragging him to the hallway. He found a more or less secluded entryway to a meeting room:

"Look, I'm sorry, but our deal is off."

"What do you mean?"

"I don't know the truth perhaps," Fairchild said as politely as he could. "But I heard..."

"You heard what?" Vince yelled, sensing what was coming.

"You know," Fairchild hesitated. "The connections, the allegations. I hadn't known."

"They are bullshit!" Vince yelled.

"They may be, they may be," said Fairchild in a loud whisper. "But can I take a chance? I came all the way over here. I brought my family here from England. The New Jersey Casino Control Commission makes you dance through hoops to get a license. Any affiliation. Any question. Any little thing can deny you. I can't take chances. You're a nice guy, I'm sure you're on the up and up. But I went through hell getting this license. Any connection, no matter how remote, to anything or anybody..." The man was going to say, "Shady," but Vince interrupted.

"Jack, I'm clean. I know nothing about these people. Please don't believe what you read in the paper." He shouted, "I'm a victim of fraud. They stole my money. The guy who can clear this up is on the lam. You'll see. Everything will be all right."

"I'm sorry, Vince, I'm sorry."

"We have a contract."

"We had a contract. Talk to your lawyer. Now, excuse me." He brushed past and without looking back returned to his lunch.

Julie said nothing as Vince finished the story. She went back to bed, leaving her husband on the porch. The next morning, hung over from the insomnia of the night before, Vince called

Clyde Woolen. Clyde's wife told Vince that Clyde went away for a couple of days, on business. "He didn't say when he'd be back."

"Where'd he go?"

"I think, Detroit."

"Please have him call me as soon as he gets back."

It was a long shot and a gamble, but things had to be brought to a head, Vince thought, as he drove north on Route 206. The clutter of the suburbs quickly gave way to the flat pines. He crossed Route 70 and turned on the road to Buddtown. On Ong's Hat Road he looked for a place to park where he could hide his truck, making sure it was a good half-mile from the "mailbox" that Feeno and Clyde had set up between them for messages. He walked the rest of the way.

This was a risk, thought Vince, a dangerous move. But he wasn't going to let his family fall apart through misconceptions or accusations, especially false ones, no matter how innocently nor politely delivered.

Vince's ugly recollections vanished when he walked into the woods and in the jungle of pines concentrated on finding the Ong's Hat mailbox, hoping to learn when Feeno and Clyde would hook up again. He felt again in his shirt pocket for the note he had written before leaving home, telling Feeno "It's important." But he could not find the tangle of pine trees with the "mailbox" drop, so he returned to his truck and drove aimlessly into the pines, up one sandy road and down another, crisscrossing and backtracking. Though he was as familiar with these remote woods as anyone living there, he knew how difficult it would be to find Feeno. And when he found him, he wasn't even sure what he would say or do.

He stopped finally when he came to the Mullica River, threading its braided way in a dozen watery trails, past and between hummocks of reeds and cattails. A blue heron stood on one thin leg about one hundred yards away, motionless, waiting for prey to glide beneath it.

Twenty minutes went by. The heron had not moved. What Vince heard was a slight rustling wind in the pines, and an accompaniment of song birds. He leaned back and began to sweat. He closed the windows and turned on the AC, losing the sense of hearing, but as he glanced at the rearview mirror, he saw the black outline of something big moving through the brush, far away. He turned, looked again, put the truck in reverse and backed away slowly from the river bank. Carefully he followed the Ford camper, which painted in black was not easy to see in detail. It moved slowly through the brush.

He kept pace, but stayed about one hundred yards behind, not daring to spook whoever it was. The cat and mouse game kept up for five or so minutes. Then the camper disappeared. Vince hit the gas, making up space until the camper once again came into view. His suspicions that the camper was Feeno's increased because whoever was driving it ran a zig zag through the woods, and no doubt the pickup following him was staying with him. He was already spooked.

Finally, the camper hit a dirt road surrounded on both sides by a cranberry bog. They drove upon a berm between the fields. Next to the road, a flatbed truck was parked, containing sprinklers and pumps.

The camper drove past slowly, followed by Vince. Up ahead was Route 563, a two-lane asphalt highway. Vince figured they were somewhere near the old village of Martha. When the camper reached the highway, the driver floored the accelerator. Startled, Vince did the same, reaching the highway in a series of bumps which smacked hard against his truck's suspension. The wheels dug and spun into the loose sand until taking hold on the asphalt. By then the black camper was a quarter mile away, heading towards Green Bank.

Vince's speedometer read seventy-five mph. He was keeping pace, now convinced that the camper was Feeno Bannon's. How long the chase would continue, Vince wasn't able to predict and did not care. He blew the horn, stomping it with his fist, pushing it into the steering wheel with force. Vince was good and pissed, a mood that started to subside with the sudden deceleration of the camper ahead, which had slowed to about forty, then twenty-five, allowing Vince to catch up.

When he was parallel, Vince looked to his right to see a startled Feeno Bannon, by now a stranger in heavy beard, ball cap and work clothes. Feeno stopped his camper, rolled down the window.

"What the hell are you doing? Are you crazy?"

"Pull into the woods, Feeno," Vince yelled. "It's important."

Feeno made sure that both he and Vince were far enough off the highway to avoid detection. He stopped the truck in a tangle of vines. He forced the camper's door into the strong branches of a pine tree and with his long legs loped to the ground.

"What the hell is going on? What are you doing here?" He looked nervously to the right, then to the left.

Vince had left his pickup and advanced to within ten feet of his old friend: "We have to talk." He suddenly felt out of breath. Feeno offered his hand to shake but Vince moved both of his to his hips and held them there.

"Talk about what?"

Not sure what to say or how to say it, Vince asked loosely, "Where's Clyde? I've been trying to reach him." His face was worn, heavy with thought. Sweat had a grip on his neck.

"What do you want Clyde for?" Feeno asked, leaning against a rear fender of the camper. He sensed an urgency and fear in Vince's voice and was making sure that the conversation, wherever it went, would be slowed down, unhurried.

"I'll get to the point," said Vince, staring hard, not taking his eyes off Feeno's. "I think you should turn yourself in, give yourself up. Enough fucking bullshit. This has gone too far."

Feeno did not reply. He looked to the ground, then to Vince.

"Did you hear what I said, Feeno?"

"I heard you, of course. What's troubling you, Vince?"

"Every fucking thing. That's all."

"You know what I'm doing, don't you?"

Vince shouted back, "No, I don't know what you're doing."

"We need time, Vince."

"We? Who's we?"

Feeno stepped toward Vince's truck. "C'mon, listen, listen. I know you're pissed. I'm not even going to ask what happened. I think I already know."

"Anybody with half a fucking brain, Feeno, would know what my family's been going through."

"All right, stop it right there, Vince." He paused to collect his thoughts, took a deep breath to push down his own rising anger and frustration. "Both of us know what got us here. Don't you think that I don't sweat every day about what happened to you. You lost your money, your dignity, and I guess its hurting your business.

"You got it right," Vince said. "What are you going to do about it?"

"Vince, if I went back into the Witness Program right now, I'd still face trial in Neptune County. I'd still have to listen to my best goddamned friend tell how I allegedly stole his money. The government won't let me take the stand to explain. They're afraid it'll tip off their case against Scalesi and the other Teamsters.

"So, I got to sit there...and take it. I also got to sit there and take it when I'm accused of setting up the disappearance of Jimmy Hoffa, for Christ's sake."

Vince said nothing, but he listened.

"Vince, I'll tell you this, but you gotta' go home, give it time. Clyde is in Detroit; he's trying to find out more about what happened to Hoffa, about what connection his disappearance had to the bank. I know nothing. I signed stuff; I know I did it carelessly at times. Back then, I was high half the time on cocaine. All kinds of money went out to Las Vegas. I didn't care as long as I got my cut."

"That's your side of the story, Feeno," Vince interrupted. "We heard it before. I got yanked into this mess because of the mistake I made of trusting you."

"Maybe that's your trouble. You trust everybody. You listen too much to other people. Right now I guess your wife is on your ass."

"If you had a family maybe you'd understand a few things."

"I do understand. I understand this. Maybe you ought to stand up for yourself once in a while. Get some backbone for Christ's sake."

Vince's right fist shot out, landing somewhere on Feeno's face, knocking him against the side of the camper.

"What the fuck are you...?"

He lunged at Vince, tackling him to the ground. He

attempted to pin his arms, but Vince, though smaller, had years of hard-work muscle on his frame. Feeno's face throbbed over his left eye. He cursed.

Vince, still lying on his back, got one hand loose from Feeno's grip and thrust the heel of the hand onto Feeno's jaw, forcing it back. Feeno lost his hold and Vince with both hands grabbed the front of his shirt, pulling Feeno off him. He stood up and with a swift kick, felt the toe of his boot land on Feeno's ribs. Feeno gasped, went to his knees and rolled over in pain.

Vince climbed into his truck without looking behind him, started the engine, put it in reverse gear and backed away through the brush, hitting the gas harder with each pound of resistance from the scrub. At a little clearing, he backed around, headed the nose of the truck towards the highway. He sped away, finally thinking down the anger, pulling his brain to relax, thinking about consequences. The truck slowed, but he struggled the next few miles to keep from mentally crushing Feeno Bannon.

The anxiety remained as he pulled into a Sunoco station and stopped at the phone booth. His heart thumped furiously. He looked in the blue pages of the fat book, swelled like a pillow with the multiple searches of callers.

When the woman answered, "FBI, this is Helen speaking. How may I direct your call?", she heard silence from the unknown other end. "Hello, how may I help you? Hello, hello. This is the FBI."

He let her hang up, cradled the phone gently and left the booth, walked inside the gas station, told the clerk, "A pack of Chesterfields." He walked outside, stepped back in his truck, lit a cigarette, took one drag and pulled the truck back onto the road, this time driving slowly. A minute later he stubbed the barely smoked cigarette out in the ash tray. He opened the side window, reached into his shirt pocket, grabbed the newly purchased pack of cigarettes, crushed it in the hand that still throbbed from striking Feeno's face with all the fury of pent-up days and weeks of nowhere. He threw the crushed pack out the window, and drove home.

Chapter 39: LITTLE LEAGUE

"Is this Mister Woolen?"

"Yes it is."

"How are you today sir?"

"Fine," said Clyde, peeved at the phone call, but suddenly he recognizes the voice.

"I'm calling, sir, from the Camden County Cancer Foundation."

Clyde answered: "Excuse me. No offense, but I usually don't respond to telephone solicitations. If you wish a contribution, please do so by mail."

"This won't take a minute, sir. Or is there a better time to call you?"

Clyde paused, by now certain of the voice.

"I won't be available again until 9 o'clock tonight."

"I'll be happy to call you back then, sir. You have a nice morning."

At nine that night, as the sun had finally lipped to the west and darkness settled, Clyde was at the Ong's Hat Mailbox. Feeno was late, as usual, but when he showed up, the two of them had multitudes of information to share. About Central Sanitation. About the pursuit in the Pinelands. About a closing net. About what to do next, especially about the new information concerning the relationship between the North Jersey Teamsters and events in Detroit the day that Jimmy Hoffa disappeared.

"I explored the Central Sanitation thing to what looks like a dead end," Clyde told Feeno. He was frowning and gripping the steering wheel of his Mustang in frustration. "I thought we had a connection to where Hoffa's body was disposed of. I even got a copy of the search warrant."

Feeno's face and eyes delivered a vacancy. In the dark, Clyde could not see the welt under his left eye.

"I think that Hoffa's funeral ceremony," Clyde continued, "if that is what you want to call it, was originally to be held at Central Sanitation, but for some reason or another, whoever killed Hoffa — Russell Bufalino, Tony Provenzano, who knows? — I think they called it off and he was buried or incinerated somewhere else. An FBI informant said that this place was used in the past to dispose of mob hits. I guess whoever whacked Hoffa suddenly realized that Central Sanitation might be the first place the feds would suspect."

Feeno stared into the deep woods, then to his hands, which were muscled and dirty with callouses he never had before. "So, we're nowhere."

He wasn't used to this. Getting answers to tricky problems were his stock and trade. Whether at the track with a trifecta, gambling on anything. He could derive what's in front of him, shuffle it, digest it, and come up with something. Anything. Now, the wall was getting higher. Nothing in sight but long shots.

"I think there's one guy," he said after a long silence, hearing in the distance the "whoo, whoo" of an owl. "It's a long shot but it's somebody who may have some answers. I'm talking about Fred Russo."

"He's a lawyer," Clyde said. "I don't trust lawyers."

"Fred is not like the others," said Feeno. "He has ten times the brains and ten times the savvy and, believe it or not, he has a touch of conscience, of morality in his background." Russo, he said, "was in it for the money. That's all."

"A lawyer in New Jersey can't make money legitimately?" asked Clyde.

"Sure, but this was big money. Kickbacks aren't taxable unless you're caught," said Feeno, reciting a description that applied to himself as well as Russo. He added that Russo "enjoyed the thrills associated with mobsters. He's a made guy, but he earned it on his brains. Consigliere. All brains. He's really a fringe guy so to speak, like me."

"I know plenty of fringe guys," said Clyde. "They're the ones who get in the most trouble."

"Don't I know it," agreed Feeno.

"I suspect that from what you tell me about Russo he likes

the top shelf," said Clyde. "Lots of women too?"

"That's where you're wrong," said Feeno. "Fred doesn't screw around. Never, never! He's strictly family. Beautiful wife, three little ones. He adores them. Believe me, I've seen girls throw themselves at Fred. He brushes 'em off."

"Loyalty to his wife and family. Is this what you mean by his touch of morality?" asked Clyde.

"You could say that, yes."

Clyde, who recognized Russo by the description given to him by Feeno, reckoned that catching Russo outside his office, preferably on the street, was the best way to actually corner the guy, even if it was open spaces. As he watched the well-dressed lawyer emerge from his law office building alone, even he was surprised at how easy it was.

"Mister Russo," said Clyde. "My name's Clyde Woolen. I'd like to talk to you."

Russo stopped, smiled and put out his hand, but his mood changed when Clyde identified himself as a private detective.

"Make an appointment, please, at my office." And he started to sidestep the big gumshoe.

"I think we should talk now," said Clyde. "In private. It's about Feeno Bannon. It's really about Feeno Bannon." Clyde stared hard into Russo's eyes.

"We can't go to my office," said Russo, now nervously looking in several directions.

"I'm not here to embarrass you," said Clyde. "Let's meet. How about six? You name the place."

Clyde drove into the parking lot and made one pass down the row of cars which were parked along the cyclone fence facing the ball field near the Summit Golf Course in Short Hills. He saw Russo near the third base line.

"Just a second," said Russo. "My kid's up to bat." Russo and Clyde were standing side by side behind the chain link fence near third base.

When the little boy struck out, Fred yelled, "It's okay Mikey, get 'em next time."

He turned to Clyde, who wasted no time getting to the point: "Raffie Quasarano and Peter Vitale. What can you tell me about them?"

"Now wait a minute," Russo snapped angrily. "Let's not forget the niceties here. Who the hell are you and who are you working for?"

Clyde apologized and told Russo that he was not at liberty to disclose his client's name but that, "Let's just say my client has an interest in this case. He has an interest in Feeno Bannon; in fact, I'll tell you this. He has some faith in Bannon and he doesn't like to see him being framed."

"Feeno can look out for himself as far as I'm concerned," said Russo.

Clyde paused, watching a slow ground ball travel under the glove of the third baseman and into left field. "I know all about Central Sanitation."

He watched Russo's eyes flicker, but Russo didn't respond.

So Clyde laid it out, with particular emphasis on the North Jersey Teamsters involvement in Hoffa's disappearance. "Sally Bugs. He was there, wasn't he? Tommy Andretta? He was there too. Both were in Detroit the day Hoffa got it. Witnesses put them there. Who got in the car with Hoffa, Fred? Was it Briguglio or one of the Andretta boys? These are all Teamsters. They're all with Local 560. One more, Local 319, Anthony Trapetto. He there, do you think? How about it? Where's Hoffa's body? Central Sanitation or someplace else?" Clyde half barked the information out with clenched teeth. He made sure that Russo heard, but no one else.

Russo forced a smile that fooled nobody, least of all Clyde, who continued, "The Health and Welfare fund. Unity Savings. Loans up the ass that are never repaid, including the $85,000 that went to Central Sanitation. "

"I don't think I'd better talk to you," said Russo, finally. "I don't appreciate this conversation."

"Well how about this?" said Clyde. "I'll leave you now, but there are a few things for you to consider."

He ticked off a list: "Crown Leasing, Atlantic Express, Rogers Transport. Ever hear of them, Fred? You should." As he talked, he kept his eyes on the playing field, diverted from Russo. "You're the guy who set 'em up. All dummy corporations, aren't they? You're the attorney of record."

"They're all legitimate companies," said Russo, unconvincingly.

"I know what they are. They're legit all right; your Teamster buddies own them and staff them with non-union drivers so that you can under-bid the union companies. You guys are screwin' your own union members."

Now that he had laid it all out for Russo, Clyde's attitude softened. "Listen, I know all of this is tough. Lots of things going down. Lots of indictments coming up. There are going to be a lot of guys taking the fall on this one. I would hate to see you among them. Most of these guys are bums. You know it. I look at you and I see a successful lawyer, a businessman, nice clothes, nice family. You have the most to lose. Feeno is going to testify some day. You know that. He also has a lot of respect for you. You have to know that too."

He looked out to left field, where a line drive had gone past the peewee fielder's glove and rolled toward the fence. "I'd hate to see you be one of the fall guys, Fred."

"I can take care of myself," said Russo, staring at the ball field, watching his two boys take the field. "Remember, I'm a lawyer." Then he turned toward Clyde and said, "I have a question for you. If you want information from me there's got to be a trade off. When are the feds going to get rolling on this? I hear that Feeno's back in custody, back in the witness program."

Clyde stared, stunned: "Where'd you hear that?"

"It's on the street," said Russo. "I'm sure you know better than I do."

Clyde was thinking hard, wondering what was going on. If Feeno were back in custody what was he doing at Ong's Hat just yesterday? Clyde stared at the lawyer with a look of wonder. Where the hell did this rumor originate? By whom and what for?

"That's all I know," said Russo.

Even though this meeting ended in a standoff, Clyde and Russo agreed to talk again. Before he left, Clyde leaned in close to Russo. "Fred, please just keep this in mind. All I'm interested in is

Central Sanitation. I wanta' know who forged Feeno Bannon's name on that loan authorization. I have the evidence on that. Was it you, or somebody else?"

On the way south down the Jersey Turnpike, Clyde wondered whether he had disclosed too much to Russo or whether he came down too hard on him. The conversation would not have suited Feeno. But Clyde picked up immediately that Russo was too clever to extend any kind of cooperation, even to his old friend Feeno. So Clyde reasoned to himself that he had to get the lawyer's mind working. Number One, Russo would by now be convinced that Clyde Woolen was working in some fashion for Feeno, or most likely Feeno's friend, Vince Berardi. Russo knew now that they had a ton of information available to them to use against the Scalesi mob. And how much of this information did the feds have?

Deep in thought as he drove, Clyde failed to pick up the car that had been tailing him until he arrived at Exit 7. The car, a dark Oldsmobile, chose the toll booth next to Clyde. After dropping his coins in the basket, Clyde hesitated.

The car in the next lane hesitated with him; its driver threw a glance at Clyde. About fifteen seconds passed until the car behind Clyde beeped impatiently. When Clyde pulled away, the car with the two men next to him continued past him, then slowed, letting Clyde pass again.

When he approached north of Vincentown, Clyde got off and continued south on Route 206, followed by the Olds, which then peeled off away toward town. Clyde slowed down. Not long afterwards a different car with two different men came into view in his rearview mirror. Thirty-five years of piled up instincts told him that these were feds. They had the resources to switch off cars when tailing someone. Things were getting tight, he thought. And he smiled because those same instincts told him that things were also warming up.

Chapter 40: TAKING LEAVE

Stan Schweitzer's mood was bad. He was late and he knew the rule: An FBI agent is late as often as his tie is crooked. As he parked and started to hurry into the Galloway Township PD building on Jimmie Leeds Road, he heard someone yell, "Yo!

"You Schweitzer?" asked the patrolman walking towards him.

"I am, you Ray Gewirtz?"

"Almost missed you."

"I apologize," said Schweitzer. "Big pileup on the White Horse Pike."

"I heard," said the officer, extending his hand. After the brief cordialities, Schweitzer got directly to the point, figuring this would be brief and he would be on his way back home in Morristown by mid-afternoon. He was tired and frustrated.

The information the officer gave Schweitzer was not only scant, but would lead to a long day. On June fifth, Gewirtz's ex-wife picked up a hitchhiker on Route 9: "Early morning, that I'm sure of. My wife was late for work as usual and I caught her barreling ass down Route 9."

But when he looked and studied the photo of Feeno Bannon that Schweitzer had handed him, he looked up, shook his head: "I really didn't get a good look at him, I'm sorry. I couldn't really say. It kind of looks like the guy, but I didn't get a good look from where I was in the patrol car."

Gewirtz told Schweitzer where he could find his ex-wife, who by this time would be finishing up her shift as the cleaning super at the Marina Casino in Brigantine. "You'll have to hurry if you want to catch her there."

A half-hour later, Schweitzer was on the phone with Mario Bianca. He held the photo of Bannon and smiled when he heard Bianca's voice.

Five minutes before, Amy Smith-Gewirtz had wiped her red hands on her apron, grabbed the photo, and said, "Yeah, that's the guy I picked up. No doubt. I remember the face. Handsome kind of guy, very polite. Real grateful that I stopped for him. He told me he lost his car keys running in the pines. He came across as telling the truth. He was a very convincing guy."

Bianca listened carefully to the story. He was excited but half-pissed that someone like Bannon could outsmart him and his Strike Force.

"She made a positive ID," said Schweitzer to Bianca. "Our boy may have been under our noses all along. Looks like he went to Atlantic City. This woman picked him up on Route 9 in the early morning after he busted out of Fort Dix. Right now, I'm on my way to Atlantic City International Airport. We'll see if he flew out of there."

"I thought we had all the airports checked," Bianca replied, jubilant over the news that the search for Feeno Bannon had narrowed but irritated that he might have slipped the noose again.

"I think we have to check again, also with Atlantic City PD, the toll clerks on the AC Expressway and Garden State Parkway, the bus terminals in particular, and listen, wire the photo down to the Cape May-Lewes Ferry. He may have gone to the Eastern Shore."

"That's where he was before," said Bianca, doubting that Feeno would go back to see his wife, who had since applied for her exit from the Witness Protection Program. "I don't think he would go back there."

"I don't either," said Schweitzer. "It's my guess he went to New York. He could get there easily by bus. Or rent a car. Or even buy one."

By the end of the week, Fish & Wildlife Agent Sid Willoughby had turned over to his boss in Trenton the license plate numbers of twenty-seven vehicles that he had spotted in the southwest quadrant of the Wharton State Forest that he patrolled in his pickup truck.

He hadn't taken too seriously the so-called "urgent need"

that was directed down to him and the other officers from his boss at F&W. It had happened before and the results were often the same. Almost never can your quarry be found in these woods.

Still, by now he had memorized the photo he kept on his dashboard. He stared sufficiently at each fisherman he encountered along the Mullica or at the many ponds scattered throughout his patrol area. He also put out the word to some of the old-time residents who called the Pine Barrens home. Only once in his thirteen-year career with F&W had he come across a missing body, either dead or alive. That was a dead one, a poor young girl whose decaying corpse he had discovered dumped beneath a bridge. It had been trapped in some fallen limbs and was swaying with the current. The girl, a teenaged rape and murder victim, had been missing from her Northeast Philadelphia home for a month.

The recent directive to be on the lookout for a tall man of about forty was on his mind, however, each time that he came across the tent of a camper or a truck with a cap. Camping in the portion of the park which Willoughby covered was forbidden except in designated areas. Still, on occasion he would find a tent tucked away in the brush. He would tell the occupants to move on to a campsite.

Willoughby was not told who he was searching for, neither he nor the other F&W officers were told who originated the directive. Originally, when the search was ordered for Feeno Bannon in the Pine Barrens, the FBI officers and state cops, who feared they would be assigned the task, shuddered. Mosquitoes, rattlesnakes and excessive humid heat was what they would encounter for sure. But Mario Bianca saved them from the assignments by calling in Fish and Wildlife.

"You guys will never find what you're looking for in that forest," said Bianca to Agent Schweitzer. "Don't even think about it. Let the guys who know the territory do the searching."

Willoughby became curious about the black Ford pickup when the driver gave it some gas as if to move quickly away. He followed it through the woods.

Feeno braced himself as the truck bounced from rut to rut.

He eased back on the accelerator, knowing that speeding up would only increase suspicion. When he hit the asphalt road, however, he floored it, easing back only when the F&W truck emerged from the woods and appeared to be gaining. Feeno slowed, then stopped.

"How ya' doin'?" Feeno piped when the officer walked up. He smiled brightly.

Willoughby saw a tall bearded man with dirty jeans and a sleeveless plaid shirt open to his tanned waist sitting behind the wheel. The man had a purple and red streak near his left eye. "Going pretty fast back there weren't you?"

"Yeah, I know. Shit. I thought youse was the law. The real law I mean."

"You better believe I'm the real law in these woods. Let's see your registration."

"That's what I mean. I ain't got it. I lost it. In a bar fight last weekend. Had my wallet on the bar when some big old guy came up and said he didn't like me lookin' at his woman. I told him kiss my butt and the next we know we is tumblin' 'round the floor. I got up and he knocked me on my ass again, and went out the door. When I got up my wallet's gone."

"Where'd this happen?"

"Dover, Delaware, after the stock car races."

"Let's have your name," said Willoughby, pulling a notebook from a back pocket.

"Robert Price, sir. P-R-I-C-E."

The F&W agent walked to the rear of Feeno's truck and jotted down the license number.

"Okay. You live in these woods?"

"Right now, yep. When it gets cold, I'll have to find me a warmer place."

Willoughby said Feeno could go.

It took less than twenty-four hours for the license number to be checked back to its alleged owner, one Alfred Peters, who had purchased the camper at the All Aces Used Car Lot on the Black Horse Pike east of Atlantic City on June 5...the same Alfred Peters whose career as a U.S. Marshal was shattered with the theft of his wallet and the escape of the man he was charged with protecting on June 4 at Fort Dix.

Evening was arriving when Feeno heard the chopper as it flew about a half-mile to the north. The rain that had begun an hour before was picking up in intensity. He got out of the rear of the truck and walked several yards to the south through the deep underbrush. He listened. Five minutes later the chopper returned, flying low except by this time it was about five hundred feet closer. No doubt, he thought, there was a pattern to its movements, and in a storm that was by now dumping solid sheets of rain, this was no routine search for forest fires.

When the chopper passed, he hastened to the truck once more, grabbed his sleeping bag, maps, compass, flashlight, his hunting knife and the new, never-used S&W revolver he purchased at the sporting goods store. He hefted the gun in his hands. He regretted telling the sales clerk that he needed a pistol for protection in the wilderness, for a camping trip he was taking in the Yukon. "Grizzly country." The thing was nearly a foot long and weighed three-and-a-half pounds, held five rounds and let loose a dangerous .500 caliber bullet. He never fired the gun. He aimed at a raccoon once, suspecting that the animal was one of the ones keeping him awake with blood chilling screeches at night. He couldn't pull the trigger. He had never aimed a weapon at a living thing, let alone shot one.

Stuffing his necessities in his backpack, he began walking through the rain, stopping and turning one time to say goodbye to his truck.

The old rundown house was about one-half mile south. He entered through the kitchen door that had said goodbye to its functioning hinges many years ago. It was easy to pry open. Thankful for the poncho he was wearing, he put down his gear, shook the water from his shoulders and looked around. This could have been the house of an iron worker or saw mill employee and his family many years before. Though small, houses like this in the Pine Barrens supported large families. This one had a brick fireplace, a living and sitting room of sorts, kitchen and shed on the first floor. Upstairs were three other rooms and a smaller one about the size of a large closet. It contained a shelf with a hole large enough to hold a basin. A small woodshed and falling down three-hole outhouse stood fifty feet from the back door.

Besides the dust and debris, vines and moss grew on the accumulated dirt. A still growing maple tree was taking over the territory of the rusted tin roof.

Lightning flashes and thunder claps roared through the pines as he waited, sitting on the dirt-strewn floor of an upstairs room. A flash caught a glimpse of torn lath and horsehair on the old walls, then thunder's boom about ten seconds later, a couple of miles away. The darkness that fell was so pervasive it seemed to have a fabric to it, a black gauze before his unseeing eyes. But the blindness gave him a blank screen of the mind in which to think: *"How much longer can I keep running?"*

He envisioned all the consequences of turning himself in: A jail cell, not just for his involvement with the Teamsters, stealing union funds through phony loans which he helped administer, but for being found guilty of stealing deposits of innocent borrowers, like from his best friend, Vince Berardi; for stealing the identity of a U.S. marshal, breaking and entering, stealing a canoe, for setting up the murder of Jimmy Hoffa. A dampness grabbed his spine at the thought of that one, a tingling of fear from his neck to his tailbone.

He touched the welt under his left eye. Still painful, but not so aching as the void it marked, the friendship lost, the trust gone of his last, best friend. He had prayed that Vince would not turn him in, but each of the last several hours spent creeping through the pines, settling in another risky hiding place, simply was part of the exhausting countdown. They would find him, a fear tempered only by the one which was worst. If the Scalesis found him first, all would be over. Maybe quickly, maybe a good thing at last.

At about ten o'clock he awoke from the brief but deep sleep that had finally caught up to his exhausted body. He stood, stretched, found his backpack and hoisted it from the floor, using the flashlight to find his way down the dangerously decrepit stairs. He kept southeast. The rain had abated and most of it had sunk into the absorbing sandy soil and into the huge, greedy reservoir beneath. He walked, hesitating at each paved road before hurriedly crossing it and resuming his trek into the forest. By now he knew many paths.

He arrived at the Bayshore Motel shortly before daylight pierced the eastern sky. The clerk on duty was an elderly woman who sat in a very worn but comfortable easy chair behind the counter. She was reading the classified ads in the *Shopper's Shore World*, and when Feeno asked for a room and put down the money, she pushed the registration book toward him, handed him the key, and said, "It's around back, toward the bay." She resumed reading.

Late the next morning, Feeno showered. He shaved away most of the beard that had given him the anonymity and protection over the past weeks. He looked in the mirror, wincing as he gently touched the awful souvenir that Vince had put upon his face. But he remarked to himself that the mustache and Van Dyke goatee he had fashioned were quite handsome. Feeling refreshed, partly due to sleeping in a bed and taking the hot shower, the first in several days, he looked beyond the window, thankful that he had a room on the rear side of the motel facing the back bay.

Carefully walking around to the front, he feigned casualness as he approached Edna's door and knocked softly. There was no answer. He knocked again and finally slid beneath the door the note he had written. Then he walked east along the highway, and at the edge of a newly built Park-and-Ride lot, which was created primarily for casino employees, he caught a bus to Atlantic City.

By noon he was sitting in the Chips & Slots Lounge of Caesar's Casino eating a bacon, lettuce and tomato sandwich. An hour later he was at a blackjack table. A red Phillies baseball cap was on his head, as were dark sunglasses and a slathering of zinc oxide upon his nose.

Chapter 41: LUCY THE ELEPHANT

Edna climbed wearily down the steps of the bus at the Park & Ride lot on Route 40 and walked the two hundred yards to the Bayshore Motel. She carried a thick loose-leaf notebook and held it tightly to her chest as she stooped to pick up the note left under her door.

She began reading it at the same time fumbling the key in the lock, and read it three more times inside, the last time just before stepping into the shower: Feeno/Bob's note of contrition, in handwriting that was apologetically florid, was the *mea culpa* of a one-night stand:

"I am sorry I left that night. I wanted to leave a note and had no paper and pencil. I'm sorry again. I should have called. I kept changing my mind about it. The memory of that night is why I am asking you to forgive and forget. Oh, bull shit, let's go to another movie."

She smiled, but tossed the note into the bathroom trash can prior to stepping into the shower, humming "I Will Survive." Ten minutes later when she toweled off, she noted in the mirror the sexy contrast of her white breasts and bikini bottom against the deep tan of her body.

She was wearing a crimson-colored Turkish bathrobe when he knocked on the door. She had rehearsed the moment in the shower, repeating to herself with different inflections, "Having no pen and paper is not a great excuse, Bob. You could have called, you know."

She opened the door and looked at a vastly different man, one with nearly shoulder length black and gray hair, a curious but neatly trimmed Van Dyke beard. He wore light blue bell bottoms, a black tee shirt fitting tightly over tanned and trim muscles. There was a white leather belt about his waist.

Suppressing a gasp at the sight of him, she said, unsmiling,

"I don't know if I should let you in."

"I know and I don't blame you," he responded, trying not to imagine what she wore beneath the red gown. He put on a mock shyness, face turned to the floor and from behind his back turned his arm and held out the bouquet of tiny tulips, protected with the giveaway cellophane of a 7-Eleven store.

"Just come with me for a ride. Please, Miss Edna," he said. "Look, it's a beautiful evening." The sun had just disappeared, letting in a cooler autumn night devoid of the close air, the high humidity of the day.

"I don't know. I need a couple of minutes," she said, quickly grabbing the door and pushing Feeno out with her left hand. "Wait outside," she said. "Please."

Edna slid the clothes hangers back and forth in her small closet, finally picking out her favorite gypsy dress, ankle-length and decorated with the print of ceramic Pueblo bowls.

She looked at herself in the mirror, brushed her hair and with a sigh, took off the dress and laid it on the bed. From the bottom dresser drawer she took out a stark white micro mini-skirt and squeezed into it. She picked out a pair of translucent plastic platform shoes, giving an image of sparkling champagne in the heels. The shoes gave her a little more height.

When she opened the door, still not welcoming him in, he glanced inside and was pleased to see the flowers sitting in a twelve-ounce glass full of water upon the little desk in the corner. The short skirt she was wearing relayed another message, that perhaps this affair was back to Square One. Not bad, he thought, as he led her to his new car, a five-year-old Mercury sedan, which he had parked on the bay side of the motel.

"Where's your truck?" she asked.

"Tranny went."

"What went?"

"The transmission." Now he smiled. "I thought you were a Southern girl. You should know what a tranny is."

As Feeno drove east on the Black Horse Pike into Atlantic City, he let her know that he was her new neighbor, newly moved in on the marshy side of the motel. She stared straight ahead, purposely nonplussed, giving him no indication that this was welcome, or even startling, news.

But a few minutes later, driving through the neat neighborhood of cottages on Atlantic Avenue flanking the ocean through Ventnor and Margate, Edna suddenly gasped and yelled, "What the hell is that?" She twisted her head around to see a large wooden pachyderm standing solitary next to the beach.

"That's Lucy the Elephant." Feeno smiled broadly, slowing down and finally braking. He put the car in reverse, then stopped. Blocking their view of the beach and ocean was an odd architectural spectacle, a good six stories high, painted gray with white tusks and bulging eyes. A large howdah sat atop the elephant, which in the fading light appeared to have a few square windows carved into its wooden flanks.

"I don't know much about it," Feeno said, "except that it's been here for decades. The story I heard is that some real estate guy built it. He was selling cottages here and that was his advertising gimmick."

"It's so big!" shouted Edna.

"You used to be able to go inside," said Feeno, pleased that the eccentric elephant, a giant Victorian anomaly — a protected and beloved architectural misfit — had come to his aid, at least momentarily breaking the mutual gloom between him and Edna. "It has stairs, and you can get a great view of the ocean and Atlantic City. At least that's what I'm told."

"I have to go inside it," she yelled.

"I'm afraid it's closed," Feeno said truthfully. "It's always being repaired and preserved by somebody. I think it's owned by one of those preservation committees. I'll tell you what. I'll check it out tomorrow and if it's still open, we'll go see it."

As they continued on down the highway and over the long, flat bridge over the Great Egg Harbor Inlet, Feeno remarked that "I'm told that you can see that elephant from about eight miles out to sea."

She looked at him with a large, sweet grin below her little freckled nose. "I have to see it," she said.

The remainder of that special evening was one that Feeno would enfold in memory thousands of times over the rest of his life, encapsulated and tucked in a corner of his mind, to be extracted and embraced on lonely days and nights.

They crossed the Ocean Drive Bridge over the inlet between Longport and Ocean City, finally stopping at a white clapboard restaurant with bright red shutters and outdoor tables on a broad porch overlooking the back bay. They laughed over the lobster dinner, letting the melted butter streak over their hands, wiping their faces on real cotton napkins after devouring corn on the cob.

"You look happy," said Feeno, leaning on his elbows.

"I am. I graduate next week."

"From the casino academy?"

"Yep."

"What's your grade point average?"

"What is what?"

"Nothing. I'm just teasing."

"Oh, I know what… Actually, I scored very high, my teacher says, in some areas. He said I have great hands. Lots of dexterity. I was the first in my group to master the shuffle and wash. You know what that is?"

"I think so."

She grinned wide-eyed. "The teacher said 'Look at that…It looks like a peacock's tail.'"

Feeno laughed aloud, as the waitress, a freckled girl with a mellifluous Irish brogue, filled their glasses with more iced tea. Edna had originally ordered a beer and was astonished to learn — in New Jersey, of all places — that alcoholic beverages were illegal in Ocean City.

"This town was founded by Methodists," said Feeno. "Big retreats here way back. But this is a very popular town. Lots of college kids come here, and at night they cross the bridge to Somers Point where the bars are. And get loaded."

They later strolled the boardwalk, Edna's big shoes clomping, ate crispy French fries from paper cups and soft ice cream in waffle cones. Feeno bought tickets for a ride at The Old Mill. They floated quietly through black tunnels on a wooden swan with seats. With his arm around her, he squeezed. She responded with a kiss. Like a gentleman, he resisted the urge to fondle.

They walked toward Wonderland Pier, which in the distance advertised itself with a big pinwheel of electric globes, a giant lit-up ferris wheel spinning slowly against the black sky. But about a block from the pier, Edna suddenly pulled Feeno toward the ocean, down the steps from the boardwalk onto the deserted beach where they removed their shoes. Edna ran and Feeno chased her to the tide line. Both splashed their feet in the cold surf as it lapped up and over their ankles. They walked in the surf for nearly a mile until reaching the boardwalk's end, where they stopped and held each other. He kissed Edna's hair, brushing it from her face. The autumn breezes grew stronger and colder. Her small body felt warm and protected against his.

"Can you come to my graduation?"

Feeno hoped that the hesitation in his voice was not detected, but his answer was sincere: "I'd love to come." That was true, he would love to come, if only...

When he left her bed that night, he said, "Thanks for welcoming me to the neighborhood. You don't know how good it feels that I don't have to leave a note and steal away in the dark."

He dressed. She walked him to the door, where he held her and whispered "Edna, sweet Edna. You can't imagine how I feel. knowing someone like you. Someone like you..." He paused, letting his head drop on her shoulder, pulling her tight.

"You make it sound like you never knew anybody like me before," she said, laughing. The porch light caught a glint in her eyes.

"The best thing about you, Edna, is that you're special and don't know it. God, I wish everyone was like that."

She hugged him tightly and looked up at his face. He noticed that her neck was tanned and muscular. Strong little shoulders.

"My mom says I take stuff too seriously. She said I bruise too easy." Her smile was forced as she looked up at his face.. "Don't run away on me, big guy." She poked his ribs with her small fist. "Stick around a while."

"I will, I will."

Chapter 42: SOUTH PHILLY

Feeno shaved and dressed, and as he combed his new beard the mirror showed that the lump of bruised flesh below the eye was diminishing. He touched it, and felt no pain, wondering at the same time if the bad feelings that his old best friend had for him were still there.

He walked to the bed, glanced out the window. He saw only a kid, grade school age, bouncing a beach ball near a station wagon loaded on top with luggage. A dad was pulling a beach umbrella and more suitcases out of the back. Seeing no one else, but jittery, Feeno lifted the mattress, and counted. New, crisp one hundred dollar bills fanned through his fingers. It had been his best night at a blackjack table since the day after his escape from Fort Dix, the day he was hustled out of the casino as a card counter after his first big score.

He sat at the small table and from the drawer removed a postcard with the etching of the Castel Sant' Angelo in Rome. On the back he wrote Vince's address and on the other side panel drew with a flourish his best imitation of Roman cursive: "Fortino's Ristorante…" On the way to the bus stop he slipped a note beneath Edna's motel room door inviting her – "Let's get a bite to eat tonight."

When Vince picked the postcard out of his sidewalk mailbox the next day and slapped it in his hand, he read it half pissed at Feeno's insolence, yet curious as hell as to what he was up to now.

Later that afternoon he told Julie that he was going to a Phillies' game, but made the mistake of announcing the lie when his two girls were in the room.

"Daddy, daddy, can we go?" yelled Patty, with echos provided by Gloria, the six-year-old.

"Not tonight," he said. "You have school tomorrow." He added a *mea maxima culpa* to mollify the list of letdowns to his children. "Besides," he said, feeling terrible about this whopper, "the way the Phillies are playing lately, this will probably be another extra inning game and we'd get home awful late."

Julie mumbled something about his past promises. "Don't keep letting them down on this. You told them you'd take them to a game soon."

"I will, I will. I promise!"

She gave him a curious look, one that asked, "What are you up to?"

The post card announced that Banone would not be performing until nine o'clock, giving Vince time to kill between the alleged arrival at Vets' Stadium on South Broad Street and getting to Fortino's. He drove around his old neighborhood in South Philly, going down Mifflin Street, wondering how people managed to thrive in the choking confinement of these row houses.

At one time, the Berardis had lived in a neighborhood whose tiny brick homes had been built upon an ash dump. The SEPTA bus would rumble by, Momma Berardi's dishes rattled and shook in her dining room cabinet. Once, the cabinet smashed upon the floor, corrected only after Vince's father wired the back of the cabinet to the wall.

Vince smiled, reflecting now how the row-house blocks were like massive dormitories, with privacy afforded only by thin walls. Just one big family, snarling for space and loving each other at the same time. Outside was even more vivid a scene of closeness. The cars were parked end to end on one side of one-way streets. Parking spaces in South Philly were so rare and valuable that disputes over rights to them were frequently settled by flying fists.

Vince drove to Pat's Steaks at 9th and Passayunk and after circling the Capitolo playground across the street, he was able to pounce upon an open parking spot just as it became empty. He backed into it just ahead of another car, a Toyota, whose driver shoved up his middle finger. Vince replied in kind.

An hour later he was in Fortino's. This time he sat at the

bar and told the hostess, who was the stunningly attractive daughter of the owner, that he would not be ordering dinner. It being a week night, the place was only half full.

He no sooner told the bartender that he might be getting a phone call, when it rang. The bartender picked it up, and said, "Hold on a minute." He looked and nodded toward Vince, whose fingers were wrapped around a glass of sherry. Vince put it down at the waiter's station and walked around to the more private hallway.

"I know it's risky calling you, but it's important, worth your while." said the voice after Vince had answered with a hesitant, "Hello."

"Important to who?" Vince asked. "Me or you."

"To you, Vince, to you."

There was silence until Vince said, "What am I supposed to be, excited or something?"

"Vince, I want to move on. I'm hanging by a thread." He added, "It's important to you Vince," said Feeno softly. "And to your wife." He added seconds later, "And kids."

"I'm not coming near you again, Feeno. You can go piss up a rope."

"Vince, Vince, please." He let his voice quiet down. "Look, just tell Clyde to pick up a package. I haven't been able to reach him. I'm afraid to call. I think his phone is bugged. Please. Just tell him. He knows how to reach me."

Vince's answer was, "I gotta go."

"Vince, tell him," came the loud voice from the other end. "Tell him, please tell him..." He heard the buzz of a hang up.

Vince walked out the side door as it was getting dark outside, streets enveloped in shadows. He had a long three blocks to walk to get to his latest parking space. The streets were shiny after a quick shower of rain and the early autumn air hung humid. None of the residents were out sitting on their front steps, as was the usual summertime custom before bedtime. The street was empty as Vince passed a closed auto parts store, which stood next to a boarded up house of a kid that he knew years ago. Vince wondered what happened; wondered where the family was now. There was silence except the drone of a plane taking off from

Philadelphia International Airport only a few blocks away, and the tiny yaps of a little dog somewhere.

Around the next corner, Vince looked up to see a man approaching, walking fast, very vast. He had his eyes fixed on Vince's. Nervously, Vince looked over his shoulder and just as quickly another form closed in behind, grabbing him by the neck and yanking him into an alley. In a split second Vince found himself pushed against a brick wall, held up high in the grasp of both men. A hand was clasped across his mouth.

"No fuckin' around now buddy! What was the phone call about? And don't scream!" Vince felt a sharp point scratching his gut. Just to make certain, the thug with the knife held it to his eyes. "Don't yell out, you bastard."

Vince's reply was a series of stammers, the gist of which was that "I don't know what you're talking about." The taller of the two men thrust his forearm against Vince's throat and lifted. Vince couldn't talk anymore even if he tried.

"Are you gonna let us know what your buddy wanted? Did he say where he is? Is he in Philly? And don't give us that 'I don't know' shit!"

After weeks of being haunted and chased, with memories of the beating with the gun, the losses and accusations, the built-up frustrations and questions — all culminated in a sudden and surprising fury. Vince grabbed one man by the crotch and pulled and twisted as hard as he could, at the same time coming down hard with his heavy work boot upon the foot of the other. Both men dropped their hands. The one with the aching balls howled. Vince reached out and grabbed him by the shirt front. Getting two hands full of jersey he spun and yanked at the same time, with centrifugal force driving the hoodlum against the opposite brick wall. Vince heard a crack as the man's head stuck the bricks. The man dropped to the ground.

Vince approached the other man, grabbed him by the head and pushed it down, at the same time coming up with his knee into his face. At this point, some dark shadows, cast by the dingy street light beyond, formed at the entrance to the alley. Immediately, two other men appeared. They were equally strangers, but one yelled, "FBI! Hands on the wall!"

The two federal agents took over the scene by quickly tripping the standing thug to the ground. Each of them grabbed an arm and bent it back up towards his head in a way that offered no compromises, and no getting away. Handcuffs went on and the assailants were yanked to their feet. Blood was trickling down the face of the one who encountered the wall. Within a few minutes, a blue car with a burp of its siren, came to a halt in the street, joined by another and then a third. The Philadelphia Police Department had joined the party.

"Are you all right, Mister Berardi?" asked one of the agents, a younger man who was breathing hard and sweating.

"Yes," said Vince, leaning against the wall and panting, wiping beads of sweat from his face with a forearm. "I never felt better in my life. Thank God you guys showed up. You must have been tailing me." He looked anxiously at one of the agents, who was indistinguishable from any other guy in the neighborhood, wearing a faded blue work shirt over worn jeans.

"Not just tonight" said the other agent, grinning. He pulled out his badge, and said, "I'm Agent Hillary. This is Agent Moore. We've been watching you for a while."

A cop in uniform approached, hand on his pistol. He was pulled aside by Hillary.

In a minute the cop walked to Vince and asked, "You want to file charges against these guys?" Both assailants were being guided, handcuffed to a nearby patrol car.

"I don't even know who they are," Vince said after a cop led him to his blue sedan with the whirling red light on the roof. By now, people had come out of their houses and accumulated on the sidewalk. Some of them bent over to get a closer look at Vince. The assailants were already driven away.

A fat man came out his front door, looked over the crowd and said to a neighbor, a woman with her red hair in curlers, "Anybody shot? Anybody dead?"

A plainclothes Philly detective drove up and eyed Vince up and down, then bent over and asked him to step outside. The detective huddled with the FBI agents for a good ten minutes, and when he came back, he said, "I'm sorry, Mr. Berardi, are you okay?" Someone had called for medical support and an EMT walked up to

Vince and said, "We think you had better go to the hospital with us, just to be sure."

Vince twisted his neck a couple of times and insisted that he was sound enough to go home.

"I'm okay." The adrenaline was still pumping. He meant what he said.

"Do you know who these two are who attacked you?"

"No. No, don't recognize them."

"Well they're familiar to us. Philly mob guys."

They decided to let Vince go home and the FBI agents said they would be right behind him, following him to Medford. Vince had plenty of time to think on the way. The fact that hoodlums other than the Scalesis had entered the picture, though evidently at the request of the Scalesis, chilled his spine and raised an anxiety that he thought he had under control.

By the time he pulled into his quiet street and into the driveway, Julie and the kids were asleep. He was thankful. He decided he would keep this little incident quiet for a while and he was comforted by the fact that the FBI guys didn't leave until a patrol car from the Medford police drove up and parked outside. "They're going to stay there all night." said Agent Hillary, handing Vince his card and adding, "If anything comes up tonight, call me. And I mean any thing and any time."

The one person Vince was anxious to talk to was Clyde, whom he called and asked to come over, even though it was late. Vince told the cop in the police car that Clyde was a friend. They sat in Clyde's car and Vince told him what happened, including his phone conversation with Feeno and that Feeno left something for him at Ong's Hat.

"Not Ong's Hat."

"What do you mean?" asked Vince.

"A few things are changed, Vince. The less you know the better. Listen, I don't want you pulling this Lone Ranger shit anymore without me going with you. Understand? These guys are more and more desperate. You could have gotten killed."

"I know, I know, I'm sorry. Believe me, it will never happen again."

"And look," Clyde said. "Stay away from the Pines.

Whatever it is that Feeno left, I'll get it."

The next day about supper time Clyde showed up with a large manila envelope, addressed to "VB." In it was eighty $100 bills, new and crisp. A note that was clipped to one of the bills read tersely, "First installment. Bal. $28,000."

A knock on the door at six a.m. the next morning alerted Vince and family to a new problem. Two FBI agents, including Stan Schweitzer, with whom Vince was growing more comfortably acquainted, stood there along with Brian Hillary, one of the agents from the night before. They wore grave faces.

Vince invited them into the kitchen, where they sat while Julie, her face full of consternation, made coffee.

Schweitzer declined to sit, standing instead in the doorway, looking at Vince, then at Julie, and back again to Vince, "We think it's best that you move your family to a safe house for the time being. As soon as possible."

"What?" yelled Julie. "What are you talking about? What on earth is a safe house? This is a safe house."

She looked at her husband: "What's going on, Vince? What happened last night. You got home late. What happened?"

Vince looked at the two agents. Schweitzer shrugged and Hillary looked at Julie. With Julie's angry eyes upon him, Vince began telling what happened. He stopped when the two girls walked sleepily into the kitchen. Emily went to the refrigerator, pulled out the half-gallon of orange juice. Vince reached into the overhead cabinet, grabbed her favorite juice glass, "The Aristocats", from the cupboard above and handed it to her. He gave a Donald Duck glass to Gloria.

"Please, let's take this conversation elsewhere," said Julie. The adults moved away, letting the kids take over the kitchen.

Schweitzer and Hillary sat on the living room sofa and remained silent as Vince explained what happened in the alley. Julie's angry face turned to fear when he described the fight. He told about the FBI agents and Philly police coming to his rescue. He mollified the attack by saying the mob guys "tried to hustle me a little.".

"Luckily, the FBI was right behind them," Vince said,

adding, "Julie, I..."

But she interrupted, looking at Schweitzer with her arms folded before her: "What do you want us to do?"

"Do you have some place to go where you know you'll be safe?" asked Schweitzer. "Otherwise, we can find a safe house for you."

"Would you mind not calling it a safe house?" she asked. "That gives me the creeps."

Vince interjected, "Maybe John's," meaning Julie's brother, John Wolyniak, the Cherry Hill cop.

"It should be someplace where someone is around all day, friends you can count on," said Schweitzer.

Julie said, "No, John's place is no good. Everybody is out of the house in the daytime. John and Kathy work; the kids are in school. I want to go to the farm. There's protection there. Mom and Dad, the help, somebody's there all day long, and all night."

Vince tended to agree that the ninety acre vegetable farm and farm stand operated by the Wolyniak family near Buena was a busy, active place this time of the year. Often the same people stopped at the highway stand on Tuckahoe Road every day for fresh fruits and vegetables. They went beyond being customers; they were friends and neighbors.

It was settled. They would shutter their house and leave immediately.

Chapter 43: NICKY NUTS

Rocco Scalesi picked up a copy of the *Star-Ledger* at a Mobil station in Carteret, hurried to the green Olds parked at the air hose with the motor running. He squeezed into the front seat and ordered Tommy Cisco, his driver, to "stay right here a minute."

He reread the Page One story three times, as if trying to pry from between the lines the possible consequences of the headline reading, "Teamsters Lawyer Arrested on Federal Charges." There was a photo and caption of "Fred Russo, the dapper attorney of the North Jersey Teamsters Union, being led in handcuffs to his arraignment in the federal court house in Newark."

The charges had to do with fraudulent transactions between the North Jersey Teamsters Health and Welfare Fund on deposit in the closed Unity Savings & Loan bank in Clifton. "Though not the brains of the scheme, Russo, a prominent North Jersey attorney, was described by U.S. Attorney Mario Bianco as 'the man who made it work'."

The article went on to titillate its readers with the background information that Fred Russo was the younger brother of the singer and movie star, Lena Russell.

"What's wrong?" asked Tommy Cisco, lighting a cigarette with the dashboard lighter.

"Nothin,'" said Rocco, who crushed the newspaper in his hands. "Nothin' except now we got another potential rat. Get going."

"Where we going?"

"Back to the house, quick."

On the way, Rocco ordered Tommy to stop at a drug store in a small strip mall in Spring Lake. He found a pay phone and called the Connerly Security Co. where he told the manager to "come to my place at the shore. I want to add some cameras."

He made a second phone call to Nicholas Campanio sixty miles down the coast in Atlantic City. With the man called "Nicky Nuts" on the phone, Rocco and he talked about the latest development.

"I felt that without Feeno Bannon to testify, our chances of springing loose from all this bullshit would be a certainty. But things are piling up."

"What are you worried about?"

"Russo, Fred Russo. That's who I'm worried about."

Rocco hadn't talked to Nicky in days. Nicky was a handy guy but he was one wiseguy that you used only when things got tough. Nicky's propensity in handling problems was to act first and don't think at all, let alone think later. A murderous lust for revenge and his subsequent lack of remorse classified him, even among hard-core Mafiosi, as a psychopath. Other mobsters were sometimes afraid to be around him.

"I'm tired of dickin' around, Nick," said Rocco. "And you know what I'm talkin' about. I need somebody who can take charge of a certain problem and make quick decisions and who ain't afraid when the going gets tough." He outlined the latest problem over the Russo indictment, plus the ongoing search for Feeno Bannon. He solicited the thug's advice: "You got any ideas?"

Chapter 44: TO GRANDMA'S HOUSE

Taking up residency, whether temporary or not, at the Wolyniak farm, provided Julie and Vince with the same kind of warm feeling that soul food does for the tummy. They unpacked in the small but cheerfully chintzy guest room. The big Queen Anne house was an oasis in the flat and often hot South Jersey landscape, surrounded by a dozen tall oak trees set back about a half-mile from the highway and the family's roadside vegetable stand. The girls had the room next to their parents and immediately settled into a laughing and tickling wrestling match on the big featherbed. Going to grandma's was an adventure, and staying overnight was an even more exotic visit.

  In addition to feelings of warmth and security, there was a shucking off of a vast cloak of worry, thanks mostly to the surroundings.

  After a while, the noisy kids' romp in the bedroom next door fell to silence. Vince guessed correctly that they had gone downstairs to forage for some homemade preserves or freshly squeezed lemonade in Grandma's refrigerator.

  He lay on the bed exhausted, occasionally rubbing beneath his chin, which his assailants from the night before had used as a handle. Julie lay down beside him, rolled half onto him and touched his cheek. She wouldn't ask about the night before, but let him talk when he began smiling and told her how good it felt to see "that bum drop to the ground when I threw him into the wall."

  Shadows cast by the big, old oaks on the back lawn splayed across the bedroom wall. They danced in a new breeze that had come up from the river and was captured and tossed throughout the room by the small ceiling fan above them. They felt the cooler air touch their skin, soothing and caressing. Who got horny first is a question of no value. The tensions of the past twenty-four hours were ripped away literally. Shoes, socks, slacks, pants, shirt, blouse, boxer shorts and panties were yanked and tossed to and fro, on the floor, the chair, the bookcase and upon the bed. Julie's bra landed atop the bedside lampshade. They clasped on the smothering downy bed, and after a few spasmodic strokes followed by mutual convulsions, Vince rolled over and looked up at the ceiling, watching the blades of the ceiling fan turn slowly.

"Wow, what happened?" said Julie, smiling and turning to touch his face. "That was like the Fourth of July!" She was sweating and panting, bosom heaving.

"Oh, ye gods, did I need that!" Vince replied in return. He looked at her face and lightly touched her right breast: "You are still the ripened plum that I knew and adored in my youth." he said.

"Thank you, that's very romantic and complimentary," she said.

"No, but you're still a plum. No, you're a cherry waiting to be plucked from the tree, a succulent grape from the vine. You never change. You're as ripe and voluptuous today as you were when I first met you. Just a wee bit sluttier. I love slutty women."

"And you're a fruitcake," she said. "I confess I'm a little fond of fruity men."

They got dressed in shorts, went down stairs, collected the girls and decided to stroll down to the stream which bordered the southern edge of the farm. Their path was a tractor's width between rows of tall corn, the kind of "horse corn" that is harvested late and fed to cows and other cattle. The green stalks were still in the humid air though they were easily seven feet high.

The stream was running low on water, dissipated by the late summer heat. Julie and Vince sat on its bank. Vince tossed pebbles, watching the rings grow and fade on the water's surface. The girls took off their sandals and waded. Vince noticed the tan of their legs and little bug bites, battle scars of the wonderful days of summer. Both girls had curly black hair which tended to lighten in the summer sun.

Patty was holding her sandals in one hand and balancing with both feet as she climbed upon a fat log that had fallen over the stream. Vince no sooner said, "Careful there, girl," when her foot slipped and she tumbled backwards into the water.

Julie yelled and stood up, but Vince sat back and watched,

knowing the water was barely two feet deep. Patty waded toward shore, soaked and laughing, wringing out her shorts with her hands. Gloria was in spasms giggling at her older sister.

"C'mon," said Julie, grabbing Patty's hand and pulling her out of the water. "That's enough acrobatics for one day." She and Patty turned toward the lane. Julie said, "We're leaving."

"I'll be along in a minute," Vince said, feeling drowsy and so very comfortable on the grassy bank, watching water bugs skating along the stream. Just a few inches above them were a couple of dragon flies, while in the cornfield some crickets were getting in their last chirps before autumn descended.

His reveries lasted only about ten minutes. It was getting late and supper would be on the table soon. He got up stiffly, stretched and took one last look at the stream and woods beyond, and headed back to the house.

Julie's mother, Marie, asked, "Have a nice swim?" Her husband, Jake, was washing his tanned arms and hands in the kitchen sink. His forehead looked strangely white from wearing his hat, in contrast to the ruddy leathered look of his sunburned face.

"You're asking the wrong person," Vince said, letting the screen door slam against his back. "That smells good," he said, noticing that he was ravenous. Afternoon sex and a lazy lie will stoke an appetite.

Julie, who came down from upstairs, followed by Patty, who wore clean shorts and a Muppets tee shirt, yelled, "Gloria, supper's ready. "C'mon, quit poking," she yelled again, directing her voice up the back staircase.

They sat at the table, and Julie said to Patty, "Will you go upstairs and see what she's gotten into?" She helped herself to mashed potatoes and passed them onto Vince.

"She wasn't up there when I came down," Patty said, and rose reluctantly, sometimes annoyed at the sister-keeper role thrust upon the oldest.

"Mom, she's not up here," said Patty, walking down the back steps. "Maybe she's out on the porch."

Vince got up from the table, threw his napkin down heavily upon his empty plate and trudged out the screen door. "Gloria," he yelled. "C'mon honey! Supper's ready."

Silence bothered him at times where Gloria was concerned. She was an active child, but given to daydreaming and at times to selective hearing, especially when called to supper or to bed.

"Gloria, goddammit! I'm tired of fooling around. Where are you? Get in here!" He walked around the house and met Julie coming the other way.

A half hour later, the supper that was cooling on the kitchen table turned trivial as Vince ran from the house to the stream, stopping and yelling, "Gloria!" as loudly as he could. He slowed down and walked slowly beside the tall corn, looking for paths that might occur when someone enters the field. Seeing no evidence, he ran back again to the creek and walked its bank about a hundred yards in each direction, looking into the water and opposite into the other cornfield. Again, he found nothing. Julie and Patty ran toward the highway and the roadside stand, where Elmer, a teenaged boy who worked there, was closing up the shutters for the night.

"Elmer, have you seen Gloria?" Julie asked.

"Not since you all drove up this afternoon," he answered. He could see by the desperate look on Julie's face that something was wrong, and so he asked, and when he learned that the little girl had not been seen for the last hour, he jumped in the jeep and told Julie that "I'll take a look around. Maybe she went out to the field barn or something."

Back at the house, everyone attempted not to panic. "Let's organize this," said Jake. "Let's start at the top of the house, search every room, and come down. She's got to be around somewhere."

Gloria was not to be found in any of the upstairs or downstairs rooms. Jake and Vince searched the cellar, then the outbuildings, checking the old fallen down corn crib and the barn and horses' stalls. He jumped up into the hay loft and peered down the hole to the stalls below. Nothing!

Jake and Vince climbed into Vince's Bronco, told the women to stay put "in case she shows up" and drove to the highway, going back and forth for a couple of miles in each direction. "It's foolish to think she'd be out here by herself," Vince said.

Jake looked at Vince with the most serious gaze. Vince

began shaking all over and had difficulty breathing.

"No, no, no, no, it can't be!" he repeated to himself.

With the sun fading from behind the tall trees to the west, Jake and Vince returned to the house and when Julie asked, Vince merely shook his head from side to side. "Nothing," he said.

"I'm calling 9-1-1," Vince said, and when the operator answered, he told her as casually as he could that they could not find their daughter.

"How long has she been missing?" asked the woman.

"I don't know, an hour, maybe two hours."

The woman paused and said, "We usually don't respond this early to a missing person problem," but Vince interrupted:

"Listen, this is an emergency. It's different, it's different. I am her father and I and my family have been receiving protective custody from the police and FBI. It has to do with a criminal investigation."

During the next three hours, two New Jersey state police cars pulled up to the house. The FBI arrived from Philly. That was when it dawned on both Julie and Vince that something terribly, terribly bad had happened. They hugged, and then Julie wept. "I can't handle this, Vince. I can't handle it!"

Vince walked out to the yard when Agents Schweitzer and Hillary had driven up. They were talking in a low key with the state police officers. "Listen," Vince said, "I can't believe that the Scalesis would be involved in this. They don't kidnap children, do they? How? I can't believe they would do this?"

"We don't know yet," said Schweitzer. "But we'll find out."

A hastily organized search team of police, FBI agents, volunteer firefighters, Boy Scouts, members of an American Legion post, 4-H Club kids, plus neighbors and high school students began searching fields and woods and the stream. It went through the night. A squad of four tracking dogs arrived and began looking for Gloria.

About midnight, Vince sank onto the wooden two-seater swing on the porch and held his head. The yard and house seemed ablaze with floodlights as searchers repeatedly went through rooms, down into the cellar and through the barn and other outbuildings.

Julie came up and sat beside him. He squeezed her hand. "We'll find her," he said with false hope. "We'll find her."

Schweitzer walked onto the porch, rubbing his sweat-filled brow with a handkerchief. "Can I talk to you a minute, Vince?"

He began to walk toward the far end of the porch, with Vince following. But Vince stopped and motioned for Julie, "You're a part of this. Come with us."

Julie followed.

"Look, this is difficult," Schweitzer began, "and I won't gloss over it. It's going to get tougher. They will call, I am sure. They will ask you to tell them where Feeno is. If you want to get Gloria back."

"This may be against procedure," Schweitzer said. "Certainly, the bureau doesn't want the Scalesis to get their hands on Bannon. But this is different. I can't advise you to put Bannon's life ahead of the safety of your daughter. Do whatever it takes to get Gloria back. You will have to cooperate with whoever calls and promise to do what you are asked to do. Let us handle the rest."

Julie began to cry and turned away. Tears filled Vince's eyes. He swallowed hard, and nodded toward Schweitzer: "Thanks."

At 3:07 a.m. the call came. They were seated in the living room — Vince in a hardback chair next to the phone on a small end table. Julie on the couch leaning forward. Schweitzer stood next to Vince. Three other agents, plus a state police captain, stood in the doorway between the living and dining rooms. When the phone rang, Schweitzer coordinated the signal, looking over his shoulder to an agent in the corner wearing headphones. Schweitzer snapped down his index finger when Vince was to pick up.

"Hello," Vince said, the word ringing hollow down the line.

It was a woman's voice: "She's fine," the woman said softly.

A different voice came on the line: "Daddy!"

When Vince heard Gloria the tears and words came flooding out of him. "Oh baby, my baby!"

"These people took me, Daddy. Please come and get me. I don't like it here."

He heard a brief rustling sound at the other end, and the

woman came on again. Her voice was incredibly soft and calm: "You tell us where he is and you get your daughter back."

The words came tumbling. Vince was a man about to drown, out of air and about to die and was frantic to grab onto anything: "He's in the Pine Barrens," he yelled. "I don't know where exactly. I'm telling you the truth. It was Ong's Hat, I don't know. I don't know. I'll help you find him. Please, please, don't harm my daughter. Please, please!"

Schweitzer yanked the phone from his grasp: "Listen, return the child and we'll let you go," he yelled. "There won't be any charges pressed." A second later, his shoulders dropped and the phone hung in his hand at his side. He looked to another agent sitting in the corner. The man shook his head: "We lost 'em."

Chapter 45: A GOODBYE

Clyde Woolen was on his way north when KYW News Radio announced "a child missing in Buena in South Jersey." When he heard the name "Berardi," he gasped and pulled off the highway at the Woodrow Wilson service area.

There was no answer at the Berardi house. He called the FBI in Philly, where he learned that the family was at the Wolyniak farm in Buena. He got the number from 4-1-1 and called:

Again the signal to answer the phone was given to Vince. When he heard Clyde's voice, he looked at Schweitzer and shook his head from side to side, letting him know that the kidnapper was not on the phone.

"Vince, I know how tough this is," said Clyde. "They'll get her back. I know they will."

He asked to speak to Schweitzer, who picked up the phone and listened, concentrating with a mix of disbelief and also of feint relief and optimism, shaking his head affirmatively. He walked out of earshot into the dining room.

"I understand what you're saying and welcome your cooperation," he told Clyde. He added: "It's possible that Bannon will come in now, if he has a conscience. We don't know. At this point, I'm willing to try anything. Let me know what you come up with."

Clyde asked to speak to Vince again. He told Vince that he was on his way north to visit Fred Russo when he heard the news on the radio. As Vince talked, he looked out the window of the living room and could see, far away at the end of the lane, a couple of TV trucks parked at the lot of the farm stand, with their antennas poking the South Jersey sky.

"I know this may sound strange, but I have a feeling that Russo can help us on this," said Clyde. "I'll be talking to you later. And if there is anything you need, let me know. I'll be in touch."

Neither of them had mentioned Feeno Bannon, the cause celebre of recent events. Where was he now? Did he know what has happened? How will he react?

As Clyde and Vince talked, a pair of helicopters was flying overhead, back and forth over the wild expanse of woods, stubby rivers and and sand hills that made up much of South Jersey. Jeeps and police cars sped down dirt roads, searching.

When Feeno heard the news of the kidnapping, his first impulse was to shoot himself on a public highway and thus put an end to everything. With his death, the child would be released and a sense of normalcy would return to some very good people whom Feeno had come to love, and at times, regret knowing.

He tried pushing back the fear that was taking over his brain. He decided that he had to get out of the motel. He needed time to think. He stared out the window to the little dock stretching into the marsh. There was a rowboat tied up. He walked to it, got in and rowed about one hundred fifty yards to a channel that led toward the back bay. It was surrounded by tall marsh grass. He pulled into it and rested, hidden and safe in the rushes.

A half hour later Feeno emerged from the marsh grass with a desperate plan. Going to the front of the motel, he took a chance. He went to her door and knocked.

"Hi!" she said with a quick smile and let him in. They embraced. She seemed particularly glad to see him. "What are you up to" she said. "Aren't you working today. I have no classes. Want to do something?"

"No, not now," he said. "There's something I have to tell you."

He stood in the doorway and watched, with deepest yearning, how she brushed her hair. He wanted to grab and hug her.

"Have you seen the TV?"

"It's been on," she said, "but I only half listen."

"About the kidnapping."

"Oh, that little girl. Oh, God, it's terrible."

"I'm the one responsible for that," he said, as she abruptly turned and stared.

"Don't get me wrong, I didn't kidnap her." He began his story hesitantly, watching as her face turned dark and bewildered.

"My name is not Bob Price. I'm not a carpenter," he said. "My real name is Joseph Bannon. They call me Feeno. I'm a bank president."

He sat on the chair in front of the small desk. On the TV a young woman holding a microphone was seen standing near a roadside stand, pointing back to the Wolyniak farmhouse: "The child disappeared from this field about dinner time last night. It wasn't until several hours later that the kidnapper called and told the child's father that little Gloria was being held..."

Feeno turned it off and looked at Edna. "It's true, Edna. All true. Listen, I wouldn't blame you if you just booted me out and told me not to come back. I understand."

She sat on the bed, staring alternately at him and the TV.

"I was married," Feeno said. "I'm still married. I lost my wife. She's with another man. We were in the Witness Protection Program."

She sat silently while Feeno told her everything. Not a sound in the room when he stopped. Outside the casino-bound traffic sped by in a senseless rush.

When he was finished, he told her, "I'm going to turn myself in, but I have to do something first." Edna remained silent, staring at the floor. He moved to touch her but she shook her head and spoke something. Her voice was a hoarse whisper.

When Feeno asked, "What?", she said gently:

"Leave. Just leave."

He got up and began to walk to the door, but turned and walked back to the bed. He grabbed her by the shoulders and squeezed her tight to him. She stood lifeless, her arms hanging at her sides. She refused to look up at Feeno.

In a rush, he said, "This may be the last time I see you. This may be the last day that I see anybody." She looked up wonderingly and slightly frightened.

"I have some things to do. I have to move fast." He held her with both hands at arms' length, staring at her stunned face, imploring: "I don't know what's going to happen. I only ask you, please, please, reveal nothing to anybody about what I told you. At least for twenty-four hours. After that I don't care. After that, I may not care about anything. That's all I ask. Give me one day, and I'll be gone."

He turned and went to the door, half-opened it and stopped. He turned to her: "Edna, I love you. I love you more than anything!"

She began to cry and looked at him through a blur of tears, her voice and chin trembling:

"Leave!" she screamed. "Get out! Get out! Get out!"

Chapter 46: THE RAIL YARD

Clyde searched ahead on the highway for signs to Exit 15E, as Russo had instructed. Driving interstate highways in this part of New Jersey demanded a sixth sense regarding which side of the highway would the exit lane be on. Often, directional signs would come up quickly, demanding sharp turns and sharp eyes in the face of a bull rush of traffic.

Russo had told him to go to Fish House Road, which was not exactly prime residential real estate. It was a neighborhood crisscrossed by rail lines in a mammoth freight yard which serviced the New York City metropolis.

Judging from the unwelcoming and shabby remoteness of the area, Clyde figured that Russo wanted privacy above all else for this upcoming conversation. He fingered the .38 beneath his jacket and was thankful that he decided to strap on a second small Beretta to his ankle. He had been told to find a dirt road going north from Fish House that crossed a double set of tracks, then turn left and stop at a deserted metal warehouse building that was overshadowed by a large rusted crane.

The tires of Clyde's Mustang crunched the dirt and gravel as he braked to a halt beneath the crane. He watched and listened. At least once every minute he heard and felt the roar of jet engines overhead. Newark International Airport was only a few miles to the south, and the rail yard was also beneath the flight paths of Kennedy and LaGuardia airports. In the distance could be heard the steady hum of highway traffic going in and out of New York.

Clyde looked down at the note he had scribbled hastily. On the phone, Russo seemed out of breath and in a great hurry. "Crane...northwest...warehouse" meant that when Clyde got to the crane he was to look northwest toward the end of the old warehouse building. He got out of the car, looked forward and backward. There was not a human nor automobile in sight, just tracks and long lines of rail cars about two blocks away in either direction.

He walked into the warehouse, which was a corrugated metal building, filthy with busted out small, filth-encrusted windows. The concrete floor was littered with glass and rusted pipes, old wooden crates and loading pallets. Clyde bypassed one area where a couple of dirty mattresses lay on the floor along with pieces of crack pipes, needles and used condoms.

"Over here," came an echoing voice. Clyde turned and saw in the shadows a tall, thin man who looked like Russo, minus the natty clothes. He was wearing khaki jeans and shirt beneath a nondescript sports jacket, and dark sunglasses. But Clyde could see that his hair was neatly combed.

"You're not looking GQ today," said Clyde smiling as he approached Russo.

"I don't feel it either," said Russo. They shook hands.

"What is this place?" Clyde asked, looking far away at the open end of the warehouse. A rusted donkey locomotive stood on faraway tracks.

"The Scalesis used it as a drop," Russo said, "Hid hijacked goods here."

He grabbed Clyde by the elbow. "Let's go over here," said the lawyer, pointing to a more secluded area behind wooden crates and pallets that had been stacked one upon the other.

"I'll tell you what," said Clyde. "Let's not." He suddenly feared a setup, and perhaps that Russo was maneuvering him into target range. "Let's move back a little around here," he said, urging Russo to a spot that could not be seen so clearly from the open part of the building.

The change in location didn't seem to bother Russo any, so Clyde relaxed a little. "What's up?" he asked casually, studying the lawyer's face.

Russo was tense and obviously distraught. "I heard about the kidnapping. I had nothing to do with it."

"Who did? demanded Clyde.

"Nick Campanio," said Russo.

"I know who he is. Nicky Nuts. He's a ruthless bastard. What the hell is Scalesi thinking?"

"They're both psychopaths," said Russo. "Rocco's paranoid. He's gone insane. I'd never trust Campanio to do anything. He was a capo once and Rocco had to bust him down to soldier."

Clyde looked long and hard into Russo's sad eyes. "What else are you telling me. Where's the girl? What's the plan?"

"I don't know where the child is. Believe me, if I did, I'd tell you. But I do know that Rocco wants Feeno to surrender to him. He'll exchange the girl for a dead Feeno."

"You guys are all crazy!" said Clyde.

Russo at the moment had no reply. He was about to speak when the crack of a rifle shot burst behind them. By the sound of its roaring echo it had come from up high and far away. Clyde ducked and shoved Russo to the ground. Clyde rolled and crouched behind a large wooden spool that had once held heavy cable. It afforded almost no protection. His .38 was out of his holster and sweeping the warehouse. The echo of the shot made it difficult to tell where it came from. Another shot rang out, followed by two more, then the sound of running upon metal. From up high near the ceiling, Clyde could see a shadow moving quickly along a steel platform. He fired, the bullet ricocheting with a metallic ping off the tin-sided wall of the warehouse. He fired again and again. The footsteps faded. He could see no one.

When he turned to look for Russo, he could see that the lawyer was gone. So it was a setup after all. He decided to wait, not offering himself as another target.

But he heard a groan from the other side of the stack of crates. Carefully, he crouched and held out his pistol long-armed in front of him. He turned a corner and on the ground before him lay Russo.

"I'm hit," he said. "The leg! Oh, Jesus Christ!"

Russo was lying on one side propped on his right elbow, his left arm reaching down toward his knee. Clyde took him by the head and shoulders and held him. He looked at the knee and saw a dark wet stain running through the torn pant leg, and pieces of skin, muscle and bone poking through the blood. The knee was shattered.

"C'mon Fred, we're getting out of here." He picked up

Russo and held him by the waist. Russo wrapped an arm around the big man's shoulders. They hobbled out of the warehouse into a blinding sun. Clyde stopped at the wide door to the warehouse and hastily scanned the freight yard. There was no sign of an assailant.

"Can you make it to the car?" Clyde asked.

"I think so," said Russo.

It was when Clyde placed Russo as carefully as he could in the front passenger seat of his Mustang that he saw the other wound in the lawyer's chest. A neat hole had torn through the jacket and khaki shirt. Foams and bubbles of red were seeping from Russo's lips. Clyde put his hand behind Russo, feeling his back beneath the jacket. Discovering no blood upon his hand, he reasoned that the bullet was still lodged inside Russo's chest, or worse, it was a hollow point, shattering upon impact.

As they sped away, Russo spat and coughed more blood from his mouth. "Hurry, hurry!" he said, gasping.

The car bounced over the railroad tracks. Russo screamed with pain.

"Hold on," yelled Clyde. They jumped several puddles and potholes, then hit the asphalt road. Clyde sped toward where he suspected he could find Route 1. As they exited the rail yard he spotted a youth walking by the tracks.

"Yo, kid!" yelled Clyde. "Where's the nearest hospital?"

The boy, aged about sixteen, appeared perplexed, then said, "Newark, I guess. Probably Saint James."

"Get in the car!" yelled Clyde.

"I ain't goin' with youse!" said the boy, now frightened when he saw the blood on Russo's chest.

Clyde pointed his .38 toward the boy and yelled again, "Get in the fucking car!"

With the teenager in the back seat providing directions, they sped as fast as the traffic would allow. Clyde leaned on the horn and never let up blasting.

"I'm gonna pass out!" Russo whispered.

"Hang on, goddamit, hang on!"

"Stop!" yelled Russo, wincing in pain. He looked over at Clyde. His eyes were glazed and Clyde could see that he might not make it. "Pocket, pocket," said Russo, moving a bloody, shaking hand up toward his shirt.

Clyde pulled to a stop.

"Pocket!" Russo gasped again. His fingers, which tapped at his heart, were trembling.

Clyde reached into the inside jacket pocket and pulled out an envelope with his name written on the outside. The edges were stained with dark red.

"What is it?" Clyde said, then added, "Shit! We gotta' get you to a hospital." He floored the accelerator, finally hitting city streets.

"Turn right up ahead," the boy in the back seat yelled. "Raymond Boulevard."

Several blocks later, the boy yelled for Clyde to "turn left onto that street."

"What street?" yelled Clyde.

Beside him, Russo gasped and spit a glob of blood onto his lap: "Hurry!"

"Cross Market," the boy said. "And there, Jefferson Street, turn here."

"Left?" yelled Clyde.

"Left, left!" the boy yelled.

Clyde was zigzagging now, blowing the horn, sweeping traffic from his path. He jumped through a red light on Lafayette Street. A block later he drove under the canopy with the dark black overhead sign reading, "Emergency".

"Gun shot wounds!" Clyde yelled to the orderlies as they carefully lifted Russo from the bloody front seat and placed him in on the gurney. "Chest and left knee."

Clyde leaned against a cement pillar holding up the canopy, breathing heavily. He noticed his fingers trembling as he lit a cigarette. As he did, the kid who got them there started walking away toward the street. Clyde saw him. "Stop," he yelled.

He pulled out his wallet and handed the puzzled and frightened boy two twenty-dollar bills, and said, "Thanks, thanks. I mean it. You got us here. What's your name?

The boy answered, "Cruz," and Clyde replied, "I didn't mean to scare you back there. You did good. Thanks again."

Policemen began filling the emergency room, and one

plainclothes detective questioned Clyde, who told him everything pertinent to the shooting, showed him his PI's license and explained that the victim was Fred Russo.

"Did you say Fred Russo?" the detective asked. "The lawyer? That guy? Angie Russell's brother? The singer? Jee-sus Christ!"

Clyde was shaking his head when a doctor wearing a white robe and stethoscope approached.

"You're the one who brought him in?" he asked. At that moment a young and attractive well-dressed woman, her eyes flushed with tears, pushed into the crowded emergency room.

"I'm his wife," she said. "Where is he, where is he?"

She shouldered past a policeman who reached for her.

"Ma'am, please ma'am, you can't go in".

Fifty feet away, Russo lay on a bed enclosed by curtains. Three doctors and several nurses, plus a cop were near the bed. Russo's shirt had been ripped open and a plastic shield placed over the hole in his chest to prevent air from being sucked into the wound to help prevent a collapsed lung. A tube was inserted into his mouth while a doctor ripped off the seal and began sponging.

The cop who had chased the woman grasped her firmly by the arm and as gently as possible, with the assistance of a nurse, began wrestling her out of the area to the waiting room. She twisted and screamed, pulling so hard that her silk blouse pulled out of her skirt. One of her high heels came off and she began kicking at the policeman's leg.

They sat her in a chair.

"I'm his wife," she said, as they finally propped her on a metal chair next to a sterilizer. "What happened to him? What happened?"

Five minutes later, nurses led the hysterical woman to a small room and sat her on a padded chair. She refused a sedative and clutched the arms of the chair. A young doctor with a dark mideastern complexion entered and sat by her side. "Mrs. Russo. I'm Doctor Hajani." Her eyes were wide, staring at the man in the green cap and scrubs. He had washed away most of the blood from his forearms but could not hide the stains on his clothes.

"I'm sorry," he said with an accent of a Pakistani or Indian.

"He didn't make it. I'm sorry." The woman jumped and ran to the cubicle. Before they caught her, she got close enough to see just the top of her husband's dark hair poking from the sheet. She wailed.

They kept Clyde at the hospital for an hour, taking down a full statement of the circumstances leading up to Russo's death. When the police were finished with the interview, he went to a rest room, a private one containing only one urinal and one toilet and sink. He locked the door and washed the blood from his hands and looked into the mirror. He saw the exhausted face of a man who should be in his backyard tending roses, and not chasing down gangsters all over the state of New Jersey.

He sat on the toilet and opened the envelope that Russo had given him with a dying breath.

Chapter 47: AFFIDAVIT FROM THE DEAD

Feeno turned left onto Carranza Road, a paved two-lane straight shot through the woods that covered several miles. The parking area at the little park was thankfully deserted; there would often be no cars traveling this section of the road for hours, even days at a time.

When he darkened the headlights, the blackness of the forest and night sky dropped like a cloak, sealing off the imagined dangers of this part of the Pine Barrens. With his flashlight, he looked at the time — 8:19. He was uncharacteristically early, due to the motivations of anxiety and fear. He even worried whether he got the message straight. The old lady at the front desk of the Bayshore Motel told him for certain that, "your friend who called said he would meet you at eight-thirty at the Carranza Bar and Grill. He said you knew where it was."

He had a little time to think about his descension into hell and how it had been a series of steps: welcomed associations with dangerous people, losing his wife, losing his friends, suspected, arrested, lying, stealing, running. Now the worst, a kidnapped child added to the list. He could barely handle his own losses, including the screaming goodbye from Edna.

He studied his watch again. He and Clyde had met a couple of times before at the Carranza Monument when Feeno was flitting about the Pine Barrens like a lost sparrow, one day here, another day there. The monument had been erected in honor of Emilio Carranza Rodriguez, a Mexican aviator whose plane had crashed there July 12, 1928, on a mission coming back from New York City to commemorate Capt. Charles Lindbergh's trans-Atlantic achievement.

There were no thoughts of heros as Feeno drove north on the Garden State Parkway from the motel, hearing the worrying chop-chop-chop of the searching helicopters above the pines.

He parked at a now-deserted camp site across the road. A chill arose on Feeno's neck as the headlights approached. He could see them several yards away. "What if it's not Clyde?" he thought, and jumped out of his car and ran to the woods, kneeling behind a bush.

Through the gloom he saw a sedan that was definitely not Clyde's green Mustang. He crouched and waited, holding his big, new wilderness revolver with two shaking hands. The trembling didn't stop until he saw the big man exit the car and say, "It's me, Feeno."

"Where's your car? I might have blown you to pieces," said Feeno, stepping from the shadows and showing Clyde his Smith & Wesson.

"Where the hell did you get the elephant gun?" Clyde asked.

"Where the hell did you get the car?" Feeno answered.

"It's a rental. My baby's full of blood."

As they drove, Clyde filled Feeno in on recent events, particularly how Fred Russo was killed. Feeno sat quietly as Clyde told how the lawyer died. No surprises anymore. Feeno thought of Fred's three young boys and his wife.

"He gave me this just before he died," said Clyde, handing the blood-streaked envelope to Feeno, he said, "Read it!" as they sped east on Carranza Road.

They drove back roads until they reached Route 70, then went east and north through Lakehurst to Manasquan Park, then turned right onto Riverview Drive. The area was full of small homes and quiet, residential streets intersecting one another. Soon they were past the urbanity and onto the shore road leading toward the ocean. Feeno used a flashlight to read Russo's letter, uttering "Holy Christ" repeatedly as he read. He ran his fingers over the notary seal on the back page and read again the beginning of the statement, "This affidavit is made and effective September 4, 1979."

Clyde took a left off an asphalt road and followed a sandy path through the dunes until they were a few blocks from the ocean. They stopped but before leaving the car, Clyde reached down to his left ankle and unholstered the little Beretta, handing it to Feeno. "Put your cannon under the seat. That thing you have will break your arm and probably bring a wall down on us."

He asked, "Ever shoot a gun?"

"Is a bee-bee gun a gun?" answered Feeno, staring at the Beretta. He put it in his waist, then removed it, looked at the weapon curiously and placed it in his back pocket. Still confused, he removed it and placed it in a front pant pocket.

"Keep the end with the little hole in it pointed away from me and you," said Clyde.

About two blocks away, they stopped when they saw the outline of the two brick pillars flanking the driveway of Rocco Scalesi's oceanside home. They looked and listened.

"I don't see anybody there," said Feeno, but Clyde clamped a hand on his elbow before he could walk away.

"Look again," said Clyde. "Just to the right of the pillar on the left."

Feeno could barely make out a red dot, moving up and down, the glow of a cigarette.

"This way," said Clyde. They retreated about a block and began a long detour toward the ocean.

They began walking through the deep sand. Civilized sounds fell off in the background, taken up instead by the buzzing and whirring of insects in the tall grass. Feeno and Clyde climbed the sand dunes awkwardly, maintaining silence along the way until they heard the crashing sound of the ocean meeting the beach.

Clyde put out his hand and stopped Feeno in a trough between two dunes. The dark sky was low overhead. Fog began to drift in ghostly waves above and around them. "Are you sure you're up to this?" he asked Feeno.

"No way I'm turning back now."

When they got to within fifty yards of the house, Clyde stopped again. They bent low behind a stone jetty. Behind the fog was the black vast expanse where ocean meets bay, and in the distance, a fog horn bellowing its lament. Rocco's house was in black silhouette except for a horizontal sliver of light coming from his study facing the sea.

Clyde whispered: "We have to be careful. He's bound to have a couple of bodyguards around."

"Yeah, but I've been here before," answered Feeno. "They're mostly out toward the land side of the property. Never back here."

Rocco was on the phone, talking softly. A lit cigar lay in an ashtray on his tidy desk. From a bookcase speaker in the background came the soft sound of a tenor singing a Neapolitan love song.

"So, I will see you on Saturday," he said into the phone. "I look forward to it, Nancy." As he put down the receiver, he felt the cold end of something metal pressing the back of his neck.

"Not a word, Rocco," said Clyde. "Not a word or I'll put a hole in your head."

The Mafia boss was startled but forced a smile. "Have we met?" He turned to face his intruder, but when he saw Clyde and then saw Feeno standing two steps behind him, his face dropped in amazement. He saw two guns aimed at him.

He pulled back a couple of breaths and thought quickly. He didn't get to be boss of one of the world's riskiest enterprises by being a wimp. "I didn't expect to see you so soon, Feeno." At the same time, Rocco bent slightly, reaching his arm under his desk.

Clyde grabbed the man's coat collar and spun him around in the swivel chair away from the desk, tumbling Rocco to the floor. "Get up, and you make another move like that and it's all over. I'll start with your knees. Feeno, take a look and see if there's a button there. He may have signaled his goons."

Feeno bent and examined the underside of the desk. "I don't see anything."

Rocco, breathing deeply with his fingers now clamping the arms of the chair, asked Clyde, "Who the hell are you?"

"Does it matter?" asked Clyde.

Rocco forced a low laugh.

"Where's the girl, Rocco? Where's the child?"

"I don't know what you're talking about."

"I know for a fact that the feds were talking to you today. You should have your answers rehearsed a little better than that."

"Little girl, yeah," said Rocco, smiling. "A shame, real shame."

"All right, let's cut the crap and get to the point," said Clyde. "Fred Russo's dead. I think you know something about that too." Clyde pulled up a captain's chair to face Rocco. He sat down, keeping the gun leveled at Rocco's chest. "I was there when he died. Too bad your shooter had imperfect aim. He lived a little while."

"I know a bluff when I see one."

"Okay, let's match your testimony against that of a dead man, a guy who was one of your loyal buddies right up until today."

Feeno stepped forward and broke his silence. He was surprised at how much power he felt waving the little Beretta. It reinforced his anger, pent up from many weeks of isolation and worry. He felt the blood rise through his neck and into his face. His eyes were narrowed. "Rocco, you don't know how close I am to pulling this trigger. I never killed a man in my life. But I could blow you away right now and feel no conscience at all."

He held his arm out straight, his right hand holding the gun two feet from Rocco's right ear. Rocco was truly startled and tried to back away in the swivel chair. Clyde clamped his foot behind one of the wheels on the chair leg.

"You don't stop at killing one of your hoodlum Mafia pricks," whispered Feeno hoarsely. His jaw was tight. "You don't stop at kidnapping little girls, and now you don't stop at wiping out Fred Russo, the guy who made millions for you."

The Mafia boss stared at Feeno, then at the gun, noticing the trembling in Feeno's hand.

"By the way, we found out who forged my signature on the loan to Central Sanitation, the dump where you guys wanted to cremate Jimmy Hoffa."

"I had nothin' to do with that," said Rocco. "I didn't forge no signature."

"Maybe you didn't put pen to paper. You didn't forge my name. We know that. We also know that Fred Russo did it. He signed my name, on your orders."

"Yeah, and look what happened to him," said Rocco, suddenly angry. But immediately he caught his wrath and checked it. "Listen, listen you two. Feeno, sit down, sit down, let's discuss this like gentlemen."

"I'll stand, thanks," said Feeno.

"What is it you want? You want my life? Go ahead, shoot me. Who the hell cares? I'm an old man. But you shoot me, what are the chances your asshole buddy..." he said, looking at Feeno, "...what are Berardi's chances of ever seeing his kid again?"

Rocco continued, sensing the conversation being tipped in his favor. "Listen, you need me, and I need you. We need each other." A sardonic grin was on his face. "What is it, money? Feeno, I probably underpaid you. I didn't appreciate all that you had done for us. Without your brains, without your bank, there'd be no crime. Just ask my lawyers. You'll find out in court anyway. You haven't got a chance of wiggling out of this, even if you didn't bury Hoffa. You dumb shit, you were so stuck on yourself."

He began an imitation whining: "Big Mafia wannabe, that's all you are. You had no idea what was going on half the time."

Feeno retreated a little, holding the Beretta with both hands.

Rocco paused, his face softened: "Look, guys, what is it? Money? I got tons of it. Five hundred grand," he said, pointing a finger toward Clyde, "and for you. Each. Swiss bank accounts, no IRS, no nothing. Perfectly easy."

"And what do you get out of it?" asked Feeno.

"You go away," said Rocco. "Your silence, that's all I want."

Clyde tilted his head and said, smiling: "You mean bang bang silence, don't you Rocco?" He added quickly, "Let's change the subject. I'm going to ask you once more. Where's the girl?"

Rocco attempted a smile, but his eyes revealed fear.

Clyde lowered his voice, and removed the envelope that Russo had given him earlier in the day. He waved it at Rocco: "This is from your old buddy, Fred Russo. It's all in here."

"What the fuck do I care?" said Rocco, swallowing hard.

"I'm going to tell you how much you care, my friend." With that, he moved to a leather chair and sat down, relaxed. Feeno stood and moved to the far end of the room, away from the ocean side. He leaned against the book case.

Clyde took his time getting to say what he planned. He wanted to see Rocco's expression.

"Let's forget what Russo pinned on you as far as your lousy little scheme is concerned," said Clyde. He spoke calmly. "Forget the forgery, forget the Hoffa deal, forget the eighty-five grand you paid to Central Sanitation to get rid of Hoffa's body. We can even forget the last-minute change of plans. I know about that too. It's in here, this little affidavit."

He read: "Bufalino considered Central Sanitation as being too obvious a place to dispose of Hoffa's body. Owned by mob guys. That's the first place the feds would look. Bufalino's thugs found another place, a better place, with a better oven, one that doesn't leave a trace. It was a funeral home near where Hoffa was shot."

He paused, and leaned toward the Mafia boss, placing his elbows on his knees and putting his face up close to Rocco's: "But that's little stuff compared with what else is in here, Rocco. Let's talk about that something else. Let's talk about Richard Gambini."

When he spoke the words "Richard Gambini'" Clyde could see the tiny flinching of the muscles around Rocco's eyes. The eyes are mirrors of the soul, they say, and what was once a blurred reflection was about to become clear. But Rocco was looking over the shoulder of Clyde and beyond into a hallway.

"Drop it," yelled a new voice, coming from the door opposite. A tall, thin man held a gun, waving it directly at Clyde. Then he held the gun with two hands and stepped back into the hallway so that only Clyde could see him. Looking at Clyde, the thug said, "I said drop it."

Clyde set his pistol down on the carpet. At the same time, Feeno leaped toward the door and fired blindly, letting loose six shots in a spray pattern. Silently, the man in the hallway, his face twisted in pain and bewilderment, fell head first into Rocco's office, his gun still in his right hand. He hit the floor, his head nearly at Rocco's feet, and lay still.

Feeno stared at the thing in his hands, then at the man on the floor. His heart was half way up his throat.

Clyde stared at Feeno in amazement, but for only a second. He picked up his .38 from the floor:

"Now, where were we?" asked Clyde, holding his revolver straight out in front of him, aiming it at Rocco's head.

"Who killed Richard Gambini?" Clyde asked.

Rocco was sweating, both eyes bulging, and in a breaking

voice, said, "I don't know nothing about Gambini?"

"Who killed the boy?" shouted Clyde. "Poor kid, going to his girlfriend's senior prom. Her high school prom. In a limousine, all dressed up. Somebody pulls up in another limo right behind him and blows the back of his head off. Right in front of his girlfriend."

Rocco began shuffling his feet. "I don't know nothing. Some guy killed him, that's all I know."

"No, you do know, don't you? You were at the funeral. You went up to the mother. What's her name? Beautiful woman. Concetta. Concetta Gambini. She loved her son. You promised her you'd find the one who killed her boy.

"You found him, all right! The Squirrel, Anthony Trapetto. That's what you told Concetta and Joe Gambini. That's who pulled the trigger and killed Richard, you said. Right Rocco?" Now, Clyde's voice was agitated, but in control. "So you found out he did it and in return you killed Trapetto and tossed him into the woods, the backyard of Feeno's friend, didn't you? Isn't that the story?"

He rose from the chair, still holding the .38. With his left hand he grabbed Rocco by the throat. Rocco pulled back but Clyde held on, "Isn't that the story?"

"Yeah, yeah, that's the story. I killed the little bastard myself. Is that what you want to hear?"

Clyde let go of Rocco's throat. The Mafia boss brushed his shirt front and twisted his neck. "Yeah, I took care of it. I avenged the death. One of my own soldiers. I did the right thing."

"You did the right thing all right," said Clyde, his voice rising. "Except Trapetto didn't fire the gun that killed Richard, did he? You were there, you were there when Richard was whacked.

"It's all here, Rocco," said Clyde, waving the bloody letter that Russo had given him. "It's all here. Listen to what Russo confessed. He wrote it all down when he found out you kidnapped the Berardi girl. It was the final straw with Fred. He was a decent man. Loved his children. He hated what you did.

"This is what he wrote." He read loudly: "We drove down the lane to the country club. We were in a limousine, right behind the limo of Richard and the girl. I was in the front seat. Anthony

Trapetto was to be the shooter. He was in the back seat on the right hand side. Rocco was seated beside him. Just as Anthony lowered the window, Rocco yelled, 'Gimme that gun. I'm doing this one myself.' He took the gun from Anthony and pointed it at the Gambini kid. He shot him twice in the back of the head."

Clyde stuffed the letter back into his inside pocket. "Russo saw it. He heard it all. You pulled the gun away from Trapetto and blew the kid's head off. It's right here, Rocco." Clyde slapped his chest. "Right here."

"That don't mean nothin,' That paper's worthless."

"Except it's not, Rocco. Russo even had it notarized. It's an affidavit, a sworn statement of facts. An affidavit from the dead, with witnesses that Russo wrote it."

Rocco yelled: "So what! So what if I did. I did the world a favor. He was scum, that kid!" he yelled. "Scum! Do you know what he did with that girlfriend of his?

He began yelling louder now: "Got her high, turned her into a junkie, made that sex movie. What would you do? You'd do the same. That little bastard dated my daughter. That little prick, he got what he deserved."

"Do you think Concetta and Joe Gambini are going to look at it that way?" asked Clyde.

"The son betrayed his mother's honor. He had to be killed," yelled Rocco, strained and sweating, his eyes wide and protruding.

"According to Russo," said Clyde, "And it's all in here, you are in love with Concetta Gambini. She trusted you."

"So what? The feelings between a man and a woman are nobody's business. I am an honorable man. I violated no code. I respect the woman. And her husband. So, what are you gonna' do about it? You kill me, the kid stays missing. Anything can happen. Nicky Nuts has her. He's a mental case. And that piece of paper you got don't mean a thing."

"I know it doesn't," said Clyde. "And it truly doesn't matter. You and I agree on that. The only thing that matters as far as you're concerned is the phone call I placed about ten minutes ago." He looked at his watch. "To Concetta Gambini, the woman you adore, the woman you look up to so much you whacked her prick of a son.

"I wonder how much she respects you now," said Clyde, arising from the chair and nodding to Feeno. "Let's go," he said. He looked at his watch again, and from his jacket pocket pulled out a roll of duct tape, tossing it to Feeno.

"Secure this piece of shit," he said to Feeno, all the while watching the sweat roll down Rocco's jowls.

Feeno started at Rocco's wrists, fastening them to the arms of the chair. Then the chest, rolling the tape around his suit jacket and the back of the chair. He went around three times.

"Get his ankles real tight," said Clyde.

Feeno was sweating but enjoying it.

"Now his mouth," said Clyde, hearing Rocco grunt. Rocco strained, his eyes bulging, his face beet red with exertion and fear. With the tape pulled tightly over his mouth, he could barely breath.

"She knows, Rocco. Concetta knows; her husband knows. They know you were the trigger man who murdered their son. I figure you have about a half-hour, Rocco. A half-hour before they get here. Maybe fifteen, twenty minutes.

"Let's go, Feeno! Let's get the hell out of here before the fun starts. I don't want to be a witness to what's going to happen."

Clyde bent and whispered in Rocco's ear, "By the time the Gambini thugs get done with you, before they put a merciful bullet in your head, you'll be a blubbering piece of bleeding meat. They'll probably use baseball bats."

He stood up. "We'll see you, Rocco. Let's go Feeno."

They reached the French door to the outside deck, opened it and felt the stiff ocean breeze as they stepped out. They heard the distant foghorn, melancholy and truly meaningful on this night. And they heard the roaring ocean waves thundering upon the beach. And they heard the muffled screams from inside the house.

Chapter 48: WHAT GOES 'ROUND

Gerry Shapiro parked her car in the shade in the far corner of the lot away from the southwest entrance to the Cherry Hill Mall. She noted the time and looked worriedly at the large rectangular banner that had been strung between two parking lot light poles. It announced a "Summer's End Clearance." And this was to be the "Final Summer Explosion" day, with some stores promising up to sixty percent off their shelf price, including Gerry's dress shop, the Bonjour. With markdowns so dramatic, shoppers would feed like piranhas. She still had a lot to do.

    Checking her watch again, she told herself to slow it down. "No sense getting riled so early in the day." Besides, the sun was advancing higher in the sky, warming away the early morning chill, perhaps creating a day too good to shop, one better suited to a final picnic in the park, a round of golf or a day at the shore. The blend of mixed gray clouds had given way to fluffs of white, and promised, later on, clear blue.

    She waved and smiled at other shop owners and clerks hustling into the mall. As she got closer to the entrance, she saw the woman who owned the Bread Basket in the Food Court, and yelled to her, "Look out!" as a car sped along the entrance road and was braked to a squealing stop.

    The Bread Basket woman jumped and yelled angrily at the driver, who ignored her and yelled something to a woman seated beside him. That woman jumped out and hastily pulled something from the back seat behind her. She hurried back into the car, a black Buick, slammed the door; the car sped ahead, loudly burning rubber on the asphalt.

    Left on the sidewalk was a child, standing near the curb appearing puzzled. She wore shorts, sneakers and a dirty pink, Tweedy Bird tee shirt. Her black curly hair was uncombed and the child was clearly at a loss about her presence there.

Gerry hastened to her, bent toward her and saw tear tracks on the girl's dirty face. "Hey there, what's your name?"

The girl looked up pop-eyed and said with all the firm enunciation that a six-year-old can muster, "My name is Gloria Berardi. I live at three-five-seven-two Twin Oaks Drive, Medford, New Jersey."

Seventy-five miles to the north, Clyde Woolen drove down Broad Street in Newark during the early morning rush hour, coming to a stop in front of the Federal Building. A jolly looking, hefty security guard standing nearby pointed behind him toward Federal Square: "Sorry, can't park here, sir. Gotta' use the lot in the back."

From the driver's seat, Clyde motioned for the guard to come closer. The man bent, cocked an ear and listened as Clyde explained his purpose to him. The guard appeared stupefied for a second, then said, "Okay. I'll let 'em know you're coming." He hastened into the building.

"Your isolation from society has ended and you are once again about to be the center of attention. Your fame has returned," said Clyde to Feeno, who had just stepped from the back seat. Feeno grasped Clyde's outstretched hand in both of his. With an uncharacteristic stammer he said, "I don't know how…I can't tell you…" He finally was able to let it go: "Without you I'd be dead."

"That'll happen when you get my bill," said Clyde, who beamed at Feeno, squinting into the morning sun. "It's been a pleasure, Feeno. I'm going to miss you."

Feeno stood straight; he was now cleanly shaved and wore a dark blue business suit and crimson necktie, suited to his next role — that of the dignified and reluctant banker who would find the courage to stand up to some of the most dangerous people in America. He felt a quiver of apprehension in the gut as he tossed one final wave to Clyde. He also grinned and waved to the back seat of Clyde's car, then walked into the federal building.

The man at the security gate looked at Feeno carefully. He scanned his body with the security wand and nodded him through the gate. Feeno was partly disappointed that no bells clanged, no lights flashed and no sirens screamed. His re-entry to the civilized world was occurring fluidly, and with uncanny quiet. But once upstairs in the outer lobby of Mario Bianca's office, he smiled after telling the receptionist, "Joseph A. Bannon reporting for duty." He saluted, accentuating the flourish with a kick of the heels, then watched the woman's mouth drop open.

She rose from her seat as if to turn and run, but plopped down heavily, and with suitable urgency, not once taking her stare from Feeno, pushed the interoffice command and announced, "Mister Bannon to see Mister Bianca."

The first words out of Feeno's mouth when a frowning and surprised Bianca came bearing down upon him were "Guess who's outside."

About three minutes later, four wide-eyed men ran to Clyde's car and surrounded it on all sides, guns drawn and aimed at the back seat. One of them reached for the door next to the curb and held it open.

"Step outside sir, hands first," said an FBI agent to Rocco Scalesi, who, scooted across the back seat awkwardly, with arms raised.

He exited the car and did as ordered when an agent said, "Hands on the roof." Another agent patted him down. Turning Rocco toward him, the agent recited, "You have the right to remain silent. Anything you say can and will be used against you in a court of law. You have the right to an attorney. If you cannot afford an attorney, one will be provided for you at interrogation time and at court."

"My lawyer's on his way," said Rocco growling. "He better be."

As he was led away in cuffs, he twisted toward Clyde, at the same time rubbing dirt from the palms of his cuffed hands. "Next time," he said to Clyde, who was smiling, "Wash your goddamned car."

"Glad to let you have the last word, Rocco," grinned Clyde, bowing deeply.

Chapter 49: JOY/TEARS

The joyful-tearful celebration that the Berardis welcomed that night in their lit-up home on Twin Oaks Drive is a trophy in their minds, a classic night that will hang in the family Louvre forever. Vince squeezed Gloria so many times and with such possessive force that she complained, "Daddy, you're hurting me."

He also hugged Agent Schweitzer, Agent Hillary, his lawyer Bernie Samuels, the pesky neighbors next door and all of the other fifty or more relatives and friends who squeezed through the front door and into their hearts and home that night. It seemed as if the whole town had a representative there, as well as the media from Philly and New York. Their lawn was cluttered with well-wishing folks; floodlights from TV trucks lent their artificial brightness to the neighborhood. Julie and Vince found each other alternating between hysterical poles of laughter and tears.

As at all good parties, the celebrants stayed close to the food and booze, in the kitchen and also circling the dining room table where lay the cold cuts, finger veggies and multiple varieties of bread.

"Some of the funniest shit happens when you least expect it." Agent Schweitzer, who was on his fifth or sixth bottle of Rolling Rock, was talking to John Wolyniak, Julie's brother, who chewed a carrot while leaning against the kitchen sink. "We got a call from a postal inspector up in Morristown one time. There was a cardboard box in the post office Dead Letter office, and it was stinkin' to high heaven. The guy said, 'You better be here when we open it.' This box was addressed to one of the Gatto brothers — Rosario — a Sicilian wiseguy. He was under indictment in Brooklyn and was about to go on trial on a drug bust. His buddies, the other guys who were indicted, were jumpin' all over the place. We had already flipped a couple.

"But somebody sent this dead fish to him, which you

know...It's a message, that so-and-so is sleepin' with the fishes. We still don't know who sent it. But they sent it to the wrong address and it ends up back at the post office. The mob guy, Gatto, had moved back to an apartment he had in Bensonhurst. So we rewrapped the box with the stinkin' fish in it and sent it on its way. Then we put a 'round-the-clock on the guy to see his reaction. The day after he got the fish he was due to appear in court. The bastard was so scared, his throat closed up. He couldn't talk; he couldn't breathe. Literally. They had to call nine-one-one and take him to a hospital." Schweitzer laughed loudly above the din.

"Are you guys still trading cop stories?" Vince asked as he took a plate of cold cuts from the refrigerator.

"I can't match that one," said John Wolyniak, popping open another beer, "but did you hear the story about Frank Rizzo and the Queen — Queen Elizabeth of England?"

Schweitzer shook his head in the negative. Agent Hillary, interested, moved closer.

"Rizzo was in his second term as mayor and the Queen was in Philly for the Bicentennial," said Wolyniak. "Nineteen Seventy-Six. I was in the Philly P.D. back then working the City Hall detail. The Mayor's office. They had this big soiree for the Queen at the Philadelphia Art Museum, and Rizzo had to give the Queen The Philadelphia Bowl. You know what it is? The Philadelphia Bowl? Great big crystal bowl, very expensive. Cut glass, Waterford or something. All the visiting dignitaries get one when they come into town. So Rizzo, Mister Sophisticate. He presents the bowl to the Queen and he says..."

John put down his beer, cupped his hands as if holding the bowl, and finished the story loudly:

"Here ya' are, Queen, this bowl holds exactly twelve pounds of rigatoni!"

About nine-thirty the uproarious part of the gathering began calming down as the well-wishers, the co-celebrants, waved and left. Remaining in the kitchen were Schweitzer and Julie's brother, who continued to trade cop stories; the neighbors Billy Ferris and Mr. and Mrs. Hibberd, plus Julie's parents and Vince's mom, who throughout the evening wept quietly and dabbed with a wrinkled Kleenex at her nose.

One person who should have been there was not. Clyde's absence caused Vince to mark the time every half hour wondering where he could be. They had saved the last bottle of champagne for him, and Vince had rehearsed the toast to Clyde over and over. This party was for him as much as for the Berardis. Without him, there would have been no party.

Julie had taken the kids upstairs to bed. Vince followed about twenty minutes later, with none of the visitors realizing they were gone. The kids' room was semi-dark. Not even the little night light on the floor was lit. The back window of the bedroom was open a few inches and an early autumn breeze flowed through and out to the hallway. He found Julie sitting in the small rocker facing the bunk bed. Her arms were folded and she was perfectly still. Gloria was a faint lump on the bottom bunk, her little head turned to the wall. She clutched Pooh Bear. Vince couldn't see Patty in the upper bunk but was assured that she was there by the sound of her tiny, wheezing snores.

He sat on the floor and rested his arms and head on Julie's leg. She put her arm on his shoulder, rubbed his head and said with a light laugh — a brave laugh, uttered in jest but perhaps as serious as stone — "I don't know if I can ever leave this room again."

"We'll get an alarm," Vince said. "I've been thinking about it. They can't cost too much." They sat still, quietly holding one another, listening. But then he added, "What the hell are we thinking? It's over!"

"It's never going to be over." she said.

"It's over, it's over, Julie," he said softly, "It's over."

In the dark he could not see her smile. But she kissed his hair and he could tell by the warmth in her voice: "You're right, it's over!"

About ten, John climbed the stairs, poked into the bedroom and said quietly so as not to wake the girls, "You have more visitors."

Vince left Julie with the kids. Downstairs in the kitchen, there he was at last.

"Christ, I've been waiting for you all night," Vince said to

Clyde Woolen, returning his bear hug. He introduced him all 'round as "the man who got Gloria back for us. Our hero!" Then he saw standing in the corner a short, young woman with light brown hair, a stranger who wore an engaging squint behind dark-rimmed, plastic glasses.

Clyde turned and introduced her: "This is Edna; she's a friend of our friend Feeno."

"Hi," said Vince, staring at the little woman for a few seconds, then collecting himself, "What can I get you to drink?"

"A beer," she smiled, while John Wolyniak turned to the cooler on the floor.

Vince looked once again into Clyde's face and hugged him once more; the tears flowed again, but not from Clyde. He smiled and shook hands all 'round. John Wolyniak uncorked the last bottle of Moet Chandon Perignon, handed it to Vince, who stumbled through his toast. Tears formed and he had to stop. Clyde smiled but was not embarrassed.

"Hey," he said, rescuing his friend by grasping a shoulder and taking him out of the kitchen to the rear screened-in porch.

Consolation came to Vince in sobering terms. Clyde told him of the final minutes in Rocco Scalesi's house, leaving out the part where Feeno shot dead the intruder friend of Rocco.

"Rocco was all tied up, scared shitless. He really believed that the Gambinis were on their way."

"Were they?" Vince asked.

"Let's leave it at that. Anyway, Feeno and I left and stood outside. We could hear Rocco screaming inside. With the tape on his mouth, he sounded like a steer in a slaughter house. We waited a good two or three minutes, then went back in."

Clyde described removing the tape from Rocco's mouth.

"He was covered in sweat and had pissed himself. He wanted to get out of there. Immediately, he was so scared, but I told him, 'No. I want to hear the phone call to whoever it is who has the girl.'

"Not until he was on the line with Nicky Nuts. He's the guy who had Gloria, did I say, 'Okay, we can leave.'"

Over the next few days and weeks the Berardis learned

some of the details of Edna and Feeno's association, mostly from Clyde but some from Edna herself. She became a casual visitor, always bringing Gloria and Patty small gifts, mostly children's books.

Clyde had told Vince and Julie about the night that he had first met Edna, and the reason why he had been late for the party. "When I dropped Feeno off and back into the Witness Protection Program he pleaded with me to go see her. At this motel down the shore.

"He let me know that he had some 'things to set straight with her'. So now I'm a mediator. The best I could hope for was that she didn't kill the messenger."

Clyde said he called the girl's motel room from the motel office phone so as not to scare her by knocking on her door where she would be confronted by a hulking stranger.

Edna was not friendly at first, though she listened patiently as Clyde explained the inner workings and necessary deceptions of Feeno's past weeks and months, who he really was and even who he had conspired to be, "a mobster" — a banker-mobster.

"Feeno liked to have it both ways," Clyde said to the troubled girl, sensing in the beginning that he was getting nowhere with his explanations.

When he began telling her of the previous night's events, however, which included the confrontation with Rocco Scalesi at his shore home in Manasquan, and Feeno's bravery, except for the shooting part, Edna didn't know whether to push Clyde out the door or await more about what happened. She decided on the latter. Clyde by now was seated in the one easy chair that the room allowed. Edna sat on the edge of the bed, her ankles crossed and her hands in her lap. She had insisted on leaving the door to the outside wide open because her experience with Feeno, the betrayal of identity, told her not to trust too many men anymore.

But she got around to liking Clyde and believing him more as he explained how Feeno was determined to set his wrongs upright and start his life over, even though it was to be with another phony identity in a tax-supported witness protection plan.

"You mean he's going to testify in court about all those gangsters?" Edna asked.

"Yes."

"My God, that takes guts!"

Clyde told Edna about Feeno's relationship with Berardi, about their growing up together in Philly and him going to Viet Nam and then to college and Feeno and Vince losing touch with each other until the day Vince asked for the loan.

"I wish I had known all this before," she said. "But it wasn't to be."

Chapter 50: THE FINAL TAKEDOWN

For many souls, the Ten Commandments notwithstanding, the most powerful moral lesson, the greatest, most persuasive rule, especially for a child growing up, is the Great Fear of Getting Caught.

More than anything, those words to live by spared Vince Berardi from countless troubles. It often meant a forswearing of some of the earthly pleasures celebrated by persons like Feeno Bannon. Of the words that Feeno lived by, his guiding motto was "Buy now, pay later, and pray that tomorrow never comes."

Despite getting caught again and again in some endeavor that would border on either insanity or an instant, immediate gratification, Feeno plowed onward. His impulsive character and his explosive laugh could light a room. The pain he caused to his friends and moreover to himself underlined a frustration and restlessness in his life that was difficult for even his best friends to understand.

What would he do next? Where would he go? Vince wondered about that probably every day in the months and years that passed. He learned tidbits about what Feeno was up to through the news. Feeno received a two-year suspended sentence, meaning he did no time in jail. The Neptune County charges against Feeno were dropped for two reasons: Vince refused to press charges and the evidence against Feeno was nullified because Rocco Scalesi admitted that it was he who stole Vince's money.

Rocco got off with ten years, which he was thankful to serve in a safe area of the Federal Prison Camp at Yankton, South Dakota. He too became a government witness, and between himself and Feeno caused a rupture in organized crime, especially in the East, that was devastating, a boon to prosecutors and mob hunters, sudden death and confinement to bad guys. Many of them were flipped as the word circulated about what Feeno had on the secretly recorded tapes, and some of those informants met death at the point of a gun. The investigations sped to Italy and the major heroin exporters in Sicily and Milan.

Evidence was delivered to secure RICO indictments against many of the top leaders of organized crime, not just in New York and Jersey but in Chicago, Philadelphia, Buffalo and Los Angeles. The Mafia's grip on several unions — Teamsters, Longshoremen and Laborers — was significantly reduced. Loansharking, extortion, gambling, prostitution, drug importation and distribution all were exposed through the influence, in particular, of Rocco's huskily treble voice from the witness stand. The Teamsters Union was placed in a federal trusteeship, to be supervised by the government. Once leadership of the union was wrestled from Mafia influences, elections of officers became democratic and true,

Feeno was absolved in the death of Jimmy Hoffa. Scalesi confessed that, "Bannon had nothing to do with it. Neither did I, Hoffa's death I'm talkin' about. All I did was pay off the people to dispose of the body."

Behind closed doors in the offices of government investigators, Scalesi laid out the plan of a huge Teamsters Union endeavor to get rid of Hoffa forever. He made the case as clear as anybody:

"Hoffa was a smart guy and a tough guy. Like all tough guys, myself included, that's what brings you down. He told us all when he got outta' jail to move over. He said he was comin' back; he wanted the presidency of the union back and he promised he was gonna' get rid of some guys. That meant us! Imagine the balls that Hoffa had. He's gonna push us outta' the way and he's tellin' us ahead of time. The miracle was that he lived so long.

"I'll tell ya," said Rocco. "The day I heard that he disappeared, we celebrated. Who the hell needed Jimmy Hoffa? The son of a bitch was a lightning rod for trouble. We had a good thing goin' with the pension fund. Without him. It was worth millions. It was the easiest pot of money in the world to skim from. Better than Vegas, better than anything."

So far as Vince was concerned, his family's troubles were over; but the normalcy that returned was in some ways a veneer.

Neither he nor Julie welcomed the additional notoriety that came their way when they testified at the trial of Nicholas Campanio, the guy they called "Nicky Nuts." He and his woman friend had been arrested within a half hour of dropping Gloria off at the Cherry Hill Mall. More than one witness got the license number. They were caught before they got back to Atlantic City. Campanio was sentenced to ninety-nine years.

Vince never saw nor talked to Feeno Bannon again, but a vision of his floppy face was a frequent visitor to his mind, in particular on the summer day when a package arrived in the mail just a year after Feeno re-entered the Witness Program, with a new name and a new life.

An overdue breeze welcomed the morning after a string of hot, rainless days. Vince had packed the beach umbrella, the folding beach chairs, the sand buckets and other toys for a day at the shore. He stood at the long kitchen counter.

The thick manila envelope he hefted contained no return address. It was postmarked "Kansas City."

"Who's that from?" asked Julie.

"I don't know. It doesn't say."

He slit the envelope and thrust in his hand, looking up at Julie wide-eyed. He gasped. She gasped. Money was pouring onto the kitchen table, an overwhelming amount of one-hundred dollar bills, Benjamin Franklin in the center, with pursed lips, and six ten-dollar bills.

When they finished counting, Julie wrote the number on the envelope: $31,060.

"He must have added interest," she said, laughing now. She held the envelope by the corner and shook it. "Did we get it all?"

Out came a small glossy brochure:

Unity Savings and Loan
Ask About Our Fabulous Rates!

~ The End ~

EPILOGUE

This book is a work of fiction. Some of the major characters, including Feeno Bannon, Vince Berardi, Clyde Woolen, Rocco Scalesi and Fred Russo are a composite of real people, but their actions and behavior within the plot are the work of the author's imagination, as is the general plot itself.

The movements and details of the really real people named in this book, including Jimmy Hoffa, Tony Provenzano, Russell Bufalino, Sally Bugs Briguglio, Frank Sheeran, Raffael Quasarano and Peter Vitale, among others, are based upon investigative and public records, and news accounts that have held up over the years. So are the facts in the book that are attributed to the FBI's Hoffex Memo, which is part of the 16,000 page file of an investigation into the Hoffa death that lasted for nearly thirty years.

Though the certainty of Hoffa's murder has never been doubted, the case has never been solved officially, including what happened to his body after his death. For instance, it has not been proven that his body was to have been disposed of at Central Sanitation, but for years much of the evidence was pointed in that direction. There are still some investigators and writers who insist that Central Sanitation played no part in Hoffa's demise, and that it is a theory to be lumped among dozens of other possibilities.

So how did Jimmy Hoffa die? In the book titled, *I Heard You Paint Houses,* (Steerforth Press, Hanover, NH, 2004), Frank Sheeran, Hoffa's good friend and a Teamster boss in Wilmington, Del., before his own death on December 14, 2003, disclosed what I think is the most convincing evidence of what happened on July 30, 1975, the last day Jimmy Hoffa was seen alive. Sheeran admitted, virtually on his death bed, that he had accompanied the former union boss to a house in a Detroit suburb.

"When Jimmy saw that the house was empty, he knew right away what it was...If he saw the piece in my hand he had to think I had it out to protect him. He took a quick step to go around me and get to the door. He reached for the knob and Jimmy Hoffa got shot at a decent range...in the back of the head behind his right ear. My friend didn't suffer."

Sheeran took no part in the disposal of Hoffa's body. He originally thought it would be disposed of at the Central Sanitation site in Hamtramck, but that Russell Bufalino called it off, sending the corpse instead to a funeral parlor with a crematorium.

Of all that has been written about the Hoffa case, *I Heard You Paint Houses*, by Charles Brandt, comprises the most convincing evidence, that this writer has seen, about how Hoffa died. The book is a "fly on the wall" account of the convulsive last days of Hoffa and of the total corruption of the Teamsters Union leadership in those days. There would appear to be no doubt that Frank Sheeran was the gunman who killed Hoffa.

The other, most authoritative work involving Hoffa's life and death remains *The Teamsters*, by Steven Brill, (Simon & Shuster, New York, 1978). Brill is a lawyer and writer who went on to found *Court TV* as well as *The American Lawyer* magazine. Brill reported how the Bank of Bloomfield in New Jersey, in exchange for Teamsters Union deposits, made many unsecured loans to mob-dominated businesses, among them $85,000 to Central Sanitation. The loan, as were many others, was never paid back.

Among other sources that served as background material for the writing of *From the Dead*, I acknowledge:

The Pine Barrens, by John McPhee, 1967, Ballantine Books, a division of Random House, Inc., New York.

The Complete Idiot's Guide to the Mafia, Second Edition, by Jerry Capeci, Alpha, a member of Penguin Group.

Mobfather, the Story of a Wife and Son Caught in the Web of the Mafia, 1993, Zebra, by George Anastasia, my good friend and former colleague at *The Philadelphia Inquirer*.

A special thanks goes to Jim DeFilippi, whose critique nudged the narrative of the book in the right direction.

John Hilferty, a retired newspaper editor and reporter, wrote about Hoffa's disappearance as a reporter for *The Philadelphia Inquirer*. He is one of a team of reporters who won the Pulitzer Prize for General Public Reporting in 1980 for *The Inquirer's* coverage of the Three Mile Island nuclear accident. He was also a team member of reporters honored with the Associated Press Managing Editors Award for coverage of the murder of Philadelphia Mafia boss Angelo Bruno in 1980.

He is the author of *Moonlight in Vermont, a Novel*, which was judged the Best Romance of 2007 by the IndieExcellence Awards, and *The Mad River Valley*, a photographic history of the Mad River Valley of Vermont, co-authored with his wife, Ellie, in 2005.

§ § §

Made in the USA
Lexington, KY
03 April 2015